PRAISE FOR IAN ROGERS

"Rogers continues to engage and intrigue with his trademark cross-over of the supernatural mystery . . . [his] writing has a cinematic quality that is fully immersive."

—*Bloody Bookish*

"Wry and stylishly bizarre, Rogers hits the mark dead on. . . . I hope he's on the job for years to come."

**—Laird Barron,
author of *Occultation***

"Ian Rogers' stories are old-fashioned in the very best sense: classic thrillers in the spirit of Shirley Jackson and Richard Matheson. *Every House Is Haunted* is full of well-crafted, satisfying twists, a fine companion for any reader of literate horror."

**—Andrew Pyper,
author of *Lost Girls*,
The Killing Circle and *The Guardians***

EVERY HOUSE IS HAUNTED

IAN ROGERS

ChiZine Publications

FIRST EDITION

Distributed in Canada by
HarperCollins Canada Ltd.
1995 Markham Road
Scarborough, ON M1B 5M8
Toll Free: 1-800-387-0117
e-mail: hcorder@harpercollins.com

Distributed in the U.S. by
Diamond Book Distributors
1966 Greenspring Drive
Timonium, MD 21093
Phone: 1-410-560-7100 x826
e-mail: books@diamondbookdistributors.com

Library and Archives Canada Cataloguing in Publication

Rogers, Ian, 1976-   Every house is haunted / Ian Rogers.

Short stories. Issued also in electronic formats.
ISBN 978-1-927469-16-3

    I. Title.

PS8635.O4264E94 2012   C813'.6   C2012-904983-2

CHIZINE PUBLICATIONS
Toronto, Canada
www.chizinepub.com
info@chizinepub.com

Edited by Helen Marshall
Copyedited and proofread by Sandra Kasturi

 Canada Council   Conseil des Arts
for the Arts   du Canada

We acknowledge the support of the Canada Council for the Arts which last year invested $20.1 million in writing and publishing throughout Canada.

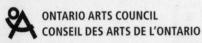

Published with the generous assistance of the Ontario Arts Council.

Printed in Canada

For my mother, Judith Anne Rogers (1946-2001)

No live organism can continue for long to exist sanely under conditions of absolute reality; even larks and katydids are supposed, by some, to dream. Hill House, not sane, stood by itself against its hills, holding darkness within; it had stood so for eighty years and might stand for eighty more. Within, walls continued upright, bricks met neatly, floors were firm, and doors were sensibly shut; silence lay steadily against the wood and stone of Hill House, and whatever walked there, walked alone.

—Shirley Jackson, *The Haunting of Hill House*

"For a minute I felt as insubstantial as a ghost. . . . The actual world was a house, with its roof falling in, dissolved so thin you could see the sunlight through it."

—Ross Macdonald, *The Sinister Habit*

CONTENTS

INTRODUCTION   11

THE VESTIBULE

Aces   21

Autumnology   42

Cabin D   46

Winter Hammock   59

THE LIBRARY

A Night in the Library with the Gods   79

The Nanny   89

The Dark and the Young   97

The Currents   126

THE ATTIC

Leaves Brown   135

Wood   150

The House on Ashley Avenue   157

The Rifts Between Us   180

Vogo   195

The Den

The Cat   201

Deleted Scenes   217

The Tattletail   227

Charlotte's Frequency   239

The Cellar

Relaxed Best   257

Hunger   270

Inheritor   273

Twillingate   286

The Candle   291

ACKNOWLEDGEMENTS

ABOUT THE AUTHOR

PUBLICATION HISTORY

INTRODUCTION

Five days after graduating from high school, I had a spinal fusion to help correct and keep my scoliosis from worsening. The surgeons used scraped bone from my hip and metal Harrington rods to fuse two-thirds of my vertebrae. I stayed in Boston Children's Hospital for one week and then spent the rest of the summer before my freshman year of college house-bound while recovering. I was alone for most mornings and afternoons with both of my parents at work and my younger siblings hanging out with their friends.

So with all of that summer me-time looming, I figured I'd have a go at reading Stephen King's *It* and its 1200 pages. Sitting in my pillow-padded rocking chair in the already sweltering living room, I read the first chapter—the monster in the sewer lures then kills the cute little brother who I imagined to be my little brother—and threw the book across the room. There was no way I was going to spend that summer alone in my house and terrified out of my gourd, so I quickly moved on to a book about Thor Heyerdahl's expedition to Easter Island. I don't remember any details from the Heyerdahl book. But I could recite to you that first chapter of King's *It* if you'd like. And yeah, after Easter Island, I went right back to Derry, Maine.

I spent most of that recovery-summer shuffling slowly from room to room looking for something to do, not that I was in any physical condition for something to do. With *It* reverberating in my head, I also spent the summer avoiding our creepy, dark, old basement, which was where we kept our ordered-by-the-month supply of important groceries like cereal and cans of Hi-C. While the basement had always terrified me as a child, that summer every room in my house held potential horrors. That summer my house was haunted.

That said, I can't pretend that I didn't enjoy my imagination running away with me; it was the only kind of running I was capable of during my long recovery. That newly minted but physically damaged eighteen-year-old about to go off to college was in awe of possibility: afraid of what might happen yet exhilarated by what could happen.

Ian Rogers' remarkable book is a time machine that carries me back to the summer when I was home alone and deliciously scared, to the summer when I unknowingly fell in love with horror stories, the very kind that Ian Rogers expertly writes. Ian's stories are explorations of the cosmic, social, and personal *what-ifs*, of the terrible and wonderful awe of possibility.

In the stunning opening story, "Aces," Toby is left to care for his irascible, charismatic, and potentially dangerous younger sister Soelle, who may or may not be a powerful witch. One of Ian's many strengths is his ability to illustrate authentic interpersonal, or more specifically interfamilial, relationships within the context of the larger what-ifs of the story. Toby and Soelle's sibling relationship is oddly warm, fraught with peril, and utterly compelling. The questions as to whether or not Soelle is responsible for the death of a classmate and for the disappearance of their parents serve as a perfect tone-and-theme-setter to *Every House Is Haunted*. Familial concerns come up again in the terrifying "Inheritor," with Danny inheriting a long-abandoned childhood home from his estranged father; a home in which his sickly sister suffered terribly and died. Here the family dynamic is as corrupt and diseased as the haunted house.

In the wildly entertaining and slightly skewed (and I mean that in the best possible way) "Cabin D," a fatigued and forlorn diner waitress serves a bizarrely dressed man his last meal(s) before he attempts to confront the haunted Cabin D. Ian observes, "But hauntings aren't restricted to houses. There are also haunted apartments and haunted trailers, haunted farms and haunted restaurants, haunted churches and haunted schools. . . ." Or, as Joe and his young friends learn in the eerie and fitting conclusion to the collection, "Twillingate," there are haunted lighthouses and haunted shorelines as surely as his characters, and by proxy us, will all be haunted by the questions of *who are you?* and *who are you going to be?*

EVERY HOUSE IS HAUNTED

"The House on Ashley Avenue" is a clever riff on the haunted house story, with an amiable psychic group who eventually does battle with the formidable house but only after detailing the potential dangers ahead. The playful interaction between Charles and Sally ratchets up tension before the final and satisfying confrontation.

The juxtaposition of the chaotic supernatural with Ian's grounded, empathetic characters is what gives his stories their heart. It's a heart that beats fast in "The Rifts Between Us" where Stanton and other scientists attempt to explore the vast alien landscape of death. Or a heart that beats unbearably heavy, as it does in "The Candle." Tom and Peggy, the weary middle-aged couple, are the source and power behind the story's palpable dread. Their ennui, regret, and dissatisfaction of who they were, who they became, and who they could've been are the ghosts in their house. Those everyday anxieties of husbands and wives are given a further, creepily arachnid spin with "Charlotte's Frequency."

Two end of the world scenarios are outlined toward the end of the collection. The first, "Hunger," is a quick and stinging jab from the point of view of a patient zero, one who narrates with a simple, cold detachment that is unnerving and unique to the other stories in this collection. If "Hunger" is the jab, then the following story, "Winter Hammock," is the twelve-round bludgeoning. An epistolary account of the world's strange end from a college drop-out who works at Radio Shack, "Winter Hammock" is H.P. Lovecraft meets Tex Avery meets George Saunders. It's a smart, savage satire of pop culture and our apocalyptic/zombie/Cthulhu zeitgeist; our haunted zeitgeist.

But you don't believe in haunted houses, Daniel.
No he didn't. Just haunted people

Looking back on my summer of recovery, I realize now that I wasn't so much haunted by King's *It* or by my house and its dank basement and empty rooms as I was haunted by my condition within the house: alone, unsure, physically fragile and vulnerable. The truth is we are all perpetually haunted by our evolving yet constant condition of vulnerability. Ian Rogers knows this and uses our vulnerabilities to move us, to make us *feel* that truth. What more could anyone want from fiction? Rogers' short story collection is a statement about the possibilities of horror short fiction as well as being a factual statement. Yes, every house is indeed haunted. Including yours.

PAUL TREMBLAY
5/17/2012

EVERY HOUSE IS HAUNTED

THE VESTIBULE

ACES

Soelle got kicked out of school for killing one of her classmates.

They couldn't prove she actually did it, which was why she received an expulsion instead of a murder charge, but there was no doubt among the faculty that she was responsible.

Soelle told me she didn't care if they kicked her out or put her in jail. She just wanted her tarot cards back.

At dinner that night I asked her if she wanted to talk about it. Our parents should have been the ones dealing with this, but we hadn't seen them in four years.

"Talk about what?" Soelle snapped. "Tara Denton is such a baby. I read her cards wrong on purpose. She wasn't really going to die!"

"But she *did* die," I pointed out.

"Yeah, because she ran in front of a bus."

"So you did predict her death."

Soelle tilted her head to the side and gave me a long-suffering look, as if she was the older sibling and I was the younger. "We all predict our own deaths, Tobias."

"Nice. Where did you get that?"

She frowned. "*Ghost Whisperer*?"

"Why don't you tell me what actually happened."

Soelle blew a strand of her straggly blonde hair off her forehead and dropped her fork on the plate with a loud clink. She was going to be sixteen in August, but she still had the mannerisms of a young child. Most people grow up; Soelle was growing inward.

"It was Algebra and I was so bored I could die. I was feeling fidgety so I took out my tarot deck and started shuffling it, practising some of those fancy shuffles you taught me. I started snapping cards down on my desk—maybe a bit too loudly, I admit—and Tara, she was sitting beside me, started giving me these dirty looks. I shot one right back at her and asked if she wanted to play. Do you know what she said to me? She said, 'I don't gamble.' Like she had never seen a tarot deck before. What a zero. Anyway, Mrs. O'Reilly put some big complicated problem on the blackboard and said she had to step out for a few minutes. I heard she's a drunk, so I figured she was heading off to the boiler room to get juiced. Robbie Moore said he saw her in the parking lot one time and—"

"*Soelle.*"

"So the teacher left and I turned to Tara. She was kind of pissing me off at that point. I snapped down a few more cards, some of the trumps, and I said, 'Do these look like *playing* cards to you, sistah?' I was expecting Tara to say something smart, but she surprised me; she actually picked up the cards, one at a time, and looked at them. She asked me what they were, and I figured, what the hell, and I started explaining what tarot is. We weren't bonding or anything—I was still thinking she was a twit—but she seemed seriously interested. I could tell because she looked kind of scared. She probably heard some the rumours about me that are always floating around. . . ."

I nodded. "Go on."

"So I asked Tara if she wanted me to give her a reading. I told her she had to ask me to do it or else it wouldn't work. I don't think that's true—in fact I'm pretty sure it isn't—but it sounded kind of occult, sort of vampirish, and she seemed to eat it up. By then a few of the other kids had gathered around us, and Tara must've known it was too late to back out. So she started acting smarmy, telling me to play her cards and read her future, or am I too scared. I didn't like that. First she says 'play' her cards, right after I told her they weren't playing cards, and she says it in this joking tone, not for my benefit, or even hers, but because we had an audience. Then, to top it all off, she asks me if I'm scared, which I found doubly insulting since she was the one who was actually afraid. But then I figured out what the problem really was. What *her* problem was." Soelle paused for a moment, possibly to take a breath, more likely for effect. "I realized she wasn't scared *enough*."

"So that's what you did?" I said. "You scared her?"

"I don't care if people disrespect me. They can say whatever they want about me. They can write it on the bathroom walls—they could write it in neon on the front of the school, for all I care. But tarot isn't something to be laughed at. The cards don't like it. They told me so."

"Uh-huh. So what happened?"

"I dealt out her spread. Then I sat there for a while staring at her cards, looking like I was concentrating really hard on them. I knew the longer I took the more agitated Tara would get. So I started her reading—her *joke* reading, I might add. It wasn't real. I made it up. I just wanted to take her down a peg, and in front of all the jerks she was trying so hard to impress. I put on this serious expression and shook my head, telling her I didn't like what I saw. I began asking these medical questions, like if there was a history of heart problems in her family, is her father a smoker, stuff like that. Tara started getting freaked out. I had her cards laid out facedown, and I was flipping them over one at a time. The first card I turned over slowly and smoothly, barely making a sound, but each one after that I started snapping them louder and louder. When I flipped the last one—a card I slipped to the top of the deck on purpose without Tara noticing—it sounded like a gunshot, and Tara actually jumped in her seat. She was really scared, Toby. That last card was Death, which, as any self-respecting tarot reader will tell you, doesn't actually mean death but change."

"I would say death is a fairly big change."

Soelle's shoulders twitched in a small shrug. She was tall for her age and tended to slouch, which gave her the appearance of someone expressing perpetural indifference.

"Tara wanted to know if I was making it up. I told her I wouldn't do something like that. I told her that the cards would turn back on me if I read them incorrectly. I'm pretty sure that's bull, too, but it didn't matter much because Tara wasn't listening anyway. She stood up and started flapping her arms like she had to pee or something. She was breathing really fast and looking all around the room. She looked at me with these big saucer eyes and asked how she was going to die. Then I realized why she was looking all around like that. She was seeing death everywhere. I told her I didn't know how she was going to die, that the cards weren't that specific. Maybe she'd slip in the shower and break her neck. Or maybe she'd get kidnapped and chopped into little pieces."

"Or get hit by a bus," I added.

Soelle shrugged again. "Or that."

"Then what happened?"

"Some of the others were trying to calm her down. They tried to get her to sit back in her chair, but she pushed them away. She started saying something really fast. I didn't understand all of it, but I think she was worried that one of the chair legs was going to break and she was going to fall backwards and fracture her skull. She started moving down the aisle toward the door, turning around and around. She bumped into Jack Horton, who was just coming back from sharpening his pencil, and she started screaming at him, accusing him of trying to kill her. She was absolute loony tunes. She started spinning around pointing at the chalkboard, the globe, even Blinky the classroom iguana—screaming about death, death everywhere. Then she ran out of the room. Nobody followed her, but some of the others went over to the windows. A few moments later we saw her come running out of the school and into the street. The buses were just arriving and"—Soelle drove her fist into her palm—"el smacko."

"You sound real broken up about it."

"Tara Denton wasn't my friend. She was some twit I sat next to in Algebra who believed too much in tarot. I didn't like her, but I didn't kill her."

"And yet you got kicked out of school."

"They've been waiting to do that for a long time," Soelle said, with a noticeable lack of resentment. "Ever since the school mascot drowned himself."

"Right," I said. "Because he thought he was a real shark."

Soelle shrugged. "That's the rumour."

"Seems to be a lot of rumours at that high school," I mentioned. "Most of them about you. Would it kill you to make some friends?"

"I don't need friends. Just my brother."

She gave me her NutraSweet grin: full of artificial sweetness.

I remember the day when I became an adult.

It was four years ago. I was eighteen and Soelle was eleven. I'd just graduated from high school. My student co-op at the paper mill had turned into a full-time job. I drove a forklift. The hours were long, the work monotonous, but it was union and the pay was decent. I wondered if it was possible to do this kind of mindless labour for the next thirty or forty years without developing some sort of psychotic disorder. I was thinking about getting my own place and finding a girl to take back to it.

One day I came home from work and found Soelle sitting on the porch swing. She was drinking an Orange Crush and reading one of her Anne of Green Gables books.

"Mom and Dad are gone," she said.

"What do you mean they're gone?"

"They're gone." She took a sip of her drink. "I went out walking this morning, and when I came back they were gone."

I looked over at my car sitting in the driveway, parked behind my parents' station wagon. "Where did they go?"

"I don't know," Soelle said. "I thought they went visiting, but they haven't come back."

"Well that's it, then. They've just gone over to the Mullens' or the Heaths'. They'll be back."

Soelle lowered her book and gave me a patronizing look. "Mom and Dad haven't gone visiting in years, Toby. Where have *you* been?"

I was beginning to wonder that myself. I felt like I had been away much longer than seven hours. More like seven years.

I left Soelle on the porch and checked the house from top to bottom. There was no sign of our parents. No sign that they had suddenly packed up and left, but no sign that they had been dragged out of the house by force, either. No sign of anything at all. It was like they had been ghosts haunting the place rather than flesh and blood people who had once lived here. My memories of them felt hazy already.

I didn't feel scared or frantic. I felt angry. I didn't know why I felt that way, and that made me angrier. Where the hell could they have gone? Why would they leave me alone with Soelle?

I called the police and they searched the house. They talked to the neighbours. They asked for phone numbers of our other relatives, but we didn't have anyone we were close to.

The police came to the same conclusion I had reached hours earlier: that our parents had left the house seemingly of their own volition, but with absolutely no evidence of having done so. Their belongings hadn't been disturbed or removed and their luggage was still stacked in the crawl space. The neighbours didn't recall seeing them leave the house, nor did they report seeing any unusual people in the area.

Time passed. Days turned into weeks, and I kept waiting for a social worker from the Children's Aid Society to come and take us away. Soelle and I would be placed in a province-run care facility until adequate foster homes could be found. They would try and keep us together, but there were no guarantees. We would eventually be passed off to different families. Over the next few years Soelle and I would exchange birthday cards, Christmas presents, the occasional letter, but eventually we'd drift apart until we finally forget we even had a brother or sister. It was stuff shitty made-for-TV melodramas are made of.

But it didn't happen. The social worker never showed up. I thought maybe Soelle and I had slipped through the cracks, as so many kids are supposed to do, if you believe the news magazine shows. The truth was much simpler.

They didn't come because I was eighteen and working. The mortgage was already paid off, and I was bringing in enough to cover the bills and keep us fed. I had grown up without realizing it. I was an adult.

Soelle had a reputation as an unusual child even before she started school.

My earliest memory of an "incident," which was what our parents called the strange things that happened in Soelle's presence, occurred when Soelle was two years old and I was nine. We were in the back yard, Soelle playing in her turtle kiddie pool, me sitting on the swing set that I was already too big for. I was bored out of my skull. I had been tasked with keeping an eye on Soelle and making sure she didn't drown herself in fourteen inches of water.

Something caught my attention in the farmer's field that our property backed onto. I don't recall what it was. A deer, maybe. I wandered over to check it out, and when I came back, no more than two minutes later, the turtle pool was gone.

The pool wasn't very big, but it was a painfully bright lime green that stood out on our parched yellow lawn like a radioactive spotlight. Still, it took me a moment to realize it was gone. Part of that was because Soelle was still right where I had left her, blonde hair in a ponytail, decked out in her My Little Pony bathingsuit, and sitting in the spot where the pool had been only a moment ago.

"Soelle," I said, "where's the pool?"

"It's gone!" She was crying and slapping at the ground, which was turning muddy from the hose that was still spraying out water.

"Where did it go?"

I was thinking some kid must have come into our yard and taken it.

"It went away!" There were tears on her face. I remember that because she wasn't the kind of kid who cried very often. She raised her hands, the hose still gripped in one of them, and sent a spray of water into the air.

I actually looked up then, half-expecting to see a green turtle-shaped pool floating in the sky over my head.

Of course there was nothing there when I looked.

But I saw plenty of other strange things over the years since then.

After Soelle got kicked out of school, she started disappearing most nights. I'd be walking past her door on my way to bed and, more often than not, her room would be empty, the bedsheets neat and undisturbed. She was always back in the morning, acting as though she hadn't left, and although I questioned her about it at first, she always gave me the same reply: "I was just out walking."

After a couple of weeks of this, I started going out looking for her. Silver Falls isn't a very big town, but it still took me a few nights to find her, walking barefoot along the banks of the Black Creek, near the Cross Street bridge. She was wearing her nightgown, and looked like an oversized child.

"What are you doing down there?" I called from the bridge railing.

"Oh, I'm just looking around," she said, her arms held out to either side, walking along the water's edge, one foot stepping in front of the other like she was walking on a tightrope.

"What are you looking for?" I spoke in a low, harsh whisper. I didn't know why I bothered. We were on the edge of town, almost into the woods, and there were no houses nearby. Even if there were, no one would have thought anything of it. Not if they knew it was Soelle.

She giggled and disappeared under the bridge. I swore under my breath and went around to where the embankment slanted down to the creek bed. Soelle was staring up at the underside of the bridge. I tried to see what she was looking at, but it was too dark.

"I asked what you're doing out here. Don't you know it's after midnight?"

Soelle shrugged. "I'm looking for dead bodies."

I wasn't sure I heard her right. The creek was very loud under the bridge.

"Did you say dead bodies?"

Soelle gave a small nod, still staring upward. "I watched a TV show about police psychics. The kind used to track down dead bodies. They said most bodies are found in the vicinity of water. Lakes, rivers, ponds. I got to thinking about it and realized I've never seen a dead body before."

"And that's a bad thing?"

"Sure. I don't like the idea of not experiencing all that life has to offer."

"So you decided to go out in the middle of the night and look for dead bodies."

"Yes."

"Anyone in particular?"

"No. Anybody will do." She giggled. "Any *body* will do."

I hesitated, picking my words carefully. "You realize how messed up that sounds?"

Soelle turned and looked at me, and I felt a momentary pang of terror. Then her brow creased in puzzlement. She was looking at something above my head. I looked up and saw something hovering there: a small white rectangle. "What . . ."

Soelle touched my arm, startling me. She was standing right in front of me now. "Give me a boost."

I hunched over and laced my fingers together. She slipped her foot into the cup formed by my hands and I hoisted her up gently. I tried to crane my head back, but it was all I could do to keep from dumping us both into the creek. I looked over at the dark water churning by. There was something strange about it; something I hadn't noticed earlier. I couldn't be sure—it was too dark—but I thought it was flowing in the wrong direction.

"Got it!" Soelle said. I lowered her to the ground. She was holding the white rectangle in her hand, flipping it back and forth between her fingers. "Now *this* is exciting," she said.

It was a playing card.

The ace of hearts.

A few weeks after that, I came home to find Soelle in the front yard holding a leash. She was dragging it back and forth across the lawn like she was walking an invisible dog. I came over and saw there was a collar on the end of the leash. It was red with the words MY FAVOURITE PET embroidered on it.

"Dare I ask?"

Soelle smiled. "I went down to the store to get a chocolate milk, and the guy behind the counter called me a witch."

"He said that," I said, sceptically, "right out of the blue?"

"Well . . ." Soelle hesitated. "I asked him if he had seen any aces lately."

"Any aces."

"Like the one I found under the bridge. I'm looking for the rest of them. I thought he might've seen one of them around. That's when he started looking at me funny. He said he recognized me and that people were talking about me."

"So what else is new?"

"They've always talked, but no one's ever called me a witch before."

"And what, you're worried they're going to burn you at the stake?"

"No, of course not. The guy in the store did say he'd call the cops if I didn't leave, though. He was a real *ace*-hole. But it got me thinking, what if he did call the cops? How would the poh-lease deal with a witch?"

"I think they shoot them on sight," I told her, "but they use silver bullets."

"That's for werewolves, you nerd."

"What does it matter? You're not a witch. People in town, they're just . . ."

"Yes?"

"They don't know what to make of you."

"Maybe I am a witch."

"You're still young. You can be whatever you want."

Soelle shrugged. "Maybe I want to be a witch."

"A witch who looks for aces. Sounds like a wise career choice."

"Thank you."

"It still doesn't explain the leash."

"Oh, this." She held it up like she didn't even know it was in her hand. "This is for my familiar. I figure if I'm gonna be a witch, I'd better start acting the part."

"You're already acting the part," I said. "That's why people think you're a witch."

Soelle nodded thoughtfully. "Toush."

"That's touché, you nerd."

Soelle started dragging the leash with her everywhere she went. This went on for about two weeks, and then one day I noticed her without it.

"Give up on the familiar?" I inquired.

"No," she said, smiling brightly. "I already found one."

"Oh?"

"He's been living with us for the last week, as if you didn't notice."

"I'm afraid I didn't."

Soelle turned her head to the side, as if hearing something I could not. "Oh," she said. "You can't see him. Only I can."

"What happened to the leash?"

"He doesn't like wearing the leash. He said it was degrading to his person."

"He actually said that? Degrading to his person?"

"Yes. The Haxanpaxan is quite sophisticated. He's going to help me find the rest of my aces."

"The Haxanpaxan?" I said. "What's that, a zebra or something?"

"It's a name." Soelle rolled her eyes at me. "And I wouldn't make jokes about it. The Haxanpaxan doesn't have a sense of humour."

"Sounds like he's a lot of fun at a party."

Soelle glared at me. "I'd watch that."

Ahh, the Haxanpaxan. How he made our lives so very interesting.

"Soelle, I told you to turn off the TV if you're not watching it."

"The Haxanpaxan's watching it."

"The Haxanpaxan is watching *Canada's Next Top Model*?"

"He likes it. He says the models remind him of himself."

"Soelle, did you leave the back door open?"

"The Haxanpaxan did. He went outside to do his business."

"Well, can you tell him to close it when he's done?"

"You don't *tell* the Haxanpaxan to do anything."

"Can you ask him, then? Pretty please, with sugar on top?"

"Toby, do you remember what I said about being funny?"

"Soelle, do you know anything about the Conroys' minivan getting smashed up last night?"

"I'm afraid not, Toby. But on a side note: the Haxanpaxan doesn't like minivans. And he doesn't like the colour lime green. He finds it offensive to the senses."

"Uh-huh. The back door was open again all night."

"The Haxanpaxan was out."

"Doing his business?"

"No, silly. He was looking for aces."

On an unseasonably warm Saturday in March, I was outside on the porch swing reading the paper when Soelle came skipping up the cobblestone path.

"Hard day at the office?" I asked.

"Look what we found."

She was bouncing around and waving something in her hand. It took me a moment to figure out what it was: a playing card. The ace of clubs.

"The Haxanpaxan was the one who found it, actually. He's very smart."

"Where did you find it?"

"Mrs. Ferguson's birdbath."

"Mrs. Ferguson?" I pictured an old woman who lived alone with her pet Rottweiler. An animal she could've thrown a saddle on and ridden around town. "You went into her back yard?"

"Duh. That's where her birdbath is."

"What about Kramer? Wasn't he outside?"

Soelle flashed me a wicked grin. "Oh, he was there all right. But one look from the Haxanpaxan and his fur turned completely white."

"Uh-huh."

"Yep. Then he ran around the side of the house and we went over and got the card."

"Aces."

"That's right." She winked at me and skipped up the porch steps and went inside. I was picking up my paper when I heard the porch steps creak. The front door swung open on its own, then closed again.

Just the wind, I thought.

❖

Soelle called me from a payphone and told me I had to come over to Mrs. O'Reilly's house.

"Who?" I asked, groggily. I had been asleep. I looked over at the clock radio and saw it was half past two in the morning. "Do you know what time it is?"

"It's not important. You need to get over here now."

"Who's Mrs. O'Reilly?"

"My Algebra teacher. Duh!"

Soelle gave me the address, but the house turned out to be easy to find. It was the one on fire.

A pair of fire engines were parked out front, blocking off the street. Firefighters ran hither and yon, dragging heavy canvas hoses. A group of rubberneckers stood off to one side. Soelle was among them.

"What the hell's going on?" I asked her in a low voice so the others wouldn't hear.

"I didn't do it," Soelle said immediately. "The Haxanpaxan did."

"There *is* no Haxanpaxan."

"The Haxanpaxan doesn't like it when—"

I grabbed her roughly by the arm. "Stop it, Soelle. This is serious."

"You're telling me."

She nodded at the house. The firefighters had stopped running and were staring at it, too.

The flames were green.

❖

"So you're saying you didn't burn down your algebra teacher's house because she was the one who confiscated your deck of tarot cards and got you expelled."

"Ex."

"What?"

"She was my ex-Algebra teacher. I feel the need to have that stated for the record."

"The record? You're not on trial, Soelle."

"Really? You could've fooled me."

"You said the Haxanpaxan did it."

"That's right."

"But there is no Haxanpaxan."

"I wish you would stop saying that. It makes him very angry."

"Was the Haxanpaxan angry at Mrs. O'Reilly?"

"No. I guess you could say he was angry on my behalf."

"And that's why he burned down her house."

"I don't control the Haxanpaxan, Toby. He knew I was upset, and I guess he just took it out on her."

"Well, that's just . . . just . . ."

"Aces?"

"No, Soelle, it isn't aces. It's the exact opposite of aces."

I got a phone call from the guy who owned the convenience store. He said Soelle was loitering around outside, and if I didn't come down and collect her, he was going to call the police. I realized this was the guy who started all the witch talk. He sounded terrified. As I got in the car and drove over, I wondered how he got our phone number.

Soelle wasn't there when I pulled into the strip mall. I parked and went around back to where the dumpsters were. I found her writing on the brick wall with a piece of pink chalk. She was drawing squares, one next to the other, one stacked on top of another.

"What the hell are you doing?"

"What does it look like?"

"It looks like you're tagging the back of the store."

"Tagging? Oh, Toby, you're so street." She snickered and kept on drawing. "And it's not graffiti. It'll wash off in the rain."

"Then what are you doing?"

"Testing a theory," she said vaguely.

She drew one final square, then walked back to where I was standing. She handed me the piece of chalk and walked further back, toward the screen of trees between the plaza and the lake. She stopped on the grassy verge, turned around, and suddenly ran full-tilt at the wall. I started to call out, but she sped past me, arms pumping, brow furrowed in concentration.

At the last moment, she leaped into the air, throwing her legs out in front of her like a long-jumper, and landed on the wall.

And stuck to it.

She stood frozen there, in a half-crouch, on the wall. Then, slowly, she began to stand up straight . . . or rather, sideways. She was standing in the middle of the first square she had drawn. She hesitated a moment, then hopped sideways and landed on the next one. I tilted my head, trying to watch her, but it was disorienting. It was one thing to see her defying gravity by sticking to the wall, but it was quite another to watch her hop up and down in a sidelong fashion. It was like watching someone walking up the crazy stairs in an M.C. Escher print.

It wasn't until Soelle reached the final square and turned around and hopped back that I realized what she was doing.

Playing hopscotch.

Things quieted down a bit after that.

Soelle didn't do anything too weird, and there were no unusual occurrences in town. It was a textbook Silver Falls summer: hot, quiet, and uneventful.

September arrived and the kids went back to school. October came and the leaves started changing colour. Everything was still quiet. I started to think maybe it was just a phase Soelle had gone through. Like puberty or something. I thought about getting her back into school, or at least helping to get her high-school equivalency. On the one hand I was surprised I hadn't received a summons from juvenile court. On the other it was just another example of how removed Soelle was from everyday life.

I had asked Soelle what she wanted to do with her life, and she told me her first priority was to find those last two aces. I told Soelle we'd have to work on that, but until then maybe she'd like to help me rake the leaves.

I told her to get started while I went down to the hardware store to buy some paper leaf bags. As I was coming out of the store, I happened to look across the street at the people lounging around in Orchard Park. They were all looking up at the sky. I went over to see what was going on. I tried to follow their collective stare, but I couldn't see anything. Then I saw it, something small and dark floating high above the trees. It looked like a black balloon. Everyone was talking in low, excited voices, some of them pointing. An old man holding a bag of bread crumbs he had been using to feed the pigeons was shaking his head and saying, "It ain't right. No sir, it ain't right at all."

Whatever it was, it started to come down closer to the ground. It bounced back up, then came down again, lower this time, and I could make out what it was.

Soelle.

She was wearing a black dress and black shoes (part of her witch's wardrobe, I assumed). As I watched her descend lower, one of the shoes slipped off her foot and fell into the park fountain with a splash.

"Heads up!" she called down in a giggling voice.

"Soelle!" I shouted. "Come down from there!"

I felt absurd saying those words. Like I was only asking her to come down off the roof.

"Are you kidding?" she hollered back. "Do you know how long it took me to get up here? I've been working on this for weeks!"

"Get down right *now*!"

"Don't be such a drag." She swung around in a lazy turn and started coming down lower. She brushed the top of one of the tall elms and called out: "Oh, wow!"

"Be careful!"

She came floating down to the ground, looking like a gothy version of Mary Poppins (*sans* umbrella). The people in the park ran away, some of them screaming.

"This can only end well," I said, watching them scatter.

Soelle waved a dismissive hand. "They're just jealous," she said. "Forget them. Look what I found at the top of that tree!"

She passed it to me.

The ace of spades.

The van showed up the day after the levitation incident.

I knew something was coming. There was a tension in the air, the kind that reminded me of the wet-battery smell before a powerful thunderstorm.

I was in Soelle's room changing her sheets. Not that there was any sign she actually slept in her bed those days. I was just going through the motions of a normal life. I was putting on the pillowcases and staring at the spider that built a web outside Soelle's window every spring. The web it had made this year was bizarre to say the least. It was all over the place, for one. It was coming apart in places and in others the webbing had been spun into strange, almost geometric shapes.

I was watching the spider running madly back and forth when the van pulled up: a white van with no markings on it except a plus sign on the side. Sort of like the Red Cross only black.

A man and a woman got out, both dressed conservatively—the man in a dark suit, the woman in a skirt and jacket ensemble. They looked like Jehovah's Witnesses. The man was carrying a briefcase, but I didn't think there were copies of *The Watchtower* inside.

I reached the front door just as they were knocking on it.

"Hello," the man said. "My name is Waldo Rand. This is my partner, Leah." He motioned to the woman behind him without taking his eyes off me. "May we speak with you?"

"About what?"

"You have a sister." It wasn't a question. "May we see her?"

I turned my head and looked into the living room. Soelle was sitting on the floor amid a drift of our father's old *National Geographics*.

"What for?" she asked gruffly.

"This won't take very long," Waldo assured me. "And it won't hurt," he added to Soelle, who didn't look convinced. "Just have a seat here." He gestured to the table in the dining room. Reluctantly Soelle came over and took a seat across from Waldo. His partner, Leah, stood in the doorway, one hand resting on her hip, fingers tapping against a bulge under her jacket.

"Do you have a lot of friends, Soelle?"

Soelle stared at him for a moment before answering. "No. I don't need any."

"Not even an imaginary one? Someone only you can see? Do you have one of those?"

"Yesss," Soelle said slowly.

"Is he or she in this room right now?"

Soelle made an effort of looking all around her, then she shook her head.

"She's burning hot," Leah mentioned in a strangely casual voice.

Waldo took out a folded piece of paper, unfolded it, and put it down with a pen in front of Soelle. "Can you draw me a picture of him?"

Soelle stared at the paper, then raised her eyes up to Waldo.

"The Haxanpaxan doesn't like to be drawn, does he?" he said.

Soelle shook her head.

"Have you ever played with tarot cards?"

"You don't *play* with tarot cards."

"I've never seen anyone shift like this before," Leah said in a low, awe-filled voice. She raised one of her hands toward Soelle, fingers wavering slowly back and forth. "I'm surprised she's even visible."

"*Leah*," Waldo said curtly. He turned back to Soelle. "Have you ever *used* tarot cards before?"

"Yes."

"A girl died," I mentioned.

"I didn't kill her! She ran in front of a bus."

Waldo held up a calming hand. "It's okay. We're not here about that."

"Then why are you here?" Soelle snapped.

"We just have one more question." Waldo cleared his throat. "Have you ever played . . . Have you ever used a Ouija board?"

"No," she said emphatically.

Waldo let out a deep breath. He wiped his brow and looked over his shoulder at his partner. She crossed her arms and leaned back against the wall. "Thank God for small favours," she said.

Waldo stood up and led me into the kitchen.

"May I call you Tobias?"

I nodded.

"Tobias, your sister is . . ."

"Please don't say special."

"I was going to say dangerous."

"That's awfully . . . frank."

Waldo frowned. "I'm afraid I don't know any other way to be."

"It's okay," I told him. "It's just unexpected. I've become sort of used to—"

"Covering up for your sister?" Waldo finished. "Making excuses for her? We know, Tobias. We know all about it."

"What do you mean by that?"

"Soelle is having an adverse effect on reality. She's out of phase. She's not supposed to be here. I'm sure you've noticed some unusual phenomena while in her presence. People and animals acting strangely, unusual weather, apports . . ."

"Apports?"

"Objects that appear seemingly out of thin air."

"What kinds of objects?"

Waldo gestured vaguely.

"Like playing cards?" I suggested.

"Sure," Waldo said. "Small objects usually."

"Soelle's been finding playing cards—aces, specifically—around town. She's become intent on finding them."

"Aces?" Leah said, coming up behind us.

"Yes," I said. "She found one under a bridge. Another in a tree—a tree that she was levitating over at the time."

"Levitation." Leah's gaze drifted away for a moment, then came back in force, boring into me. "Has she found them all?"

"No. She's found three of them so far."

Leah turned to Waldo and said, "We need to move quickly."

Waldo cleared his throat and turned to face me.

"Tobias, we have a man in our employ. A psychic. He has the ability to the see future in his dreams. He lives in one of our most remote stations, in Lhasa. That's in Tibet. The Roof of the World, they call it. We have him there because the high elevation causes people to dream in extremely vivid detail. It makes his ability that much more potent."

"What does this have to do with Soelle?"

"This man," Waldo said, "he's been dreaming of her. In those dreams, Soelle destroys the planet."

"She's not supposed to be here," Leah muttered.

"Where is she supposed to be?" I said. "Tibet?"

Waldo shook his head. "It's not important. All you need to know is that she can't stay here." He reached out and gave my shoulder a firm but comforting squeeze.

"Tobias, your sister needs to come with us."

Soelle didn't put up a fight. In fact, she wanted to go.

"I have to widen my search," she said. "You understand."

"Sure," I said. You could have filled a barn with all the things I didn't understand at this point.

I offered to help pack her stuff, but Leah said it wasn't necessary.

"We'll get her new clothes," she assured me. "We'll take care of her."

Waldo shook my hand and thanked me. I didn't know for what, but I said "You're welcome" anyway. Then they stepped outside to let me say good-bye to Soelle.

"Take care of the Haxanpaxan for me," she said.

"He's not going with you?"

"Leah says there's only room for me."

"Too bad."

"Yeah, but at least neither of you will be lonely."

I nodded. "Be good, Soelle."

She gave me her NutraSweet grin. "I'll try." Then she did something she hadn't done since she was little: she kissed me on the cheek.

Then she was gone.

I watched the van drive away. The plus sign on the side was gone. In its place were three wavy lines. I didn't know what that meant.

One more thing to add to the list.

After a while I went upstairs. As I was passing Soelle's room, the door slammed shut. I tried to open it, but it wouldn't budge.

The door still doesn't open, and I haven't been in her room since.

No one ever questioned Soelle's disappearance. I never called the police, and no one ever came around asking about her. I think it was more than just the town being glad she was gone. Maybe she really didn't belong here.

I heard from her only once. I got a letter. It was postmarked from a town in Mexico, some place I couldn't even pronounce. It contained two items. One was a colour photograph of a Mayan pyramid. On the back she had written: *I found it, Toby. It was here all along.*

The other item was a playing card.

The ace of diamonds.

Autumnology

I never knew his real name. No one did. When I first started delivering his groceries, I told him mine, thinking he would do the same, but he shook his head.

"Names aren't important," he said. "Only the work is important. There will be no names between us. You will be 'the Boy' and I will be 'the Professor.'"

I was sixteen at the time and didn't particularly like being called a boy. But the Professor was so unusual, so different from any adult I'd ever known, that I didn't give it much thought. Of course now all I can do is think about him.

I started to ask him about his "work," but he was already gone, out the back door. I watched him walk into the woods—a common sight, I would eventually discover.

Most people thought he was odd from the moment he arrived in town. For one thing, he referred to himself as a "professor of autumnology"—which is where the nicknames came from—and for another he was from "Away," which is what we say on Cape Breton Island to describe someone who wasn't born here.

He had moved into an old house on the outskirts of New Waterford. It was probably the best place for him. It made the townfolk comfortable with him in a way they might not have been otherwise. It's one of the simple truths we live with out here on the East Coast. The clouds are in the sky, the fish are in the sea, and the weirdos are on the edge of town.

People still wondered how he could live out there, with no electricity and no water except what he brought up from the well. I thought about these things too, but mostly I wondered about his "work," and why it was so important.

And it was important. I could see it in the Professor's eyes when he spoke to me. I still see that look in my dreams. I feel it burning a hole through me, but I never turn away from it.

It was on a day in November that he showed me the tree.

I had gone out to deliver the week's groceries, letting myself in through the front door since the Professor wasn't always around to hear me knocking. If he was home, we'd talk for a little while, usually about the weather. If he wasn't, I'd stick around for a bit anyway, unpacking the groceries and telling myself I was just being helpful, that I wasn't being what my mother called a Nosey Ned.

He wasn't around that day, so I set to restocking the pantry from the two big paper bags I had carried from town. While I was reaching up to put a box of powdered milk on a high shelf, the back door suddenly opened with a loud screech. The box slipped out of my fingers and bonked me a good one on the head. I didn't feel it, though. I was too busy gaping at the Professor standing in the doorway, his cheeks rosy as polished apples, the breath fuming out of his mouth in great frosty plumes.

"Someone has to see it," he gasped. "So I know I'm not crazy."

He did look a bit crazy, I had to admit. His eyes had the thousand-yard stare you sometimes see in fishermen who have spent their entire lives working on the sea. The eyes of someone who is looking at everything and nothing at the same time.

I was reaching down to retrieve the box of powdered milk when he grabbed my hand and pulled me toward the door. I managed to grab my wool cap off the kitchen table, and then we were outside, headed into the woods.

The dead, naked branches of maple and white birch raked at us like long, bony hands, making harsh scraping sounds against our coats, while our feet kicked through ankle-deep drifts of humus, decaying leaves with bright colours long faded. A branch snagged the wool cap out of my hand. I started to turn back for it and was almost pulled off my feet.

"No time," the Professor said in a low, desperate voice. Then he uttered a shaky, distracted laugh. "What am I talking about?"

I couldn't answer that question, and it seemed he couldn't, either.

We walked for a long time. The overcast sky grew darker by slow, almost imperceptible degrees. The smell of the leaves was almost overpowering. To me it was the smell of seasons dying.

The Professor began to speak. I couldn't hear everything he said, and the things that I could make out didn't always make sense. He said there were places in the world where it was like summer all the time, and spring, and winter—*but not autumn*. Oh no, he said, there was no place in the world where it was like autumn all the time. That's what made it special.

I began to feel afraid. It was getting dark and I was alone in the woods with a strange man who was dragging me God-only-knew where. I could feel the sky pressing down on me. The trees crowded in like co-conspirators in my own abduction. I wanted to leave, I wanted to go back home to my mother.

I was breathing rapidly and I eventually became aware of a smoky smell in the air. Up ahead the trees became less dense and it looked like one of them was on fire. But there was something strange about it. Something I couldn't pinpoint right away.

We broke into the clearing and stared up at it—an enormous elm with a thick trunk and branches that curved upward like the arms of a candelabrum. It was not like any tree I had ever seen before. It was almost artificial, like a piece of art—a concept that became even more cemented in my mind when I realized the flames which engulfed it weren't moving.

Something finally clicked in my head. It was like one of those migraine-inducing three-dimensional paintings where you have to sort of cross your eyes to see the hidden image.

There was no smoke because the tree wasn't on fire.

What I had at first taken to be flames were in fact leaves. The tree hadn't lost them yet, which was strange in itself, but made even stranger by the intensity of the colours themselves. Starburst yellows, candy-apple reds, and oranges as bright as the vests worn by the hunters who regularly tromped through these woods in search of deer and moose. They were almost too bright to look at.

"How . . ." I began.

The Professor shook his head.

"*When*," he corrected me, and placed his hand on the rough, almost ornate, bark. "And the answer, my boy, would be autumn. Forever autumn. Right here. In this spot."

He was exultant, almost reverent, like a priest who has come upon the very first church ever constructed. I thought he would fall on his knees and pay worship to the tree. For a moment I thought I might, too.

"Can you imagine it?" he breathed, staring up into the conflagration of leaves. "A place where it's like this all the time?"

I didn't want to imagine it, not then.

It's hard to explain why the tree frightened me so. I think it was what it represented. A place where it was always autumn. There was something unnatural about the idea. My fear lay in the root of that concept. Unnatural. Un-nature. The tree was something that shouldn't be. It was a tree out of time. A living monument that shouldn't exist, and yet at the same time couldn't be ignored.

I inched back to the edge of the clearing. The tree wasn't on fire, but a part of me still thought I would get burned if I stood too close to it. I started to back away, and the Professor turned, holding me in his gaze for a moment. There was something in his eyes. Disappointment, maybe. But then he turned back to the tree. When I realized the Professor had no further interest in me, I simply slipped into the woods and left.

I didn't think I'd be able to find my way back, but I did. I saw my hat hanging on a branch and grabbed it as I ran past.

I never saw the Professor again. I guess he got another boy to deliver his groceries.

That was many years ago. I'm an old man now, as old as the Professor was then. I have a son, and from time to time I see a look of curiosity on his face that is very familiar. It's like looking into a mirror to the past. I see that look on his face and I find myself thinking back to the Professor's final words to me, and the world I was too afraid to imagine.

It doesn't scare me anymore. In fact, it's a comfort to me now.

I see it when I close my eyes.

A world where the sky is cloaked in perpetual overcast, the scent of woodsmoke is always in the air, and the trees that burn there burn forever.

CABIN D

I

When the man in the houndstooth jacket stepped through the door, Rachel knew he was going to be trouble. It wasn't until later, after he had dropped the biggest tip she ever received, that she learned trouble was, in fact, where he was going.

It was a few minutes past eight on a Friday morning and Rachel was nursing a cup of coffee and leafing through the Sutter County *Register*. The breakfast crowd had come and gone, and she expected things to pick up again, oh, sometime tomorrow morning. The Crescent Diner did a good business in the hours between six and eight AM, but afternoons and evenings were deader than disco.

At the moment, the only sounds in the diner were the low gurgling of the Silex and the whisper of the ceiling fans turning overhead. Reg was out back having a smoke and the jukebox (which contained such golden oldies as "Gangsta's Paradise" and "Mambo No. 5") was mercifully silent.

The bell over the door jingled, and Rachel was so surprised by the sound that she almost dropped her coffee cup. She looked up from the newspaper and saw a man standing in the doorway.

"Morning," he said, and gave her a sunny grin. He squinted his eyes in order to read the orange, moon-shaped name-tag pinned to her blue rayon uniform. "Rachel." He raised a hand in greeting. "I'm Henry."

The waitress's first thought was that the man, Henry, had crawled out of a Salvation Army donation bin. In addition to the houndstooth jacket, he wore a paisley shirt, a plaid tie, and a pair of tan slacks so short they looked like flood pants. He was also wearing mismatched socks—one brown, one yellow and covered with a pattern of lobsters. She wondered idly if the circus was in town.

She was about to head out back and tell Reg they had another homeless person in the diner, but something made her wait. She stared at the man a moment longer and realized that, despite his ragged, clownish attire, he clearly wasn't one of the homeless vags who wandered in from time to time in search of food or money. He was in his late twenties or early thirties. He was thin, clear-eyed, and clean-shaven, and he didn't give off the stink of either cheap wine or puke.

"Hi Henry," she said finally.

"I just hitched in." His jacket opened a bit as he jerked a thumb over his shoulder, and Rachel caught a glimpse of rainbow suspenders. "A trucker named Eddie Ray said if I wanted a good meal I had to stop in at the Crescent."

"You found it," Rachel said. "In all its glory."

"Do you have an extensive menu?"

Rachel blinked. In the five years she had been waitressing, she had never heard that question before. "I'm sorry?"

"Well, I have some time to kill—and an appetite to kill, for that matter—and I was just wondering if your menu has a wide selection. I brought a newspaper—" he patted the rolled up copy of the *Register* under his arm "—and I plan to bivouac in one of your booths for the day. If that's all right by you."

"Bivo-what?"

"Bivouac," he said. "Camp out."

Rachel was speechless. She was tempted to look out the wide front window and see if there was a camera crew out there. She felt like she was on one of those reality TV shows where they play practical jokes on unsuspecting people.

"We have a pretty good menu . . . I guess." She made a vague gesture. "Would you like to see it?"

Henry held up his hand. "No need," he said, still smiling. "I trust you."

Rachel watched as he went over and took a seat in a corner booth. He put the newspaper on the table and picked up a laminated menu. He began looking it over with the wide-eyed exuberance of a scholar perusing a rare folio edition.

Five minutes later, he summoned Rachel over.

"All set?" she asked.

"Yes. I'd like the Full Moon breakfast—scrambled eggs, sausage, hash browns, toast (white bread, please), melon, and orange juice. I'd also like an extra side of bacon."

"Coffee?"

"Constantly," Henry said, and grinned.

Rachel didn't like that grin. There was something artificial and a little unsettling about it. It stretched too tightly across the skin on his face. Like a skeleton's grin.

She turned away and went through the swing door to the kitchen. Reg was just coming back in, taking off his coat and hanging it on the wooden peg next to the door.

"We have a customer," Rachel told him, and recited Henry's order.

"Really?" Reg said, amused. "Hell must have frozen over." He slipped his apron on over his head.

"Guy looks kind of weird. Says he hitched in with Eddie Ray."

Reg dipped his head down so he could see through the partition in the wall. "He looks harmless enough. Although I don't know many bums who ever used a newspaper for anything other than a blanket."

"I don't think he's a bum," Rachel said. "He seems kind of . . . strange."

Reg shrugged. "Strange or not, he's got an appetite."

‖

Ten minutes later, Rachel emerged from the back with Henry's order on a large serving tray. As she dished it out, Henry moved each plate around like chips on an oversized bingo card. When he had everything where he wanted, he looked up at Rachel with that same beaming grin.

"This all looks great. Really great."

Rachel smiled politely, tucked the empty tray under her arm, and returned to the kitchen.

Henry picked up his fork and knife and began to cut up the four sausages on one of the side plates. When he was done, he cut up his eggs, forked some hash browns on top of them, and began to eat.

Rachel watched him through the partition. Henry didn't seem

to be aware of her staring, and that was good because she couldn't seem to make herself stop. She followed his fork as it scooped up eggs and sausage and hash browns and deposited them into his mouth. He chewed mechanically, as if he were a machine and the food was his fuel.

He seemed to relish the food, closing his eyes and letting out long, satisfied sighs of pleasure between bites. It was like sex. He wasn't just eating the food; he was savouring it. Like he had never eaten before. Or might never eat again.

Like a death-row inmate, she thought.

Henry took a big gulp of coffee, tilting his head back to get the last drop. Watching from the partition, Rachel noticed dark smudges under his eyes. At first glance Henry had seemed full of buoyant, invigorating energy, but upon closer examination she saw he was quite thin and pallid, almost sickly. The phrase *death-row inmate* clanged in her head, and Rachel reassessed her initial observation.

No, he looks like death. Or someone close to death.

Regardless, Henry continued to eat steadily throughout the day. After finishing his breakfast, he ordered a tuna-fish sandwich on rye and a glass of milk. Rachel topped up his coffee—almost filling it past the overflow point in her daze—and went back to Reg in the kitchen with his order.

"Maybe he's one of those food critics," Reg said, taking an enormous bottle of mayonnaise out of the big, steel-doored walk-in. "Sometimes they travel in disguise."

"I don't think so," Rachel said.

By the time noon rolled around, Rachel had filled Henry's coffee cup at least a dozen times. He had polished off the tuna-on-rye and ordered a side of French fries with gravy. He told Rachel that you could tell a lot about a restaurant by the quality of their gravy.

At three PM, Josie Sutton pulled up in her lime-green VW bug with the bumper sticker that said TENNE-SEEIN' IS TENNE-BELIEVIN'! She was wearing her waitress uniform and the magenta hoop earrings that she had bought off eBay because they supposedly once belonged to Tammy Wynette.

She gave Henry a passing look as she strolled through the swing door. She was reaching for her time-card in the slot on the wall when Rachel stopped her.

"What's wrong?" Josie asked.

"Do you mind if I take your shift today?"

"What? Why?"

Rachel told her about Henry. Josie raised one pencil-drawn eyebrow. "You got a crush or sumthin'?"

"No," Rachel said, flushing slightly. "I just know that if I go home now I'll be wondering about it for the rest of the week."

Josie thought it over for a second—which was about as long as Josie ever thought about anything—and said: "Okay. Sure. Whatever. Matt Damon's gonna be on Oprah today, anyway." And she left.

An hour later, Rachel came out of the kitchen to wipe down the counter for about the forty-seventh time that day. Henry was reading his newspaper.

As she moved along the counter, Rachel turned her back to him. When he spoke she dropped her cloth and almost cried out in surprise.

"I've been in here for just over five hours and I haven't seen a single person come in."

Rachel let out a long, steadying breath as she crouched down and picked up the cloth. "Things fall off pretty quick after the morning crowd leaves," she said. "You're really making me earn my minimum wage today."

"If you don't have many customers, then why such a big menu?" he asked. "Not that I'm complaining."

Rachel turned around and leaned against one of the counter stools. "The owner, Reg, is also the cook. He says offering a wide variety of food puts a certain amount of creativity into an otherwise mundane job."

"Seriously?"

"That's what he says," Rachel said, aware that Reg might be listening.

"Well," Henry said, raising his voice slightly, "he's an absolute artist in the kitchen." He folded his newspaper and picked up the menu again.

"More?" Rachel couldn't quite mask her surprise.

"Shocking, isn't it?" Henry smiled again; this one was thinner, not as forced as the others.

"It's just . . ." Rachel contemplated for a moment, then threw caution aside. "You're eating like a condemned man."

"Condemned," Henry repeated, and looked away. "That's funny." But the look on his face said it wasn't funny at all. "I'm not condemned. This is all voluntary. Very, very voluntary." The look went away and the thousand-watt smile came back on again, like a switch in his head had been flipped. "Could I get the meatloaf? Mashed potatoes, roast carrots, and a tall glass of milk?"

III

As Reg went to work on Henry's meatloaf, Rachel drifted back to the partition. Henry had taken a single piece of newspaper and was folding it carefully and methodically. Curiosity finally got the better of her and she went back to the booth, under the auspices of refilling Henry's coffee cup. As she topped him up, he raised his head.

"Do you know what this is?"

On the palm of his hand was a folded-paper animal. A cow, she noticed, complete with tiny paper udders. Its head was lowered as if it were cropping.

"A cow?" Rachel guessed.

"That's right." Henry set it on the table. "Origami. The Japanese art of paper-folding."

"Paper-folding, huh? I thought they just made electronics."

"This is a much older craft."

"Secret of the Orient?" Rachel asked.

"Something like that," Henry conceded. "It can be traced back to the sixteenth century. Can you believe that knowledge of something like that could be kept for so long, passed down from one person to the next?"

"The only thing passed on in my family is insomnia and an old moth-eaten quilt that my great-grandmother made while she was snowed in one winter."

Henry chuckled.

Rachel eyed him suspiciously. "I'm sorry, but I have to ask: have you been drinking or something?"

Henry chuckled again, louder this time, then stopped suddenly.

"I thought about drinking today," he said in a solemn, thoughtful tone. "I thought it might be for the best to, I don't know, *sedate* myself, before the main event." He shook his head ruefully. "But I decided not to. It seemed kind of . . . cowardly."

He is *sick*, Rachel thought. *I knew it. It's cancer, or something like it.*

"The way I see it, nobody dies with a clear conscience, but I plan to go out with a clear mind." He looked down at the origami cow. "I'm afraid the only thing I planned to get drunk on today was cholesterol. And why not? Long-term health effects are not exactly my concern anymore. Hell, the long-term in general isn't my concern."

Rachel gave him a long, considering look. He didn't sound self-pitying or self-deprecating. He was speaking lucidly, almost clinically, as if he were talking about something he had read in the newspaper spread out before him. He had taken his time eating the food she had served; he hadn't wolfed it down. He had made it last. He acknowledged each forkful before putting it into his mouth. Like he was counting the bites. Like he knew there were only so many more he was ever going to take.

The sound of Reg dinging the order-up bell almost made Rachel jump. She went over to the partition and retrieved Henry's meatloaf dinner, delivering it to him without comment. Henry didn't say anything, either, just smiled that damn smile of his and started eating.

When he was finished it was almost eight o'clock. Like the rest of his meals at the Crescent Diner, Henry had made his dinner last.

After clearing his empty plate, Rachel came back and filled his coffee cup. "Dare I ask?" she said. "Dessert?"

Henry was breathing heavily now. Rachel thought it was a wonder his sides hadn't split.

"What kind of pies do you have?"

"Apple, blueberry, strawberry-rhubarb, peach, and pumpkin."

"One of each," he said without smiling. "Please."

Nothing surprises me at this point, Rachel thought on her way back to the kitchen.

But she was wrong. After she brought out the pies, Henry

surveyed each one, picked up his fork, and began to eat. Rachel couldn't watch any longer. Henry was sick, this whole thing was sick, and she didn't want to look at it anymore. She felt like she was participating in an execution. She wished she hadn't taken Josie's shift.

She was turning away when Henry said, "This is a good place."

"What?"

"The Crescent Diner. This is a good place. Good food, good service. I like it."

Rachel stared at him.

"I'm fit to burst," he said. "There's no way I'm going to be able to finish these."

She looked down and saw that he had taken a single bite out of each piece of pie.

"There was a guy from around these parts, name of Mundy or Mindy, I can't remember which. He wrote a book about bad places."

"A food critic?" Rachel asked.

"Something like that," Henry said dismissively. "He had a word for these bad places. He called them 'pressure points.' I knew a girl once who called them something else. A much more appropriate word, in my opinion." He paused in remembrance, or maybe for effect. "She called them 'tornadoes.'

"Do you read?" he asked suddenly.

Rachel shook her head. "Only the expiry dates on the milk cartons at the Food Mart," she said, and Henry laughed.

"Can I get my bill?"

Rachel took her order pad out of the pouch on the front of her uniform. She flipped through the sheets on which she had scribbled Henry's orders throughout the day. She couldn't remember the last time she had to add so many numbers. Finally she scribbled a total at the bottom of the page and plunked it down on the table.

Henry reached into his houndstooth jacket and produced a thick wad of bills bound with a rubber band. He paid the bill and then placed the still-considerable stack of cash on the table. He smoothed it out and placed the origami cow on top of it.

"That's for you," he said.

And then without another word, he stood up, ignoring Rachel's stunned expression, and left the diner.

Rachel turned around in time to see the door swing shut. She heard the sound of Henry's shoes on the crushed gravel in the parking lot, and a second later she saw him pass in front of the side window on his way around to the back of the diner.

The next time she saw him he was on page four of the Sutter County *Register*.

IV

There are haunted places in the world. Dark places. Shunned places. Forgotten places. All existing in reality and every bit as tangible and accessible as the house next door. Sometimes it *is* the house next door.

But hauntings aren't restricted to houses. There are also haunted apartments and haunted trailers, haunted farms and haunted restaurants, haunted churches and haunted schools, and, on Lake Shore Boulevard in Toronto, there is even a haunted fish-processing plant.

In the unexpunged edition of *The North American Guide to Haunted Architectural Structures and Supernatural Pressure Points* (Horsehead Press, 1949), paranormal researcher Dale Mundy declared that the most haunted building south of the Mason-Dixon Line was not a house but a cabin. Cabin D, to be exact, at the Crescent Moon Motel in Tennessee.

According to Mundy, no one who stayed in Cabin D—the Crescent Moon's honeymoon suite—lived to see morning. The cabin had been built away from the others in a clearing in the woods, the thought being that seclusion equalled romance. Mundy didn't mention exactly how many newlyweds had died in Cabin D, but he soliloquized on vast numbers of young lovers who never even had the chance to consummate their wedding vows. Eventually the owner stopped renting it out, and then, in October of 1923, a hurricane dubbed "The Southern Banshee" tore through Sutter County and reduced every cabin at the Crescent Moon to splinters. Every one except Cabin D.

Some people in Sutter County said the destruction of the Crescent Moon cabins was a blessing; others went one further and called it "nature's exorcism." The following summer, the land was bought by a developer and a motel was put up in the cabins' place—not directly on the site of the demolished cabins but closer to the highway. The new owner was never told about the existence of Cabin D because the old owner wasn't around to tell them. The Southern Banshee had exorcised him, as well.

The new motel opened in the fall and Cabin D was left to rot quietly in the woods. It had always been a dark place, a shunned place, and now it became a forgotten place.

Occasionally it reminded the world of its existence. Hobos and transients in search of shelter from Tennessee's brutal thunderstorms sometimes came upon the lone cabin in the woods. Most of them were struck dead before they could get within ten feet of the front door. A few made it inside, but as the saying goes at the roach motel, *They check in, but they don't check out.*

Despite the lofty theories of pundits like Dale Mundy, Cabin D was not hungry for blood, or souls, or Hostess Twinkies. It simply didn't like visitors. It had stood in the woods beyond the Crescent Moon Motel for over eighty years, and, like Shirley Jackson's Hill House, it might stand for eighty more.

But some people—those who had not forgotten about Cabin D—decided they couldn't take that chance.

V

When he reached the edge of the parking lot, Henry kicked off his shoes and continued on barefoot. The grass was cool and damp under his feet. It was incredibly refreshing, and it took his mind off the gargantuan meal he had just eaten . . . and the cancer that was eating *him.*

It also took his mind off the thing that was waiting for him in the woods. The thing that had been masquerading as a dilapidated cabin for the last eighty years.

Cabin D hadn't killed anyone in seven years—not since a seventeen-year-old runaway named Justin Dugby came upon the cabin one rainy night—but the group Henry worked for decided enough was enough. It was time to take Cabin D out of the game.

Except we can't do that without taking one of ourselves out of the game.

Henry recalled something one of his science teachers had said, about how energy could neither be created nor destroyed. The poisonous cloud that Cabin D had existed within all these years operated under a similar principle. It could not be destroyed, as such, but the malefic energy that thrummed through its walls could be negated.

Travis had given him the means to do that very thing. A small post-hypnotic trigger that—if it worked—would snuff out both the cabin's influence and Henry's life. A fair trade, he thought. The authorities would find his body, eventually, and he'd be written off as just another dead vagrant. He wasn't carrying any identification, not that it would have mattered anyway. He had been legally dead since he joined the group eleven years earlier.

Passing through the grass and into the dense woods, Henry could feel the pressure building up around him. His ears felt stuffed with invisible cotton. The sound of his footsteps seemed distant, not his own. As he pressed on, the pressure continued to build until he thought his head might explode. Cabin D didn't like visitors. Travis had shown him a satellite photograph of the woods behind the Crescent Diner, pointing out a number of black dots in the clearing where Cabin D stood.

Birds, Travis had said with a dark grin. *Makes you kind of glad there are no commercial flight routes that cross over it, huh?*

That was part of the reason Henry had volunteered to take out Cabin D. Yes, the cabin was mostly cut off from the world, and yes, more people died each year from lightning strikes and shark attacks, but those were natural occurrences. There was nothing natural about Cabin D. And things could change very quickly. Cabin D wasn't sitting on prime real estate now, but who could say what would happen ten, fifteen, or fifty years from now? The possibilities were as endless as they were disturbing.

The last few weeks leading up to his departure, Travis had started calling Henry "The Amazing Psychic Suicide Bomber." Henry didn't mind. At least Travis was still talking to him. By that time, most of the others in the group were ignoring him completely. In their minds he was already dead. He was like a ghost walking among them. They knew what he was planning to do and they were afraid for him.

And now here it was.

Henry stepped out between two hoary oaks and into a sea of tall grass that wavered gently in the night wind. Cabin D stood about forty feet away.

The wind picked up and the cabin seemed to creak scornfully.

Henry cleared his throat and spoke in a loud, carrying voice.

"Think of this as the return of the Southern Banshee. Back to finish the job."

He felt the pressure around his body intensify, like he was being squeezed within a giant invisible fist. Cabin D didn't like visitors in general, and it absolutely hated him. Henry could feel it. That was his freak, his wild talent, the thing his mother had called his "little extra." It had allowed him to converse with the dead, to read portents in broken glass and animal bones, and now it was the thing keeping him from dropping dead like the birds or any of the unfortunate souls who had travelled into Cabin D's noxious orbit.

Henry bore these intangible touchings as he waded through the tall grass toward the cabin. He went up the short flight of steps to the front door. He raised his hand and saw the veins sticking out on his arms like bas-relief. He opened the door—it wasn't locked—and stepped inside.

The air was dry and still. Galaxies of dust motes revolved slowly in the moonlight that filtered in through the windows. Henry realized with a kind of dim awe that he was the first person to step inside Cabin D in over eighty years.

There was still furniture in the cabin: an old horsehair sofa, two puke-green easy chairs, and a wooden coffee table that had been warped so badly by eighty years of moisture that it now resembled some strange piece of modern art. Hanging over the sofa was a painting of a summer landscape that was so sun-faded it could have now passed as a winter scene.

Stepping further into the room, Henry felt the pressure around him turn up a notch. Invisible fingers scrutinized the rondure of his skull like the shell of a hardboiled egg. He went into the bedroom.

The bed was neatly made, though the sheets lay in their own funky miasma of mildew. He went back out into the main room and sat down on the sofa, sending up a cloud of dust that caused him to cough loudly. He leaned his head back and closed his eyes.

All alone in the honeymoon suite, he thought. *It doesn't get much lower than this.* He felt the Cabin probing his eyesockets, his ears, the smooth trunk of his neck, looking for leverage, access.

In his mind he pictured the trigger. Except it didn't look like a trigger; it looked like a metal ring. He felt the pressure increase again, the hands scampering frantically over his body, patting him down, looking desperately for some way in. The ring was attached to something. In his mind Henry raised an invisible hand and slipped a finger through the ring. He let out a deep sigh and flexed his mind.

Henry slumped down on the couch, a small thread of blood trickling out of his nostril. He wondered dimly if it worked. His eyes flicked to the window as a cluster of shingles fell off the roof and landed in the tall grass. A crack appeared in the front door with a loud splintering sound. A floorboard snapped upward like a drawbridge. There was a low groaning sound that might have been the cabin settling. To Henry it was sound of something dying. He smiled and closed his eyes.

Winter Hammock

November 29

The power went off today. Which means my days of writing on the laptop are officially numbered. The battery will die, and there's no way in hell I'm going back across the bridge for another one. Not with those things wandering around.

I found this ledger in a desk, and it'll do the job fine. The job of what? I don't know. Writing my story, I guess. Isn't that what the guy in my position is supposed to do? Leave some sort of record behind about how things used to be before they got fucked up royally. So the people who come after can learn from our mistakes. It sounds like a good theory, except I'm not so sure there's going to be any "people after." Not now. Maybe not ever.

But I have lots of time. Oodles of time! Not much food, not much water, but time coming out of my ears! Time to kill, you could say. And I guess there's no harm in writing a few things down. For posterity, right? Ha-ha!

I'm not going to rewrite everything I put on the laptop. Writing this down is like reliving the past, and I just can't do it. Living through it once is bad enough. So you'll have to excuse me if I break into the program-already-in-progress. I'll give you a few highlights.

My name is Reggie Norris, formerly of 425 West Hill Street, Oakridge, Washington, currently of . . . I don't know. It's a warehouse on the dark side of the moon—by which I mean the far side of town, near the coast. That's all I can really say. I don't even know what they ship or receive at this place. Except for a few crates, the warehouse was empty when I got here.

Most of the Oakridgers worked at the factories and plants on the other side of the Town Bridge. I'd been trying to get on with one of them, but apparently you needed to be related to someone who already works here or know the secret handshake just to get an interview. I didn't want to work in a factory, driving a forklift or unpacking crates of computer parts, but I didn't have much of a choice.

I came here to go to school, and dropped out before my first year was up. I wasn't a party guy, and I didn't fall in love; I just didn't have what it took to make the grades. It happens, I guess. My parents didn't disown me, but they didn't want me to come home. I made my bed and I'd have to sleep in it, were my father's words. So I got a job at Radio Shack. Some life, huh?

It's funny. Trying to justify my existence as a drop-out while the world slides slowly into hell.

November 30

I worked the evening shift with a guy named Barney Tobermeier. Barney was a townie. He was fifty-four and lived in a trailer with a sign over the door that said CASA BARNEY. He wasn't a bad guy, but he couldn't see beyond his next paycheque or his next hangover. Mostly we goofed off. The nights were dead, except for the odd yuppie looking for fuses or a coaxial cable or a cell phone charger. We talked a lot. Barney liked to say he was wise in what he called "real-life truths." These were secret (and usually useless) tidbits of information that the public wasn't privy to. Things like which reality TV shows were actually scripted and which were real; which music albums contained secret lyrics when played backwards; and of course, which girls in town were worth a lay and which he wouldn't touch with a ten-foot pole.

It was all pretty dumb shit, and even if I wasn't smart enough to stay in college, I was smart enough to know that much. I was smart enough to leave town, too. When the news started to get bad. When it started to get weird. Really weird.

Hold on, I want to check something.

(later)

I was working on the night things went strange. Barney and I were swapping blonde jokes and listening to a college radio station out of Olympia. They had a decent Saturday night jazz show, and one of the deejays was a Wolfman Jack wannabe whose voice was still breaking. It was pretty funny stuff, though we didn't do much laughing that night.

Thelonius Monk was tickling his way through "Straight, No Chaser" when the broadcast was interrupted by the host's quavering voice. "We apologize for the interruption, but we have important news that affects everybody in Olympia. We have just received a report that several streets have become overrun with snakes!"

"Snakes?" Barney said. "Are those kids toking?"

I turned up the volume.

"Police and emergency crews are on the scene, but we have yet to receive any information on the origin of the snakes or if anyone has been injured. One listener who called this station sad he saw thousands—I repeat—*thousands of snakes coming out of sewer grates along Center Street*. We will be interrupting the program periodically to bring you further updates."

Thelonius Monk came back on. Barney and I exchanged puzzled looks.

"Snakes?" he said again. "What the Christ does that mean?"

"I haven't a clue," I said.

"It's gotta be a joke, right? College kids playing a prank?"

I shrugged.

We closed up and left in Barney's rattletrap K-car. We had the radio on and were awaiting "further updates." Barney got anxious and started running the dial across the band, trying to pick up another station. We got some tunes, but no news. When he pulled up to my apartment on Oak Hill, Barney found a raspy woman speaking in a frantic voice.

"This is Lois Davies with a special report. Police are advising citizens to stay indoors after hundreds of snakes were reported coming out of the sewers and drains in Seattle, Spokane, Olympia, and Yakima. A city official has described this event as '*a scourge of biblical proportions*,' and said they are doing everything in their power to contain and investigate this emergency."

Barney turned to me and said: "What do they mean 'biblical proportions'?"

I shook my head, but I was thinking about the final book of the Old Testament. Revelation. The end of the world.

Barney had paled considerably. He waved a hand that was not completely steady in a dismissive gesture. "I heard this same shit back in the seventies when I was working for Public Works in New York. Only then it was alligators! It's a humbug. Snakes can't live in sewers. Only rats. And they don't hardly ever come out into the open."

I nodded, but I wasn't convinced. I wasn't sure of anything. Not in a world where tabloid newspapers regularly printed headlines like FACE OF SATAN SEEN IN TORNADO and LIZARD BOY CAUGHT IN FLORIDA SWAMP. I usually didn't give those stories a second glance. I figured they were all lies—or "humbugs," to use Barney's word. But now I didn't know what to think. All I knew was that I was scared.

I'm still scared, but I have a better idea of what's going on now. People talk about fear of the unknown, and I get it, I really do. I get how it's scarier not knowing. But I tell you, there are days when I wish I didn't know what I do. That I never lived to see what I've seen.

December 1

I can't remember how long they kept calling them snakes. After a few days of watching nothing but CNN, I started to tune out. By then they were appearing in cities all over the country. All over the world.

I remember the last newspaper I saw before I came to this warehouse. It was the *Seattle Times*, and the headline said PANDEMONIUM! The front page was dominated by a picture of downtown Seattle. It could have been Any City, U.S.A. except for the Space Needle in the background. Many of the buildings in the picture appeared to have been completely overgrown with thick creeper vines. The caption said: *"TENTACLES" OF UNKNOWN ORIGIN OVERRUN DOZENS OF BUILDINGS DOWNTOWN.*

I watched a televised argument between two scientists. One of them was against calling the things "tentacles," because they hadn't yet determined what they were attached to. The other scientist didn't see how that made any difference. He was right, in his own way. It turned out the tentacles were only the opening act.

And frankly, I think it's a good thing we don't know what they're attached to.

December 2

Let me tell you a bit about my life here at Casa Warehouse. It's a fairly static existence, except for the newspapers. I find them sometimes, and looking at them is like looking at relics of a lost civilization. I guess that's what they are now. We've become the Incas and the Mayans; the lost Roanoke Island colony and those poor suckers on Atlantis, if it ever existed (Barney was positive it did).

I have a routine of walking around the warehouse twice a day, once in the morning and once in the late afternoon (I never go out at night). I don't do it for the exercise. I do it because of what the old-timers call cabin fever. The warehouse is huge—about a million times bigger than my studio apartment on Oak Hill—but there are still days when I feel like climbing the walls.

So I walk. Like an old man going for a constitutional around the block. Sometimes I find things. Mostly junk blown across the bridge from town. Sometimes I find newspapers stuck to the side of the warehouse. Seeing them like that always reminds me of the leaflets you see stuck under windshield wipers.

I peel them off and keep them. I never go out looking for more. That would be a bad idea, especially now. I've already drawn the attention of the ramblers, and even though I can't see them, I can smell them. That sharp sweet smell of rancid meat. They're out there, lurking around. I can feel them.

December 3

The "experts" had all kinds of theories, but no answers. Some of them said it was a government experiment gone awry. Others blamed a tear in the fabric of reality. Some wag even blamed Global Warming. And of course, the saucerheads blamed UFOs.

Then, for a period of about forty-eight hours, the various nations of the world turned their attentions on each other. The U.S. blamed terrorists; so did England; France and Germany blamed Russia; Russia blamed Japan; the countries in the Middle East blamed each other.

Martial law was declared in almost every major U.S. city. The Army and the Navy rolled out and got rolled over; same for the National Guard. Things started to break down. Then they started to slow down. The phones died. The TVs showed only test patterns, then static. People left the cities en masse, only to get stuck on the highways.

None of it mattered to the tentacles and the ramblers and the rest. To them a meal on the road was just as good as a meal at home.

I didn't own a car, and although it would have been easy enough at that point to steal one, I felt the key to survival wasn't in leaving town . . . at least not exactly.

I put myself into one of the situations they give you in college entrance exams—the kind I had done so well on before I got here and flunked out. I put myself in the position of the monsters. I tried to think the way they did. If I wanted to eat, where would I go? Where the food was, of course. Where the people are.

So I packed a bag and went where there were no people. I almost made it, too.

Almost.

December 4

I don't know what the ramblers are. Zombies, I guess. They look human: they have human facial features, however disfigured and grotesque. I came upon five of them just as I reached the Town Bridge. I saw them and they saw me. Only a couple of them had eyes (most only have dark pits where their eyes should be), but that didn't seem to bother them. I could feel them looking at me, scrutinizing me. They each had a nose, or the vestiges of a nose, and long, jagged fangs that punctured their cheeks and shredded their lips as they snapped their mouths open and closed. They were standing in front of a burned-out deli, filling their filthy maws with the spoils from the shattered display window.

I stood frozen for a moment when they started toward me. Not walking, not running. Rambling, as it were.

I ran. I looked back once, but kept running. On the other side of the bridge, the road bent to the north and I lost them behind some trees. I'd put about a mile between them and me, and I thought that would be enough. They don't move very fast.

I was panting and sweating and laughing. It was not good laughter. It was the kind of laughter they put people away for. I forced myself to stop.

I started walking again until I reached the industrial section of Oakridge. Warehouses, factories, and other soot-caked buildings. Smoke stakes pointed into the sky like silent cannons. Broken glass twinkled in the weeds that grew up from the cracked cement. Concrete culverts channeled rust-coloured water. A set of old train-tracks on a railway embankment.

In a word: heaven.

December 5

I brought a bag of books with me from home, but I lost it when I was running from the ramblers. I suppose if I get bored enough, I might actually go looking for it. It might come to that. There is ABSOLUTELY NOTHING TO DO HERE! I'm not so bored that I wish something would happen. I know if I did that the next thing I'd know there'd be a knock on the door. Ding, dong! Avon calling! Except the Avon Lady would be an Avon rambler with a dirty pink pantsuit, empty eyesockets, and a mouthful of broken glass for teeth.

I found some letterhead in one of the desks. My new home is— or *was*—called DTS Shipping. I haven't been able to find out what DTS stands for. I'm not sure it matters, but it's something to do.

There's an enclosed area at the rear of the warehouse which houses a row of offices. I've turned one of them into my living quarters, which is just a glamorous way of saying I unrolled my sleeping bag on the floor and my Garand is propped in the corner. There's also a men's room and a ladies room and an empty vending machine.

The walls are cement cinderblock and completely windowless. There's a skylight in the ceiling that provides enough light to see by day, and enough shadows to jump at by night.

I should have brought candles.

December 6

Found a new door today.

When I first came here I made sure to check all the possible ways in or out of the warehouse. Thankfully there was only one door in the entire place that wasn't a fire door or a loading door— by which I mean a door that a rambler or a tentacle could open from the outside. I use a few of those leftover crates to barricade it at night before I go to sleep.

The new door I found is at the end of the hall near the washrooms. It was on the other side of the vending machine, which is why I missed it. It leads out into what I presume was a smoking area. It's a fenced enclosure about twenty feet long and fifteen feet wide. Not quite enough room to have a dance party, but it sure beats staying inside all day.

December 7

Winter's coming, it's official. The wind is getting colder, sharper. It reminded me that I haven't shaved since I left home. I've grown a beard and didn't realize it.

In the effort to combat boredom, I decided to open the crates that are lying around here like some giant kid's toy blocks. I am now the proud owner of a set of patio furniture—four plastic chairs, one plastic table with a folding umbrella, and a hammock.

I'm going to set everything up in the pen out back. I've lived in an apartment my whole life, I think it will be nice to have a backyard for once.

December 8

Spent the morning rearranging furniture. The table takes up a considerable amount of space—so much I ended up hucking two of the chairs over the fence. I thought about keeping only one, for me, but you never know when company might drop by. Ha-ha!

I set up the hammock between two of the fence posts, so that it hangs diagonally across the enclosure. If I lie in it one way I can see the train tracks that run through the industrial area; if I lie in the other direction I can see the smoke rising from town.

At least I can't hear the screams anymore.

December 9

Been outside lying in the hammock. It's not exactly hammock weather, but I'm bundled up with blankets. It's nice just to be outside in the fresh air. Living in the warehouse is like . . . well, living in a warehouse.

I wish I had a razor. This beard business must be an acquired taste.

December 11

I found a newspaper today. It's the December 4th edition of the *Seattle Times*. The headline says, U.N. DECLARES STATE OF INTERNATIONAL EMERGENCY. There's a photograph of the U.S. president standing before the General Assembly. His shoulders are slumped and he looks tired and defeated.

There's another photo, this one of a weary-eyed man the paper identified as the U.S. Surgeon General. The caption is a quote that says: "We have no contingency plan for something like this, but we're all praying for a quick resolution." When the government tells you to start praying, that's when it's time to worry.

The paper also contained several "exclusive" photographs. One particular image has burned itself onto my mind. It shows a creature that looks like an enormous shark with six or eight crab-like appendages extending out of its underbelly. The caption says it washed up on the shore of Newfoundland. In the bottom left corner of the picture, a trio of kids can been seen poking the shark thing with a stick.

December 13

It's raining outside. The sound it's making on the corrugated tin roof makes me feels like I'm living inside a Jamaican drum. I thought I heard a dog barking last night, but it might have been a dream.

Speak of dreams, I had a real doozy last night. Dreamed I was talking to God on the telephone. We made small talk for a little while, then I started telling Him about everything that was going on right now—the tentacles, the ramblers, the shark-crabs (or crab-sharks, if you like). He seemed genuinely concerned, but right before he was about to speak, I heard a click.

"Call waiting," He said. "Can you hold on?"

Then I woke up.

Can you hold on?

December 14

Heard the barking again last night. It's not a dream. I know because I had just woken up from one. Could be a dog out there, maybe even a wolf.

In the dream I was having another telephone conversation with the Lord Almighty. This time He answered the phone with "Complaint Department, how may I help you?"

I told him that cities are burning, tentacles are tearing people apart, and the dead have risen and are eating the living.

When I was finished, I heard Him blow air over the receiver. "Holy moly," He said. "Would you like some cheese with that whine?"

I asked him if there was another god, a *caring* god, who I could speak with instead.

"All the gods are busy," He told me. "They're sleeping."

(later)

Let sleeping gods lie.

Is that funny or have I been in this warehouse too long?

December 17

Feeling better today. Things were getting a little scary there for a while. Cabin fever, I guess. I scoffed at it before, but now I am converted, praise God, hallelujah!

Did I tell you that Barney died? I stopped by his trailer on my way out of town. I banged on his door, the one with the CASA BARNEY sign, but he didn't answer. I went inside and found him lying on the bedroom floor, naked except for a pair of underwear. There was an empty bottle of sleeping pills on the nightstand. I was going to ask him to come with me, but I guess he didn't want to go anywhere with anyone. I covered him with a blanket. On my way out, I saw his Garand rifle propped in one corner. I took it with me.

No happy ending for Barney. Mine is still under consideration, ha-ha. Sitting in my hammock helps me forget about things. For a little while anyway. It's nice to be outside without having to look over my shoulder every two seconds. The view leaves something to be desired, but it's better than nothing.

I'd very much like to see a train.

December 18

Good news and bad news today.

The bad news is that the ramblers have found me. The same group of five I saw outside the deli.

The good news is that I've reduced their number to three. Had my rifle with me (like your American Express card, you should never leave home without it) and managed to pop two of them before they could get too close. Barricaded the door with a couple of crates, and that seemed to hold.

The bastards were standing together on the south side of the warehouse, in the spot where I've been finding the newspapers. Like they were waiting for me to show up.

December 20

Going to do a little Christmas shopping today. Got up early and watched the sunrise from my "backyard." Almost felt like a normal morning, except for the two dead shamblers on the ground about fifty yards away. I've got to get rid of the bodies, but I don't dare touch them with my bare hands. God only knows what kind of germs they carry. I'm hoping to find a pair of gloves in one of the abandoned cars on the bridge.

If this ends up being my last entry, then I want to say . . .

Wow, I really can't think of anything. How pathetic is that?

I guess I should pray.

Hail Mary full of grace, help me win this rambler race.

If I should die before I'm found, then I wish this warehouse burned to the ground.

(later)

Back.

No sign of the remaining ramblers (maybe I scared them off, ha-ha). No tentacles, no giant spiders, no dinosaurs trampling along the interstate. It was, all things considered, a fairly quiet day.

I made it to the bridge and spent the next few hours searching cars like a raccoon digging through garbage cans. One thing I noiced that bothered me: I didn't see a single dead body. It was like everyone simply got out of their cars and strolled away into the Twilight Zone. I guess that's a mystery for another day.

My haul from the cars included: canned food (beans, mostly), instant coffee, waffles, powdered milk, powered eggs, and those instant potatoes that taste like instant crap. Candles, matches, and gloves (yes!). I also found a case of bottled water, but I couldn't carry it with the rest of the stuff. I'll have to go back for it. No big deal. Tomorrow is anutha day!

December 21

Went back for the water this morning. Should last me another month, as long as I ration it. I'll need to make another trip for supplies before the snow really starts coming down. It could be any day now.

Found something else when I went back to the bridge, in a station wagon packed full of camping gear. It was in a long, battered cardboard box that had seen some long years of use. I knew there was a Christmas tree inside even before I opened it. Not a real one, of course, but beggars can't be choosers (that's become my motto these days). I also found a box with ornaments, tinsel, and lights—no juice to power them, but they'll still look nice on the tree. I set it up in the backyard, and it looks great!

Spent the rest of the day in the hammock, whistling Christmas carols with the Garand across my lap.

Three ramblers rambling! Ha-ha!

December 24

It's a good thing I got my shopping done early. No milk or cookies for Santa, but I left out a can of Spam and a bottle of water. Maybe he'll bring me that AK-47 I asked for.

December 25

No assault rifle under the tree today. But there were a couple of ramblers trying to climb the fence. I think if I had gone outside two minutes later, the backyard would have become a killing pen.

One of them had managed to pull himself to the top of the fence. I shot him in the chest and he fell into the enclosure. He landed on the patio table, flipping it over and snapping the umbrella off. That made me angry. The other rambler had dropped back to the ground on the other side of the fence. I snapped a shot at him, but he disappeared around the corner of the warehouse.

There was no sign of the third.

Dec 26

I discovered something new today. Remember the animal I heard howling in the night? The one I couldn't decide if it was a dog or a wolf? Looks like I was wrong on both counts. Sort of.

Turns out it was a dog—or at least, it was at one time. Not quite a hound from hell or *Night of the Living Dog*, but something in between.

It was chowing down on the dead rambler, the one that broke my umbrella table. I'd tossed the carcass over the fence the other day, with the intention of moving it later on. Now this thing that looked like a dog was tearing off hunks of its putrid flesh with a horrible canvas-ripping sound. The dog thing looked up at me and seemed to hesitate before hightailing it around the corner. It'll be back, I have no doubt. And when it does, it's dogmeat. Ha-ha!

Dec 27

Laid a trap for *el poocho* today. Instead of disposing of the dead rambler, I dragged it closer to the fence. Then I climbed into the hammock with my Garand, covered myself with blankets, and waited. It had started to snow and I spent the next hour or so catching flakes on my tongue.

At some point I fell asleep. I woke up sometime later to the sound of canvas ripping. I didn't move. I made sure the safety on the Garand was off, then I slowly peeled back the blankets and looked out.

The dog thing was there, by the fence. Its head was down and its jaws were working in a mad frenzy. It didn't eat like a normal animal—it didn't chew. It was like a machine that had caught something in its gears and was now ripping it to pieces.

I must have made some kind of sound, because it suddenly snapped its head up and glared at me. I raised the rifle, socking the butt into the crook of my shoulder, and fired. The bullet went through the dog thing's mouth and out the back of its head.

It fell on its side, twitching. My second shot caved in its chest. There was no blood. Not even a drop.

Dec 28

The days are getting chilly. Something that tends to keep people indoors. Not me! I spend most of my days outside, in the hammock. If it weren't the danger it is, I'd probably sleep out here.

The dog didn't bleed. That thought keeps coming back to haunt me. I don't have any answers. I don't even have theories anymore.

The tentacles found me today. They came over the railway embankment. One big one and four or five little ones. The big one stayed on the tracks. I prayed for a train to come. The little ones were farting around in the cinders at the foot of the embankment. One of them found an old rusty shopping cart and dragged it back over the tracks. Finders keepers.

I've come to the conclusion that the tentacles are not guided by any deep-rooted intelligence. This comes after spending the day watching them fight over the patio chairs I had tossed over the fence . . . what? A month ago? Has it been a month?

They seem to operate solely on instinct—which is why I haven't taken any shots at them. Not until they give me a reason. They took the chairs back over the tracks and I haven't seen them since.

Will they be back? I wonder. To which Barney would have said: Does Howdy Doody have wooden balls?

December 29

Tentacles stole my Christmas tree.

Sounds like one of those tabloid headlines, doesn't it? Except this one is true.

Of all the post-Christmas chores, taking down the tree is the one people put off the most. Not me! I came outside this morning to do that very thing and found half a dozen tentacles (including the big one) dragging it over the fence. They didn't even knock the angel off. Who do you call to get rid of your Christmas tree? 1-800-T-E-N-T-A-C-L-E-S!

Looks like I won't be staying outside anymore.

December 30

Dreamed of God again last night—several of them, in fact. They were asleep in a warehouse very similar to my own, lying in row upon row of hammocks. There must have been hundreds of them. On the wall was an enormous digital alarm clock ticking that cast an eerie red glow over everything. Next to the clock was a sign that said QUIET PLEASE.

I gotta find a way to wake them up.

December 31

Stayed outside last night. Was curious to see if anyone would light off any fireworks. Didn't see any.

It's becoming harder to stay indoors. I was sitting in the hammock, staring at the stars, and they didn't look right. I don't know anything about constellations, but I can't shake that feeling. They just don't look right.

The tentacles are getting closer. They're sliding along the outside of the warehouse right now. The sound is driving me crackers.

I'm going to try and sleep. I've got work to do. No snooze button for the gods. Time to roll them out of their hammocks.

January 3?

The gods are not in my dreams—they are here! I think that's the message—what Barney would have called the real-life truth.

I know what the tentacles are. They're not attached to anything. They're the highways to the gods! And the ramblers are their disciples, travelling door to door and spreading the word and selling Avon products.

I will survive, I will survive, I will survive.

Was Gloria Gaynor ever an Avon Lady?

Jan 34 (?)

Soooo tired.

Hammock rejected me today. Spit me out like a watermelon seed. God, I want a watermelon. If I can only hold on until summer.

Tentacles are loud tonight. They could wake the dead, ha-ha!

I will hold on . . . for watermelon . . .

The Library

A Night in the Library
with the Gods

First there was darkness. Then a series of deep, ratcheting clicks and clacks, followed by a low hiss of escaping air that buffeted his face and tousled his hair. Then, slowly, the darkness not so much lifted as swung away to his left as if an enormous door were opening.

Lights sputtered to life from somewhere overhead, and he saw it *was* a door. A big one. Not quite as large as the one on a bank vault, but similar in appearance.

He stepped into a long, windowless room with five tall metal bookcases at the far end. Before him was a long table. Not the fancy kind like in an executive conference room. Just an ordinary reading table like you'd find in a library.

Was he in a library? He had an idea he was, but he didn't know for certain. He couldn't seem to recall exactly where he was—or how he had gotten here. There was something strange about the bookcases. It was so slight that he couldn't tell precisely what it was, but there was definitely something odd about them.

He heard someone cough, and turned to see a tall woman standing in the doorway behind him. She was dressed entirely in black—black topcoat, black blouse, black slacks, black gloves, black pointed-toe shoes. Her face was a pallid mask that only served to make her red hair that much brighter.

"Good evening," she said in a cool, crisp voice.

"Is it?"

"Well, it's more of a greeting than a description."

"No, I mean, is it the evening? I can't seem to remember." He looked down at himself, saw that he was dressed in a ratty plaid bathrobe and a pair of slippers. "I can't seem to remember very much, actually."

"I apologize for that," the redhead said, and slipped past him into the room. Her poise and demeanour exuded an air of indifferent professionalism. As if she belonged in that executive conference room rather than this strange little library. "I realize all of this must be very unsettling. But I assure you, the alternative is much worse."

The man in the bathrobe nodded, even though he still had no idea what was going on. "Who are you?" he asked. Then: "Who am I?"

"Names aren't important."

"Are you sure?" The man's voice wavered. "Because I think it's actually pretty goddamn important."

The redhead waved her hand dismissively. "There's a difference between knowing a thing and understanding a thing," she said. "*Knowing* isn't as important as *understanding*. In this instance— in regards to all of this"—she indicated the entire room— "understanding is key."

The man gazed into her cool green eyes for a long moment. His mind felt like a newly washed chalkboard, and the redhead was the teacher about to impart some important lesson. Strangely, he found it wasn't difficult at all to put things aside and simply go with the flow.

"First," she began, "I will tell you something—something you don't necessarily need to know, but maybe it will help to put you at ease."

The man nodded mutely.

"You're not in trouble," she said in a voice that was both calm and firm. "I'm not with the police or any government body. Nor have you been kidnapped. Your life is not in danger." She raised her hands again. "You're standing in a little-known room within the Fisher Rare Book Library." She added: "That's at the University of Toronto."

The man nodded even though he didn't know where that was exactly.

"To those who know of its existence, it's simply called the Restricted Collection. You don't need to know *what* it is, but you need to understand *why* it is. Understanding is key. It's very important that you're here tonight."

The man nodded again.

"You won't be called in often," the redhead went on, "but those times that you are will be extremely important. I can't stress to you how important—and there would be little point even if I could—but I can assure you that your involvement is integral."

She turned slightly and swept her hand across the room. "Notice anything unusual?"

"Something," he said in a low, ruminative voice.

She motioned him to follow her, and they walked around the long table to the middle bookcase. Closer now, he could see what made these cases different from the ones he had seen before—the shelves were encased in glass. On the left side of each shelf there was a raised metal panel.

"Hermetically sealed," the redhead explained, then startled him by slamming her gloved fist against the glass. "Shatterproof."

"How do you open it?"

"See the pad?" She pointed at the raised panel. "Put your finger on it."

The man in the bathrobe started to raise his hand, then hesitated.

"Go ahead," she said. "It won't bite you."

He raised his hand slowly, extended his index finger, and placed it gently against the panel. There was a sharp, ratcheting click (not unlike the one he heard before entering this strange little room), and then the long glass panel rose up like a garage door and slid back into the housing in the top of the shelf.

"Abracadabra," the redhead said.

"Did I do that?" the man asked a little timidly.

"You did that," the redheadsaid. "Only you."

He turned his head and looked at her. "What does that mean?"

She ignored the question and continued to stare at the line of books. "Take one out," she said. "Any one."

The man fidgeted. The books looked very old and delicate. "Don't I need gloves or something?"

She shook her head. "It's okay."

She said that, but he couldn't help but notice that she herself made no gesture toward the shelf, as if there was something in there that might bite. Until now she had made gestures as she spoke, at the room, at the bookcases, but now, standing in front of one of the open shelves, she kept her hands strictly behind her back.

He felt a sudden need to leave this place, to just turn around and walk out. Something made him stay. He was supposed to stay. He didn't know why.

He reached up and pulled down a large book. It was bound in leather that was cracking in several spots. The pages were yellow and uneven, some of them sticking out unevenly, as if the book had been constructed in haste, or maybe by a publisher who didn't know his craft. There was no title on the cover, which was withered and shrunk like the skin on some strange dried fruit. It was a heavy volume, and he carried it over to the reading table with both hands, holding it close to his chest. He breathed deeply and inhaled a musky aroma of mildew and millennia.

The redhead came over and stood behind him on his left side. She watched over his shoulder as he opened the book. The first page was blank. He turned to the next page, and it was blank, too. He flipped further ahead, then back again. They were all blank.

"Is this a joke?" he asked.

"Keep going," she said. Her breathing was faster and deeper.

He continued to turn the pages. After a few moments of finding nothing but more blank pages, he looked up and saw someone standing in the doorway. She was a short elderly woman who would have looked at home in a country kitchen baking banana bread. She was plump in that pleasant way only elderly women seem able to pull off. She had a round, friendly face and her grey hair was done up in a tall Tower of Babel beehive that almost reached the top of the doorway.

"Spank my ass and call me Betty!" she cried out in a voice that seemed incongruously soft compared to the words she had spoken. "What have you got this poor, young man doing? Are you mad, woman?"

"I'm in the middle of his orientation." The redhead's voice remained cool and calm, but the man in the bathrobe detected something beneath that polished surface . . . something that sounded a bit like fear.

"I need to speak with you," the old woman said urgently. Her eyes moved fretfully between them.

The redhead let out a frustrated sigh. "Keep looking," she said to the man in the bathrobe, and went around the table to talk to the old woman.

The man watched them. He tried to figure out what they were saying, but they spoke in low, hushed voices. He looked back at the book, expecting to see another blank page, and saw this instead:

DO YOU SEE RED?

The lettering was so ornate he almost couldn't read it. The first three words were printed in black ink, while the fourth word, RED, was printed in red. So he supposed he was seeing red.

He looked up from the book, and he was seeing red again. The redhead. He looked back down at the book, and the words had changed. Now they said:

DO YOU SEE HER BLOOD?

This time the word BLOOD was printed in red—and not just red, but *dripping* red. The ink (if that's what it was) was running down the page in thin rills like . . . well, like blood.

He raised his head and started to say something to the redhead, but she cut him off with a briskly upraised hand. He looked down at the book again, and the word HER was bleeding now. He looked up at the redhead and then back down at the book, and what he saw written there this time was enough to cause his breath to catch in his throat.

DO YOU WANT TO?

He stared at this question, feeling a strange species of shock, not because he was looking at a book that appeared to be writing itself before his very eyes, but because a part of him *did* want to see her blood. It was a small part, to be sure, but it was there, and he could feel it growing within him like a tumour.

As he continued to stare at the page, the words changed . . . unravelled . . . as if they were made of string. The black and red lines streaked across the page like contrails. Reaching the top of the page, they began to move in more purposeful manoeuvres—loops and curlicues and smooth curves that seemed to have no meaning at first. He soon realized that this was because they were not forming words this time, but a picture. The black lines were becoming the portrait of a woman's face—*her* face—while the red lines spun themselves like eldritch silk into her hair. The finished product was a simple but perfectly executed sketch of the redhead.

Below the sketch, the black lines that formed her long, slender neck began to unravel. They sagged down like falling spiderwebs and twined together to form words:

OPEN HER UP

They unravelled again and reformed.

SEE HER BLOOD

The man let out a low sigh that was almost a moan. He felt nauseated. His legs threatened to buckle and spill him to the floor. There was something stupidly evil about those words. They reminded him of those children's readers, the ones that told the adventures of Dick and Jane and their dog Spot. *See Dick run. Run, Dick run.* Except this was the adult version. *Open her up. See her blood.*

Scarier than the thought of a book that not only wrote itself but wrote such horrific things, was that growing desire to do exactly what it said. It was a desire strong enough to be considered lust—bloodlust. He lusted to open her up and see her blood. But another part, one that seemed to be growing smaller and distant with each passing moment, told him it was wrong, it was inhuman. That other voice was like a transmission sent from deep space; it was becoming more garbled and incoherent as he stared at the book.

He shut his eyes tightly, counted to five, and opened them again, hoping the words would be gone. They were, but new ones replaced them.

EVERY HOUSE IS HAUNTED

STOP THINKING ABOUT IT AND DO IT!

The letters unravelled (more harshly this time, almost impatiently) and reformed, except now they were in a jagged, less attractive script.

KILL HER! OPEN HER UP!

The man in the bathrobe looked up from the book. The desire was like a bushfire burning in his head. It was, he realized, the best idea he had ever had in his life—the only idea, really. It was so great that he couldn't figure out why he hadn't thought of it before. It didn't matter. It was there now, beating a poisonous pulse in the centre of his mind. He could feel the vein in the middle of his forehead standing out like some strange brand. He could see himself doing it. Dragging her down to the floor, driving his hands into the smooth pale skin of her chest, ripping, tearing, punching through her ribcage and then pulling it open like an old book. He could even hear the sound it would make: a crunching, ratcheting sound like a key turning in a lock.

He slammed the book shut with a loud, portentous boom. His hands were slick with perspiration, and he could feel drops of sweat running down the sides of his face. Part of him wanted to open the book again—the same part that wanted to take the redhead apart like a Thanksgiving turkey—but it was becoming the dimmer voice now, the one moving farther down the dark tunnel of his mind.

Gradually, he felt his mind reasserting itself. He took a deep, steadying breath and let it out. *See Dick walk*, he thought as he went around to the other side of the table. The redhead and the old woman had finished talking. The old woman gave him a fretful look, then turned and left the room.

"Well," the redhead said in a bright, cheery voice, "where were we?"

She walked over to the table and placed her hand on the book, fingers tented on the cover. The man winced a bit when she did that. He hadn't liked touching the book himself, and watching someone else do it wasn't much better. It was like watching someone stick their hand in a terrarium full of tarantulas.

"What do you think?" she asked.

The man looked at her quizzically. "About what?" he asked.

"About the rising gas prices," she said seriously. Then she laughed and shook her head. "About the book, of course." She tapped the cover and the man felt his stomach do a backflip. "What did it say to you?"

The man opened his mouth but nothing came out.

"Did it say *Hello*? Did it say *Mars Needs Toilet Paper*? Did it tell you to save air miles?" A strange little smile crept across her face. "Did it tell you to kill yourself? Or Lorna? Or me?"

"Who's Lorna?" he asked.

The redhead nodded toward the door. "The librarian," she said. "She's also your driver."

"My driver?"

"She'll take you home shortly. We're almost done here."

"We are?"

"Yes."

"How does she know where I live?" he asked suddenly. "*I* don't even know where I live? Or who I am! What the hell is going on here? *Who are you people?*"

The redhead continued to smile. "What did it say to you?" she asked again.

"Can you please not do that?" He was looking at her hand, the one resting on the cover of the book. "Can you . . . take your hand away? Please?"

"Oh, I'm sorry," she said, sounding genuinely sorry, and took her hand off the book. "Now, can you tell me . . .?"

"*It said I should kill you!*" the man in the bathrobe cried out in horror and shame. "It said I should open you up . . . open you up so I could see your blood."

"Did it now," the redhead said in a musing tone. The expression on her face was not one of fear or anger or disgust, but of thoughtful amusement. She suddenly let out a loud, full-bodied laugh and gave her head a rueful little shake, the kind that says *Oh well, boys will be boys.*

"Don't worry about it," she said. "That book has said worse things to me. A lot worse. Sticks and stones." She glanced over her shoulder at the row of bookcases. "They all have."

EVERY HOUSE IS HAUNTED

The man followed her glance. "Are they all like that?" he asked incredulously.

The strange little smile reappeared on her face. "Oh yes," she said. "Of course, some are worse than others."

"God," he muttered in a low voice.

"Gods, actually," the redhead corrected him. She shook her head in good-natured reproof. "It never fails to amaze me the number of people who think there's only one. It's such a small-minded view."

"Those things . . . they're not books."

"Nope," she said. "You've heard the expression 'Never judge a book by its cover'? Around here it's sort of a warning. If I could, I'd put it in neon letters about five feet high right above those bookcases."

"Then, what are they?"

"I could tell you," she said conspiratorially, "but then I'd have to kill you."

"Really?"

She spread her hands and grinned. "No," she said. "It's difficult to explain. It helps if you think of them as phone cards."

"Phone cards?"

"*Inter-dimensional* phone cards," she clarified.

"Reach out and summon someone," the man in the bathrobe said in a dazed monotone.

"Yes!" The redhead laughed and clapped her hands together. She picked up the book, carried it back to the stacks, and reshelved it. Then she pulled the long glass cover down and locked it back in place. "You won't have to look at one of them ever again. I can assure you of that. I just wanted you to understand the gravity of the situation." She saw that he was about to speak and raised her hand. "Yes, yes, I realize you don't *know* what's going on, but some part of you understands. Doesn't it?"

The man swallowed dryly. "I suppose I do at that," he said. "Although I don't see what good it is to understand something I don't know about."

"That's all right," the redhead assured him. "It's not your business to know. From time to time you will be brought here to open the Restricted Collection. Once you've opened the door, you're free to wait in the outer hall. There's a coffee machine that's

87

quite respectable." She saw the look of frustration on his face and added: "You're not going to remember any of this anyway. Clean wipe, kitty-cat. I promise."

"Are those books . . . are they safe here?"

"This is one of the largest university libraries in the world. They're very safe here."

"I don't know if I'll ever feel safe," the man said, "knowing those things exist."

"Sweetie, it's better if you don't think about it."

A few minutes after midnight, a man in a flannel bathrobe walked out of the Robarts Library to a car parked on the street with its engine running. He hesitated a moment, then opened the passenger door and climbed in.

"Good evening, sir," said the old woman behind the wheel. Her name was Lorna. *Lorna the librarian*, the man in the bathrobe thought for no particular reason. He tried to grasp the thread of this thought, but it slipped through his mental fingers like smoke.

"Good evening," he replied, fastening his seatbelt.

"I must apologize for the lacklustre transportation. It's not much to look at, but it will get you where you want to go."

"Where do I want to go?" the man in the bathrobe asked automatically.

"Why, home, dear," Lorna said, and pulled away from the curb.

"Home," said the man in the bathrobe. He didn't know where that was exactly, but for some reason that didn't bother him. Knowing wasn't nearly as important as understanding. Knowing was highly overrated, but understanding . . . understanding was key.

THE NANNY

Jodie made the turn onto Ash Street and started looking for 823. She had one hand on the wheel, the other holding the open file in her lap. She squinted , trying to read the numbers on the houses, some of which were only half-built, but it was too dark. She finally pulled over in front of a house with no lights on, and turned off the engine.

She was about to get out when there was a sudden rap on her window. Jodie let out a frightened squeak.

"Sorry," Brian said, looking chagrined on the other side of the glass. "I thought you saw me."

Jodie slung her purse over her shoulder, picked up the file, and stepped out of the car. "You scared the crap out of me," she said, with a nervous giggle. "Which is not to say that I scare easily."

"It's my face, I know." Brian rubbed his unshaven cheek. "I've been meaning to go out and buy a paper bag for my head."

"I hope you don't mind me saying, Brian, but you look like shit."

"Thank you, dahling," he said, wrinkling his nose with theatrical indignation. "And I thought flattery was a lost art."

Jodie smiled, but it was true. Brian Torver, normally the most dapper and well-dressed of men, looked like something that had crawled out of the gutter. His eyes were bloodshot, his cheeks were stubble-dark, and the shirt he was wearing had a yellow, lived-in look.

"This is bad, isn't it."

"I wouldn't have dragged you out here to the willywags if it wasn't."

"How bad is it?"

"Not good, kiddo. Not for me, not for Mags, not for business."

"What business is that?" Jodie asked. She felt a slight stab of guilt for not keeping up with Brian and Maggie's affairs. She got their e-mails, but only glanced at them briefly, and almost never replied. It was hard to focus on anything external when she was working, and her schedule for the past two years had been rigorous, moving from site to site after the completion of each case.

"Behold!" Brian spread his arms expansively. His voice sounded cheerier, almost jovial. "My legacy."

"Ash Street?" Jodie said.

"Ash Street, Oak Street, Maple Lane, Spruce Crescent." He ticked them off on his fingers. "We own the whole damn subdivision. Dumped everything we have into it. Silver Woods Estates."

"Very nice."

"People are moving up here in droves—and not just the seniors. We've got lots of young professionals, some with families. Nice, hardworking people who want to raise their kids away from the cities. Peterborough is getting too big for them. Ninety thousand people, according to the last census. Silver Falls has got a population of ten thousand. Those who want real country living are coming here."

Jodie looked up at the dark house. "Is this the one?"

"Yeah." Brian jovial tone turned sullen and troubled. "The thorn in my ass."

"Has there been any outside exposure?"

"I've done a pretty good job of squashing any rumours," Brian said judiciously. "It's not easy, what with all the houses being sold. People are having to wait for new ones to be built, so yeah, I guess there's probably some curiosity about why this one is empty. The numb fuck who used to live here—some computer geek who works in Markham—actually went to the local press, if you can believe that. Like shooting yourself in the foot."

"Did they believe him?"

"It didn't matter. Bob Hardy, the editor over at the *Examiner*, killed the story. He lives on Maple Lane and knows what a story like that would do to property values in the area. The geek should have known better. He won't get a good price on his house if people think it's haunted."

"You never know. Some people might consider it a selling point."

Brian's face darkened. "Yeah, well I don't. And I don't plan on taking any chances." He sighed and ran a hand through his thinning hair. "I'm sorry. I'm tired and stressed out. This isn't just our investment. Mags and I live here, too. Right around the corner. I think that's the only reason I've been able to keep this thing quiet for so long. Every time something happens, I've been able to quash it right away."

"Things like what?"

"The usual. Broken windows. Vandalized cars. Mrs. Bettingham, the old bat who lives next door"—Brian gestured at the house on the left side of 823—"she called me one morning and said her picket fence was missing. I came over and the whole damn thing was gone. I replaced it out of my own pocket on the condition she didn't talk to anyone about it."

"Are people seeing anything? Hearing anything?"

"Not too much. Some bright lights I've been able to explain away as construction crews working late. Some loud booming sounds that they probably think is just thunder."

Jodie nodded. "You have been lucky."

"Yeah, and I think it's running out." Brian clenched his hands into fists. "Fucking kids. I could strangle them."

"I don't think so," Jodie said absently, staring up at 823 Ash Street.

"You think you can do something?"

"Only one way to find out."

Jodie started up the cobblestone path to the house. On the porch she opened her purse and took out a pair of oversized glasses with dark lenses. An electrical cord ran from one of the bows to a small power-pack that she clipped to her belt. She checked the boost and gain levels, pressed the power button and put on the glasses.

"Knock, knock," she said in a low voice. "Here I come."

It was dark—darker than it was outside, where the stars had provided at least some fledgling light. Inside the blackness was total. The glasses had an infrared setting, but Jodie chose not to use it. She preferred to let her eyes adjust naturally, which took longer because of the dark lenses.

"Hello?" she called out. "Is anyone home?"

She didn't expect a reply, and none came. She stepped forward, holding the file in one hand, while she waved the other in the air before her like a blind person. She touched something hard and spherical. The newel post at the foot of the stairs. She looked up toward the second floor and caught a flash of luminescent green in her peripheral vision. She snapped her head to the left, but it was already gone.

"I'm not going to hurt you," she said in a carrying voice, moving toward a doorway that led into either a living room or a dining room, depending on the layout of the house. "I just want to talk to you."

She heard something that sounded like a sharp intake of breath. She looked up and saw a glowing green shape on the ceiling.

"Why don't you come down from there?" she said, and the glowing shape immediately fell to the hardwood floor with a thump and went running out of the room.

Jodie followed slowly, taking her time. "It's okay," she said. "I just want to see you."

She looked over her shoulder and saw another green shape—this one taller than the first—peeking around the corner of the main foyer. She turned back, pretending not to have noticed, and removed the glasses, unclipping the power-pack and putting everything in her purse. She didn't need them anymore. She could feel herself moving into the proper range. It was like stepping into a warm bath, except instead of feeling it around her body, she felt it around her mind.

She moved into the kitchen. Her eyes were beginning to adjust to the dark and she could see a bit better now. She could make out the straight edges of the counter, the dull gleam of the chrome appliances. There was a faint antiseptic smell in the air.

Crossing the room she heard a series of thumps—the sound of someone racing up stairs. She went down the main hall to the foyer, just in time to catch a glimpse of two shapes zipping down the second-floor hallway. She grinned.

"I can see you," Jodie said in a low singsong. "Here I come."

She went up the stairs and stood at the foot of the hallway. There were four doors, but only one of them was open. She went over and stood on the threshold. A small boy, perhaps six year old, stood in the middle of the room. He was wearing pyjamas with dinosaurs on them. There was a dark stain on the front of his shirt, as if he had spilled something on it, although Jodie knew that was not the case.

"Well hello there," she said pleasantly.

The boy stared at her with an expression of mingled curiosity and concern. "Are you dead?" he asked.

Jodie smiled. That was a new one.

"No," she said. "I'm afraid not."

A female voice called from the hallway behind her, giving her a small start, and a second later she felt something brush past her, leaving the entire left side of her body numb. She lost her concentration for a moment, and the boy seemed to swim out of view. She squinted her eyes, focusing, and he came back, along with a young girl. She was about a foot taller than the boy, but she had the same wide, dark eyes. Older sister.

She spared Jodie the briefest of looks, then turned to her brother. "What are you doing?" she snapped. "Misty is waiting for us."

"This lady," the boy said, pointing at Jodie. "She can see me."

The girl turned her head and gave Jodie a slightly longer look. "No, she can't."

"Yes, I can," Jodie said. "I see you quite clearly. You're wearing a nightgown with a bear on the front. The bear is wearing a bonnet and a dress. She almost said *The dress is red*, then stopped herself. The dress wasn't red. It was blood, from the stab wound that had killed the girl, identical to the boy's.

"Who are you?" he asked.

"Shut up," his sister said sharply. She made as if to hit him, then grabbed him by the arm instead. "You know what Misty said. *Don't talk to strangers*."

"That's good advice," Jodie told her. "So how about if I do all the talking? You don't have to say anything, just listen."

"Misty knows about you," the girl said. She fixed Jodie with a stare that she felt like an icy hand gripping her heart. "She knows all about *you*."

"Really?" Jodie said. "I don't recall ever meeting her."

"Who are you?" the boy asked again, and his sister gave his arm a hard shake.

"I'm the new sitter. My name is Jodie."

"There is no new sitter!"

The force of the girl's scream seemed to hurt Jodie's mind more than her ears. She heard the distant sound of glass breaking and knew one of the windows in the house had just been blown out.

"Okay," Jodie said slowly, placatingly. "I apologize. I didn't know you still had a sitter." She gripped the file in her hands. *That's why they won't leave*, she thought. *The sitter won't let them.* "Why don't you think of me as your nanny, then?"

"What's the difference?" the boy asked. The girl looked like she was about to take off again, but the boy's question seemed to catch her interest, at least temporarily.

"Oh, not much really," Jodie said. "A sitter is someone you call when your parents are in a pinch."

Both kids looked at her as if she had started speaking Latin. *They don't remember their parents*, she realized. *Sweet Christ, it is bad.*

"What does *that* mean?" the girl asked truculently.

"It means when they're desperate," Jodie said. "They hire a sitter to come take care of you. On a temporary, short-term basis. A nanny is a much closer acquaintance. Sometimes they even live in the house with the kids. She's like a mother when the real one isn't around."

"You're not my mother," the girl declared, and Jodie had to repress an urge to say *Are you sure?* But that wouldn't help her case. It wouldn't help anyone, except maybe Misty.

"And you're not living here," the girl added, crossing her arms for emphasis.

"That's okay. I have friends I can stay with."

"What does a nanny do?" the boy asked.

"Oh, all kinds of things. She takes care of the kids, plays with them, reads them stories . . ."

"Misty tells us stories," the girl said. "Good ones."

"I'm sure she does," Jodie said, hoping the contempt she felt didn't seep into her voice. She opened her purse, put the file inside, and took out a book. The faded cover showed a little girl peering into a hole in the ground.

"This is one of my favourites," Jodie said. "It's called *Alice's Adventures in Wonderland*. Have you heard it before?"

The boy shook his head. The girl stood impassively, arms still crossed.

"It's about a little girl who travels to another world through a rabbit hole."

"That's stupid," the girl said. "Rabbit holes don't go anywhere."

"Not all of them, that's true. But this one does. There are many different ways to travel to other worlds."

"Like on rockets," the boy piped.

"That's right. Rockets, rabbit holes—there's even one you can get to through a magic wardrobe."

"I know that one!" the boy said. "Misty read us that one before she turned red."

"Did she?" Jodie said. "Then you know what I'm talking about. There are lots of different doorways to other worlds." She paused, licking her lips. "Sometimes they look like ordinary things. Like a wardrobe, or a fogbank, or even just a bright light. Have you seen any bright lights in the house?"

The boy's lower lip began to quiver. "Misty says the light is bad."

"Does she?" Jodie said, tilting her head thoughtfully to the side. "Why is it bad?"

"She says it burns."

"Oh, I see. Does it burn you?"

The boy looked confused. "I don't know. We don't go near it."

"The light always seemed warm to me," Jodie said offhandedly. "But I've never been burned by it."

The girl scowled. "You don't know anything," she said. "You've never seen it. You *can't* see it."

"It's a white light," Jodie said. "Or at least that's how it looks at first. But as you get closer, you can see it's actually made up of many different colours. Maybe all the colours in the universe."

The boy nodded slowly.

"And if you stare at it long enough, it seems to sing your name, over and over again."

"Yes!" he cried out, then covered his mouth. "That's it."

"You don't know anything," the girl said, but she didn't sound so sure now.

"You don't have to believe me." Jodie held up the book for them to see. "But maybe you'll change your mind after hearing about Alice."

"She doesn't know anything either."

Jodie shrugged. "Okay. I'll make you deal. If you aren't convinced, I'll come back tomorrow and read you another story. And if you're still not convinced, I'll come back again the day after that and read another one."

"I don't care about rabbits or rabbit holes," the girl said.

"Okay," Jodie said. "Tomorrow I'll tell you a story about a garden."

"A garden?" the girl said sceptically.

"A *secret* garden," Jodie clarified. She thought back to the case she'd just finished in Redlands. She had read eighty-four books before the kids had finally trusted her enough to pass on. She hoped this case would tie up faster than that. Brian didn't have that kind of time. But then this wasn't the sort of thing one could rush.

"Is the garden magic, too?" the boy asked.

Jodie opened the book and turned to the first page.

"You'll have to wait until tomorrow to find out," she said. "I suppose we all will."

The Dark and the Young

1

Human innocence in its purest form is a newborn child.
It usually wears off in six to eight weeks.

2

Wendy sat in the dry, airless sauna of her car, rubbing her finger over the bright yellow sticker on the corner of the windshield and thinking: *That was the weirdest job interview I've ever been to.*

One of her professors at Stanford had helped to set it up. *It's a translation gig,* he had said. *Perfect for someone with a doctoral degree in applied linguistics. Ancient language decipherment.* He was right. It was right up her alley. She wasn't really interested in teaching, and she hadn't found any other research gigs that interested her. Ancient language dicipherment was hard to come by outside of Greece or the Middle East. The pay wouldn't be great, and she'd have to move to Nevada, but the job was in her field, and lodgings were included. Besides, she thought, it might be good to get away from California for awhile. So she called the number her prof had given her and spoke to a woman who told her to hold please while her call was redirected. A man came on the line and gave Wendy directions to their "training centre." *We look forward to seeing you,* he said in a chipper voice.

Wendy headed east on I-80 and spent the night in a Reno hotel that advertised COOL OUTDOOR POOL and ADULT MOVIES & KIDS VIDS. The following day she got up early and put on her nicest outfit, a dusty rose blouse and a khaki pencil skirt. She applied what she hoped was a liberal amount of makeup, and was out the door.

After picking up a toasted bagel and a bottle of grapefruit juice, she got back in her old Dodge with its fickle A/C and continued east on I-80. The Nevada scenery was as dull and lifeless as the surface of Mars. There wasn't much to see except sand, rocks, and the tenacious desert plants that added a small splash of colour to the landscape. California wasn't so far removed from the desert, but this was particularly bleak. And the heat! California was hot, but Nevada was *stifling*.

Passing through the town of Lovelock, Wendy grabbed her purse off the passenger seat and rooted around inside for the directions the man on the phone had given to her.

Wendy was one of those people who never seemed to have pen and paper at hand when she needed to write down important information. She found the paper napkin on which she'd written the directions, and saw that the words, scribbled in eyeliner pencil, had smudged in the desert heat. In fact, the small stockpile of makeup in her purse appeared to be undergoing the Revlon equivalent of thermonuclear meltdown.

"*Shit*," she muttered, tossing her purse back onto the seat. She almost missed her turn-off, and reduced her speed. She checked her rearview mirror, but there was no one behind her. No one coming in the opposite direction, either.

Mars, indeed.

3

The "training centre" turned out to be a dusty, weather-beaten trailer with plastic sheets covering the windows. It was standing in the corner of a crushed-gravel parking lot off the side road Wendy had turned onto after leaving the Interstate. A wooden sign on the post, as faded and dusty as the trailer, said WEATHER MONITORING STATION 7.

She looked at the napkin and confirmed that this was where she was supposed to be. She stepped out of her car, and the heat fell on her like a heavy cloak. She walked hesitantly toward the trailer, went up the creaking wooden steps, and knocked on the door.

"It's open!" a familiar voice boomed from inside.

Wendy opened the door and stepped into a small, unfinished room. A plank table and two plastic contour chairs were the only furnishings—unless you counted the rows of miniature cacti that lined the window sills.

Sitting in the chair on the other side of the table was the chipper man she had spoken to on the phone. He was barrel-chested, thin-faced, and had a crewcut so short his pink scalp showed through. He was wearing white pants and a bright green blazer that looked about two sizes too small. COYOTE SPRINGS OUTDOOR SERVICES was embroidered in gold thread over the breast pocket.

"Mr. Vanners?" Wendy asked, a little doubtfully.

"Please, have a seat." He gestured to the empty chair.

Wendy sat down. Outside, the wind howled around the eaves and whipped sand against the plastic sheets that covered the windows.

"Thank you for coming," Vanners said. "I know you've come a long way."

"No problem."

"So. You like books?" he asked in a way Wendy had found was typically reserved for people who didn't. Vanners certainly didn't sound—or look—anything like the beetle-browed academic she had been expecting. She didn't like to generalize, but at the same time she got a very distinct vibe that Vanners was an operations man and the research position didn't overly concern him.

"Uh, yes," Wendy said, trying to readjust to the tenor of the conversation.

"Excellent, excellent," Vanners said, smiling. In his bright green blazer, with his hands folded neatly on the table before him, he looked like a salesman for a landscaping company.

"So what kind of work would I be doing?"

"Oh, just some basic decipherment. You might have to dabble in a little Egyptian, Greek—maybe even a little Arabic—whatever the work requires. Nothing one of Wilkins' kids couldn't handle."

"You know Professor Wilkins?"

"Oh sure. He's sort of a talent scout for our organization. I'm the recruiter."

Wendy nodded, but like all of her responses to this man, it was tentative and unsure. She felt as if she were being graded in some manner that she didn't quite understand. As if Vanners were speaking in some kind of . . . well, code.

"What kind of company do you work for?" She glanced again at his jacket. COYOTE SPRINGS OUTDOOR SERVICES? It didn't sound like the kind of organization that needed a freshly minted linguistics expert, not unless Bigfoot had turned up speaking ancient Sumerian.

Vanners steepled his fingers under his chin and leaned back in his chair. "We're a research firm with a few government contracts."

"That's kind of vague."

Vanners grinned. "But kind of exciting, too, isn't it? I mean, aren't you curious?"

"How long is the contract for?"

"It's research," he said with a shrug. "Could be two weeks, could be two years. A lot of it depends on you."

Wendy thought about it for a moment.

"Did you happen to notice any buildings around here once you got off the Interstate?" Vanners asked suddenly.

Wendy shook her head. "No. Not a thing. In fact, I don't think I've ever seen so much nothing in my life."

"There's a road," Vanners said, "about ten miles north of the turnoff you took to get here. It's little more than a trail, full of chuckholes and washouts, and you'd have to be looking for it to see it. It runs exactly twenty-five-point-four miles to a building. Once upon a time it was a glove factory. Now it belongs to us."

Vanners reached into his jacket and took out a square yellow sticker. It looked like a miniature road-sign, except the symbol on it wasn't one Wendy recognized. It showed what appeared to be an erupting volcano. Vanners handed it to her.

"The glove factory is a secure facility. Unless you have one of those stickers on the windshield of your car, you can't get within thirty miles of it. The security detail is very tight. No fences, no guard patrols, no watchtowers, but they're always watching. And if they see someone coming down the road and they don't have that sticker showing . . ."

Vanners flashed a wicked grin and spread his hands in a way that suggested all kinds of things, none of them pleasant.

"I suggest you put that on your car before you leave today," he said, nodding at the sticker in her hand.

"So I got the job?" Wendy said.

"Your qualifications check out, and you said you like books. That's enough for now."

This is completely absurd, Wendy thought. But when Vanners reached across the table and offered his hand, she shook it. It was a job, after all. And if she didn't like it, she could always quit. Right?

4

Wendy put the sticker on her windshield before she headed back to Reno.

Entering her room at the hotel, she found a thick booklet with a red vellum cover lying in the middle of the double bed. She stared at it for a long moment before picking it up.

On the inside cover was a Post-It note with a message written in a looping hand: *Think of this as the first of two books that will change your life. This one's our standard non-disclosure package. Read it, sign it, and bring it with you on Monday.—V.*

Wendy went to the small bar fridge and took out a Coke. Then she sat down at the kitchen table and began to read. After she was finished she sat quietly with her hand resting on the cover of the booklet.

After a moment, she got up and began looking for a writing implement. Something better than an eyeliner pencil.

5

The following Monday, she drove out to the glove factory. She went over a rise, and there it was, at the bottom of a wide valley.

It was an old army Quonset hut—*old* being the operative word. The roof was full of holes, some of which looked big enough for Wendy to drive her car through. The wooden rafters supporting the centre of the building had collapsed sometime in the building's long existence, giving it a hunched, shoulder-shrugging indifference. *Yeah, I'm old*, it seemed to say, *but what can you do?*

Wendy drove down the flank of the hill and turned into a sand-covered parking lot. She pulled up alongside a silver pickup truck that made her Dodge look like a soapbox racer by comparison. There was a yellow sticker in the corner of the pickup's windshield.

Taking up her purse and the non-disclosure booklet from the passenger seat, she stepped out into the dry heat of the morning and walked over to what she assumed was the building's entrance—a splintering wooden door that looked as if it would fall off its hinges if someone so much as breathed on it.

It was unlocked. She pushed it open and stepped inside. The shadowy interior was broken by spears of light coming in through the holes in the roof. The ancient smells of oil and leather suffused the dusty air, thick and cloying. A row of light bulbs was strung across the raftered ceiling, sagging in the spot where the roof had caved in. A large generator thrummed in the far corner, and thick insulated cables ran from it to an elevator that stood in the centre of the large, cavernous room.

The doors stood open.

Down the rabbit hole I go, Wendy thought, and stepped inside.

6

The elevator doors opened on a long hallway that ended at another door. As she walked slowly toward it, purse clutched in one hand, the non-disclosure agreement in the other, the door opened and Vanners appeared. He had traded in his green blazer for an oxford shirt and chinos, and there was a red plastic card hanging on a lanyard around his neck.

"Wendy!" he said, beaming. "So glad you could make it."

"Good morning," she said, a little uncertainly.

"Please forgive the cloak-and-dagger bit." Vanners led her through the door into another hallway. "I assure you we keep all of that business aboveground. Down here things run like any other office."

As they walked, the wall on the left side of the corridor turned into a glass partition, and Wendy saw that Vanners wasn't kidding. From the tone of the non-disclosure agreement, she had been expecting Area 51. But what she saw on the other side of the glass was nothing more sinister that an office building that just happened to be underground.

Vanners took her through a door that led inside.

"This is Research and Development, where you'll be working," he said. "The project's still in its conception phase—something we're hoping you'll kickstart along once you get settled. We're only operating at fifteen-percent capacity, as you can clearly see, so feel free to pick whatever cube you want."

Wendy nodded absently, looking around at the few inhabited cubicles. Each one was decorated with family photographs, *Far Side* calendars, plush toys, and anti-work slogans like I'D RATHER BE DRINKING and ALL WORK AND NO PLAY MAKES JACK A DULL BOY.

In one cubicle, a large model of Godzilla stood atop a computer monitor. Wendy stopped to admire it, and noticed a sticker on the wall that said TOO MANY IDIOTS, TOO FEW SERIAL KILLERS.

"Thumper," Vanners said by way of explanation.

"What?"

"Never mind. You'll meet him later."

They continued across the room to another glass door that led down another long corridor. They passed other parts of the facility: the supply closet, the copier room, the cafeteria. There was even a modest-sized gymnasium.

"It doesn't have all the comforts of home," Vanners said, "but what we lack here we more than make up for in Coyote Hills."

They came to the final stop on the tour—a door in a corridor that ended at another elevator.

"Where does that one go?" Wendy asked.

Vanners shook his head, and motioned to the door before them. Wendy gave it her full attention. She saw it was the only room on the floor that didn't have windows looking in on it.

It was also the only room with an electronic card-reader next to the door.

"This is the library," Vanners said. He slipped the lanyard over his head and slid the card into the scanner. A green light came on, and the lock disengaged with a sharp snapping sound.

"Go on in," Vanners said.

Wendy looked at him questionably, then stepped inside.

The room was dimly lit, almost cozy, like the libraries she had known as a kid. But to call this place a library was, in Wendy's opinion, a huge overstatement.

There was only one book in the entire room.

It lay closed atop a wooden pedestal, looking very important within a glass case not unlike the kind used in restaurants to preserve cakes and pies. A single overhead pot-light cast a soft, orange glow on the book, emphasizing the deep furrows in its dark cover.

"You can take it out of the cradle," Vanners said from the doorway.

Wendy carefully removed the glass lid and picked up the book.

It was extremely old, that much was apparent. She half expected it to moulder and crumble in her hands, as some Egyptian mummies were said to have done after their crypts were opened and exposed to fresh air. And it was heavy, too, for something the size of a hardcover novel but as thin as a newspaper. The book was bound in a way she had never seen before, and though the edges of the binding were frayed, it was still in unbelievably good condition.

The spine crackled as she carefully opened the book. She was startled to see that each parchment page had retained its velvety-smooth texture, and had none of the stiffness or warping that was the eventual fate of most writings this old.

Wendy felt such awe at the remarkably preserved condition of the book that she scarcely paid any attention to the contents. Crude pictograms and symbols, it seemed. Like nothing she had ever seen. Some of the text ran horizontally, but some also ran vertically and even diagonally. Some text was wound into drunken spirals, and some started on the left side of the page and then jumped across to the right.

Her overall impression of the artefact was of a shoddily constructed scrapbook. Something a disturbed kindergarten student might have made.

And there was something else. An indefinable sensation she got just by holding the book in her hands. A dark feeling she didn't much care for.

Wendy returned it to the cradle, replaced the glass lid, and rejoined Vanners in the hallway.

"What is it?" she asked in a voice that trembled slightly.

"We call it Black Book," Vanners replied. His voice had also lost some of its *joie de vivre*.

"Yes, but what *is* it?"

Vanners grinned, but there was no warmth in it. "Think of it as the other book that's going to change your life."

7

"Did you feel it?" Vanners asked as they walked back to the elevator.

"I felt . . . something," Wendy said in a low voice.

"We've pointed every damn instrument we have at the thing and all we know is that it was written in ink made from some kind of charcoal and vegetable gum, and it's in incredibly good shape for a book that's over six thousand years old."

"Six thou . . ."

"We've carbon-dated the pages and binding and it checks out."

"That would make it early Sumerian."

Vanners nodded. "That's what we think."

"It's like nothing I've ever seen. I don't know how something like this could have existed, let alone survived in that condition. . . . You don't have any idea what the symbols mean?"

Vanners gave her a look as if the answer was obvious.

"That's why you're here, kid."

8

After they returned topside, Vanners took Wendy out to Coyote Hills, a housing development for employees of Project Wellspring.

She followed Vanners' silver pickup along another nameless desert trail that suddenly and inexplicably turned into flawless, black asphalt.

She was so absorbed by this unexpected change that it took her a moment to notice the houses passing by on either side of the road. Large, picturesque bungalows and quaint little cottages, each with its own luxurious green lawn, and on each lawn a sprinkler system spraying out twirling fans of water.

Vanners turned into the driveway of a quaint little Cape Cod with lots of gingerbread trim, and a flower garden that seemed to be thriving in spite of the harsh desert conditions.

Wendy parked behind him and got out of her car.

"Welcome to Coyote Hills," Vanners said proudly. "Population: 16. But we're a town on the grow!" He sounded absurdly official, as if he were the mayor of this tiny town. "If you decide to stick around, you'll be number seventeen."

"This is your place?" Wendy asked.

"Nope, this one's yours. I live over on Maple Lane." He pointed further down the street.

"I get to live here?" she asked skeptically. "This is my house?"

"One of the perks of the job. If you choose to take it."

The chance to study the oldest book in the world *and* a considerable trade-up from the one-bedroom dormitory she'd expected? Suffice it to say she took the job.

9

On Tuesday, Wendy was introduced to her supervisor, Professor Horowitz. A tall, skinny man in his early sixties with pale skin and a prominent bone structure that gave him the appearance of a skeleton in a lab coat.

He didn't seem to like Wendy very much, and he didn't seem overly concerned about hiding the fact, either. Vanners told her it was because Horowitz saw her as an affront to the quality of his research to date on Project Wellspring.

"What exactly is the purpose of the project?" Wendy asked as they entered the office area.

"For now it's a straight decipherment deal," Vanners explained. "Put another way, in R&D we're currently doing a lot more R than D. We've got plenty of ideas for application, but we can't work on implementing any of them until we unlock the damn book."

"Unlock the book?"

"There's a general feeling among the experts who have had a chance to examine Black Book that it's not only written in a language we don't understand, but also some form of code. What kind of code, we don't know exactly. The thing doesn't match up with any comparable linguistic data we've managed to get our hands on. Horowitz doesn't know what it means, and neither did the three guys who worked here before him."

A metallic thumping sound caused Wendy to jump. She looked over at a young man with shaggy red hair bending down to get a can of Sprite from one of the vending machines.

"Sorry about that," he said, smiling sheepishly. "Sounds like someone racking a shotgun, doesn't it?"

Wendy smiled politely.

"Thumper, this is Wendy Harris. Wendy, Thumper."

"Charmed," he said, tipping her a little salute with his can of soda. "Welcome to the cave. Your eyesight will adjust in a few weeks. 'Course by then you won't be able to go back out into the sunlight."

"It might be for the best in your case, huh, Thumper?"

"Touché," Thumper said. "If my mother could only see me now. A lab technician who spends his days feeding hundred-year-old manuscripts into a computer that is, alas, my only friend."

"What about Tara?" Vanners asked, nodding at a narrow-faced woman sitting in a cubicle on the far side of the room.

"Tara doesn't talk. I might as well have a conversation with Godzilla."

Wendy recalled the model she had seen perched on the computer monitor the other day.

Vanners clapped his hands together like a teacher calling his class to attention. "I'll let the two of you get acquainted. If you need me, I'll be in the cafeteria with Horowitz."

10

Thumper's situation turned out to be almost identical to Wendy's. After graduating from UCLA with an advanced degree in computer science, he had come here after hearing about the job from one of his professors. He had been on Project Wellspring for eight months and still didn't have any clear idea as to the nature of the work he was doing.

"It's research," he said, offering the same reply (and the same shrug) that Vanners had given her. "I run ancient texts through an optical scanner. But it's a living."

Thumper also told her about Tara, the narrow-faced girl who didn't talk.

"Well, she talks, but not very often. I say 'good morning' to her every day, and I get a response maybe ten percent of the time. It could be worse. My father's typical attitude in the morning was to whip bottles of Jack Daniels at my head."

Wendy stared at him.

"It wasn't so bad," he said, giving her hand a reassuring pat. "It was only the full bottles that really hurt."

11

Over the next two weeks, Wendy fell into that depthless chasm of the working class—the daily routine.

Monday to Friday she woke up at six, showered, dressed, and stuffed a piece of toast or an apple in her mouth before driving the twenty-five miles to the glove factory. She spent the morning struggling with the perplexing symbols of Black Book, jotting notes on possible leads, then hashing them out with Thumper and Tara in the afternoon. By the time four o'clock rolled around, the three of them were wandering the halls like undead ghouls in a George Romero movie.

A month went by, and Wendy was still no closer to understanding the book's strange language. The work was going very slowly—something Horowitz pointed out every chance he got. He likened Wendy's progress to the speed at which the polar icecaps were melting. *For your sake, Ms. Harris, and for the sake of all humanity, I sure hope the solution to global warming isn't in that damnable book, because we'll all be living on rafts and backstroking to work by the time you find it.*

"You should feel sorry for him," Thumper told her one day.

"Feel sorry for him? The guy's a total jerk."

"He's a Skeletor," Thumper said, as if this explained everything. "His skin's two sizes too small for him. He walks around like he's wearing jeans that just came out of the wash. Rides up in the crotch. Bound to make anyone miserable."

"Thanks, Thumper."

It would have been easier to take Horowitz's comments in stride if they were only off-the-cuff jabs made by an angry, old man. But the truth was, she was no closer to figuring out Black Book, and however mean and pejorative Horowitz's criticisms might be, inaccurate they were not.

The only thing she had come up with, the only theory that Thumper and Tara had yet to shoot down, was that Black Book might be a primitive arithmetic primer. Some of the symbols bore at least a passing resemblance to basic syntactical structures she had seen in other ancient texts of the same period, but it always felt as if there were something missing, some basic layer of information she hadn't figured out how to interpret.

There was something else, too. It was a minor thing, but she couldn't help feeling it might be significant.

The first time she had handled Black Book, she had done so with her bare hands, and the book had left charcoal stains on her hands. Every time after, she had been wearing latex gloves, and it had left no marks.

Maybe it was because the gloves just didn't pick up the charcoal, but she wondered. She wondered a lot.

12

She was still wondering about it as she was getting into her car at the end of another fruitless day. Thumper and Tara had taken the afternoon off to go to the movies in Bartonville. Wendy had been invited, but she didn't feel right about leaving early on yet another day when she had failed to produce any results.

She rummaged in her purse for her car keys and felt something wet and sticky touch the back of her hand. She pulled it out and saw the old napkin she had used to write down the directions to the job interview. The eyeliner she used had caused the napkin stick to her hand.

She recalled how angry she had been that day when she saw the directions had been smudged. The writing was totally illegible now. She could no more understand the words on the napkin than she could the symbols in Black Book.

She stared at the eyeliner stain on the back of her hand for a long time. Then a smile slowly spread across her face.

She hopped out of the car and ran back to the glove factory. She took the elevator down and searched all of the rooms on Sub-Level One. Horowitz wasn't in any of them, which meant he was probably in the lab on Sub-Level Two. Wendy's key-card didn't give her access to that floor, and Horowitz never answered his phone.

She went to her desk, booted up her computer, and fired off an e-mail to the good professor, telling him of her discovery.

His laconic reply came a moment later: *I'll check your notes in the morning.*

Wendy stuck her tongue out at the screen and dropped her finger ceremoniously on the delete key. "Take that, Skeletor."

What she proposed was impossible, of course. Completely impossible. But the Black Book itself was impossible on so many levels she had given up trying to document them. When you bent the rules of physics once, why couldn't you do it again?

She shut off her computer and went back down the hall. She stood outside the elevator, tapping her foot and looking back the way she had come. She could go to the library and test her theory herself, but something told her that might not be a good idea.

In fact, it might be a bad idea.

Black Book was a dark book. *Dark* as in threatening. *Dark* as in sinister. And she didn't want to be alone in a room with anything that transmitted such malefic signals.

If Horowitz wanted to wait until morning, that was fine by her.

She would go home and sleep the sleep of the just.

Or try to.

13

It was still dark out when she woke up to the sound of someone banging on her front door. She slipped into a robe and went downstairs.

The banging resumed, accompanied by a voice: *"Wendy! Wendy, wake up! It's Vanners!"*

Wendy opened the door and let him in. A pair of security officers in black combat fatigues followed closely behind him. They wore ski-masks and goggles that she assumed were of the night-vision variety. They were carrying assault rifles, which, for the moment anyway, were pointed down at the Turkish rug that covered the foyer.

"What is this?" Wendy demanded.

"It's Horowitz," Vanners said in a strident voice that didn't sound like his own. "He's dead."

14

Wendy had never been in Horowitz's study before—she didn't even know where he lived (on Maple Lane, it turned out, two doors down from Vanners). But even if she had, she didn't think she would have recognized the place now.

It looked as if a tornado had ripped through the mahogany-panelled room. The heavy oak desk had been reduced to splinters, the lamps lay shattered on the floor, and all of the books had been pulled off the shelves and thrown every which way.

Horowitz, or rather what was left of him, was sitting in his executive swivel chair. If the room looked like a tornado had hit it, then the professor looked like someone who had swallowed a hand grenade. His arms and legs, clad in striped flannel pajamas, were held together by a bloody, pulpy mess that was no longer recognizable as a human body. His head, miraculously still attached to his neck, lolled to the side, as if he couldn't bear the sight of his own horribly mangled body. Not that he could have seen much, anyway. Whatever had caused his body to rupture in such a gruesome manner had done the same to his eyes. They lay across his cheeks like white jelly.

"What the hell happened to him?" Wendy asked.

"I don't have the slightest clue," Vanners replied. His voice seemed unable to decide whether it wanted to be scared or angry.

A couple of security officers were taking surface swabs and photographs. Another was crawling on the study floor, picking up the fallen books and stacking them in neat piles.

Vanners looked over at Wendy. "When was the last time you saw Horowitz?"

Wendy stammered. "I . . . I e-mailed him just before I left the glove factory. I didn't actually see him, but he sent me a reply."

"What did you e-mail him about?"

Before Wendy could answer, the security officer on the floor flipped over a hunk of wood and uncovered a familiar, dark-covered book.

"Found it!"

"Oh, thank Christ," Vanners let out a deep breath. "That was too close. Too damn close."

The security officer handed him the book. Vanners clutched it to his chest. Watching him, Wendy was once again reminded of the first time she had held the book. She remembered that feeling of power—dark power.

"Vanners," she said, "you might not want to hold it so close."

15

"So explain this to me again."

Wendy folded her arms and looked over her shoulder at the drawings she had made on the white board. Thumper and Tara had remained silent throughout her presentation, but Vanners and Summerhill, the chief of security, had asked questions throughout.

Vanners' queries chiefly consisted of clarifying certain details and points throughout her narrative. Summerhill's, on the other hand, bordered on accusations of murder—or at least accessory to murder.

"Which part do you need explained, Mr. Summerhill?" Wendy asked crisply.

The security chief sat up in his chair (he had been slouching further and further into his seat as Wendy attempted to explain her theory of what may have happened to Professor Horowitz). "The hocus-pocus bit," he said. "The part where the professor's little black book goes boom."

Wendy gave Vanners a look that said *How much longer am I supposed to humour this fool?*

Vanners nodded sympathetically and motioned for her to be patient for just a little bit longer.

"First of all, it wasn't anyone's little black book that did this." Wendy pointed to a glossy black-and-white photograph on the wall that showed the scene in Horowitz's study. "*That* is Black Book, and *that* is a deadly artefact."

"What is this 'deadly artefact' bullshit?" Summerhill quipped. He looked at the others for support, but didn't find any. "I mean, it's a *book*, for Christ's sake. Books don't kill people."

"I don't think this one meant to. Not exactly."

"We're going around in circles, Ms. Harris, and I'm sorry, but this isn't making any sense to me."

"This is a bomb," Wendy said, and picked up the plastic evidence bag that contained Black Book. "And this is the trigger." She picked up another evidence bag, this one containing a sheet of paper from Black Book. It had been found on the floor of the study near the professor's body. "I believe the professor used his key-card to remove Black Book from this facility and took it home with the intent of using the information I supplied him to carry out an experiment that ultimately cost him his life."

Summerville pointed a finger at her. "So that means you might have had some complicity in Professor Horowitz's death."

"I told him what I thought it was," Wendy said in a low voice. "I told him what we had been missing. What was needed to activate the book. But I had no idea what it would do . . . the kind of power it had."

"But how did it happen?" Vanners snapped. "It's all so . . . backwards. It feels like we just invented nuclear power and now we're trying to figure out how to split the atom."

Thumper visibly trembled and Tara let out a deep sigh. They were both looking at Wendy. For what? Comfort? Reassurance? She didn't think either one was on the menu today.

"I think Professor Horowitz tapped into some kind of energy source contained within Black Book, and I think he did so by physical contact."

"But we've all handled the book before," Thumper said. "I've flipped through the damn thing dozens of times."

Wendy said, "I don't think simply touching the symbols is enough. I think Horowitz took an entire page from the book and applied it to his bare chest."

Everyone was silent for a moment.

Then Vanners said: "What difference would it make where the contact was made?"

"I'm not sure the precise location matters, but I think the contact has to be total." She picked up the baggie containing the single page and pantomimed pressing it against her chest. "All along we thought it was some sort of language barrier. Or code. But that's not it at all. It's a . . . formula. An equation. And I think this energy, this force, is only activated when the entire formula has been imprinted. It's not enough to get some of it on your finger or your hand. I believe that the purpose of Black Book was to use human flesh as a conduit for whatever energies it contained."

"And what energies would those be?" Summerhill asked.

"I don't know," Wendy replied. "But I think we should make it a priority to find out."

16

In the wake Professor Horowitz's death, things began to move very fast on Project Wellspring.

In a week, the number of personnel at the glove factory doubled. Vanners gave Wendy the probationary title of Supervisor of Research & Development and put her to work on determining a way to safely test the power of Black Book without anyone else getting killed.

The symbols in the book were difficult to crack, but it turned out she was right. Black Book was, in actuality, a collection of ancient formulae. Thumper started calling it The Great Cook Book from Hell, since one of the key symbols in these formulae was indeed human beings (as Horowitz had posthumously confirmed). It was a disturbing discovery made that much worse by the book's clear description of exactly what kind of human beings it preferred.

Namely, young ones.

17

"Oh *God!* Are you saying it's made of people?"

"It's not *made* of people," Wendy said. "But people make it work. They're like . . . the main ingredient."

It was Saturday, and Wendy and Thumper were walking down Main Street toward Maple Lane.

"But still, if people go in, and something comes out . . ." Thumper shook his head to dispel the horrific images in his mind.

"That's the theory."

"So when Horowitz slapped that piece of paper on his chest, what? Some tentacled nasty materialized in the room and gave him an appendectomy?"

"I think Horowitz was a victim of . . . electrical feedback."

"How's that?"

"The page he took from the book was part of a set. You know those pages where the symbols run from the left page to the right?"

"Yeah."

"Well, I think the equation only works if you use both pages on two separate people. Horowitz used only the one and the damn thing, well, malfunctioned."

"That's one way of putting it."

They walked for a bit. Then Wendy asked: "Did Vanners tell you about the test subjects?"

"Yeah, he said they were volunteers. I figure, they must not know what happened to old Skeletor, or else they would have kept their mouths shut."

"Not if they thought they were getting something out of it."

"Like what?"

Wendy stopped and turned to face him. "They're death row inmates, Thumper. Vanners made some sort of deal with the state. The cons know the whole situation. He had them sign non-disclosure forms and everything."

"*What?*"

Wendy nodded. "Vanners said they have nothing to lose, which is why most of them agreed. But . . ." She shook her head doubtfully. "Testing on humans. It's not right."

"Hell," Thumper said, "nothing's been right around here for weeks. And it doesn't show much sign of getting any better."

18

On a hot day in August, four months after Wendy first came to the glove factory and Coyote Hills, Project Wellspring received its first two human volunteers.

Johnny Spartan and Elroy McIntyre were on loan from the Nevada correctional system. Dressed in orange prison overalls and leg irons, they trotted into the testing area flanked by a pair of security officers.

The guards took them over to where Thumper and Tara were waiting for them, each with a page of Black Book in one latex-gloved hand, and a device that looked like a miniature paint-roller in the other.

Wendy watched from the observation booth that overlooked the room. Her arms were stiffly crossed, and she was feeling extremely tense. Vanners stood beside her, and she thought she could feel the same nervous vibes coming off him. His eyes were slightly puffy, too, as if he had slept poorly last night.

He thumbed the intercom. "Let's get this thing rolling."

In the testing area, Thumper gave him a thumbs-up, though the look on his face was dark and grave.

Wendy watched as both of the convicts unsnapped the clasps on their overalls and exposed their bare chests. One of them said something to Tara, and she flushed and turned away. The guard standing behind the con gave him a quick jab with the butt of his rifle. The con smiled and stood up straighter.

The guards nodded to Thumper and Tara and they stepped forward to do their part. They each placed their page flat against the chest of their respective volunteer. Then they ran the miniature paint-rollers over the pages a few times for good measure.

Wendy watched it all with utter amazement. *It's sticking to their skin. It's nothing but six-thousand-year-old parchment and charcoal, but it's sticking to their skin.*

Tara and Thumper stepped back and exchanged a look. *What happens now?*

Wendy turned to Vanners, but he was staring at the readout of one of the hundred or so pieces of monitoring equipment packed into the small room. He must have seen something he didn't like, because he came back to the window in a rush, pushing a lab technician out of the way. He stabbed the intercom button.

"Tara, Thumper," he said briskly, "please vacate the room."

Tara and Thumper exchanged another look, and started toward the door set in the tempered steel wall. Thumper cast one look back over his shoulder at the two cons. They had come in swaggering and smiling. They looked different now, although he couldn't say exactly how.

A moment later, Tara and Thumper joined Wendy and Vanners in the observation booth. Vanners' attention was once again glued to the readout of one particular instrument.

"Something's happening in there," he said.

Wendy couldn't tell if it was fear or excitement she heard in his voice—probably a little of both.

She turned back to the window and saw that something was happening to the cons, all right. One of them seemed to be okay, but the other had dropped to one knee, as if he were proposing marriage to his buddy.

Whatever he was doing, the guards didn't like it. They had moved a discreet distance away and raised their rifles held to high port.

"He thought he was getting a rub-on tattoo," Tara said in a low, childlike voice. The others turned and looked at her. "That's what he said to me in there."

Wendy looked back into the testing area just as the other con doubled over. He was trying to peel the page of Black Book off his chest, but it wouldn't come off.

The security guards backed further away, toward the door. Vanners was on his way to the intercom to tell them to hold their position when the event that would be referred to as "realization" in top-secret government reports suddenly took place.

There was a brief flash of light that seemed to have no source. The scene in the testing area seemed unchanged. Then the group in the observation booth realized that although they could see the convicts, writhing on the floor in soundless agony, they could also see *through* them, as if they were ghosts.

But you don't usually see ghosts in so much pain, Wendy thought.

The pages from Black Book were now lying on the floor of the testing area.

Why not? They've already done their part.

The apparitions began to shrink and collapse into themselves. Because the observation booth was soundproof, the entire sequence played out in silence. It was like watching a clip of some special-effects-laden movie for which the soundtrack had yet to be recorded.

There were now two spheres of shimmering blue light hovering over the floor of the testing area. Great spikes of electricity crackled off them. The spikes grew taller and taller until they met in the centre of the room. Something began to happen, some sort of reaction.

It's happening, Wendy thought. *I don't know what* it *is but it's happening!*

Something that looked like a swarm of fireflies began to materialize in the space between the two spheres. They grew larger as the spheres channelled energy into them. The fireflies started to merge with one another to form an expanding ball of red-orange light. It spread across the air like a festering wound, and by the time the blue spheres had fizzled out, their energy spent, the ball of light filled the entire room.

There was another flash, and in the half-second before it disappeared, Wendy glimpsed an enormous silhouette against the red-orange glow. Then she was looking at something her eyes refused to transmit to the receptors in her brain. Something that at first glance looked like some strange new species of whale.

It lay on the floor of the testing area, unmoving, in about a foot of steaming green water that must have been brought from whatever place it had been snatched.

A thirty-foot-long creature with the basic shape of a whale, but with the plates and ridges of a rhinoceros. Its mouth, crusted with things that might have been barnacles, hung slightly open to reveal rows of triangular shark's teeth, each one as big as a human fist.

Of the convicts, there was no sign.

19

Over the next two weeks, several more guests of the state of Nevada came to Project Wellspring and stood shirtless, smiling even, as pages from Black Book were applied to their chests. They never smiled for very long. The entities that appeared in their place were a rogue's gallery of nightmarish entities and hellish abominations. They shared only one common similarity.

They all showed up either dead or dying.

To anyone who saw one of these creatures suddenly appear in a room where there had been only a pair of men before, this would have seemed like a blessing. But Vanners only grew more annoyed as the experiments went on.

With the exception of the whale-thing, Wendy saw none of these creatures. Since she, Thumper, and Tara were technically part of R&D, they were not authorized to be on Sub-Level Two, where the experiments took place. Vanners had only invited Wendy that first time as a courtesy—perhaps because he wasn't convinced anything was going to happen.

What little she learned about the experiments, she gleaned from the hushed (and horrified) conversations she overheard from those in the Applications department.

According to one worker, the reason the creatures were showing up dead was because their DNA was in such a state of flux that they couldn't live any longer than a few minutes before undergoing complete cellular breakdown.

One creature that showed up must have been especially bad because Vanners gave the entire Applications department the rest of the day off.

Afterward, he had gone to Wendy and asked her about the pictograms in Black Book, specifically the ones that denoted the human form. Wendy brought up a high-resolution scan of the symbol on her computer.

"Why's it so small and bent over like that?" Vanners asked, pointing at the curled, almost comma-shaped symbol.

"Thumper thinks it might be symbolic of the act of realization," she lied. "The bent-over figure representing the subject undergoing the . . . process."

Vanners nodded but his eyes had a faraway look.

He walked off, zipping through the cubicle-maze like a man on a mission.

Wendy supposed that was probably close to the truth.

Over the following weeks the stories she heard were no longer about convicts.

They were about children.

20

They arranged to meet at Wendy's house. She was on the porch when they arrived, pacing back and forth.

"Do you think it's safe to talk out here?" Thumper asked.

"The insides of the houses are almost certainly bugged," Wendy said, "but I can't see them bugging the outsides. It doesn't matter anyway. What I want to do—what I *have* to do—is going to happen tonight, and they won't have time to stop me."

"*Tonight?*" Thumper exclaimed. "Jesus, Wendy. If what we've heard is true, then we have to do something, yes, of course—but *tonight*? We need to plan this out, we need to—"

"I have a plan," Wendy said, in what she hoped was a confident voice. "If we do it quickly, I think we can get away with it. But it has to be tonight."

"But how do we know the stories are true?" Tara said. "How do we really know they've started using children in the experiments?"

"I told you what Vanners said," Wendy said. "He asked me about the human pictograms in Black Book. I'm almost positive he was testing me, trying to feel out how much I knew. He's figured out that the key to bringing over live creatures from whatever godforsaken hell they come from is not scum-of-the-earth death row inmates. It's children. The younger the better, I'm willing to bet."

Tara paled. She lowered her eyes and nodded, as if she had known the truth all along but needed to hear it spoken aloud.

"The day before Vanners came to see me something happened. Something that may not have tipped him off to the truth, but it certainly put him on the right track."

Thumper perked up. "What was it?"

"I can't say for certain," Wendy said, "but I'd be willing to make a guess."

She let them think about it for a moment.

"Oh God," Tara blurted. "You think they killed an innocent man."

Thumper ran a trembling hand over his face and sat down hard on the porch steps. The thought that Black Book had been able to do what a jury of a man's peers had been either unable or unwilling to do made him feel sick to his stomach.

"I don't think it happened on purpose," Wendy said. "But I think it clued Vanners in on what Black Book really wants."

"You're talking about babies." Tara said. "You really think they'd do that? Kill babies?"

"I think Vanners will do whatever's necessary to bring those things over alive and healthy."

"But why?" Thumper said. "What the hell do they want with them?"

"My guess would be military applications."

"What, you think they're going to harness them? Train them like attack dogs? Do you think those things can be housebroken?"

"No," Wendy said, "but I think they're going to try."

21

Wendy moved stealthily down the corridor to the gymnasium, constantly looking over her shoulder, waiting for the men in the black fatigues to pop out and arrest her. What would happen then? Would she be charged under the Secrecy Act? Or would she be shot on the spot and buried somewhere in the desert?

Tara and Thumper were back in the office area, sitting in their cubicles and waiting for her. Since the experiments had begun, the R&D staff had switched to a rotating evenings-and-midnights schedule. So there was nothing unusual about them working late.

Wendy slipped quietly into the dark gymnasium and over to the equipment closet.

There was an electronic card-reader on the door. It was a recent addition.

The reason for the heightened security was related to a story Wendy had heard from the Applications rumour mill.

Since they had switched from convicts to children, the experiments had been successful. Supposedly the armoury on Sub-Level Three had been converted into some kind of holding pen. It was here that the creatures—the *live* ones, that is—were being kept.

Wendy had no intention of going down to Sub-Level Three, which the Applications people called "the Zoo," but she had been very interested in the part about how the weapons and ammunition in the armoury had been temporarily moved into the large and mostly vacant gymnasium equipment closet.

She took out her key-card, crossed herself with it, and slid it into the reader.

The green light came on and the lock snapped open.

Wendy muttered a prayer of thanks and stepped into the dark room.

22

Her second stop was to the storage closet where all of Horowitz's belongings had been stored following the investigation into his death. Since it was located on Sub-Level One, Wendy's key-card gave her access to it.

She found the stack of cardboard boxes that contained all of the books and papers and other assorted items that had been taken from the professor's study. She found his wallet in a plastic evidence bag, and took it out. The leather crackled when she opened the wallet, making her think of the way the pages of Black Book had crackled when she opened it for the first time.

Just as she had hoped, the security guards hadn't bothered to catalogue the wallet's contents. If they had, they surely would have confiscated the red plastic card with "S3" printed on it in gold letters.

23

When Wendy returned to the office area, Thumper and Tara popped out of their cubicles like a pair of jack-in-the-boxes.

"Did you get them?"

Wendy slipped her hands into the wide pockets of her coat and took out a pair of nine-millimetre pistols. From her inside pocket she produced a number of extra clips. She hadn't bothered to grab one for Tara. She had never fired a gun before, and they all agreed that tonight wasn't the best time to start.

Thumper picked up one of the pistols. "I can't believe we're doing this."

They stood in silence for a long moment. Then:

"My mom always says you do the thing you're most afraid of first, and then you get the courage afterwards."

Wendy and Thumper looked at Tara. It was the most either one of them had ever heard her say at one time.

24

They walked in single file down the corridor to the elevator that would take them to the lab. Professor Horowitz's key-card opened the doors, and they stepped inside. Wendy looked at the control panel, and her face crumpled.

"It's what I thought," she said, indicating the buttons. "This lift doesn't go to the surface. Once we get the kids we're going to have to take this elevator back up here, go back the way we came, and take the other elevator up to the glove factory."

"That sounds like an awfully long walk," Thumper said.

The elevator doors opened on Sub-Level Two. Wendy, Thumper, and Tara stepped out into a corridor they had been down only once before. There was a large pressure door up ahead on the left side—the entrance to the testing area, they knew. At the far end, the corridor took a left turn and continued on to the observation booth.

They moved quickly, passing the pressure door and continuing around the bend to the entrance to the observation booth. Wendy took a deep breath, then swiped Horowitz's key-card through the reader.

Thumper moved quickly into the room, followed by Wendy, with Tara taking up the rear.

Wendy had been expecting a roomful of armed sentries and important-looking bureaucrats in expensive suits. What she saw was the same thing she had seen the last time she was here: Vanners and a young lab tech running the whole show. Only this time Vanners had an incredulous look on his face that quickly turned to blackest hate.

"What the hell is this?"

Wendy shoved the gun in his face. "We're shutting you down, Vanners."

The lab tech's hand was inching slowly toward a red button on the console before him. Thumper saw it, and brought his fist down hard, breaking a few of the young man's fingers by the sound.

Vanners smiled snidely. "Do you really think you'll get out of here alive? With only a couple of handguns between you?"

Wendy moved over to the console and pressed the button that sealed the testing room door. Below, the six guards in the room continued working, unaware that anything was going on in the observation booth.

They were positioning a small fleet of what looked like pedestals on wheels. Wendy counted ten of them. Surmounting each one was a child's bassinet. One guard standing off to the side was holding a thin sheaf of papers.

"You're here for the kids?" Vanners growled.

Thumper grabbed him by the back of the neck and pushed him toward the glass partition. Wendy put her gun to Vanners' temple and pressed the toggle switch on the intercom.

"Hello, gentlemen. I'm afraid we're going to have a change of plans tonight."

Six pairs of eyes stared up at the tableau within the observation booth.

"This is what's going to happen. First, you're going to put your weapons on the floor. That includes the sidearms on your belts, and the pages of Black Book. Secondly, you're going to back up against the far wall and stay there until I say you can move. If you fail to do either of these things, I'm going to pull the trigger. No warnings."

"This won't stop anything," Vanners said. "You think we can't get more kids?"

Wendy reached down and picked Black Book up off the console where it was lying. "They're not much good to you without this, are they?"

Vanners clenched his fists and said nothing. His breathing was heavy and there was a burning sun in each cheek.

"Maybe you could open a nursery," Thumper added.

25

After collecting the security guards' and Vanners' key-cards, they opted to tie them up and leave them. They had gotten what they came for, and they saw no point in executing anyone in cold blood—although, Thumper pointed out, that was precisely what would happen to *them* if they didn't get out of the glove factory before the next shift of guards showed up.

Wendy and Tara carried three babies each, while Thumper, using one of the bassinets, took the other four. They went back up the elevator, through Sub-Level One, and up the other elevator to the surface. It was coming on midnight by this time, and the moon was up.

They piled into Thumper's Jeep Wrangler, taking a moment to arrange the kids safely and securely in the back seat with Tara. Thumper sat in the shotgun seat with the basinette in his lap, while Wendy drove.

She pulled Black Book out of her jacket pocket and handed it to Thumper.

"It's not exactly Dr. Seuss," he said, opening the glove compartment and jamming it inside.

"What are we going to do with it?" Tara asked.

"We'll think of something," Wendy said noncommittally.

"What are we going to do with these?" Thumper said, hefting the bassinet. "I mean, it looks like a family exploded in here."

"Looks like it," Wendy agreed.

"Where are we gonna take them?" Tara asked.

Wendy thought about it for a long moment. "New York?"

Thumper gave her a questioning look. "Do you think that's a safe place to raise a child?"

Wendy looked at him, and started to laugh. Thumper's face broke, and then he was laughing, too. Tara joined in. The babies, all ten of them, only stared and gurgled.

They were still laughing when they reached the Interstate.

THE CURRENTS

They found him on the banks of the Black River, behind their clapboard house in Oxford. He lay facedown on the muddy shore, not sprawled out but curled up as if he were only sleeping. Bright bars of late-afternoon sunlight lay across him like a striped blanket. The three members of the Abraham family approached him slowly, warily, as if he were a slumbering bear.

"Is he drownded?" Trevor whispered. He was eight, and at a point in his life when death was something that fascinated rather than frightened him.

"It's 'drowned,'" said his twelve-year-old sister, Bessie.

"Is he?" Trevor sounded almost hopeful. "Do you think so?"

Bessie looked at her mother, but her mother's eyes remained fixed on the tall man. Trevor goggled back and forth between them, like a spectator at a tennis match.

Claire Abraham knew that strangers weren't common in this part of Nova Scotia. Oxford may have been advertised as the wild blueberry capital of Canada, but it didn't attract many tourists. Even if they were used to seeing strangers in town, they wouldn't have expected to find one passed out on the riverbank behind their house.

"Give me a hand, Bessie," she said finally.

Together mother and daughter crouched down and rolled the tall man onto his back. It was not the first time they had performed such a manoeuvre. They had had to roll George Abraham over on more occasions than either woman cared to remember. It was not the drinking that pained them; it was the remembering. George had been a silly drunk, a stupid drunk, but never a mean drunk, and it was the least his wife and daughter could do to keep him from choking to death on his own vomit.

The tall man was wearing a denim jacket, a light blue chambray workshirt, and blue jeans—all of which were soaked through and clung to him like a second skin. His arms lay across his chest in an X, reminding Trevor of pictures of Egyptian mummies he had seen in his father's *National Geographic* magazines. He looked like a man who knew death was near and wanted to make it as easy as possible on everyone involved.

As Bessie pulled him into a sitting position, she saw he had something clutched in his arms—a pair of old scuffed workboots. She pulled his arms away from his body, and the boots tumbled to the muddy ground. Trevor, wanting to be helpful, swooped down and picked them up.

With Bessie propping him up, Claire clapped the tall man on the back. The wet slapping sound, coupled with the deep mineral smell that seemed to roll off him in waves, made Bessie think of doing laundry in the summer. Scrubbing clothes in the Black River and wringing them out, flinging them against the rocks and leaving wet marks in great manta shapes on their long, flat surfaces.

The tall man let out a series of dry, wracking coughs; despite looking like a drowned rat, it seemed he hadn't taken any water into his lungs. His face was waxy-white. He had sharp cheekbones, and his wet hair lay in ropy runners on his cheeks like seaweed. His lips were a thin blue line, and when he opened his eyes, they were blue, as well. A rich, pure blue like the heart of an ice floe.

The three Abrahams each took an unconscious step backward. Those eyes were not natural. They seemed almost to glow. Bessie felt a sudden warmth in her chest, like the comforting pressure of a hot-water bottle. Looking into those eyes was like standing on the edge of Edgar's Cliff and looking down at the reservoir.

Claire helped the man to his feet, watching him cautiously as he took the hand she offered. His grip was cold and slippery—*like gripping a fish out of the river*, she thought. She felt the furrows in the pads of his fingers, the marks of one who had spent much time in the water; and when his jacket sleeve slid back slightly, she stared, transfixed at his marble-white arm shot with blue veins.

The tall man was able to walk on his own, with an arm slung around Claire's slender neck to keep him steady and pointed toward the back of their ramshackle house. Bessie walked ahead of them, while Trevor trailed behind, swinging a boot gaily in each hand.

Bessie opened the screen door, and Claire led the tall man into the kitchen, depositing him in the straight-backed chair next to the wood stove. Trevor put his boots down next to him and, without needing to be told, started building a fire, wrapping the kindling in newspaper so that they looked like oversized party favours before sticking them in the black iron maw of the stove. He got the fire going as Claire and Bessie drew up chairs on either side of the tall man—partly to prevent him from falling over, but mostly because they sensed he was ready to talk.

"Thank you for your kindness." His voice was thick and seemed to come from a distance. Like an echo floating up the stone throat of a well. "It's been some time since I've been treated so well."

The fire crackled pleasantly and began to suffuse the room with a heavy, somnolent warmth.

"Did the river carry you off?" Trevor asked. "Is that why you weren't wearing your boots?"

"Yes." The tall man nodded. "The river carried me off."

"What's your name?"

"Name?" he said, as if the concept was alien to him. "I'm a travelling man, son. Travelling men don't have names."

Trevor smiled. He liked the idea of a travelling man. He never got to go anywhere. "What do your friends call you?" he asked.

"Travelling men don't have friends, either," the tall man replied.

"Oh." The boy looked perplexed. "Well, where do you come from?"

Claire gave the boy a reproving look that he pretended not to see. Normally she would have reprimanded him for such forwardness, but the questions he was asking were the same ones in her own mind. And she could see the answers in the tall man's eyes, but she didn't think he would give them over easily, if at all.

"Where I'm from doesn't matter," the tall man said dismissively. "Where I'm going doesn't matter, either." He smiled, and it was like an eclipse over an arctic wasteland. Cold and beautiful. "What matters, if anything does, is how I get there. Most travelling men ride the rails or the roads. I ride the currents. The rivers. The streams. The creeks. Far as I know, I'm the only travelling man who does." Not proud or ashamed: a man simply stating an ordinary fact of life. "That's why I took my boots off. My feet need to be immersed in water for me to ride the currents."

"Why?" Trevor asked.

"Don't know the why of it. But growing up I can tell you I took a lot of showers with my galoshes on."

The boy smiled and the tall man leaned into the warmth of the stove. A puddle was forming under his chair from his dripping clothes. He picked up his boots and held them in his lap like a sleeping cat.

"It takes a lot out of me."

"Then why do you do it?" Trevor asked.

The tall man stared at him reflectively. "Oh, it's not so bad. Just tires me out some. Like a man who walks the roads gets blisters on his feet. 'Cept mine get me here"—he pointed to his chest—"and here." He pointed to his head. "When I was a baby, my mother used to bathe me in the kitchen sink. One day I disappeared right before her eyes—or so she told me. Scared her something fierce. Said my father searched the whole house, muttering curses in Gaelic, which was the only time he used the old tongue." His lips turned up again in that arctic-eclipse grin. "Found me in the basement, dripping wet and fast asleep next to the water heater."

Trevor stood up and fed another stovelength into the fire. The flames threw dancing shadows across the tall man's face. Claire and Bessie sat quietly on either side of him like bookends.

"I've always been able to find the currents." He raised his hands and spread his fingers wide. "Some people can see the future in people's palms. I see maps." He lowered his hands to the cracked leather hide of his boots. "Some people can find water with a forked stick. I can, too, except I don't need a stick. Mine's up here." He tapped the side of his head. "It's like having another set of eyes in my head. Shows me things sometimes. Some of 'em beautiful, some . . . some I don't ever want to see again."

"Like what?" Trevor asked, a little timidly.

The tall man stared thoughtfully at the stove. "There was one time—I don't remember dates. All my stories start the same: *There was one time*. I woke up on the edge of a great lake. Not *the* Great Lakes. I've never ever ridden the currents off the coast of Nova Scotia. Never stepped foot in the Atlantic—too scared of where it would take me. This was a great lake, though—the Bras d'Or. I recognized it, but only for a moment. I started to see it differently, like someone had opened a door into hell. I saw hands, thousands of hands, each one as white as a salmon's belly, reaching up out of the water. And I could see through them, like they were ghosts. I think that's what they were. The spirits of those who have died in these waters."

The tall man closed his eyes. His hair was still wet, but his clothes had dried considerably. The water had darkened the colours, and now they looked faded. With his eyes closed, the tall man looked faded, too.

"Are you a ghost?" the boy asked.

"Nar. But I think we walk some of the same back roads. Close enough to see each other from time to time."

Claire started to speak, but her voice came out in a croak. She cleared her throat and began again. "My husband—their father—died at sea."

"Was he a fisherman?" the tall man asked.

"Yes," Claire replied, "but he wasn't on a fishing boat when it happened. He was out at Horsehead Cove, fishing off the end of the pier, and it chose that particular day to collapse. It was an old, rickety thing, but it must have been there sixty years or more. My Da used to take me and my sisters out there when we were kids. George, my husband, was alone that day, so we didn't find out what happened for a few days. The police went out to Horsehead and saw the pier was gone. George washed up on the breakwater near the lighthouse. He was a good swimmer, but they figure he hit his head and was knocked unconscious when the pier collapsed."

They sat in silence for a long time, staring at the stove. The heat from the fire was like another presence in the room.

"They found his creel, but his pole was gone," Claire added, as if this was an important detail.

The tall man craned his head around and looked out the window above the sink. The somber late-afternoon light had turned the rich azure of early evening. The shadow of the old pump house stretched across the back yard.

"I've stayed too long."

"No," Trevor said, almost desperately. "You have to stay!"

"Nar." The tall man's voice was gentle but firm. "A travelling man is like a shark. Has to keep movin' or else he'll die."

"But I want to hear more about the currents."

The tall man looked at the boy, and Claire saw something pass between them. There were more stories he could have told them, of that she was sure, and while some of them were probably quite wonderful, she also knew there were plenty that that would give Trevor nightmares for weeks to come. Tales that would have made the ghost stories her grandparents used to tell her seem like nursery rhymes. That story about the white hands reaching out of the Bras d'Or was only the tip of the iceberg. She knew that to be true, in the same way she knew the tall man was leaving for their sake as much as his own.

"Listen to the river," he said, and rose from his chair. Trevor expected him to tousle his hair as other adults did after giving him some piece of instruction, but he didn't. He just looked at him for a moment. It was only a brief meeting of their eyes, and yet something seemed to spark between them. Trevor didn't understand what happened, and the tall man didn't say anything. He just stood up, gave Claire a strangely formal half-bow, and walked out the back door with his boots cradled in his arms.

Trevor stood up so abruptly he almost knocked his chair over. He started to follow the tall man, but Claire grabbed him and told said, "Let him be. You can't go where he's going."

The boy pulled free and bumped into the chair where the tall man had sat, knocking it over. The puddle of water underneath it had evaporated. He went past his sister, giving her a wide berth although she made no move to stop him, and out the back door.

Outside the twilight was segueing quickly into night. The wind had turned cold and feral, nipping at Trevor's bare arms. He ran past the pump house and down the steep bank to the river.

The tall man was gone. Back to the currents. Trevor walked along the shore until he came to the spot where they had found him earlier that day. Nothing left but two impressions in the muddy riverbank.

Footprints.

THE ATTIC

LEAVES BROWN

Sheldon Carey woke up to the sound of his grandson screaming. It was a high, wavering sound, almost inhuman, but he still waited an hour before going to check on him.

Sheldon cared greatly for the boy (he was always "the boy," never Benjamin or Ben, and how that drove his mother up the wall), but he was a superstitious man, had been all his life, and old ways died hard. He couldn't make himself get out of bed until the shadows had retreated back into the corners of the room. Over the years he had become gradually more aware of shadows and their slow, insidious movements. It wasn't quite dawn yet, but the tiny scrap of sky out his window had begun to brighten. He could feel the sun coming, especially this time of year, the way he could feel it when a big storm was going to sweep in and give the coast a good thrashing.

He swung his long legs out from under the covers and slipped into the fur-lined slippers on the floor next to the bed. He stood up, joints creaking like the gears in a piece of machinery that has been running much longer than expected, and shuffled over to the low, east-facing window. He craned down (he was a tall man and an old man, but had never developed the hunch that was the curse of most tall, old men) and looked out on the back yard: the clothesline swinging in the early-morning breeze, the autumn-empty trees, the roiling steel-grey waves of the Atlantic. His thoughts were like the water this morning—deep, dark, and restless.

He heard a thump from the next room and thought: *I should talk to him today.* But then the old doubt came swooping in like a bird of prey, settling on his shoulders and digging its talons in.

He's too young. He won't understand.

He pulled on yesterday's blue jeans, faded almost white from a thousand trips through the washing machine, and a chambray workshirt he'd left draped over the back of the armchair which was the only other piece of furniture in the room. Sue would have chewed him out for not putting his clothes away. It didn't seem like that long ago he would have done the same thing to her. The psychological notion that kids grow up to become their parents only accounted for part of it. The other part was fuelled by anger—anger at his coming back to Pond Hill, anger at his living in the house again. So much anger. And he supposed he deserved it.

It was funny the way things could change so drastically with the passing of a season. Simple things like the view from a window, and complex things like the ties that bind family together. They could change, completely and irrevocably, as time passed from spring to summer, summer to fall.

It has to be today. If not today, then when?

It was true; he couldn't put it off any longer. The boy's screams last night had been the worst yet. It was a wonder his mother hadn't already said something. He had no doubt she heard him. Those cries could have woken the dead. Or something worse.

Sheldon crept slowly down the stairs, so as not to wake the rest of the house or the arthritis dozing in his hands. It had been good lately, though he knew those days were numbered. This was the time of year when the arthritis really got down to business.

Stepping into the kitchen, he saw his efforts were all for naught. Sue was already up and dressed and puttering around the kitchen in high gear.

"You're up early," Sheldon said as he shuffled over to the wood-burning cookstove and began the ritual of getting it started. He noticed the boy had done the thing with the newspapers again, and smiled. He had started doing it a few weeks ago, as if he had known his grandfather's arthritis was getting worse with the cold weather, although Sheldon had never said anything about it.

"Some of us have to work today." She kept her back to him as she made sandwiches at the counter.

Sheldon frowned but didn't take the bait. If she wanted to start the morning off with a fight, then he would have to leave her wanting. Sue hadn't been like this growing up—although he admittedly wasn't one to speak authoritatively on her childhood years—and it saddened him to see the angry and bitter person she had become. He supposed she had every right to be this way. She had been married to a man who loved drinking more than his wife, and had ended up leaving her about a year ago. But he couldn't help but think that it was the boy who suffered most of all.

"Thought I'd go for a walk up the coast today," Sheldon said, scratching a wooden match across his thumbnail. "Thought I'd take the boy with me."

"Fine," Sue said. "After he rakes the yard and finishes repairing the shutter." She turned and fixed him with a steely gaze. "And I don't want you helping him. He broke it so he'll fix it. He needs to start doing things for himself."

Like you are?

The words seemed to hover in the chilly early-morning air between them. They both heard them although no one spoke them. They had danced around a thousand fights since Sheldon came back to Cape Breton, never quite going the full distance to set each other off. Sue had her own reasons, whereas Sheldon kept his mouth shut because he was a guest in her home—was paying rent, even—and he knew it was pointless anyway. You could sooner change the weather than you could the past. And even if you could, who's to say the new decisions you made would be any better than the ones you made the first time around?

On one occasion when they had come close to butting heads, Sue said: *You've stayed out of my business for so many years, you might as well stay out of it forever.* Sheldon hadn't argued with her, in part because of his reluctance to fight, but also because he agreed with her. If her life had ever been his business, it wasn't now.

But the boy . . . they both had a stake in his future.

There was nothing he could do to improve the boy's relationship with his mother, but he *could* help him with the things that were keeping him up nights. Dark things of which Sheldon was something of an authority. Things that would frighten him, disturb him, but left unmentioned could drive him off the island as Sheldon had been all those years ago.

The boy needed his help. He didn't know he needed it, but that was okay. Most folks could be drowning in trouble and never even think to ask for a life preserver. Trouble had a way of latching on like a leech, silent and undetected. The boy had a goodness about him—Sheldon saw it in things like wrapping the stovelengths in newspaper so that he didn't have to do it and work his arthritis into a frenzy—but it could be stifled as easily as blowing out a candle flame.

By the time Sheldon got the fire going and put the kettle on, Sue had finished making her lunch and was slipping into her coat. "I won't be back till late," she said, turning up her collar. "You can make dinner for yourself and Benjamin?"

"I can."

"Good." She went out the side door without saying another word. No *good-bye*, no *have a nice day*, no *take care of Ben*. Sheldon heard the engine on her old Buick cough and sputter into wheezy life, the sound fading as it lurched down the gravel driveway to the old dirt track that led to the main road.

It was very quiet in the kitchen, then. The only sound was the soft rustle of the flames in the stove and the low, intermittent shriek of the wind. Sheldon sat and sipped his tea, holding the cup in both hands like a child. He leaned back and the chair squeaked. He let his mind wander.

It drifted up the stairs, walking on invisible feet that brought no creaks from the old worn steps, and down the hall with its faded wallpaper peeling at the top and bottom like long pieces of parchment. The house needed a lot of work, but as Sue was quick to point out, money didn't grow on trees. No, it didn't, and speaking of trees, he could see the one through the window at the end of the hall, still wearing some of its red and gold leaves. Down the hall to the boy's room, passing through the door, no need to open it, and there was his grandson, sitting on the edge of his bed, dressed in a hooded sweatshirt and grey cargo pants, tying the rawhide laces of his boots with hands that wouldn't stop shaking.

It must be today.

He set his cup on the table, nothing left but the leafy detritus at the bottom. When he was a boy, Sheldon had known a woman who could read the future in those leavings.

He heard a thump from upstairs. A moment later the boy came clomping down the stairs. He looked around for his mother; seeing that the coast was clear, he smiled and said, "Morning, Grandpa."

"Morning it is, b'y. You must be one of those educated fellows, eh?"

Ben grinned and went over to check the fire. Grandpa had been off the island more years than Ben had been alive, but his Cape Breton accent was still the strongest one he had ever heard. He liked to listen to his grandfather talk, even though he didn't catch every single word. There was something calming, almost reassuring, in the way he rounded his r's, the way he said *b'y* instead of *boy*.

"Your ma wanted me to remind you of your chores," Sheldon said. "She wanted you to get started first thing, but I thought you might want to join me for a stroll up Horsehead Cove."

Ben shrugged. "Sure."

"We'll see how far up the trail we can go. I don't like the look of those clouds." He nodded at the darkening sky outside the kitchen window. "They look sketchy."

Ben snickered as he lifted one of the hotplate covers and dropped in another piece of kindling. Another thing he liked about his grandfather was his seemingly endless supply of strange sayings. *The sea's having a hissy today. The trees caught the autumn fever something fierce. Those clouds look sketchy.* Ben sometimes wondered what the world looked like through his grandfather's eyes. Sometimes, if he concentrated hard enough, he thought he could actually see it. It wasn't a trick he tried very often. Sometimes he didn't like what he saw.

Sheldon kicked off his slippers and stepped into his old, scuffed work-boots. He took his coat off the wooden peg by the door, slipped it over his bony shoulders, and went outside.

The day was almost perfectly still—an eye-of-the-hurricane day—and Sheldon took this as a good sign. It had been long years since he had paid attention to the subtle nuances of the weather. The world beyond the island had lost whatever interest it once had in the portents that could be gleaned from such things as the sound of the wind before sunset or the colour of the clouds at dawn.

The air was redolent of pine needles, wet leaves, and wood smoke. Underlying it all was the salty scent of the Atlantic. Sheldon took a series of deep breaths and watched as the air poured out of him like smoke. The joints in his hands were tying themselves into tight little knots, but even that couldn't take the smile off his face. It was a perfect fall day.

Behind him, he heard the squeak and wheeze of the screen door opening, followed by the rifle-crack as it snapped closed. If the boy's mother was around, she would have yelled at the boy, maybe ask him if he could possibly make any more noise. Sue Carrey was definitely of the opinion that children should be seen and not heard.

The boy stood on the stoop with his hands in his pockets, looking at Sheldon expectantly.

"Ready?" Sheldon flipped up his collar and immediately felt his fingers scream out in pain.

"Yeah," Ben replied. "You sure it's not too cold for you?"

"Too cold for me?" He feigned surprise. "I decked on the ore boats in the Great Lakes for twice as long as you've been alive, b'y. Now *that's* cold."

Sheldon started down the path to the woods. "I was going to ask you the same thing," he said over his shoulder. "Out of concern, you understand."

Ben hurried to keep up with his grandfather's long-legged stride. "Concern for what?"

"Well," Sheldon said ruminatively, "going up to Horsehead isn't exactly a stroll or a wander. It's not as serious as a hike or a marathon; it falls somewhere in betwixt. And I don't have a saw, y'see."

"A saw? What do you need a saw for?"

"Oh, it's not for me. It's for you."

They walked in silence for a little while, as if the conversation had reached its natural conclusion. Ben knew otherwise, but he tried to wait his grandfather out. It was a pointless endeavour. His grandfather was a master of the waiting game.

Finally he asked: "So, why do I need a saw, Grandpa?"

"Whassat?" Sheldon looked around, bewildered, as if he had been woken from some deep reverie.

"The saw." Ben tried to inject a tone of exasperation into his voice. "Why do I need a saw?"

"Oh! Right! The saw!" He gave his grandson a sly, sidelong look.

"Why, for your arms, of course."

"My arms?"

"Sure. I see you're wearing the boots I bought you for your birthday, and I know for a fact they're plenty warm enough. But you're not wearing a coat, just that hoodie."

Ben looked down at his sweater a little guiltily. "It's not that cold out."

"True, true," Sheldon agreed. "But the frostbite has a way of creeping in. And once it does . . . well, like I says, we pro'ly should've brought the saw."

"What, so I could saw my arms off?"

"No, course not," Sheldon said. "So *I* could saw 'em off." He stopped walking and looked off thoughtfully into the distance. "Though I suppose you might be able to do the one and I could do the other." He turned and looked at his grandson. "What say we work that out later on?"

"Maybe if you got frostbite in your legs I'd be able to keep up with you."

"My, what an awful thing to say," Sheldon said reflectively. He saw the blanched expression on the boy's face and slapped him companionably on the back.

They entered the gnarled, black-branched embrace of the trees. Their boots made rustling sounds as they walked through the knee-high drifts of leaves. It made Ben think of the snow he'd be trudging through in another month or so. Winter seemed like the one season that always demanded a little more of you—from the extra layers of clothes (and the extra time it took putting them on and taking them off) to the extra energy spent on even the most menial of tasks, like walking. Winter, he thought, was the greediest season of them all.

"It's not greedy," Sheldon said. "It's just bitter."

Ben's head swung around. He was still walking and didn't see the root sticking out of the ground. He tripped over it and fell flat on the ground. Leaves went flying in a burst of red and gold.

Sheldon came and stood over him, but made no move to help him up. "I guess you didn't say that out loud, eh? Sometimes I get so caught up in the flow I forget when someone's workin' their mind instead of their mouth."

Ben rolled onto his side and looked up at his grandfather. Sheldon offered his hand, and Ben took it and pulled himself up. Wet leaves clung to him like strangely coloured leeches. He brushed them off absently as he rose to his feet, his eyes never leaving his grandfather.

"I asked you out here for a reason." Sheldon sounded almost guilty about it. "I'm usually an upfront kind of guy, but this ain't something I ever talked about before."

Ben opened his mouth to say something, but nothing came out.

"It's okay," Sheldon said. "You don't understand, and that's to be expected. This ain't part of growing up. You ain't gonna hear about this at school. But you do need to be told about it."

They started walking again, Sheldon moving slower now, and Ben was able to keep pace with him. He stole glances at his grandfather while looking out for more protruding roots.

They came out on the other side of the woods. The path turned to the left and wound along the edge of the cliffs. Further down the shore, at the end of the curiously shaped breakwater that gave Horsehead Cove its name, stood the lighthouse.

They stood for a moment and admired the view, feeling the salt-scented wind wash over them, listening to the sound of the crashing waves below.

"Looks just like it did on the day I left," Sheldon said.

"The lighthouse?" Ben asked.

"All of it."

"Why did you leave, Grandpa?" Ben asked suddenly.

Sheldon smiled and started walking again. Since he came back to Pond Hill, people had asked him all sorts of questions—where did he go, what did he see, why did he come back—but no one seemed curious to know why he had left in the first place. Edie St. Paul from across the road had taken to calling him "Sheldon from Away," even though she knew very well that he had been born and raised on the island. She used to sit for him when he was little. *She sees the mark on me,* he thought, *like the one God put on Cain before sending him into the Land of Nod. The Mark of Away.*

A few people knew why he had left, and the rest . . . well, they didn't want to know.

"I guess I left because I was scared." His voice didn't sound like his own. It had a strange hollow quality that Sheldon had never heard before.

"What were you afraid of?"

"Things no one else could see." He continued to stare at the dark cliffs and the inexorable ebb and flow of the tide. "Dreams mostly. Like the ones that are keeping you up nights."

Ben paled and lowered his head. Sheldon turned and looked at him. "Nothing to feel bad about," he said. "Everyone has nightmares. But the kind we have are different, as you're probably already figuring out. I didn't leave the island just because of things I saw while I was sleeping. I left because I started seeing them when I was awake."

Ben seemed to consider this.

"You know Edie St. Paul 'cross the road."

"Yeah," Ben replied, unable to suppress the disdainful note in his voice. When he was little, Edie St. Paul used to chase him with a broom handle when she caught him playing in her yard. She was unbelievably fast for a woman her age. "Mom says she's the oldest woman in town."

"Probably the biggest bitch, too," Sheldon said offhandedly.

Ben stared at his grandfather with an almost comical expression of shock on his face.

"She is," Sheldon said, grinning. "I don't mind saying it— though I wouldn't do so to her face. Ain't polite. She's pushing a hundred, but I'm willing to bet she's still strong enough to beat me to a bloody pulp if she had a mind." Sheldon looked back the way they had come, back to the screen of trees and the vague shape of the house through the branches. "She used to chase me with that broom handle, too, you know. When I was your age." He paused. "But that's her way, and she can't change it any more than you can change your brown eyes. You could say that being a bitch is her *natural* way."

"Mom says she could be nicer if she tried."

"Maybe so," Sheldon agreed. "But you can't be the way others want you to be. There are plenty of people in the world who live their lives based on the expectations and demands of others. That don't mean it's right for Edie St. Paul to be the way she is, but it's a helluva lot more right than her acting a way that don't come natural to her, isn't it?"

"I guess so," Ben said, confused.

Below them the waves broke on the black rocks and sent up a huge cloud of spume.

"I left the island thirty-four years ago," Sheldon said. "I don't remember the exact day, but it was toward the end of October. The dreams are worse that time of year, and I always hated that because I really love the fall. In my opinion, it's the best time of the year. And I'm not talking calendar fall, because calendar time don't mean shit to Mother Nature. She comes around when she's damn well ready. But you can always tell when fall has arrived. The leaves change, yes, but that's not all of it. Fall is waking up one morning and finding frost-ferns growing on your bedroom window. Fall is the smell of wood smoke on a chilly day—not cold, mind you, but chilly. Do you understand?"

Ben smiled and nodded.

"Some people don't like the fall. They think it's nothing but a preview of winter, and I feel sorry for those people because it's one of the prettiest times of year. Fall has its own charm. It's also the shortest season, and that makes it extra special because nothing in life that's good lasts for very long."

Sheldon turned and gave his grandson an appraising look. "Tell me, what do you think makes fall so special?"

Ben's mind went blank. He wasn't expecting to be quizzed. He looked at the ground. He looked at the cliffs. He looked at the grey water smashing against the rocks. He looked at the skeleton trees behind them. He looked at the leaves cartwheeling along the path.

"Well," he said, "The way everything . . . changes. I guess." He felt like a grade-A nimrod, but it was the best he could come up with.

His grandfather didn't appear to be disappointed. He clapped Ben on the back. "You're close, b'y, very close." They started walking again.

"You can travel to places in the world where it feels like summer all the time . . . or spring . . . or winter. But there isn't any place on the planet where it's always fall. *That's* what makes it special. Fall is meant to be enjoyed in small doses. If the seasons were a four-course meal, then fall would be the dessert."

Ben smiled. "I can see that."

"Good. I knew you would. Fall's in your blood, you know, just like it's in mine. Other people might say fall is their favourite season, but for folk like us . . . it's almost like we're *related* to fall." Ben laughed and Sheldon nodded. "I know, it sounds crazy, but trust me, it'll probably be the least crazy thing I tell you today."

They walked on for awhile without talking. The sky overhead continued to darken like an enormous bruise.

Sheldon kicked at a pile of leaves. "Some folks say the fallen leaves are souls of those who have died over the past year, and the autumn wind comes to carry them off to the afterlife."

"You mean like ghosts?" Ben asked.

Sheldon looked down at the boy to see if the question has been asked in jest, but the expression on his face was serious and sincere.

"It's . . . complicated."

"Are there ghosts on the island?"

"Yes," Sheldon said, "there are." He took a deep breath, steeling himself. "But that's like saying there are animals in the zoo. *Ghost* is a very broad term that means lots of different things. People hear that word and they immediately think of dead people, some part of their lifeforce that stays behind. That type of ghost is more rightly called a *spirit*. Most folk use those words interchangeably, but the fact is ghosts and spirits are not the same thing. *Spirits* are people—or they used to be—but they're just one type of ghost."

"There are other kinds?" Ben asked, a trifle uneasily.

"Yes." Sheldon licked his lips. "That's what I wanted to talk to you about. The truth is I *need* to talk to you about these things. About the island, about the fall . . . and about the unnaturals."

"Unnaturals," Ben said softly, almost reverently.

"It's a word my grandfather used. Unnaturals are the most dangerous kind of ghost."

Sheldon sat down on the edge of the cliff, letting his feet dangle over the side. Ben sat next to him, the wind blowing his hair back in a shaggy brown wave.

"You see that over there?"

Ben followed his grandfather's long, gnarled finger to the breakwater further up the shore.

"The lighthouse?"

"Yes. This thing we have—the thing that's keeping you up nights—is like a lighthouse in your head. It's big and bright and it sort of swings around and throws its light on whatever happens to fall in its path."

Ben stared at him numbly.

"I don't know what to call it," Sheldon went on. "Some say it's a gift, others call it a curse. I guess it's like second sight, though I've never experienced any premonitions. If I did I figure I would've won the lottery by now." He chuckled. "My grandmother, your great-great-grandmother, just called it the sight. Some mornings she'd say to me, 'Don't make too much noise today, Shell, your grandfather was up late with the sight.'" He saw the boy's stunned expression and clapped him on the shoulder. "It's not a bad thing. Don't ever think that. It's a talent, like drawing or singing, except this one works on the inside, like another set of eyes that see things nobody else can."

"What kinds of things have *you* seen, Grandpa?"

Sheldon pursed his lips. In November of 1978, he had crewed on an ore-boat called the *Dennis Murray*. He had gotten up one night, sleepless, and gone out onto the foredeck. While he was standing at the rail, enjoying the cold breeze on his skin, he had seen a huge glowing shape come sliding soundlessly out of the fog. It was a phantom ship, an ore freighter like the *Dennis Murray* only much larger. Sheldon was the only one on deck at the time, but he was sure no one else would have seen it even if the entire crew had been there. The ship had drifted by as if it had every right to be there. Then, in a matter of seconds, it had slipped back into the mist and was gone. They were on Lake Superior, and Sheldon was certain that the boat he had seen was the *Edmund Fitzgerald*. After that night, he couldn't listen to the Gordon Lightfoot song without his stomach shrivelling up into a tight little ball.

"I've seen all sorts of ghosts," Sheldon said. "Some were nice, some weren't, and we can leave it at that. The point is, you're going to see these kinds of things whether you want to or not. Just like old Edie St. Paul is going to chase after you with a broom handle every time she catches you in her yard. That's her natural way and this is yours."

Ben nodded glumly.

"I've seen ghosts all over the world, but I've only ever seen the unnaturals in one place—and that's here, on this island. Maybe they like it here, or maybe something keeps them from leaving. It doesn't really matter. What matters is that people like us, those who have a lighthouse in their head, can see them sometimes, usually in dreams, and we see them most often in the fall. I don't know why that is any more than I know why they can't cross the Canso Causeway for a weekend in Halifax."

"Other people really can't see them?" Ben asked timidly.

"No," Sheldon said. "Some people feel their influence from time to time—like when they get a chill on a hot day or when they feel sad for no reason—but that's it."

"Where do they come from?"

Sheldon sighed. "I don't think anyone knows the answer to that one. And I doubt anyone ever will. Same as they probably won't ever know exactly why the druids built Stonehenge, or how those Incas knew more math than most other people did at the time."

Ben was quiet for a long moment. He looked out toward the lighthouse. Finally, he asked, "What do they look like?"

"Well," Sheldon said, "that's sort of difficult to say. Those of us who can see them—and I've only met two or three others who can—we all see something a little bit different. As a boy I seen one walking out on the water at the far end of the cove. Sun was behind it and it looked as black as the ace of spades. It had long thin legs, and more arms than an octopus, and it was waving them every which way. I was with some friends at the time, and none of them could see it. They thought I was having them on. There was another one, I didn't see it but I heard it. A horrible screaming coming from the woods. Long, god-awful screams like you wouldn't believe. I told myself it was just some animal caught in a trap, but deep down I knew it was an unnatural. My parents were home at the time, and neither of them heard it. Just me."

"Have the unnaturals ever hurt anyone?"

"Sure, folk been hurt," Sheldon said. "But the unnaturals don't usually interfere with people. They do prankish things, trip people up, throw things around, break windows. Things that look like accidents. The unnaturals hardly ever attack folk directly."

"But . . . people like us . . ."

Sheldon nodded grimly. "The sight is a two-way street. You see them and they see you. But if you make like it's not a big deal, then they'll treat you like *you're* no big deal. Do you understand?"

"I think so," Ben said hesitantly.

"Your ma doesn't have it, in case you were wondering. I guess that particular gene doesn't get passed along to the ladies in the family. Lucky for them, I say." He exhaled unsteadily. "We learn to deal with it. We learn to live with it."

They sat and watched the waves for awhile without speaking.

"I wish I could tell your mother why I left," Sheldon suddenly said. "I wish I could tell her that the only thing harder than leaving was staying." He looked at the boy. "It's important that you remember this. I can't stress that enough. You can't let them drive you away. There's a writer who said you can't go home again. He was only partly right. You *can* go home again, but when you come back you find out home isn't home anymore. It's just a place where you used to live. It's lost something, but you can't tell what it is. It's like an itch that you can't scratch. I think that's what the unnaturals want. I think they want me, and people like me, to leave the island. I think they want this place for themselves."

Ben looked out across the water.

"*You must remember the fall,*" Sheldon said emphatically. "When the days shorten and the leaves brown, that's when you need to be strong. The dreams can't be stopped—everybody has to dream, God knows why, but we do—but you'll get used to them. You need to stay here and you deal with it, Ben, because nothing good comes from running. Your dreams will run with you. You need to push them to the back of your mind where they can't bother you. Focus on the natural."

Ben considered this for a long moment, then nodded.

"Just keep in mind that thinking about the unnaturals is exactly what they want. They *want* to be seen. They *want* to get inside your head. *Don't let them.*"

"I'll try, Grandpa."

"Good."

Sheldon felt a drop of rain land on the back of his neck. He looked up at the dark, heavy clouds and said, "What say we head back and get us some cider? I got a hankering for some."

"Okay," Ben said.

They started back along the path. Before they entered the woods, they turned and looked back toward the breakwater. The lighthouse stood at the end of the point like a sentinel, sweeping its beam endlessly back and forth, throwing its light on all things natural and unnatural alike.

Wood

They sat around the campfire like old friends, although they were not: friends to themselves, perhaps, and the games they played, the stories they told, but hidden from one another, alone except for the wary, suspicious looks they exchanged.

"Everyone toasty?"

Court was crouched in front of the fire. His head was lowered and his features were cloaked in shadow. He threw on another log and looked over at Harry, sitting quietly with his board. The planchette was kept safe in an inside pocket of his coat for fear that one of the others might accidentally (or deliberately) mistake it for kindling.

The fire blazed bright with the fresh fuel, outlining the previously shrouded shape of their third, Beth. She sat on an angle to the others, almost with her back to them, working meticulously on a five-hundred-piece jigsaw puzzle. Her thick robe was not for warmth, as the fire provided more than adequate heat, but instead to provide a shield against the wind which threatened to blow away the puzzle pieces scattered before her on the ground.

"Well then," Court said, fingering the wooden charm around his neck. "Who's first?"

Beth didn't say anything. She found a piece of the border and was moving it along the edge of the mostly completed frame. Court turned to Harry. He had taken out his planchette, a small object no bigger than his hand, and placed it on the long oaken board that lay across his lap like a dinner tray. It was not like any planchette Court had ever seen, and that bothered him for a reason he could not articulate. It was covered in runes and cabalistic symbols and strange protrusions, like knobs of varying size, and for some reason it reminded him of the sewing board his mother used to have when he was a boy. She'd run different-coloured yarn around the knobs so that when she began knitting, the colours would turn out in the desired pattern. Court had once tried to use the board to make a throw rug for the laundry room where the floor was so cold, but the mismatched green and yellow he had used turned out so deformed that everyone who saw it was inclined to ask what had been spilled on such a nice rug.

Harry shifted his position, tilting forward slightly so that the light from the fire illuminated the board. His face was not that of a twenty-four-year-old man, but that of someone who had seen the horrors of previous campfires and the games of other players. "Why don't you start, Court?"

"That's a great idea. Is that okay with you, Beth?"

Beth continued to fiddle with her puzzle pieces. "Fine with me," she said with a small shrug. The image was gradually taking form before her: a forest setting with a large oak tree protruding into a clearing.

"Excellent," Court said happily. "I shall begin then."

There once was a boy made of wood, who had been so unhappy with his appearance that he had taken to carving himself into the images he desired as his tastes changed. Soon he was left with a body barely large enough to fill a box of toothpicks.

So into the woods he went and found a great oak tree. "This will give me many bodies for days to come," he cried with glee. "Or maybe even one large body that could last me a million carvings."

Indeed, the tree was clearly the largest and strongest in the forest with a trunk the size of an elephant and roots like thick tentacles.

The boy picked up his axe and prepared to chop it down when a voice like a sleeping giant suddenly bellowed out.

"Why would you cut me down, boy?"

The boy was shocked to hear the tree talk and almost dropped his axe. He quickly gathered his wits. Of course it can talk, he told himself. This is the strongest tree in all the forest—if any tree could talk, surely it would be this one.

"I'm sorry," the boy stuttered. "I meant no harm. I only wanted to chop down a tree so that I might carve myself a new body. I'm not whole you see, barely even a boy." He bowed grandly to the tree, showing it the top of his head. "Count my rings and you'll see, barely a boy I am, but the body I have still."

The tree made a loud creaking noise as it straightened to its full height. The boy of wood watched in amazement as it nearly doubled in size.

"You will not cut me down," it growled. "I will not allow it."

The boy looked ashamedly at the axe in his hands and hid it behind his back. "Surely you don't think I would cut down a talking tree. I meant no harm. I will cut down one of your speechless kin instead."

The tree stood fast. A large knot hole seemed to watch the boy like an abyssal eye. A pair of thick branches crossed themselves in a concerned gesture.

"A tree that does not talk is still a tree."

It bent over at the trunk, creaking and cracking, and studied the boy's face. "Do you understand, boy?" As it yelled, a powerful gust of wind blasted out of its knot hole, buffeting the boy's carved face.

Instead of being scared, the boy smiled. "Of course I do," he said, beaming. "I was once a tree and I don't think I would like it very much if someone were to chop me down."

"Good," the oak tree said, slumping back to its original, slightly canted position. "Then don't let me see you go against your word or else you may find yourself without the body that you have now."

The boy continued to smile like it was painted on his face. "I won't," he said. Then added: "I promise."

Harry interrupted: "I think I should continue from here."

Court smiled and nodded assent. "Please do."

The great oak tree watched as the boy walked away, twirling his axe in the air as if it were a walking stick.

That night as the boy sat in the clearing that was his home, he thought to himself: *Why shouldn't I be allowed to chop down a tree that does not talk? A normal tree would not scream the way I imagine the great oak would had I taken my axe to it.*

So it was that then that the boy decided the great oak, which had clearly become senile in its old age, didn't know what it was talking about when it came to talkless trees. The boy could speak of axes and carving knives since he knew them well, and the great oak could speak of other great oaks because it knew them well, but for a talking tree to speak on behalf of those that could not talk—well, that was just plain wrong.

That night with conscience clear, the boy crept back into the dark forest and chopped down one of the talkless trees. He continued to take one tree every night until the only one left was the great oak.

The boy was still unhappy with his body, so he picked up his axe and went back to the forest . . . or rather, the place where the forest once stood. *Why shouldn't I cut down the great oak?* he thought. *It is just a tree after all, and it serves no real purpose in this world. I will give it purpose, as I did the others.*

The great oak was waiting with its mighty branches crossed when the boy arrived and raised his axe once more. He brought it down against the thick trunk with a mighty chop, but the oak did not scream. Most unusual, the boy thought, and swung again. Still nothing.

Then, when the boy had chopped halfway through the trunk, the great oak spoke:

"I told you not to cut down my brothers and sisters and you did. Now you would cut me down?"

The boy explained that he was give the great oak a purpose, something it never had before. "I'm doing you a favour," he said. "You should be thanking me."

"A favour indeed," the great oak said, snort air through its knot hole. "Then a favour to you I will return one day."

The boy heard the great oak's words but did not listen. He was not thinking of consequences. He was thinking of all the bodies the great oak would give him. Bodies for years to come, maybe a million if he used it sparingly (although he knew he would not).

When he finished chopping, the great oak fell with a mighty crash that echoed across the land that had once been dense with trees. Immediately the boy set to carving the first of what was sure to be several handsome bodies for himself.

After he finished, the boy left his tired old body and entered the new one. It was glorious! Never before had he felt so strong and able. His hands, more agile than any he had carved before, would surely be able to craft even greater bodies now. His legs were those of an athlete, his body almost as thick as the great oak from which he carved it. It was a most impressive body indeed!

"You did not think I would stand idly by while you murdered me, did you?"

The voice was that of the great oak, but it did not come from its fallen body. The sound seemed to come from . . .

"Well then, maybe you did. After all, it was the same stupidity that cut me down which has now used me as a vehicle."

The boy spun all around, searching for the source of the voice, but he was the only one there. The voice seemed to have come from right over his shoulder. He reached around with both hands, feeling along his back, and found a knot hole. His mouth fell open in horror, destroying the smile he had carved into his face.

❖

"My turn," Beth said.

❖

"Dear God," the boy cried, "what have you done to me?"

The knot hole hissed at him. "I am returning your favour!"

The boy looked down at his hands as they began to move by themselves. He watched, frozen and helpless, as he picked up his carving knife with one hand while the other pressed against his chest like a sculptor getting a feel for his medium.

"What's happening?" he screamed.

The knot hole did not respond. In fact, his back was completely silent as his hand went about etching lines all over his body in intricate detail. The carving knife stayed below the neck, covering the rest of his body with sharp, precise cuts.

Finally, the hand went limp and dropped the knife. The boy looked at himself.

"What have you done to my body?"

"Your body indeed!" the knot hole bellowed. "I have done to you as you have done to me. I have created you in my image as you destroyed me in yours. To you I was a tree no different than the rest, fit only for your abominable wardrobe. Now you are a puzzle because I know not the reason for the things you do. I have left your head intact so that your mouth may cry and your eyes may weep, but never again will your tears take shelter in wooden palms, nor will you be able to run away from the things that scare or sicken you. Forever now, you will remain a wooden head with no body as you have existed before with no soul, no longer able to rob others of theirs. This is the favour I return to you."

The boy uttered a high, wailing scream as he watched as his body began to disassemble itself into hundreds of small, segmented pieces.

The boy's head tumbled to the ground, lying on its side so he could watch as the pieces scurried away like ants.

His head lies there still, watching, waiting, sometimes crying, sometimes screaming, with nothing left to consider except the stretch of land where the trees once grew, and past that, endless time.

Court shook his head. "Geez, Beth, do you always have to throw in a puzzle somewhere?"

"I like puzzles," she said. "Besides, what do you think these are made from?" She scooped up a handful of puzzle pieces, then turned her hand over and let them fall back to the ground. "Or that charm around your neck. And Harry's precious board."

Harry had returned the planchette to his inside pocket. Now he unconsciously placed a hand over it like a man swearing an oath.

"So what does it look like?" Court asked. He was excited, but he knew not to look over Beth's shoulder; the last time he did that she had slapped him so hard his ears rang. "I've given you the past and Harry's given you the present. Now, tell us what lies ahead?"

"I don't want to know," Harry burst out. "I want to get out of here."

Court turned to him. "What's wrong with you?"

Harry's eyes darted back and forth. "I don't like this place. The trees. There's something wrong with them."

Court snorted. "Beth, your story scared poor old Harry. Can't you tell him what happens next and calm his nerves?"

Beth looked down at the almost-finished puzzle. The campfire scene was almost complete. Even in the small picture, Court's wolfish grin was clearly visible. So was the dark, foreboding shape of the trees that leaned in toward their circle, as if they had been listening to their triptych story.

"Will you please finish that thing and tell us the future?" Court sounded impatient, almost a little frightened.

Beth fingered the final piece of the puzzle. She looked up at them with dark, dancing eyes. "I don't think I see one."

THE HOUSE ON ASHLEY AVENUE

1

Charles and Sally pulled up to the house at a quarter of eight. They sat in the car, basking in the air-conditioning and the picture-postcard view before them. It was one of those perfect Toronto summer evenings, with the setting sun bathing everything in a rich orange glow. Ashley Avenue looked as if it had been dipped in bronze.

Charles turned off the ignition and shifted uncomfortably in his seat. Sally glanced down at the bulge in his pants pocket. "You okay down there?" she asked.

Charles ignored her. "Let's go," he said gruffly, and opened his door.

Sally smiled devilishly to herself and opened hers. The humidity hit her like a physical force; she felt invisible hands press against her chest and force the air out of her lungs. A warm breeze buffeted her bare arms and legs.

It was only the middle of June and Environment Canada had already issued half a dozen humidex warnings. A lawn-watering ban was in effect, but you wouldn't have known it to look at the verdant lawns on Ashley Avenue. The only exception was the one at number seventeen—it was dead as the people who had lived inside.

Sally looked up and down the street. According to Charles, who had become her de facto tour guide since she had moved to the city a year ago, they were in Rosedale, one of Toronto's most affluent neighbourhoods. Occupied by the sort of personage who could get away with ignoring a city-wide lawn-watering ban without getting fined, or who could easily afford to pay it if they did.

Number seventeen stood at the end of the street, next to an overgrown lot that looked as if it might have been a Little League field once upon a time. Sally could just make out the diamond-shaped remnants of the baselines. The house itself was a large two-storey dwelling with a wraparound porch and a tall elm in the front yard. A set of flagstones made a path to the porch. The Westons had died here four days ago, but one would never have known it to look at the place. There was nary a police cruiser nor piece of crime-scene tape to be found. Sally wasn't surprised. The residents of Rosedale paid for a great many things here, but she didn't think scandal was one of them.

"Unassuming, isn't it?"

Sally shrugged. "Looks like any other house on the block. Except for the lawn."

"Just remember what it really is," Charles said. "How did Jimmy put it?"

Sally smiled thinly. "He called it the architectural equivalent of a great white shark."

Charles frowned. "Not entirely accurate, but close enough at any rate."

"It doesn't look dangerous," Sally remarked.

"Did you expect it would?"

She gave the house a long considering look, then said: "No. I . . . I don't know what I expected."

"Expect nothing." Charles's voice was calm and collected, but Sally thought she heard something else underneath—nervousness. "Don't allow your mind to focus on any one part of it. If you start to feel funny, close your eyes and imagine you're walking a tightrope. Think only of keeping your balance."

Sally glanced down at her shoes, a pair of high heels she had purchased earlier that day. "That shouldn't be too hard."

Charles heard the wry note in her voice and gave her an appraising once-over. "You'll do fine. You look great. Just hang back and let me do most of the talking."

Sally nodded and looked at the house again. *One of the Eight*, she thought. *I can't believe I'm really going inside one of the Eight.*

After smoothing down his tie and checking his suit for wrinkles, Charles finally opened the waist-high gate and started up the flagstone path. Sally followed. She found it was easier to not look at the house if she was moving. She needed all of her concentration to keep from falling down and busting an ankle.

She wasn't used to wearing heels, but today's assignment required professional attire. It wasn't a problem for Charles, who had probably popped out of the womb in a suit and tie. He always referred to his clothing by their manufacturer: his Armani suit, his Saki tie, his Gucci loafers. Sally, on the other hand, wouldn't have known the difference between Donna Karan and Donna Summers. She tended to dress for comfort rather than style, and thus owned nothing that qualified as "professional attire."

Charles reached the front door, and Sally had to hurry to catch up. He knocked, and a moment later the door was opened by a young man who looked as if he had been sleeping in his business suit for the last couple of days.

"Mr. Weston?"

The young man nodded. "Ted. Ted Weston. You're with the city?"

"We're with the Mereville Group," Charles replied. "An insurance company working on behalf of the city."

Ted Weston nodded, but the vacant look in his eyes said he wasn't registering this new information. "Please come in," he said, and stepped aside.

As she followed Charles across the threshold, Sally realized she had been holding her breath, and let it out in a long exhalation. They were standing in a small foyer. Sally heard gentle sobbing to her left and looked into the dining room, where two women were sitting at a long mahogany table. The crying woman was thin with mousy hair that looked as if it hadn't seen the business end of a brush in about a week. The other woman was short and fat and draped in a ridiculous orange sarong that, in Sally's opinion, made her look like an enormous beachball. The fat woman was patting the thin woman's hand and muttering words of consolation.

". . . s'okay . . . let it out . . . normal to feel this way . . ."

It was hearing the fat woman's platitudes that helped Sally get over the initial shock of being inside the house on Ashley Avenue. Watching the metronomal rise and fall of her meaty paw as she patted the crying woman's hand had the effective of a hypnotist's command, snapping her out a daze she didn't remember entering.

From behind her, Ted said: "That's my sister, Dawn. She . . . she hasn't been so good."

"That's understandable," Charles said. "This is not a good time. We apologize for this intrusion."

Ted led them into the dining room, clearing his throat to announce himself to the two women. "Excuse me, Ms. Morningside."

The fat woman stood up and gave Charles and Sally a cool, appraising look. Then she reached into her pocket, took out a business card, and handed it to Charles. It said:

TANYANKA MORNINGSIDE

SPIRITUAL CONSULTATIONS AND COMMUNICATIONS

"You are also family of the departed?" Morningside inquired.

"My name is Charles Courtney, and this is my partner Sally Wakefield." Sally raised her hand and wiggled her fingers in a small wave. "We're insurance investigators with the Mereville Group. We're here on behalf of the city."

"Investigators?" the psychic said suspiciously. "I don't understand. You're investigating *me*?"

"Not at all. The police informed us of the deaths of Mr. and Mrs. Weston. One of the detectives mentioned that the children of the deceased were concerned about the circumstances surrounding the death of their parents and had decided to pursue—how shall I say—'alternative avenues of investigation'?"

The psychic seemed to inflate with rage. "If you're implying that I'm—"

Charles held up his hand, cutting off her words. "I'm not implying anything, Ms. Morningside. We're not here to interfere. Just to observe."

The psychic's face became infused with colour. "I am a . . . I have worked with the police on several occasions . . ."

Charles's lips spread in a warm grin. "Then we shouldn't have any problems."

"I still don't understand why you're *here*."

"Ms. Morningside, if I may speak frankly." Charles raised his hand, placed the first and second fingers to his lips, and cleared his throat. "You're here, I presume, to contact the spirits of the deceased persons in this house, in the hope of better understanding the circumstances under which they died. I will go one step further and say that you are probably operating under the assumption that this house is haunted."

The psychic started to speak, and Charles cut her off a third time with his upraised hand. "The Mereville Group has no interest in the supernatural. That includes communicating with the dead or investigating haunted houses. We are perfectly neutral in this matter.

"But one thing *our* client, the city, does care about is Rosedale. If you yell shark at a beach, everyone runs out of the water like their asses are on fire. If you yell haunted house in a neighbourhood such as this, a lot of people are going to be placing calls to their friends on the city council. Are you starting to see things from where I'm standing?"

"Yes, I think I do," Morningside said. "You're talking about covering up what happened here." She crossed her arms defiantly. "I don't care if you're here on behalf of an insurance company, the City of Toronto, or the King of Siam, *I* am here on behalf of these people." She gestured grandly to Ted and Dawn Weston.

Charles clapped his hands together like a teacher calling the attention of his class. "Fine, okay, I didn't want to do it this way, but here goes." He cleared his throat in a theatrical manner. "Since Mr. and Mrs. Weston are deceased, the house is once again the property of the city. As representatives of the city, Ms. Wakefield and myself have more right to be here than anyone. Now while I wouldn't dream of telling Ted or Dawn Weston to vacate these premises, I feel I must tell you, Ms. Morningside, that the Yellow Pages are full of psychics, and if you have a problem with us being here, then I'm sure we can find someone else in your line of work who would be more . . . accomodating."

The psychic stared into Charles's icy blue eyes for a long time. Her cheeks were very red. A thin glaze of sweat had formed on her forehead.

"I need to work in absolute silence," she said finally.

Charles exchanged a look with Sally. "We won't say a word."

The psychic looked at them both steadily.

Sally ran an invisible zipper over her lips. "Not a peep," she said.

"Fine," the psychic said. "Let's begin."

2

They sat around the mahogany dining room table. No one said a word. They were all watching the psychic. They weren't clasping hands, but Sally figured it was only a matter of time. The table was astringently bare under the glow of the single overhead light fixture. It made Sally think of old gangster movies, stool pigeons sitting in bleak interrogation rooms, while grizzled, chain-smoking cops paced back and forth.

The psychic stared around the table at them with dull, heavy-lidded eyes. She looked as if she were about to go into a trance . . . or maybe she was trying to remember if she unplugged the iron before she went out. Finally, she pulled a pen and a sheaf of blank paper out of a satchel bag on the floor next to her chair and placed them on the table before her.

"Clear your minds," she intoned.

Sally thought, *That shouldn't take you very long*, and the psychic's head snapped back as if she had been slapped. She stared at Sally. Sally looked back with innocent surprise—an expression she had down pat. She practised it in front of the bathroom mirror in her apartment. A slight widening of the eyes, a rising of the eyebrows, a gentle tilt of the head. *Oh, goodness, is something wrong?*

Charles gave her a sidelong look and kicked her foot under the table. Sally couldn't help it. She had an impish side to her personality that seemed to embody that age-old maxim, the one that said you can dress them up, but you can't take them out. She liked to think that was part of the reason she had been recruited. Besides her other, less tangible qualities.

A slight breeze blew across the table and rustled the papers in front of the psychic. "The spirits are with us," she said.

Or someone left a window open, Sally thought.

Charles was watching her intently. He shifted in his seat and the object in his pocket bumped against his groin. He groaned inwardly.

The psychic closed her eyes, picked up the pen, and began to draw a series of loops. When she came to the end of the page, she dropped down to the next line and began again, as neat and orderly as the copy from a teletype machine.

Sally had witnessed automatic writing on a few other occasions, and recognized this kind of behaviour. Drawing loops was a sort of psychic holding pattern; it was supposed to keep the writer in a trance-like state until they began to receive messages from The Other Side. The supernatural equivalent of a secretary taking dictation from her boss.

With her eyes still firmly shut, the psychic began to speak.

"I am addressing the entities residing in this house. If you are with us tonight, please give us a sign."

The house was silent for a long moment. Then, from somewhere close by, there came a loud thump. It sounded as if something heavy—like a sandbag, for instance—had been dropped on the floor.

"Good," the psychic said, satisfied. The pen in her hand continued to execute an endless series of barrel rolls.

She's certainly the tidiest automatic writer I've ever seen, Sally thought. *Much neater than the one who used crayons and construction paper.*

"Please identify yourself," the psychic said. "Tell us your name."

They all watched as the pen jerked in the psychic's hand, dropping down to the bottom of the page. It spun around in a double-loop and made a cursive letter B. This was followed by an R . . . I . . . T . . .

"Jesus . . ." Ted muttered.

Dawn crammed a fist against her mouth, stifling a cry.

Charles and Sally stared expressionlessly.

The psychic seemed oblivious to what her hand was doing; her eyes were still closed and her brow was wrinkled in deep concentration. Her hand paused for a moment, then began again, writing with a flourish, leaping from one perfectly executed letter to the next. It was like watching a spider spin a web in fast-forward.

When she was finished, the psychic dropped the pen and let out a gasping breath. The others at the table leaned over to read the final message. Charles shot Sally another sidelong glance, while Ted and Dawn looked on with matching expressions of consternation.

Charles looked up from the piece of paper to the psychic's own startled face and said, "If this is some sort of joke, Ms. Morningside, I don't think anyone at this table finds it very funny."

Four pairs of eyes bored into the psychic. She seemed to shrink under their collective glare. In her voluminous orange sarong, she looked like a gas planet undergoing some catastrophic gravitational implosion.

Finally, she looked down at the words on the paper. Her eyes sprang open and she gave out a small squeak.

"I don't understand," she said. "I . . . I . . ."

"I think your work is done here," Ted said, rising out of his chair. "Please leave."

The psychic's chubby cheeks turned red again, out of embarrassment this time rather than anger. "N-no! This isn't right. I've . . . I've consulted on dozens of police cases—*police cases! Hundreds of them!* I have an eighty-five percent accuracy rating!"

Whatever that *means*, Sally thought.

The psychic looked at Sally again as if Sally had spoken aloud. "It's not my fault," she protested. "There was interference. Yes, *interference!*" She latched onto the word like a drowning woman latching onto a life preserver. "Interference from the *house!*"

The psychic reached out to Dawn, but Charles was suddenly there, gripping the psychic's upper arm and lifting her out of her chair. She tried to pull away and the strap of her sarong slipped off her shoulder. Her chair screeched across the hardwood floor and fell over.

"You heard Mr. Weston—your work here is done." With his free hand, Charles picked up Morningside's satchel-bag. The psychic glowered at them each in turn as he directed her toward the door.

"*Sneaks!*" she hissed. "You're all a bunch of dirty, rotten *sneaks!*"

"Thank you for coming out tonight, Ms. Morningside," Charles said as he stuck the psychic's bag in her hand and ushered her out the door. "Your insight was most educational. Good night."

The psychic opened her mouth to reply, but Charles had already closed the door on her. He went back into the dining room, experiencing a momentary sensation of déjà vu as he saw Sally standing over Dawn and patting her hand. The difference was that Sally was the real deal.

"I'm so embarrassed," Dawn fretted. "I can't believe I brought that woman here, into my parents' *house!* I feel like I've polluted this place."

This place was polluted long before your parents moved in, Charles wanted to say, but didn't.

"You had questions," Sally said, "and that woman claimed to have the answers. There's nothing embarrassing about wanting to know the truth."

Dawn wiped her nose on her sleeve and nodded reluctantly.

"But sometimes you have to come to terms with the fact that the truth may not be altogether satisfying."

Dawn looked up at her with rheumy eyes. "What truth?" she asked.

"That there is no mystery." Sally gave her hand a reassuring squeeze. "As much as you might hate to admit it, your parents were the victims of a terrible accident. But accidents don't have reasons; they just happen."

"But I've heard stories about this house," Dawn said. "I've heard—"

Sally squeezed Dawn's hand again, cutting off the other woman's words. "I know," she said. "We've heard them, too. That's why we're here, remember? Every neighbourhood has its haunted house, the one where bad things happened, the one kids cross the street to avoid. Even in a place like Rosedale. But they're just stories. There are no secrets here, no hidden truths, and no answers." She picked up both of Dawn's hands and placed them in her lap. "You don't need to like it. It's a shitty deal. But you need to try and accept it."

Dawn nodded, but it was a perfunctory gesture. She wasn't going to be accepting this, not today or tomorrow, maybe not ever.

"I need some air," she said, springing out of her chair and almost knocking it over. "I'm going for a walk. Then I want to leave this place and never come back again."

Sally nodded and looked over at Ted. He stepped forward, took his sister's arm, and led her outside.

When they were gone, Sally took out the psychic's business card. "Tanyanka? Is that Russian?"

Charles said, "If she's Russian then I'm Winnie the Pooh."

Sally tore the business card in half and dropped it on the floor.

Charles wandered over to the table and turned the pile of papers around so he could read the psychic's message.

"Britney Spears?" he said dubiously.

Sally shrugged. "Projecting at that woman was like throwing rocks at the side of a barn."

"She gave you a look."

Sally shrugged. "I goosed her," she said. "To see if she was a receiver."

"Was she?"

Sally tilted her head from side to side. "Yes and no."

"Yes and no?" Charles said, pretending incredulity. "The psychic is giving me a yes-and-no answer? What a scam!"

"Fuck you," Sally said amiably.

"So was she?"

"Eighty-seven percent of the world's population are receivers, Charles. But less than point-zero-one percent are tried-and-true psychic. This particular woman was a receiver, of that I have no doubt, but beyond that, it's hard to say. I suspect she has something, or else I wouldn't have been able to influence her automatic writing. But she doesn't have much, and she doesn't know how to use it."

"An unschooled talent," Charles said, staring thoughtfully out the window at the darkening street. "Is it worth informing the Group?"

"Couldn't hurt to put her on the watch list," Sally said, "but she's too old to train. You've got to get them when they're young." She fluttered her eyes coquettishly.

"That just leaves the house, then." Charles went out to the foyer. He looked down the central hall to the kitchen, then up the stairs to the second floor. "Do you pick up anything?"

"Nope," Sally replied. "Safe as houses." She raised her eyebrows devilishly, but Charles ignored the comment. One time she had asked him if his sense of humour had been surgically removed as a child. Charles had looked at her blankly and said he would have to get back to her on that one.

"But I probably wouldn't feel anything anyway," she went on. "These places have triggers, right? Something that sets them off and makes them go all Amityville on people?"

"It doesn't matter," Charles said. "Things are winding down. No one's going to live here ever again."

"No one should have been living here in the first place."

"Check." He went over to the window to see if Ted and Dawn were coming back, but the street was deserted. The arc-sodium streetlights had come on, washing Ashley Avenue in a sickly jaundice colour. "Matters are being corrected as we speak. The agent who sold the house to the Westons will be found."

Sally pictured an overweight, unshaven man in a piss-yellow suit with dark circles under his eyes and sweat stains under his arms. A man on the run . . . and with good reason.

"They're going to string that bastard up by his balls when they find him," Charles said. "For starters."

"If they find him."

"They will," Charles said confidently. "They put the snoops on him, and they've never come back empty-handed."

Sally hugged herself, thinking of the snoops but not picturing them. She had never seen them and never wanted to.

"So you don't pick up anything?" Charles asked. "From the house?"

Sally placed her hands against the small of her back and stretched. "I don't know," she said. "I could take a quick look around before we leave."

"No way," Charles said firmly. "Once the Westons get back I'm locking the door and we're out of here. And if we never see the inside of this place again, we should count ourselves lucky."

"Come *on*," Sally cajoled, "this is one of the Eight. I've never been in one before. Have you?"

"No." Charles licked his lips. "There's a reason no one lives in any of these places. You'd do well to remember that this is not a house. It's a slaughterhouse masquerading as a house."

Sally wandered into the living room. It had been decorated in a style she thought of as "Toronto Trendy." Imitation antique wood furniture, Robert Bateman prints on the walls, and an honest-to-goodness wood-burning fireplace that looked as if it had never been used. A living room straight out of the Country Living section of the Pottery Barn catalogue. Designed for those who had not spent any significant amount of time in cottage country but who wanted visitors to their home to think they did.

"I can't see the harm in taking a quick walk around. I won't touch anything."

Charles shot her a look. "If you knew what this place was capable of you'd know how stupid you sound right now." He pursed his lips. "This house has been empty for over sixty years. Exactly one day—" he raised his index finger "—after the Westons moved in, they were killed."

"I'm not talking about moving in. I'm just talking about a quick tour."

Charles paced back and forth in the foyer. Through the leaded glass panes in the front door, he saw Ted Weston standing out on the porch.

"They're back," he said brusquely. "I'm going outside to have a quick smoke and get rid of them. Why don't you come out with us?"

"No thanks," Sally said. "Nicotine screws with my biorhythms."

"Bullshit," Charles said, and opened the door. "Make it quick. And don't touch *anything*."

Sally gave him a two-fingered salute and went up the stairs.

3

When Charles stepped outside, Ted was sitting on the porch steps and smoking a cigarette. He had taken off his suit jacket and loosened his tie.

"I'm worn out," he said, scrubbing one hand down the side of his face. "It's official."

"It's allowed," Charles said, sitting down next to him. He produced a gilt cigarette case from an inside pocket, took out a cigarette, tamped it. "You have my permission."

"Thanks." Ted produced a lighter and lit Charles's cigarette. Then he leaned back on his elbows and let out a deep sigh. "What a day."

Charles looked around for Dawn but didn't see her.

"She wanted to be alone," Ted said by way of explanation.

Charles stood up and went down the steps to the flagstone path. He found himself conscious of making direct contact with the house and avoided it whenever possible.

"Heading out tonight?" he asked.

"Eleven-fifteen back to Calgary," Ted said, exhaling smoke. "Would've left this morning if Dawn wasn't so set on hiring that so-called psychic."

"That was her idea?" Charles asked.

Ted looked slightly offended. "Sure wasn't mine. But it's not her fault. Not entirely. The neighbours were on her the moment we got here. Whispering about haunted houses and spooks."

Charles put his hand in his pocket. "Why do you think she was so quick to believe it?"

Ted held his cigarette between his thumb and forefinger and stared at the smouldering tip. "Your partner got it exactly right, Mr. Courtney. What happened to my parents was an accident—a strange, fluky accident—but an accident nonetheless. I can accept that, but Dawn can't. Or won't."

"But why blame the house?" Charles wondered. "Of all the possible explanations she could have gone with, why pick one with a rather unbelievable angle?"

Ted shrugged. "Because they had just moved into it, I guess. We both thought it was kind of strange, how fast they sold the old place and bought this one."

"A house in this neighbourhood is usually considered a steal," Charles offered. "They don't come up that often."

"Yeah, that's what I figured, too. But the thing is, they didn't even tell us they were looking. They never said a word to us, and Dawn and my mother talked on the phone every Sunday. Last week Dawn calls me and says our parents got a sweet deal on a house in Rosedale. They closed escrow in a week. Before I became a criminal lawyer, I used to deal in real estate law, and I never heard of anyone closing escrow in a week."

Charles said, "It's strange but not completely unheard of."

"I know," Ted said, "and that's why I'm willing to accept what happened. I don't like it, but I'm not about to blame their deaths on ghosts." He gave Charles a long, steady look. "Of course, that doesn't exactly explain why you're here, though."

"It doesn't?"

"You said you came to protect the reputation of the neighbourhood. You don't want some psychic-for-hire going to the newspapers saying a house in Rosedale is not only haunted but responsible for the deaths of two people who were living there at the time. But if that's true, then why was it the neighbours who put Dawn onto the idea in the first place? Wouldn't it have been in their own best interests to keep their mouths shut?"

Charles looked down at his shoes, pretending to give the matter serious thought. "I think some people can't help but talk. Tongues like to wag."

Ted continued to look at Charles with that steady look in his eyes. "You might be right," he said finally. "The fact remains that only two people know what really happened in that house, and both of them are dead. I don't like that either, but that's the way it is."

Charles smoked his cigarette and said nothing.

They heard the clicking of Dawn's shoes as she came down the sidewalk. She stepped up to the front gate, but didn't pass through it. "Ready?" she asked.

"Yeah." Ted turned to Charles and offered his hand. "Thank you for stopping by. Good luck with your investigation."

"Have a good flight," Charles said.

He watched them drive off. When they were out of sight, he took the object out of his pocket.

It was an old, scuffed baseball. Part of the red waxed stitching had come loose and a flap of the nicotine-coloured rawhide hung loose. To Charles it looked like the dried scalp of a shrunken head. The letters T.R.T., faint but still legible, were printed on the side in childish block letters.

The baseball had come from the Mereville Group's private collection of paranormal artefacts. It had been found in the house after the Group took ownership in 1944. Jimmy Dumfreys, one of the whiz kids in R&D, the same Jimmy who called 17 Ashley Avenue the great white shark of haunted houses, thought it might be an "apport"—a solid object which seemingly appears out of nowhere. Its significance, if it had one, was unknown. Charles had signed it out that morning, and it was due back by midnight. If it wasn't returned, the snoops would be paying him a visit.

Right after they caught up with Dustin Haney.

Haney was the real estate agent who had sold the house to the Westons. Except Haney was no more a real estate agent than Charles and Sally were insurance investigators. They all worked for the Mereville Group—on the surface an ordinary multinational insurance company, below the surface a clandestine organization with interests in paranormal research. In addition to their various projects and investigations, the Group was also the caretaker of a handful of properties that were known collectively as "the

Eight." Over the years, with the assistance of individuals on the city council, they had managed to keep the properties secure, maintained, and off the real estate markets. The house on Ashley Avenue was not the most dangerous of the Eight (that honour belonged to an old fish-processing plant on Lake Shore Boulevard), but it was certainly the most attractive. As the operative in charge of visiting the house on a weekly basis and making sure it hadn't "gone Amityville" on anyone (to use Sally's phraseology), Haney would have been familiar with the neighbourhood and known how valuable the property would be to a couple who didn't know its dark and bloody history.

The real question was why did Haney do it?

The Group was still trying to figure that part out, but Charles knew they weren't really interested in the answer. What was done was done. They had learned a few facts. That a listing for 17 Ashley Avenue had appeared on three real estate websites over the past two weeks. That the name attached to the listing was one Dustin Haney. And that Haney stopped coming to work five days ago, which also happened to be the day the Westons closed escrow on their new home.

Charles wished he could have told Ted and Dawn the truth. He took no pride or pleasure in lying to people, though he acknowledged it as a necessary part of his duties. But the truth wouldn't give them closure; it would probably have the opposite effect. It would have acted like a battering ram to the fragile doors of perception, and once those doors were open, it was impossible to close them again. Charles knew this from personal experience.

On the other hand, he felt not even an inkling of sympathy for Haney. It was hard to feel for a man who had taken advantage of a retired couple who had wanted nothing more than a home in which to spend their twilight years—twilight years which had turned out to be twilight days. The Group's think-tank were still scratching their heads over Haney's motive, but Charles figured it was because they were looking too deeply. He was willing to bet Haney had been motivated by nothing more than simple greed. Why he thought he could outrun and outwit the snoops was the real question.

As these thoughts raced through Charles's mind, he discovered his feet had carried him around to the back of the house. From here he could see down into the Don Valley and the dark sprawling expanse of the old Brick Works. With its sooty brick and spire-like smokestacks, it would have made a better haunted house than the house on Ashley Avenue.

But looks are deceiving, aren't they, Charles, m'boy?

Oh yes. In fact, that was the first thing they taught you at the Mereville Group. It could have been their slogan.

He bounced the T.R.T. baseball in his hand and stared down into the valley of dark twining shapes and rustling leaves. He had meant to give the ball to Sally before he left the house, but Ted Weston had picked that moment to show up on the porch and then Sally was already up the stairs.

And here you are still outside while she's inside.

Charles clutched the ball in a death grip. The voice in his head had managed to do what half an hour in the house had been unable to accomplish.

It had scared him.

Here he was promenading around the yard while Sally was inside—*inside*—the house.

He started back at a quick trot.

By the time he reached the front yard, he was running.

4

Sally was twenty years old when she was recruited by the Mereville Group. On that particular day she had been standing outside the Red and White General Store in Antigonish, drinking an Orange Crush. She looked up when the car with the Hertz sticker in the corner of windshield pulled into the gravel parking lot and the man in the expensive suit stepped out. Not Charles. She didn't meet him until a month later, when she began the Group's year-long training program in Toronto. This man, who moved not toward the store but directly over to where Sally was standing, introduced himself as Edward Reed and then proceeded to ask if she had given any thought to her career.

Sally had stared at Edward Reed for a long moment. *Next he's going to ask if I ever thought of being a model.* She had heard stories about strange men who approached girls and offered them work as models. Unfortunately, most of those men turned out to be El Pervos who were interested only in girls willing to take off their clothes. Of course, they didn't tell you that up front. Oh no. First they had to butter you up, tell you how beautiful you are, and how much money you could make—and so easily!

That thought was going through Sally's mind as she reached out to shake Edward Reed's hand. The moment they touched it was jerked out of her mind (she jerked her hand back, too), and was replaced with a sudden and inexplicable amount of knowledge about the man standing before her.

His name isn't Edward Reed; it's Winter. Dan Winter. Daniel Clarence Winter. He's thirty-eight years old, he lives in Barrie, Ontario, and he's left-handed. Once, in his senior year of high school, he cheated on a trig final.

Sally dropped her Orange Crush and stared agog at Dan Winter, a.k.a. Edward Reed.

"It was a calculus final, actually," Dan Winter said. "But you were close."

Sally continued to stare. She'd had episodes like this before, but never one so strong, so *intense.*

Mr. Winter told Sally what was by then clearly evident: she was a telepath. Then he asked her again if she had given any thought to her career. Sally had replied in her mind: *My career as a telepath?*

Dan Winter grinned at her: *Yes.*

And the rest, as they say, is history.

A year later, Sally had finished the psychic's equivalent of preparatory school and was given her first assignment— bloodhound work at Pearson International Airport. Using her "wild talent," she picked out potential recruits from the crowds of people departing and arriving. She had been there only a week before the Group pulled her out. They were concerned that in the wake of 9/11, airport security would be on high alert, and that it was only a matter of time before someone noticed that Sally was never meeting anyone or taking any flights herself.

So they sent her to the mall. Five of them, to be precise, on a rotating monthly schedule. Same assignment, sniff out potential psychics for the Mereville Group. Sally did that for six months, spending her days pretending to window-shop, eating her meals in greasy food courts (she put on fifteen pounds), and staying under the radar of mall security (who were not nearly as astute as their brethren at the airport). The Group called this sort of work "trawling." Sally called it boring.

When Charles had come to her with the Ashley Avenue assignment, Sally had done more than jump at it—she had pole-vaulted over it. Anything to get her away from the mind-numbing Muzak and the El Pervos in the food court who seemed to come not so much to eat as to ogle the teenage girls.

Looking up at the house on Ashley Avenue for the first time, Sally had wondered if she hadn't bitten off more than she could chew. But now, as she walked aimlessly through the rooms on the second floor, she found herself feeling strangely relaxed, almost at peace. It was not the sort of feeling she would have expected to feel in a place with the reputation that 17 Ashley Avenue had. Instead she was experiencing the same kaleidoscopic mix of emotions she had felt on her first few days in the Group's training facility: a heady cocktail of curiosity, excitement, and nervousness.

She wanted to do a good job here—because she took pride in her work, but more because she didn't want to go back to the mall. It was trite, but it was true. She'd had her fill of malls and was ready for something new, something marginally more exciting than "trawling." And she hoped after today, the Group would feel the same way, too.

She considered opening her mind, just a little bit, to see if she could pick anything up from the house. But that probably wasn't a good idea. In fact, it might even be a bad idea. To do such a thing in a place like this was like raising your chin to Mike Tyson and saying *Come on, big boy, gimme your best shot*. 17 Ashley Avenue was not the heavyweight champeen of haunted houses, but it probably still packed a wallop.

Sally wandered into the bathroom where, according to the police report, Mr. Weston had had his "accident." The mirror over the sink was gone, and she could see the contents of the medicine cabinet. This struck her as an invasion of privacy, and she averted her eyes, turning instead to the old-fashioned clawfooted tub.

It was here that Mrs. Weston had found her husband, covered in broken glass, his throat slit. The report suggested that Mrs. Weston had panicked at the sight, went to call 911, and fell down the stairs, breaking her neck.

It was a good story, but Sally had a couple of problems with it.

For starters, the report said Mr. Weston had been standing on the edge of the bathtub to hang a shower curtain and lost his balance. As he fell he reached out blindly and grabbed the mirror over the sink, pulling it off its hinges. When he landed in the tub, the mirror shattered, and a piece of it slit his throat.

Sally supposed such a thing was possible, but not very likely.

The part about Mrs. Weston going downstairs to call 911 didn't make sense, either. If that's what she was really doing, why didn't she use the phone in the master bedroom? It was closer.

She was scared. She panicked.

Yes, and in her agitated state she tripped over her own feet and fell down the stairs.

Again, it wasn't an impossible scenario, but an extremely unlikely one.

Sally went into the master bedroom. All of the furniture was draped with white sheets. Sally went over to a tall, slender piece, pulled off the sheet, and let out a frightened gasp when she saw her reflection in a gilt-framed mirror. The sheet caught on the bottom corner and rocked the mirror back on its feet. Sally reached out and caught it before it fell backwards. She didn't need seven years of bad luck, thank you very much.

As she was replacing the sheet, she heard Charles in her head admonishing her: *Don't touch anything.* She stuck her tongue out at her reflection, which responded in kind. She flung the sheet onto the bed and went over to the window that looked out on the overgrown lot next to the house. From this vantage point the diamond shape of the old baseball diamond was even more apparent.

She turned to her left and took the sheet off the piece of furniture standing next to the window. It was an old vanity bench. It was beautiful. She didn't know anything about antiques, but it looked expensive. The wood was cherry and polished to a high gloss.

Sally sat down on the bench and looked into the mirror. Another mirror. Mirrors all over the place. Two mirrors in the bedroom, a broken mirror in the bathroom.

An idea came to her then, in much the same way as the one about opening her mind to the house had come earlier. Closing her eyes, she reached out and placed her hands on the surface of the mirror. Sometimes she could pick up impressions from inanimate objects. It was called psychometry, and the Group held it in very high regard.

The glass was cool under her hands. There was an abrupt cracking sound that Sally heard not with her ears but with her mind. A psychic sound. The crack of a bat. A baseball bat.

Her eyes flew open. A whitish blur came flying in through the open window and struck the vanity mirror. There was another sound—the unmistaken crash of breaking glass—and Sally felt a sharp pain in her left eye. Her vision in that eye immediately turned red, as if a filter had been placed over it. She clamped her hand over it and felt something jagged and sharp cut into her palm. *There was a piece of glass sticking out of her eye!* She opened her mouth to scream but all that came out was a dry squeak. She stood up, her hand still clamped over her eye, and tripped over the bench in her rush to escape the room and find help.

She tried to keep her balance and probably would have succeeded if her foot hadn't come down on the baseball that had broken the mirror. Her foot went backward while the ball shot forward. Her legs were swept out from under her—prompting a sudden strange association: her airplane ride to Toronto, her first airplane ride anywhere, and the mechanical vibration as the landing gear was pulled into the main body of the plane—and then she was falling . . . falling face-first onto the hardwood floor. The shard of glass sliding directly into her brain, killing her instantly.

Sally took her hands off the mirror and opened her eyes. She wasn't blind or dead, but she was crying. Suddenly she didn't want to sit here anymore. She didn't want to be in this house anymore.

She stood up abruptly, knocking the bench over. She held her arms out for balance, then walked around it, give it a wide berth, and made a beeline for the hallway.

Her attention was so focused on the bench that she didn't notice the gilt-framed mirror had inexplicably moved across the room— right into her path of travel. She saw it at the last moment, tried to dodge around it, but her foot clipped the bottom corner and sent it crashing to the floor.

Sally swore and crouched down to pick it up. The frame was

empty. All the glass was on the floor. As she stared at it, something strange happened.

The pieces started to move. Not very much at first, but they *were* moving. As if the floor was vibrating and causing them to dance ever so slightly.

Then one piece flew into the air and hung there. Another piece leaped up and joined it. Then another. And another. Soon glass was flying into the air like grease on a hot plate, joining the growing mass which hung there.

The floor was bare in a matter of seconds, and a vaguely humanoid shape constructed of broken glass stood before her. It was a flat, dwarfish form, with stumpy arms and stumpy legs. But there hadn't been that much glass to work with.

Staring at the thing which had been a mirror until a few seconds ago, Sally was reminded of another wayward girl who had wandered into a place she probably should have left well enough alone. But she didn't think Alice had ever encountered a looking-glass creature like this one in her travels through Wonderland.

It took a step toward her. Its foot made a crunching, tinkling sound on the hardwood floor. The overhead fixture sent wild flashes of light along the walls as it took another step toward her. Sally thought of Mrs. Weston and her trip down the stairs.

She hadn't gone running for the telephone, Sally realized.

She had been chased.

5

Charles ran around the side of the house and up the porch steps. He experienced a brief nightmare moment when he thought the front door was locked, but then he pushed instead of pulled, and ran into the main foyer. He saw Sally lying on the floor at the top of the stairs. Her eyes and mouth were open wide in what was almost a burlesque of fright. It was an expression Charles has seen on a hundred horror movie posters: the terrified starlet cowering before the monster. Sally was no Julie Adams, but that was okay, because the thing standing over her was no Creature from the Black Lagoon, either. It short, squat body that seemed to be composed entirely of broken glass.

As he watched, the creature swung one of its jagged hands in a glittering arc that opened a long red line on the palm of one of Sally's upraised hands.

Charles's heart seemed to freeze solid in his chest. He clutched at his chest, and realized he was still holding the T.R.T. baseball. Then, without realizing what he was doing or why, he turned to his side, dropping his arm as he did so, and leaned into a position he had seen a thousand times on ESPN. He adjusted his hold on the baseball, made sure he had a firm grip, and turned his head to the left (looking for the catcher's sign, he guessed). A half-second later the rest of his body started to turn; his arm came around last, snapping through the air in a whip-like motion that ended with the release of the ball.

It shot through the air like a bullet fired from a gun, striking the glass creature dead centre and exploding its strangely fragmented body into a thousand pieces. Shrapnel flew everywhere. Sally still had her hands raised and was able to protect herself from the worst of it. Charles raced up the stairs and looked her over. Three fingers on her left hand were sliced open and would require stitches; on her right hand, a piece of glass was embedded in the webbing between the thumb and index finger. Another piece was sticking out of her thigh.

"Can you walk?"

Sally nodded and took Charles's hand. He started to lead her down the stairs, but she stopped him and turned back around. She crouched down, teetering on her injured leg, and picked up the T.R.T. baseball sitting amongst the broken glass.

As her fingers made contact with the old rawhide, she saw a flash of images. *The vanity. The open window. The scratch baseball game taking place outside. Kids hollering and laughing. "Eddie's OUT, Eddie's OUT!" The crack of a bat, followed by the crash of broken glass. Then everything turns red.*

The images faded away.

Sally clutched the baseball to her chest and for a moment Charles thought she was going to start reciting the Pledge of Allegiance . . . or maybe a couple of verses of "Take Me Out to the Ball Game." He took her arm again and led her down the stairs and out of the house.

He put her in the car and fastened her seatbelt.

"She was trying to make herself pretty," Sally said in a low, dreamy voice. She gripped the baseball close to her chest and looked up at Charles. "But she was never pretty again. *She was never pretty again, Charles.*"

Charles closed her door and went around to the driver's side. As he slipped behind the wheel, he realized he forgot to lock the door of the house. He took the key out of his pocket and ran with it outstretched in his hand to the porch. He locked the door and ran back to the car.

As they pulled away from the house, Sally looked over at the overgrown lot. She clenched the baseball tighter. Her blood dripped across the old, cracked rawhide. The baseball didn't mind. It was like coming home.

THE RIFTS BETWEEN US

Stanton was almost out of air and the suns were coming up. He glanced down at his digital chronometer again, and the luminous red numerals seemed to scream at him.

"All right, boys. Pack it in."

Fydenchuck was down on one knee, collecting a sample of the cobalt-coloured soil. He looked up and stared off at the horizon. "We're gonna miss a real romantic moment here, bwana."

"Oh, sure." Klein came over, waving his telemetry wand through the air lackadaisically. He looked like a cut-rate magician bored with his craft. "If your idea of romance is getting chopped into coleslaw."

Fydenchuck tilted his head in mock consideration. "Susan might be down with that. I have a theory she was raised by a pack of rabid wolverines."

"Susan?" The wand dipped a bit in Klein's hand. "What happened to Julia?"

"Julia . . ." Fydenchuck shuddered. "She belongs out here."

Klein shook his head. "You're sick."

"Hey, she might survive. It's entirely possible. I tell you, that girl is *fierce*."

"Pack it up," Stanton repeated, a bit more impatiently this time. He was referring to their equipment, but he also meant their shtick. As the team leader he tended to refrain from taking part in the banter and frivolty which was, he knew, really more of a defence mechanism than anything else. That aside, Stanton didn't joke about the rifts. There was nothing funny about them. Not one little thing.

He checked his chronometer again. "The neural signal is breaking down. Get ready to shift. At five . . . four . . . three . . . two . . . one . . ."

Klein and Fydenchuck disappeared. Not in a flash of light or a confluence of strange energies or even a theatrical cloud of stage smoke—they simply winked out of existence as though they were never there.

"This now concludes our broadcast day," Stanton muttered as he depressed the button on the back of his glove, and then he was gone, too.

There was a brief sensation of displacement, like a tugging in the middle of his chest, and then he was back on the dais in the broadcasting chamber. Klein and Fydenchuck had stepped down to the main floor to make room for him. The small platform was barely big enough for two men, much less three. They would install a wider one for the next stage of the project, no doubt, after additional funding had been approved, after the board decided to send over bigger teams of explorers. Not that it would make any difference. They hadn't found much of anything in the rifts, and Stanton didn't think sending larger groups of people would change that.

Fydenchuck kicked the dust off the soles of his heavy boots, first one and then the other, while Klein took off his gloves, being mindful of the cords that fed power to the shifter buttons on the back of each one. They took off their masks in unison and breathed the cool air that was pumped into the chamber from the large industrial vents overhead. The chamber had an extremely high ceiling, with rows of windows set high up on either side, one row for the gallery, the other for the control room. Having so many people looking down on them always made Stanton think of the amphitheatres in hospital operating rooms. Except in here the patient never made it.

He tried to ignore the watchful eyes above him by looking around the rest of the room. Situated around the dais like pieces of absurdist art were a number of secondary experiments that were being run in conjunction with Project Seal.

There was an enormous aquarium filled with fish and underwater plant life that spanned one entire wall; a cage in which a pair of primates named Mickey and Minnie grunted and hooted and occasionally cavorted on a stainless-steel jungle gym; a crate housing a golden retriever named Rex, and another one with a grey tabby named Hobbes; glass containers stacked on metal shelving in which various species of insects creeped and crawled. And there were plants. Lots and lots of plants.

To Stanton, the room looked like a zoo exhibit designed by someone of the opinion that all God's creatures should occupy the same space all of the time. Noah *sans* the ark.

The purpose of this motley crew was to determine the side effects of the neural transmissions that Stanton and his team used to access the rifts. So far—none.

The seal door opened with a hiss of escaping air and Dr. Finley, a harried-looking man in a lab coat, entered the chamber.

"She's gone," he said without preamble. He tugged at the knot of his tie with a hand that trembled slightly.

"We noticed," Fydenchuck replied curtly, unslinging the oxygen tank strapped to his back.

"She held on a long time," Stanton said. "We were going to have to come back anyway. We were almost out of air."

Finley spared a quick look at his watch. "Yes. She was very strong, very . . . committed."

Stanton stopped in the middle of coiling a rubber air hose. "She knew she was terminal." He hesitated. "Didn't she?"

"Yes, of course," Finley said. "I meant she was committed to the project."

Stanton stared at him a moment longer. "Yes," he said, finally, "they all are."

The seal door opened again and an intern came in, almost bouncing with excitement.

"Dr. Finley, we just came back online. We got video." He gave a victorious grin which sagged into a pained grimace when he turned to Stanton.

Dr. Finley tugged at his tie again, but his hand was no longer trembling. "We've got video," he repeated to himself. A small, satisfied smile rose on his face.

He left the room, chatting animatedly with the intern until the seal door clipped off the sound of their voices. Stanton, Klein, and

Fydenchuck went back to removing their gear. They took their time, storing it neatly and securely in their lockers. The video feed didn't interest them. They didn't need to see it. They had been there.

Stanton sat on the edge of the dead woman's bed, holding her hand. Cold and smooth as marble. Her face was serene, her wrinkles light pencil sketches on tissue paper. The neural net hung from its mobile over her head like a glittering golden spiderweb.

Her name was Abigail Brennan. She was sixty-four at the time of her death, which came as the result of colon cancer. Many of the project's participants were cancer patients. Too many of them, in Stanton's opinion. He had talked with Abigail on several occasions, had sat in this exact spot at her bedside, but this was the first time he had held her hand. Why was that? Because he didn't want to get too close? Finley and the other project leaders didn't like it, didn't want them to have any contact with the participants at all, but that would have gone against the whole purpose of the project. If they were going to understand death, then they had to face it on every level, including the personal.

The sound of someone clearing his throat jerked Stanton out of his reverie. He turned and saw the intern standing in the doorway.

"What is it?"

"Dr. Finley has called an emergency meeting."

"When?"

"Uh, right away, sir."

"We haven't held the service yet."

The intern was silent for a moment, trying to pick his words carefully. "It's . . . an emergency. Sir."

Stanton turned his back on him.

The intern went on. "Dr. Finley feels . . ."

"Does he?" Stanton said in a low voice. "I have to wonder sometimes. Finley is familiar with the procedure—he should be, he helped write it—and procedure says we hold the service immediately after the rift closes. No exceptions."

He took a deep steadying breath to stave off an impulse to reach across the room and grab the kid's quavering throat and squeeze.

"But I don't need to quote the scripture, do I? Because even if we didn't have all these rules written down in our neat little handbook, there's still this thing called respect. Are you familiar with it?"

He turned back around and fixed the intern with a firm, dark stare. The intern nodded furiously, his Adam's apple bobbing up and down.

"Good. If Finley has any objections, maybe you can remind him."

The intern left and Stanton turned back to the dead woman. He laid her hand next to her side and pulled the coverlet up over her head. Finley could wait. There would always be more rifts. Forever and ever. Amen.

After the service, the committee held their emergency meeting. It took place in the west wing conference room because it was on the side of the building that didn't look out on the cemetery which occupied a large part of the institute grounds.

The dead are still with us, Stanton thought, *even if we don't want to be reminded of it.*

The view from the conference room was infinitely less morbid. From here one could see the duck pond, the stables, and acres and acres of untouched woodland. All of it seeming to burst with life and all of its possibilities.

Stanton sat and waited for the others to show up. He looked at the somber portraits that lined the walls. Elderly men and women mostly, except for one of a young girl dressed in what were presumably her Sunday best. Klein's sister. Eight years old. Leukemia.

All of the people in the portraits were dead now. Finley's uncle had been the last to go. He had been a kind, gregarious man with a silver tongue able to make even the most stone-faced nurse flush bright red.

The project had continued after he died, although Stanton hadn't been sure it would be possible. They started working with volunteers sent to the institute by special referral. Their arrival by air-lift helicopter was always an occasion of some ceremony. At first, Stanton thought it wouldn't be the same, travelling to the rifts of people with whom he had no personal connection. But it turned out everyone was related in death.

The room began to fill up, and everyone rose when Rebecca Marcos, silver hair, grey eyes, Armani suit, swept in on a breeze of jasmine perfume. She took the chair at the head of the long gleaming table and everyone resumed their seats.

The meeting began, and during the course of it Rebecca Marcos asked Stanton in her sweetly assertive manner that if he intended to hold up another emergency session of the committee, then could he please do it at another company. Like Wal-Mart, perhaps.

Stanton replied that he would do everything in his power to keep from delaying another emergency meeting. He could tell it wasn't the complete and total acquiescence that Rebecca Marcos wanted, but she smiled warmly just the same and the meeting continued.

He had no misconceptions or delusions about his position at the institute. He was a good man to send into the rifts, but he could be replaced—just as he himself had replaced the late Justin Cooper.

After the meeting, Stanton caught up with Finley as he slipped quickly out of the conference room and pulled him into an empty office.

"If you have a problem," Stanton said, "take it up with me. Don't cry to mommy."

Finley blinked. "I have just as much to lose in this as you, Stanton."

"Go behind my back again and you'll lose a lot more. I promise you."

"Don't get sanctimonious with me. I came here with an Elder, just like you."

"The Elders are dead, Finley—all of them—and it seems like your respect died with them."

"I have respect for the dead," Finley said hotly.

"But you don't have any respect for the dying," Stanton fired back. "That's your problem, Finley. What do you think, it isn't personal anymore so it's okay to treat these people like lab rats?"

"You're putting words in my mouth."

"Words are all you've got." Stanton's voice vibrated with anger and disgust. "Do you even remember why we're doing this?"

"We're trying to bridge the gap between life and death. We're . . ."

"Save me the metaphors and the euphemisms."

"What do you want from me?"

"Tell me what we're doing here!" Stanton screamed into his face.

"We're pushing back death," Finley said frantically. "We're exploring the borderlands. We found a frequency that the brain gives off before it dies. We can ride that signal into the rifts, the veritable waiting room of death, and explore it."

"We haven't found out a thing."

"Not yet, but we've only been transmitting for a year. We can build better neural nets, ones that can boost the signal even higher, show us more of what lies out there on Death's doorstep."

Stanton shook his head wearily. "Don't read me the brochure."

"We're explorers, Stanton, as much you might not like to admit it. The final frontier isn't space. It's death and whatever lies beyond it."

"Didn't you hear me? We haven't found anything. Just a lot of open real estate."

"That's still something," Finley insisted.

"Did you ever stop to think that maybe we're not supposed to know what happens after we die."

"How can you say that after all the progress we've made? If we weren't meant to explore the rifts, then why were we able to find them? Why were we able to develop the technology to piggyback on the death frequency and explore it? Why, if not to figure out the truth behind the eternal question: What happens after we die?"

"Maybe Cooper could tell you," Stanton said.

Finley flinched. "I'm scheduling another trip tonight."

Stanton felt his anger slip down a notch. "Who?"

"Bill X."

Stanton's gaze drifted away. "Bill . . ." Seventy-eight years old. Former insurance salesman. He was always telling elephant jokes. The only thing he had asked for in his room was the complete set of A.A. Milne's Winnie the Pooh books. Visitors weren't permitted at the institute, but he had received dozens of letters from his daughter in Sarasota.

"The cancer's spread into his lungs," Finley went on. "It won't be long now."

"He's fading?"

"Not yet," Finley admitted. "But his signal is at low ebb. I don't expect he'll last the night."

Stanton nodded absently. "I'll put the team on standby."

They went their separate ways, their argument forgotten in the rush to get back to work.

❖

"You're going to wear that tape out."

Klein snapped his head around; his face stood out like a full moon in the darkened theatre.

"It's on disc," he said.

"I know," Stanton said. He came down the aisle with its dim track lighting running along either side. "I was trying to get a laugh out of you."

Klein turned back to the screen. "If I wanted a laugh, I wouldn't be watching this."

"True enough."

He moved sideways along the row of seats and sat down next to Klein. "Why are you watching this?"

Klein shrugged. "I don't know. Research, I guess."

"Find anything?"

Even in the dark, Stanton could feel the look Klein was giving him. "Give me a break."

From behind them a voice muttered: "Holy shit."

They turned around and saw Fydenchuck's unmistakable silhouette in the lighted doorway.

"Am I interrupting something?"

"We're doing research," Stanton said. He felt Klein giving him that look again.

"Is that what the kids are calling it these days? My, I *am* getting old."

Fydenchuck sauntered down the aisle, hands in his pockets.

"I thought you had a date," Klein said.

"You're my date tonight, K-man."

He slipped past Stanton and flopped down in the seat on Klein's other side, propping his feet on the back of the seat in front of him.

"I like you better when you're getting laid," Klein said.

"And why is that, babyluv?"

"Because it usually means you're somewhere else."

Fydenchuck looked up at the screen. "I wish I was, now," he said. "Why in the hell are we watching this depressing shit?"

"I told you," Stanton said. "It's research."

"Research?" Fydenchuck frowned. "We've watched this thing a thousand times. So have the geeks. They went over it with a microscope, frame by frame, and they didn't find a thing."

"There has to be something," Klein said. "It's the only footage we have of what happens after . . . afterwards."

Fydenchuck turned and looked at both of them. "You want to know what happened?" He pointed at the screen. "That dipshit refused his call and decided to stick around to watch the suns rise. The patient died and Cooper got dragged along for the ride. Only it wasn't his time, see, and whoever—or whatever—it is that governs death chewed him up and spit him out."

"They say he had a brain tumour," Stanton said in a low, ruminative voice.

"Oh, right," Fydenchuck said with a derisive snort. "He wasn't crazy, he was suicidal. He was a terminal case—just like all of the patients in our happy little project—and he decided to hitch a ride into the great beyond? I don't buy it."

"Why not?"

The death of Justin Cooper had become a part of the institute's apocrypha. After receiving the call to transmit out of the rift he was exploring, Cooper, for reasons known only to himself, decided to stay. Or that's what they think happened. It was possible his suit had malfunctioned, although it was extremely unlikely. Every suit was equipped with three return buttons, one primary and two back-ups, and the chances of one or two failing, much less all three, were infinitesimal. An equipment check had been done before he left and everything was in proper working order. The other two members of his team were completely perplexed. They reported no unusual behaviour on Cooper's part and pleaded total ignorance of any plans he might have had to remain in the rift after the suns came up. It wasn't long before stories began to circulate that Cooper had been diagnosed with a brain tumour prior to his trip. The reason for his staying behind was narrowed down to one of three possible scenarios. One: he wanted to confront his own mortality and felt the only way to do it properly was through experiencing death by proxy. Two: he was hoping to obtain some knowledge which would somehow stay his own death. Three: he simply wanted to commit suicide.

The last was deemed the most likely explanation . . . that is, if Cooper really did have a brain tumour. The jury was still out on that one, and would be forever. His remains had never been recovered.

"Nobody knows what happens when those suns come up," Fydenchuck said. "All we know is that when the sky starts to turn pink, then it's time to pack your bags and get the hell out of there. If you want to kill yourself, you run a warm bath and find a dry-cleaning bag, or you swallow a bunch of sleeping pills. You don't travel out to the borderlands of death and say, 'God—or whoever—please take me!' I don't buy it for a minute."

"Maybe that's why he did it," Klein said in a low voice. "Because it wasn't a sure thing."

"Please." Fydenchuck shook his head in annoyance. "Cooper was a romantic. He thought he was Christopher fucking Columbus. He wanted to stand importantly on the shores of Death and look off into the distance as the suns come up. Well, he did it, and he paid the price for it."

Stanton nodded at the remote control in Klein's hand. "Play it again, Sam. But kill the sound, if you would."

"Yeah," Fydenchuck said, sliding down into his seat. "I don't need to hear that broomhead screaming. I hear it enough in my dreams."

"Take a knee, boys."

Fydenchuck and Klein got down on one knee. Stanton stood over them, holding his helmet in the crook of his arm. They were on the dais in the broadcasting chamber. The seal door was maglocked and the air had already begun to change. There was a charged calm in the air, like the buildup before a powerful thunderstorm.

In a solemn voice, Stanton recited: "O Lord, guide us through the shadow lands which lie before us."

"Lord, guide us," Fydenchuck and Klein said in unison. Their voices were a soft, hissing murmur inside their face masks.

"Show us the truth of your design, the mortal coil, the ribbon of life and death."

"Lord, show us."

"Keep us from the rifts between us until the time of our natural end."

"Lord, keep us."

"And bring us home safely."

Stanton extended his free hand and Fydenchuck and Klein covered it with one of their own.

"Lord, bring us home," they intoned.

Stanton put his helmet on, locked it in place, and flashed a thumbs-up at Finley standing at one of the gallery windows.

He pressed a button on the back of his gloved hand and Bill X's frequency thumped into life. An electronic heartbeat. A death knell in stereo surround sound.

The three men activated their transmitters.

The sky was a deep, velvety blue. The landscape was dark and featureless in every direction.

Klein unholstered his telemetry wand.

Fydenchuck took out his little shovel.

Stanton watched them for a moment, then looked off toward the bleak horizon. He stared at one spot for a long time. He took the Zeiss-Ikon binoculars slung over his shoulder and raised them to his eyes. He adjusted the focus-knob, stared a bit longer, then lowered them. He cleared his throat, and spoke into the hands-free microphone that was recording the audio portion of this trip (video was running, too, but for reasons unknown, it didn't always turn out).

"Looks like we've got something on the horizon," he began. Fydenchuck and Klein looked up from what they were doing.

"It appears to be a dome-shaped structure. Can't make out any external features." He added: "Going to get a closer look."

They stared at him for a long time.

"All right, boys, let's go for a little run."

They stood up but they didn't run. They were loaded down with too much equipment, including the thirty-pound oxygen tanks strapped to their backs. But they went along at a steady trot, their breath hissing loudly through their respirators.

Ten minutes later they stopped to catch their breath. The dome-shape was closer now and more clearly defined: it was the same cobalt blue as the soil that Fydenchuck so assiduously took samples of. Except where the soil was rough and gritty, the dome was as smooth as a freshly laid egg.

Stanton started off again, and the others followed, keeping pace a few steps behind him, their eyes staring fixedly ahead. They reached the dome and walked slowly around its circumference in a tight group, almost stepping on each other's feet in their subconscious need to stay close together.

The dome was about forty feet tall, Stanton judged, and about the same in diameter at its base. He looked over at the others. "What do you think?"

Fydenchuck shook his head. "Could be a natural formation, I guess."

Klein shot him a cynical look. "Give me a break. We've been to dozens of rifts and never seen any formations, natural or otherwise."

"It's dark over here, in case you didn't notice. Maybe we just never saw anything until now."

"You don't think this is unusual?" Stanton asked him.

Fydenchuck shrugged. "It's weird, but everything over here is weird. There's no wind—no air currents of any kind. Somehow I find that weirder than this."

Klein looked at his wrist computer. "Neural frequencies are breaking down." He looked over at Fydenchuck. The young man's face had paled considerably in the last few seconds. "Station's going off the air, and fast."

Stanton glanced at his chronometer, then turned his eyes up to the sky. It was growing lighter at an alarming rate. It was like watching a nuclear bomb go off in slow motion.

"This is new."

"I hate new," Fydenchuck said, a little frantically. "New is highly overrated."

"Agreed," Klein said. "Let's get out of here."

"All right," Stanton said, "I guess this concludes our broadcast . . ."

He was cut off by a sharp cracking sound. It seemed to come from all around them, loud enough to make all three men fall on their knees and clutch their heads in a futile attempt to block it out.

"Go!" Stanton yelled. "Break transmission now!"

He looked over at Klein and Fydenchuck. He blinked and they were gone. He pressed the button on the back of his glove, and just before he shifted, he looked up at the dome and saw where the sound was coming from.

The perfect smooth curvature of the dome was marred by a long jagged crack.

Klein and Fydenchuck were sitting on the floor of the chamber when Stanton appeared on the dais.

"What in the sweet hell was that?" Fydenchuck said, taking off his helmet.

"I don't care," Klein replied. "So long as I don't hear it again. It felt like my skull was being split open." He put a hand to his head, as if to make sure it was still there and in one piece.

Stanton stepped off the dais. "I don't like it," he said.

Fydenchuck glanced at him. "What's to like?"

"That dome . . . how quickly the suns started coming up . . ." He shook his head. "I can take one surprise, but not two."

"What do you think it means?" Klein asked.

"I think it means something's changed," Stanton said cryptically. "Something big."

Before Klein could ask him to explain, Finley came in, his lab coat billowing out behind him. "What happened? What did you see?"

"No video?" Stanton asked.

"Nothing. Not even static. Bill's condition deteriorated unexpectedly fast."

"We noticed," Fydenchuck said shortly.

Finley was about to say something when the intern's frantic voice came over the chamber intercom.

"Dr. Finley," he said, "I'm getting some extremely unusual telemetry up here."

"What is it?"

The intern's voice squeaked over the intercom again.

"Receiving! We're receiving!"

All heads turned to the dais. At first it seemed as if nothing had happened. Then Stanton saw it. He thought it was an optical illusion at first, one that confused the eyes until the brain finally caught up and made sense of it.

There was one more shadow on the dais than there should have been.

Staring at it, Stanton thought of Peter Pan and his runaway shadow.

That's what this is. A runaway shadow.

Except that wasn't entirely accurate, he realized, as the shadow took a soundless step forward. It turned to acknowledge the four men staring at it in silent awe.

It was a shadow person. A three-dimensional silhouette.

"What is it?" Finley rasped. He turned to Stanton with an almost accusatory look. "Did you bring it back with you?"

Stanton ignored him and took a tentative step forward. "Cooper?" he said. His voice was tentative, too.

The silhouette turned to face him. It seemed to consider him for a moment, and then slowly shook its head.

The shadow person walked over to one of the other experiments—a vase of flowers standing atop a stone pedestal. It extended a hand that looked as normal as anyone else's except that it was jet black, and ran its fingers delicately across the petals. They immediately curled and blackened and turned to dust.

"What is it?" Finley repeated.

The shadow person backed away from the pedestal. It looked almost chagrined.

Stanton had a pretty good idea what it was, but he didn't say anything. They'd been exploring death for so long they thought it was a one-way street. They were wrong. Now the shoe was on the other foot. The rifts had responded to their unspoken challenge. The proof stood before them. Death had sent its own explorer.

Stanton took a step toward the shadow person. He wondered if the others would ask the same questions of him they had asked about Cooper. Was it a death wish? Was there something wrong with his brain? Or was it just plain curiosity, that desire to push the boundary, to reach out to something wholly new and wholly alien.

Another step forward. They were less than twelve inches away from each other. He thought about all the patients waiting beyond the corridor, waiting for death, waiting to see what was on the other side in a way he would never be able to until his own ticket was punched. Six inches now. The emissary's hand moved. Stanton waited.

Vogo

There's nothing to do in Moose Paw on a Friday night. Ryan suggested driving over to Chelmsford—he knew a girl who could hook us up with some weed—but Alex shook his head, which immediately nixed that idea. We were cruising in Alex's car, and even if we weren't, he was our unspoken leader.

"I'm not going to chance getting busted just for some shitty Ontario green."

"Then you pick something," Ryan groused.

"I will." Alex put one finger to his lip, like he was thinking deeply, and that made me spit out the beer I had just sipped. I had snagged us a couple six-packs of Bud from my old man's beer fridge. Alex turned his head and looked at me thoughtfully. I thought he was going to punch me in the throat for spilling beer in his car, but he grinned instead.

"We're going to steal a boat."

We headed down to the docks and found a rowboat no one would miss for a few hours. After frigging with the knot for a few agonizing minutes, Alex finally cut the line with his Swiss Army knife and told us to hop in.

Ryan and I each took an oar and we paddled out onto the lake. Alex sat back and barked orders at us. "Row, droogs! Row!" That's what he was calling us lately. He was on a *Clockwork Orange* kick. Said it was the funniest movie he'd ever seen.

By the time we reached the middle of the lake, Ryan was already whining about going back. "I don't like it out here," he said. "It's too dark!"

"Don't be such a nancy," Alex snapped. "What are you afraid of? Vogo?"

We laughed, perhaps a bit too hard. Everyone in town knew about Vogo, although I didn't know anyone who'd ever seen him.

Sometimes a tourist passing through town would take a picture of something he claimed to be Vogo, but it always turned out to be a log or an otter. There had been no major sightings since the 1950s. If there ever was a Vogo, he was long dead.

We sat in the middle of the lake for the next couple of hours, finishing the six-packs (Alex called them our "stores") and watching the moon make its way across the sky.

It's hard to describe what happened next. I want to say something came up out of the water, but that's not exactly what happened. One moment our boat was bobbing in the water, and the next a great silvery shape came rising up next to us. Breaching, I guess you would say, considering the size of the creature. It was as big as a whale, but that's where the similarity ended. I didn't know what it was. I'd never seen anything like it.

It had a long, tapering neck, which I at first took to be a tentacle. Then it turned toward us. I wasn't sure what I was looking at. A long silvery appendage with two coal-black dots on the tip. Then they blinked and I realized they were eyes. I had never felt so small as I did at that moment, sitting in that boat, out in the middle of the lake, on that dark night. So very small.

The creature continued to rise out of the lake, as if in slow motion, leaving the water long enough for us to see the fins on the sides of its luminescent body. Each one was as big as a man. Then it came back down, like a shimmering torpedo, and disappeared into the water.

That's not the strangest part, though.

Whatever it is that lives in Hob's Lake—Vogo, I guess—I don't think it's alive.

You see, the creature that rose up next to our boat never disturbed the water, not even a single ripple. And when it left the water, when it hung for a moment in mid-air, I could see the moon.

I could see the moon through its body.

THE DEN

THE CAT

Brenda said the dead mouse was normal.

"They're always doing stuff like that," she said. Her voice sounded cool and calm, but John could tell by the look on her face that it still grossed her out. "They bring back dead animals to show that they're protecting the family. It's how they show love."

"Fair enough," John said. "But remind me never to let the cat make us dinner."

He looked down at the big, lean tabby, standing in a wide bar of sunlight coming in through the kitchen window. The tabby looked up at John for a moment, then began licking his paw and using it to bathe the top of his head.

"What are we going to name him?" Brenda wondered aloud.

"I don't know," John said. "Nothing stupid like Patches or Muffin. Something original—but not *too* original. We don't want people to think we gave the cat some deep and meaningful name just as a conversation piece. I hate people who do that. There is such a thing as being too clever."

"You've never had that problem, babe."

John ignored the jibe. "Grey cat . . ." he said thoughtfully. "How about Thunder?"

"How about Greybeard?" Brenda said.

"Maybe we should let Sally name him."

"If you do that, the cat will definitely be named Patches or Muffin."

John turned to her. "I thought she was still going through her angsty-teenager stage."

"She is," Brenda said, "but she's focused mainly on skipping meals, staying out late, and hating her parents."

"She doesn't hate us." John looked concerned. "Does she?"

"It's normal. She'll grow out of it." She looked down at the cat. "How about Hunter?"

"As in 'hunter-gatherer'? How about H.G.?"

"H.G. Wells?"

John winced. "That's getting into deep-and-meaningful country."

"How about just plain Wells?"

John tilted his head side to side, weighing it over. "Not bad."

"You're taking this awfully serious. I mean, it's just a cat."

John frowned at his wife. "Cut me some slack. I've never had a pet before. My parents didn't even let me have a goldfish. Do you want to give it some stupid name like that mutt next door?"

The neighbours in question were Dave and Petra Robichaud. They owned a Chihuahua that weighed perhaps five pounds soaking wet—and that included her pink glitter collar. Her name was Rambo.

Brenda giggled. "God no."

John sighed. "This could take awhile."

They stared at the cat as it continued bathing itself in the sunlight.

The next day the cat—still unnamed—left a dead bird on the back porch.

Three days after that, he left a dead garter snake.

John started keeping the dust-bin and a garbage bag next to the screen door.

One night a week later, John woke up to the sound of a dog yipping outside their bedroom window.

The sound cut through his head like a band saw. It was those high-pitched barks that could probably make a man sterile if he listened to them long enough. *Cheaper than a vasectomy*, he thought drowsily.

The dog continued barking. It went on and on without taking a breath. John recognized it as the not-so-dulcet tones of Rambo the Wonder Mutt.

He rolled over and looked at the clock on the night stand. 4:07 AM. That was just great. He had to be up for work in less than two hours. Fucking Rambo. Why didn't Dave or Petra take her inside? How could they not hear that? Were they so tuned out to that yapping that they could actually sleep through it undisturbed?

The answer: yes, apparently so.

John let out a heavy sigh and turned on his side. Brenda was still asleep, her breathing soft and even. John felt a strong urge to wake her up. Misery loved company, didn't it? He reached out to pinch her arm and—

Something landed on the bed.

John almost screamed; his mouth fell open but nothing came out.

It was the cat. It looked at him curiously with its wide yellow eyes. *Problem?* it seemed to ask.

Yeah, John thought, *you just about gave me a heart attack.*

He sat up and stroked the cat's back. It arched up to meet his hand, purring contentedly.

"How about you go next door and kill Rambo for me?" he suggested. "Earn your keep around here, huh?"

He laid back down and felt the cat curl up next to his feet.

Rambo went on yipping.

Sometime later John fell back asleep.

"Gross-*out!*"

John lowered his newspaper and looked over at Sally, standing in front of the open screen door. She was wearing a pink shirt that was too tight, and a black skirt that was too short. Of course these were the opinions of a father, but if he couldn't comment on what his daughter wore when she left the house, then who could? Of course, the irony of the situation was that if he should ever voice his opinions, the result would almost certainly be tighter tops and shorter skirts. He reluctantly kept his mouth shut as he stood up and came over to see what she was staring at.

There was a new dead animal lying on the back porch.

Except "dead" was really too light a word. "Slaughtered" would have been more accurate. Or mutilated. The carcass was so badly mangled that at first John couldn't tell what kind of animal it was. It wasn't until he eased Sally aside and crouched down for a closer look that he realized it was a dog. And not just any dog, but one with a glitter collar.

"Oh shit," he muttered. "Rambo."

The dog's fur was drenched with blood; only a few tufts of white remained. The body was covered in a brutal crosshatch of claw marks.

John felt his morning coffee gurgling unpleasantly in his stomach. He opened his newspaper, draped it over the dog's body, and went to call the Robichauds.

"I just can't believe it," Dave Robichaud said, shaking his head.

"Neither can I," John said.

They were standing in John's garage drinking beers from the fridge he kept out there.

After John told him about Rambo, Dave had come over with a broom and a garbage bag. Together they scooped Rambo off the deck, both of them wincing at the sticky tearing sound the dog's body made as it came off the wood planking.

"It must have been some sort of animal," Dave reasoned.

"Must have been." John nodded and took a sip from his bottle.

"But why would it leave her on your porch?"

"No idea. But why does an animal do anything?"

Dave nodded. His summer tan had turned the colour of curdled milk.

"Petra's at her sister's place in Huntsville. She's coming back tomorrow." He looked at John with wide, stunned eyes. "What the hell am I going to tell her?"

John shook his head. He didn't even know what to tell himself.

A couple days later, John found two dead birds and a dead garter snake on the back porch. He cleaned them up without even thinking about it. Picking up the cat's deliveries had become a part of his morning ritual. First he'd put on coffee, then he'd fetch the paper off the front lawn, then he'd open the back door to see what the cat had left for him. Most days there was nothing, but once every week or so he'd find a dead mouse or a dead bird or a dead snake. One time he found something he couldn't identify. He went and got Brenda and she told him it was a woodchuck. Then she elbowed him in the ribs for getting her out of bed.

John rustled his newspaper and Brenda looked up from her crocheting. She glanced over at the clock on the mantel. It was almost 9:30 PM.

They had been sitting in the living room for almost two hours. The only sounds during that time were the rustle of John's newspaper, and the creak of the floorboards in the hallway as the cat passed by on his way to the kitchen.

At 9:42 PM the front door opened and Sally slunk in.

"Where have you been?" Brenda said, bounding out of her chair. "You missed dinner."

"I'm home before curfew."

"That's not what I asked."

"I was out."

"Out where?" Brenda pressed.

"Just out." Sally gave her an indifferent shrug, the kind that comes naturally to teenagers and small-time criminals. Then she slipped upstairs. A moment later they heard her bedroom door slam shut.

Brenda looked over at John. "She's lying."

"You think?" John said sarcastically.

"It's going to stop."

"Good luck with that."

"We should talk to her."

"Go right ahead."

Brenda glared at him. "You won't talk to her?"

"What's the point," John said. "You said she hated us. *And* you said it was normal."

"She doesn't hate *you*. You guys used to talk all the time. You were thick as thieves," Brenda added with an undisguised note of jealousy. "Maybe you should try taking her out for ice cream."

"Ice cream?" John lowered his newspaper. "She's fifteen, Brenda. A father is no longer allowed to take his daughter out for ice cream once she starts getting breasts. It's like a national law."

Brenda frowned. "She may hate us, but she still has to respect us."

John raised his newspaper again. "I don't think she got the memo on that one, dear."

The following morning, the cat left a dead blue jay on the back porch.

That night, Sally came home at 11:30 PM. Brenda grounded her.

The night after that, Sally came home at midnight.

Brenda didn't say anything.

John and Dave were outside raking leaves on their respective lawns. Autumn had come early, along with a week of gale-force winds, and every tree on the street had dumped its load.

After awhile they leaned on their rakes and talked over the low hedge that separated their yards.

"How's Petra been? I haven't seen her around lately."

"She's okay," Dave said. "She's still pretty upset about Rambo."

John nodded sympathetically.

"Do you think you'll . . . you know, get another dog?"

Dave gave a tired shrug. "I suppose so. I mean, Petra loved Rambo, and she wouldn't want to replace her, but she needs something to, you know, fill the void. I could go either way. Although I suppose it's good to have an animal around to protect the property."

John made no comment. The idea of Rambo protecting anything, or anyone, was ludicrous. About as ludicrous as the idea of a cat killing a dog and leaving it on the porch.

He coughed into his fist and was about to resume raking when Dave spoke again.

"I don't know how to say this, John, but, well, you might want to keep an eye on Sally."

John's eyebrows went up a notch. "Sally? What for?"

Dave sighed. "It's none of my business, but I've seen Sally walking home lately with Kris Dunn."

John shook his head to say he didn't know who that was.

"He's that kid who lives at the end of the street. Well, he's not really a kid. That's why I thought I should mention it. Sally's what, sixteen?"

"Fifteen," John corrected him.

"Yeah. I just thought it was strange, seeing her hanging around that guy. Ruth Meyers says he's a drug dealer."

John snorted. "Ruth Meyers thinks every kid on the street is a drug dealer. Or a terrorist. Or a serial killer."

Dave nodded. "Yeah, she's not the most reliable source, I know, but I have seen a lot of people coming and going from his house. Not just kids, either. Older guys, too. It's a little strange."

"What do you think, he's running a grow op or something?"

"Maybe. This is the kind of neighbourhood where they do that kind of thing these days."

Dave went back to work. John leaned on his rake, deep in thought.

"You can't tell me where I can and can't go," Sally said indignantly.

"You bet your ass I can," Brenda told her. "Until you're eighteen you don't go anywhere without either my or your father's permission."

John didn't think the *While you're living under my roof* speech was the best approach, but since he couldn't think of an alternative, he opted to sit with his newspaper and keep his mouth shut. Brenda was taking the lead on this one; all he could do was back her play and hope it didn't make the situation worse. He had a father's nightmare vision of Sally in tears running to Kris Dunn, complaining about her asshole parents and then asking Kris to take her virginity. The ultimate act of rebellion.

"I don't need to tell you where I am every single minute of the day."

"Wrong," Brenda snapped. "That's exactly what you need to do."

Sally's gaze drifted off to the side.

"Bitch."

She whispered the word, barely loud enough for her mother to hear it. But hear it she did.

Brenda's hand seemed to move under its own power. It came up in a flash of motion and slapped Sally hard across the cheek. The sound was very loud in the quiet living room. Mother and daughter stared at each other, stunned. They looked like two strangers who had bumped into each other on the street. Then they both dropped their eyes and stared at Brenda's hand, as if it were a handgun that had discharged accidentally.

Brenda stammered. "I . . . I didn't mean . . ."

But Sally was already running upstairs.

Brenda started after her, then stopped. She stood there, gazing up the stairs with an expression of complete and total bewilderment. She looked over at John, still sitting in his chair with the newspaper draped across his lap. Her mouth opened and he waited for her to blast him for not saying something, for not stopping her, but she didn't say anything. After a long moment of painful silence, she wandered down the hallway to the kitchen.

John stood up to go after her. He tripped over the cat just as it was coming in from the dining room, and grabbed the wall to keep from falling. He looked down at the cat and for a fleeting moment imagined how life would be so much easier if their roles were reversed. What did a cat have to worry about? Eat, sleep, and sit in the sun all day. Go out hunting every night, drop a dead bird or mouse on the back porch on occasion. When you thought about it, the suburban house cat really had it made.

John preferred not to think about it. Thinking was getting him nowhere.

It was time to *do* something.

The following morning, Saturday, John got up early, showered, put on an old pair of jeans and a paint-spattered sweatshirt, and walked down the street to Kris Dunn's house.

That was how he thought of it, although Kris must have had parents. Right? John had never seen them—had never even seen Kris Dunn, for that matter—but he assumed the kid was too young to live on his own.

Or was he?

As he passed the Robichaud's house, then the Smythe's, John got to wondering just how old was Kris Dunn. As his estimates grew higher, John found himself getting angrier.

His hands were clenched into fists when he arrived at Kris Dunn's house. The garage door was open and John could see three young men standing inside. They might have been anywhere from eighteen to twenty-five years of age. The one in the middle had a proprietary air about him, and John figured this was Kris Dunn. He was about John's height, but thinner around the middle, with strong arms, shaggy black hair, and small dark eyes. His friends—a couple of deadbeats, John observed, just like Kris himself—stood on either side of him. The one of the left had blond dreadlocks and a tattoo on his forearm that said BITCHSLAPPER. The one on the right was tall and gangly and was wearing a black t-shirt with the word SLIPKNOT on it. John thought *Slipknot* was the name of a horror movie.

As he walked up the incline of the driveway, John noticed the three young men had already begun the day's drinking. Kris and his buddies were each holding a can of beer, and there was a half-empty case on the concrete floor, next to a stack of boxes partially covered with an oil-stained tarpaulin.

It wasn't even noon yet and these kids—as John thought of them—were already well on their way to getting sloppily drunk. Where the hell were the parents?

John stepped into the garage and immediately noticed a strange smell in the air. At first he thought it was beer, then realized it was something else. It wasn't a yeasty smell; it was sharper, like turpentine, maybe, or rubbing alcohol.

"Hey, look who it is!"

Kris Dunn and his buddies noticed John standing in the garage doorway. They grinned at him like a pack of jackals.

"How ya doing, Dad?"

"I'm not your dad," John said.

"Yeah, but we're like practically related. Sal and I have been getting close, you know." He covered his mouth in a gesture of mock embarrassment. "Or maybe you don't."

Kris's friends snickered.

"I don't want you seeing my daughter anymore," John said. He tried to make his voice sound firm and strong. "Whatever there was between the two of you, it's over now. I'm not asking you—I'm telling you."

Kris exchanged a look with his friends, then all three of them burst into loud, troll-like laughter. Kris slapped one hand across his forehead like he had never heard anything so funny. The fluorescent lighting in the garage gleamed on the silver fang-shaped ring he wore on one of his fingers.

"Oh, Dad, you're *telling* me," he said, wiping away a faux tear. "That's great."

"How old are you anyway?" John asked.

"Old enough, Dad," Kris replied cryptically. "Old enough."

"Good, then you should be able to understand that I'm not fucking around here. If I see you with my daughter again, I'll call the cops and have you charged with statutory rape."

Kris snickered. "You oughta give your little girl more credit, Dad. She gives head like a champ."

John's face darkened. "You little fuck."

"Shit, man, that girl could suck the chrome off a trailer hitch." Kris winked. "Hey, if you don't believe me just ask one of these guys—"

John lunged at him.

The kid in the Slipknot t-shirt stepped out of the way, and John thought, *Good, his friends are going to stay out of this. They're not as stupid as they look.* Then the leg snapped out into John's path. John tripped over it and did a face-plant on the cold concrete floor. He felt his nose crunch and fill up with blood. He snorted it out as he pulled himself quickly to his feet.

Just in time to catch the arcing, underhand punch thrown by the kid with the blond dreadlocks.

John expected Kris to get in a lick of his own, but it didn't happen. He staggered backwards, blinking his eyes against the pain in his cheek and nose, and saw that Kris had moved back next to the door leading into the house.

"There's someone else here who likes your little girl, Dad. I'm sure he'd love to say hello."

And with that Kris opened the door and an enormous Rottweiler came firing out like a sleek, black-furred torpedo.

John watched the dog coming at him and thought, *What a lousy way to spend a Saturday morning.*

"I said I don't want to talk about it," John said, and winced as Brenda pressed the frozen steak against the dark swollen skin puffing up around his left eye.

The kid with the dreadlocks had done that. The one in the Slipknot shirt had hoofed him a good one in the balls, and John figured he'd be spending the next week or so scraping them off the roof of his mouth.

Kris's dog, Shredder, had bitten him on the right calf, and John felt lucky to have gotten away with just that. The Rotty had looked mean enough to chew nails and spit tacks. Kris had pulled him off after that one love bite, maybe realizing that anything more might get him into serious trouble. Those punk kids had a great sense of self-preservation.

"You look like you got mugged," Brenda said. "Was it the Girl Guides?"

John gave her a wry look. "Hardy-har."

"Well, if you're not going to tell me, I'll have to come up with something to tell our friends and family. Was it Mr. Petersen? Did he catch you walking on his lawn and beat you with his walker?"

"I'll beat you in a minute," John said, without force.

"Please," Brenda scoffed. "You couldn't beat up a Care Bear in your condition."

She touched his ear gingerly, and John hissed in pain. Kris had punched him in the side of the head, and the fanged ring he wore had cut his ear. The blow had knocked John to the ground, and then the three fuckers had quite literally kicked him out of the garage. He didn't think any ribs were broken, but it wasn't for their lacking of trying.

"Are you going to call the police?"

John didn't answer right away. He had thought about calling the police. Of course he had. Kris Dunn had sicced his dog on him. He had been assaulted. He pictured himself telling all of this to the police. Unfortunately he also pictured what would almost certainly happen next. Kris Dunn telling the cops that John had stormed onto his property—*trespassing* was the word he would use—and the dog had attacked him in defence of its owner. Of course, the only injury the dog had caused was the bite on John's leg, but who's to say the dog didn't do the rest of it as well? Especially with two other witnesses who would undoubtedly back up their friend's story.

John had gone off half-cocked and he had no one to blame but himself.

"I'm not calling the cops," he said. "I'll handle this myself."

"Okay," Brenda said, a bit coolly. "Then I guess you can take care of yourself, too." She stood up and put his hand on the frozen steak. "Hold it there. And keep it wrapped. That's our dinner tonight."

John watched her leave the room, then his gaze drifted over to the cat. He was standing on the arm of the easy chair, licking his chops and staring at John with an unreadable expression.

"I know what you're thinking," John said. "You think you do a better job of protecting this family than I do." He sighed deeply. "And I think you might be right."

He looked past the cat at the telephone on the side table.

"Should I call the cops?" he asked himself.

He watched the cat jump off the chair and saunter into the hallway. His gaze drifted up to a pair of pink-socked feet on the top step of the stairs.

He called out "Sally?" and the feet disappeared.

John sighed and picked up the phone.

❖

The cops didn't find anything.

Brenda served the two uniformed officers coffee while they spoke to John in the living room.

"Are you sure you smelled drugs in the house?" one of the officers asked.

"I wasn't actually *in* the house," John clarified. "I was in the garage."

The officers exchanged a look.

"But you did smell drugs," the officer prompted.

"I . . . I think so." John hated the uncertainty in his voice. "I thought so at the time."

"Was it marijuana that you thought you smelled?"

"No, it was a sharper smell. I couldn't quite identify it."

"But you were sure it was drugs."

John muttered a reply. He could see how this was going, and he wished now that he had made an anonymous call. It was so humiliating. He felt like Ruth Meyers, the old biddy who thought the Girl Guides were putting LSD in the cookies they sold door-to-door every year.

The cops stood up and headed toward the door.

"We appreciate your concern," said the officer who had done all the talking. "There's nothing wrong with making a mistake. It's perfectly harmless."

John nodded dimly as he saw them off.

Harmless? He'd have to wait and see about that.

John put down his paper and picked up the ringing phone.

"Yes?"

"Hey, Dad, how ya doing?"

"What do you want?"

"I just wanted to say thanks for sending the cops over to my place. I really appreciated that. It's a good thing I'm an honest citizen. Too bad for you, though. I imagine the file they got on you has a nice little stamp at the bottom of it. Something about the boy who cried wolf."

John clenched the receiver so tightly his knuckles turned white.

"I thought I might drop by some night. Have us a man-to-man chat. You know, seeing as I'm the guy boning your little girl."

"Fuck you, you little shit."

John slammed the phone down.

John didn't sleep well that night. He stumbled through a series of dark dreams in which he found himself entering various rooms in his house, and every time, in every room, he came upon Kris Dunn. Sitting in his chair in the living room. Reading the newspaper in the kitchen. Sitting on the toilet in his and Brenda's en suite.

Hey, Dad, just thought I'd stop by for that man-to-man chat.

He woke up sweaty in a tangle of sheets. He went downstairs to the kitchen, half-expecting to find Kris Dunn sitting at the table. But the kitchen was empty. The first faint glow of dawn was coming in through the window over the sink. John put on coffee and started back to the hallway to fetch the paper off the stoop. Then he stopped.

He looked over his shoulder at the back door. He went over to it. Opened it. Looked down.

He looked for a long time.

The police came to the house again, but this time they brought the circus.

Brenda was upstairs with Sally in her bedroom. John was in the living room, going over his story for about the thousandth time. How he had woken up, come downstairs, and found Kris Dunn on the back porch.

Most of him, anyway.

John recalled standing in the doorway, staring down at the ragged, bloody mess that used to be a human being. His gaze had drifted over to the bottom of the steps where a trio of worms were lying in the grass. Not worms, he realized. Fingers. He wouldn't have recognized them as such if not for the silver ring on one of them. With an eerie sense of clarity he saw there was blood on the ring's fangs.

The police asked John about his "confrontation" with Kris Dunn a few days earlier. That was their word for the encounter. John did his best to explain, and under other circumstances they might have shown more suspicion toward him. But there was the state of the body to consider. And the preliminary findings of the coroner.

John overheard the man talking to a pair of detectives in the hallway.

"An animal of some kind," he proclaimed. "Something small, I'd wager, from the size of the teeth and claw marks. Maybe rabid, I don't know. We'll have to wait for the blood work to know for certain."

John didn't think anything would be known for certain. He had an idea the results would be inconclusive. Kris Dunn certainly wouldn't be talking.

You could say a cat got his tongue.

"I don't know what you're crying for," John said. "That kid was bad news and you know it."

"You didn't know him!" Sally screamed.

"I know he was dealing drugs."

His words were like a slap in the face. *And I didn't even have to lay a hand on her*, John thought.

They were upstairs in Sally's room. John wanted to talk to his daughter privately, away from the police. Away from Brenda.

Sally sniffled and said nothing.

"Yeah, I know about that," John went on. "The police were at Kris Dunn's house this morning. You know what they found? The setup for a meth lab. It turns out the police knew someone in the neighbourhood was cooking drugs; they just didn't know who. I told them to check out Kris Dunn's house a few days ago. Did you know that? They didn't find anything that time, though. Why do you think that is, Sally? Why didn't they find that stuff the first time?"

Sally remained silent.

"Did you tell that son of a bitch I called the police?" John took a step toward her. "Did you tip him off?"

Sally glared at him blackly, then turned and faced the window, arms crossed.

John sighed and went back downstairs. The cat was sprawled across his newspaper. He stared down at the cat and prayed it was all over now. He hoped that with Kris Dunn dead, Sally would clean up her act. He worried about what would happen if she didn't.

He knew he couldn't protect his wife and daughter from everything in the world, but there was someone else in their family who was more than capable of picking up the slack.

DELETED SCENES

Joe Courtney was sitting in the office of his agent, Barton Collins, discussing all the work he wasn't getting.

"I'm getting you work," Bart said defensively.

"Porno work, Bart."

"That's work!"

"I don't want to be in porno. It's greasy. Once you do porno, you can never go back."

"Yeah, but think of the chicks."

"I'm thinking of the venereal diseases."

"You're a pessimist, Joe. You've gotta look at the upside."

"I can get chicks, Bart. That's not my problem. Paying my rent is the problem."

"Porno pays, man. Porno pays well."

"I'm not doing porno! Get me a real acting job!"

Joe hesitated, then picked up a slip of paper sitting on his otherwise empty desk. "Well, I have something. It's not much, but . . ."

"I'll take it."

"You don't even know what it is."

"Is it porno?"

"No, it's . . ."

"I don't care. At this point I'll take anything."

The address was for a soundstage Joe had never been to before, which he found a little strange. In the seven years he had been working as an actor, Joe figured he had been to every soundstage in Toronto.

Once inside he saw this one was no different from the others.

Half a dozen furnished sets, big lights mounted on tripods, cameras on dollies—the usual. There were people running around looking busy, others lounging near the craft service table drinking coffee out of Styrofoam cups. And none of them were naked, Joe noted.

He saw a woman who wasn't wearing a headset or racing around like she had a job to do. A fellow actor, he assumed. He got himself a coffee and wandered over. She was reading a script. Joe hadn't seen one yet, didn't even know what the movie they were shooting was called.

"Hi there."

The woman looked up and smiled shyly. "Hello."

"I'm Joe."

"Sarah."

They nodded at each other in lieu of shaking hands.

"You're an actor?"

"Most days," Sarah said, with a laugh. "The rest of the time I'm a mild-mannered temp. My older sister calls it my secret identity. Sort of like Batman, except the pay is shittier."

"I don't think Batman gets paid for fighting crime." Joe shrugged and took a sip of his coffee. "If it makes you feel any better."

Sarah smiled. "It kind of does, actually. I bet Batman doesn't get medical coverage, either."

"Nope. Which is a shame, because he probably needs it more than us. He's always getting into fights."

"That happens on set, too," Sarah pointed out.

"True enough. I'll make you a deal. I'll keep my monstrous ego in check if you promise not to drive over me with your Batmobile."

Sarah shook her head. "I don't have a Batmobile. Just an old Chevette."

"You have my condolences."

"Thank you."

Joe nodded at the script. "So, what are we shooting today? My agent didn't give me any details."

"Oh, the usual. More footage that will never see the light of day."

Joe frowned. "Direct-to-video?"

"Nooo, it's a deleted scene." Sarah tilted her head to the side and gave him a curious look. "I don't think I've seen you around. Have you done cut work before?"

"Cut work?" Joe said, confused.

"Deleted scenes," Sarah said. "You know, the stuff they remove from the final cut of a movie. Usually it's done to speed up the pacing, or cut down the run-time, but there are all kinds of reasons why a scene might get chopped."

"I know what a deleted scene is," Joe said. "What I don't get is how we can be shooting one. How does the director know the scene we're about to do is going to be cut? And if he knows, then why the hell are we shooting it in the first place?"

"Those are production questions," Sarah said in a dismissive tone. "I don't concern myself with that stuff. You'd have to talk to the director."

Joe sighed and looked around the set. He spotted a woman wearing a headset and a laminated I.D. badge that identified her as Sharon Biggs. She was directing a pair of men who were lugging a tall piece of lighting.

"Excuse me."

The woman gave him a quick, impatient look. "Yes?"

"Hi. I'm Joe Courtney. I'm an actor."

"Congratulations," Sharon Biggs said coolly. "What do you want?"

"I understand we're shooting a . . . deleted scene?"

"Yeah. So what?"

"So it's true."

"What?"

"We're really shooting a deleted scene?"

"Yes."

"A scene that won't be in the final film."

Sharon stared at him for a moment. "That's what a deleted scene is, slick."

"So what we're doing here won't be seen by anyone."

"That's right."

"Then why are we doing it?"

"Talk to the director, guy. I've got a set to light."

Joe started to ask where the director was, but Sharon was already barking orders at the two workmen.

He went back over to Sarah. There was still about half an hour before shooting began. He wasn't very good at small talk so he ended up asking that question which is the fallback of every actor.

"So, have I have seen you in anything?"

Sarah shook her head. "Oh, no."

"So this is your first gig?"

"No, I've shot deleted scenes for lots of films." She ticked them off on her fingers. "I was in *Passing Lane, Black Thursday, 13 Shades of Night*." She smiled. "Well, I wasn't actually *in* them, because . . ."

"They were deleted scenes," Joe finished.

"Right."

"Doesn't it bother you?"

"What?"

"That you're acting in scenes no one will ever see."

"Not really. Deleted scenes are an important part of the filmmaking process."

"How do you figure?"

"Well . . ." Sarah quirked her mouth and thought about it for a long moment. "You see that piece of lighting over there?" Joe nodded. "Well, you won't actually see it in the final film, but you'll see the set that it's lighting. You'll see its effect. That's how it is for me. You may not see me in the movie when it's finally up on the screen, but you'll see my effect. Even if you don't know you're seeing it."

Joe felt the beginning of a migraine. "But we're *actors*," he said in a harsh, frustrated tone. "It's our job to be noticed, even if we're only extras hanging out in the background. We're part of the picture. That's our role."

"Sometimes it's about what you don't see," Sarah said. "Now if you'll excuse me, I really have to go over my lines."

Joe watched as she wandered away. "Right," he said under his breath. "You wouldn't want to disappoint your ignoring public."

❖

Joe eventually managed to get his hands on a copy of the script. It didn't make any sense. It was nothing more than a collection of the deleted scenes they were shooting that day. Short vignettes with seemingly no relation to one another that gave absolutely no clue as to the overall plot of the film. It might have been a romantic comedy or a gory slasher flick.

Joe tried to resign himself to the fact that his agent had screwed him again. He ignored the fact that he might be partly to blame; if he had bothered asking what the job was before he took it, he might not be in this mess. Regardless, he figured it was best to just roll with it. This was work after all, he was getting paid, and on the plus side, he didn't have to bang some girl with silicone breast implants and a name like Misty Mountains.

The director, once she finally showed up on set, was as unfamiliar to Joe as the rest of the actors he had met that day. He had never worked with her before, and didn't even recognize her name. Maybe they got special obscure directors to shoot these deleted scenes, he thought. A secret society version of the Directors Guild. It added the final lunatic touch to an already surreal day. He felt like he had wandered into an urban myth.

They were getting ready to shoot the third deleted scene of the day. In this one, Joe entered a car-rental agency and threw a set of keys at the young girl behind the counter. Then he was supposed to start ranting about their charge-by-mile rates, the ever-rising gas prices, and then segue into a philippic on OPEC and the conflict in the Middle East. It was going to be a good scene: the kind that would really show off his acting chops. Too bad no one was going to see it.

While Joe was waiting for Sharon to finish arranging the lighting, he spoke with the director.

"Why don't we get you to talk through this entire scene?" he suggested wryly. "Discuss the cinematography, the lighting. We could record the audio commentary track for the DVD at the same time we shoot the movie."

"You're a pretty funny guy," the director said in a tone devoid of amusement. "Now shut up and get on your mark."

Suddenly the lights went out. Everything was silent except for a particularly loud burst of profanity from Sharon Biggs.

"Vic, did you plug in that switch I told you not to?"

"I didn't touch it!" whined another voice in the darkness.

The red emergency lights came on with a loud snapping sound, making the entire soundstage look like the inside of a volcano. Joe heard the sound of raised voices coming from one of the other sets. Sarah came running over. Her eyes were wild with terror.

"It's the geeks," she said in a breathless voice. "The geeks are here!"

"What?" Joe said, confused. "What's going on?"

"The film geeks. They broke into the soundstage. They found us!"

"The film geeks?" Joe looked around wildly. "This is supposed to be a closed set. Isn't it?"

Sarah staggered away from him. "Run for it, Joe," she called back over her shoulder. "Run for your life!"

Joe was used to hearing melodrama like that, but not until the director called "Action!" He didn't know what to make of it. People were starting to run. Joe looked around for the director or Sharon Biggs, but they had both taken off.

In front of a nearby set, two men tackled one of the other actors Joe had been working with that day and dragged him off.

Joe turned to run and clipped the table with the large plastic coffee urn on it. He reached out instinctively to keep his balance and ended up grabbing the urn in a desperate bear hug. He tumbled backwards with the additional weight, and hot coffee splashed across his arms and chest. Joe let out a high-pitched scream that undoubtedly told everyone in the darkened soundstage exactly where he was.

After pushing the urn off and climbing painfully to his feet, Joe dashed toward one of the glowing red exit signs. Ten feet from the door, a dark shape interposed itself between Joe and his escape route.

He was just a kid. No more than eighteen years old. He was holding something in his hands. Something round that looked absurdly like a manhole cover.

"I've got one!" the kid yelled in a high, wavering voice.

He came at Joe with the round object raised over his head. Joe realized what it was a split second before it smashed into his face.

A film canister.

Consciousness returned in what Joe thought was a very cinematic fade-in of details. First everything was blurry and wavering, like the dissolve before a flashback. Then they gradually became clearer, details filling in, shapes taking on sharper, more definite forms, until he got a complete picture of his surroundings.

He was in a movie theatre.

Of a sort.

It was a dark, cavernous room with aisles and seats and a big screen, but that's where the similarities ended. The walls were covered in what Joe first took to be photographs—Polaroids, he thought, isn't that what psychos always put on their walls?—but when he squinted at them he realized they were a combination of screen shots and storyboard stills. The high walls of the theatre were covered with them.

"Where the hell am I?" Joe asked, rubbing his head. He was lying on the stage in front of the screen. Below him, on the floor between the stage and the first row of seats was a group of young people, one of whom he recognized as the kid who brained him with the film canister.

"You're in our sanctuary," the kid said in a squeaky voice that robbed it of any reverence.

"Your what?"

"The place where we come to pay worship."

Joe felt a cool tingle of fear. "Are you Scientologists?" he asked.

"No," the kid said. "We're Cultists."

"Oh Christ," Joe muttered. He looked wildly around the theatre. On the back wall, above the square hole where the camera peeked out of the projectionist's booth, was a red neon sign that said THE CUTTING ROOM FLOOR.

"We are the Director's Cult." The kid saw Joe's face and held up a calming hand. "It's just a play on words. We're not really a cult. We don't worship Satan or kill people or anything."

"Good to know," Joe said feebly.

"Our mission is to show the world the cinema that has been hidden for too long. To part the red velvet curtains of ignorance and deception. To reveal the truth about deleted scenes and alternate endings. The Unseen Hollywood."

"The Unseen Hollywood," the other Cultists said in low, reverent voices.

"What does that have to do with me?" Joe's voice trembled as he struggled to remain calm. "Why did you kidnap me?"

"We didn't kidnap you," said the Cultist. "We liberated you from those who would take your work—your *art*—and lock it in a vault, never to be seen."

"What are you talking about?" Joe said. "Most DVDs feature bonus features, including deleted scenes."

The Cultist shook his head regretfully. "Nothing more than a useless gesture. People don't really *see*. They don't *know*. We're going to show them. We're going to make them see. Make them realize a movie is more than just the sum of its parts. It's also the pieces that don't make the final cut."

Joe swallowed dryly. Sarah's words echoed in his mind: *Sometimes it's about what you don't see.*

The lead Cultist signalled to the others and they came forward.

One of them grabbed Joe's arms, the other his legs, and together they lifted him up and onto a low platform he hadn't noticed behind him. There was a mechanical whirring sound and the screen began to rise up into a slot in the ceiling. Behind it was an enormous machine that looked a bit like the Play-Doh Fun Factory Joe had played with as a kid. He struggled harder.

The Cultists bound him to the platform with some sort of crinkly, shiny material that Joe's frantic mind realized was film stock. These guys were crazy. Didn't they know everything was done digitally these days?

The platform to which Joe was bound was positioned underneath the towering machine. From his vantage point Joe was looking up at what appeared to be an enormous lever. The kind a giant might use to squeeze juice from an orange. Or in this case, Joe.

"Christ!" he shrieked. "You said you didn't kill people!"

"We're not killing you," said the lead Cultist. "We're *deleting* you."

"How is the public supposed to learn the truth if I'm dead?"

"You won't be dead. You will live forever in the eternal heaven of the silver screen."

"The silver screen," intoned the other Cultists.

"You will be a symbol for deleted actors everywhere. A symbol that the studios will be unable to ignore. They may take your lives, but they will never take your freedom!"

Joe frowned. "That's from *Braveheart*."

The lead Cultist shrugged and signalled to one of his brethren.

The other Cultist picked up a control box dangling from the ceiling by a thick insulated electrical cord. He pressed a red button and the sound of heavy machinery powering up filled the theatre.

Joe didn't know much about the production side of filmmaking, but he knew what he was looking at . . . what he was lying directly beneath. It was a larger version of a device that some might say was the real thing that made movies.

A film splicer.

Joe closed his eyes. He told himself this was only a movie. This wasn't real. Soon someone would yell "Cut!" and he'd be having coffee with Sarah and the other actors. Every action was followed by a cut. This is what he told himself while the sound of the machine grew louder.

All he had to do was be cool. Stay in character.

And wait for the cut.

Six months later, Barton Collins received a package in the mail.

He was in his office making phone calls. He had met a couple of actors at this year's Toronto International Film Festival who hinted that they might be interested in new representation. It was good for them, but especially good for Bart. He needed clients. He was losing clients like fleas off a dead dog. He sent them out on jobs, but they didn't always come back. Most of them he figured left the business out of frustration, or decided to move to New York or L.A. to be closer to the action. Actors could be so flakey. Sometimes Bart wished he had listened to his mother and become a chiropractor.

He opened the package while he punched in a phone number he had written down on a bar napkin. Inside was a DVD. He vaguely recognized the title; probably a flick featuring one of his actors. He checked the cast list on the back of the box, but didn't recognize any names. He looked at the cover, which said this particular DVD was a "Special Limited Collector's Edition." That meant it had all kinds of bonus features, like behind-the-scenes documentaries, audio commentary tracks, deleted scenes. Stuff he never bothered watching.

The phone number was out of service. Bart swore and slammed down the receiver. He dropped the DVD in the wastebasket next to his desk and went to put on a pot of coffee. He thought about calling his mother.

THE TATTLETAIL

"Dad, I need a demon."

John Smith put down his copy of *The Paranormal Times* and looked at his son: twelve years old but small for his age; soft blue eyes magnified by outsized horn-rimmed glasses; thin, almost feminine lips, carefully neutral, nothing like the petulant frown Lizzie used when she wanted something.

"A demon? Whatever for?"

"The school's putting on a talent show for pets. Demons, bogeys, familiars—as long as they're not classified as dangerous with the Registry, anything can be entered."

John folded his paper, crossed his left leg over the right, and steepled his fingers thoughtfully under his chin. "Well, a talent show certainly sounds like fun, and while I've encouraged you to take an interest in the Academy's extracurricular activities, I'm not sure owning a demon is a good idea."

"Why's that, Dad?"

John smiled inwardly. Ever the judicious debater was his son. "Owning a pet is a big responsibility," he explained. "And a demon! Your mother would throw a fit!"

"I'll feed it and take care of it," Tad said. He removed his glasses and calmly wiped them on the hem of his dress shirt. "I'll keep it outside. You and Mom won't even know it's there."

The Demonology Department at Blackloch Academy looked more like an aisle in a library than an office. The walls were top-to-bottom bookshelves, the lighting was virtually nonexistent, and the air was so still that to the casual observer the room seemed to exist in a total vacuum. The only furnishings were a small roll-top desk and a straight-backed chair, over which a Blackloch Owls varsity jacket was draped.

When Tad entered, Professor Dandridge was standing in the middle of the room with his hands behind his back, almost as if he were expecting him. He was certainly an odd man, both in looks and demeanour. One of those unfortunate people who was both very tall and very skinny, with rails for arms and stilts for legs, his head seemed to float in a nimbus of silver hair that some students opined made him look like a mad scientist. According to the Blackloch rumour network, that hair had been fire-engine red until Dandridge spent a night in the Ivy-Lesper mansion in Lotusville. And that was just one of the many stories floating around about Blackloch's demonology professor. Another said that Dandridge got his suits at the local mortuary . . . with a spade and shovel. Tad didn't think that particular yarn was true, despite the Demonology prof's admittedly fresh-from-the-grave wardrobe.

"Young Tad Smith!" Dandridge beamed. "To what do I owe the pleasure?"

"Hi, Professor," Tad unslung his backpack and took out a hardcover book with a frayed binding. "I came to return your book."

"Capital!" Dandridge's hands emerged from behind his back and came together in a hollow clap. "*Sea Serpentry and the Bermuda Triangle*."

"I liked it," Tad said, handing it over. "Dr. Cody has some interesting theories on migratory habits. Was he ever able to prove any of them?"

"He tried," Dandridge said with a dark grin. "Oh, how he tried! He used to teach here, you know. Advanced Biology, aquatic species, of course. He went on sabbatical—oh, it must have been three or four years back—to the Fuqua Islands."

"In the North Pacific?"

"Yes, that's right. He was about to start a year-long study of the Marianas Trench." Dandridge patted the book with one of his long, cadaverous hands. "He believed there was a portal located at the bottom. If true, it would've gone a long way to proving a lot of the theories in this book."

Tad gave this what he hoped was a respectful amount of

consideration. Then he said, "Professor, I was wondering if I could borrow another book?"

"Oh? Did you have one in mind?"

"*Demons, Deities, and Demi-Gods.*" He coughed into his hand. "The advanced edition."

Dandridge folded his arms and leaned against one of the book-lined walls. "That's a serious book," he said evenly. "Would this have anything to do with the school's talent contest?"

Tad looked down at his shoes.

"I thought so. Well, I don't see the harm in lending you that particular volume. It's not as if it were part of the Restricted Collection. But I don't think I need to tell you that demons classified as 'dangerous to humans' are strictly verboten in the talent show. And only a handful of Portentas are—"

"I know, sir. And yes, I was planning to enter the contest. I just . . . I wanted . . ." He frowned. ". . . I didn't want to use something out of the primer, sir. That's what everyone else will be doing. I wanted to be different."

"You wanted an edge." Dandridge's colourless lips spread in a vulpine smile.

"Yes," Tad admitted, "I wanted an edge."

"I would never keep a pupil from learning—" As he spoke he turned to the shelf he had been leaning against and selected a volume bound in dark red leather. "—especially one as bright as you, Smith. And as I said before, I can't prohibit you from borrowing it. But I will remind you to stay within the rules of the contest—"

"I will, sir."

He held the book out to Tad.

"—and don't even contemplate purchasing anything dangerous—"

"I won't, sir."

Tad took the book.

"—and above all else, be sure to have an adult present."

By the following evening Tad had gone through the book six times and kept coming back to the same entry—*Cordovian Tattletail*. The book described it as a mimic that takes on the characteristics of whatever it eats. Tad didn't know exactly what that meant; like many of the books about demons he had read, vague descriptions seemed to be the rule rather than the exception. But he figured that as long as he kept its diet simple, then there shouldn't be any possibility of a gruesome bloodbath.

There was only one place that he could purchase a demon locally. The Mall, as it was called in most circles, was a pocket portal not unlike the one Dr. Cody theorized was at the bottom of the Marianas Trench. Quite literally a tear in the dimensional fabric of reality, which in this instance also happened to be the most popular hub of commerce in magic artefacts in the Tri-State area. Tad had been there with his family a few times. One of those trips had been to Heads and Tails, a pet shop that specialized in rare demons. They had gone for Lizzie's birthday, and she had picked out a sinister-looking fish, called a Striped Shadow, which had lived for about one week. (At the toilet-side service, Tad pontificated aloud on the health and safety of Lizzie's kids, should she have any one day, and was summarily sent to bed without his dinner.)

Tad was confident he would be a better pet-owner than his sister. And because the talent contest was being sponsored by the Blackloch Academy, he was able to convince his mother and father to foot the bill for the Tattletail in the interest of his budding education. "But you know the rules," his father said from behind his newspaper. "If it turns out to crave human flesh, you have to banish it." Tad agreed. But as long as he kept the Tattletail on the vegetarian diet he had planned out, it wouldn't be a problem.

No problem at all.

"It smells," was John Smith's first and only comment on the matter of Tad's Cordovian Tattletail. And, to be fair, there wasn't much more that could be said. In comparison to some of the other entries in *Demons, Deities, and Demi-Gods*, the Cordovian Tattletail was no great shakes—at least not in the looks department.

It was the size of a large puppy, with smooth, grey skin and a long slim body. Its eyes were the colour of dull rubies and stared out from beneath a thick precipice of brow. One moment it appeared to be scared; the next it seemed decisive, thoughtful. It was a Lesser Demon and a Portenta, the latter meaning it could turn into something more than the former. If given the proper motivation.

Tad named it Dennis. Not because it looked like a Dennis or because he thought Dennis was a particularly good name. Dennis was merely the first one that came to mind. That was how Tad's thinking worked most of the time. On those very few occasions when his projects resulted in failure—like the time he brought the futon to life and it went through the big picture window in the living room, never to be seen again—he invariably gave his father the same answer: *It seemed like a good idea at the time*. Tad was not aware that these seemingly random decisions were in actuality communiqués from his subconscious, and that his decision to purchase a Cordovian Tattletail and name it Dennis came from the same place as the decision to enter the talent contest in the first place. Nor would he have cared. If Dennis turned out to be a Great Old One, one of the unspeakable deities that could destroy entire galaxies by blinking, and inadvertently brought about armageddon, Tad would have offered up the same explanation.

It seemed like a good idea at the time.

He took Dennis out to his mother's greenhouse. The vegetarian diet was to begin today, but first he needed to pick up a few groceries. As he escorted Dennis to a huddle of potted ferns, he made a mental note to secret the veggies off his dinner plate. Waste not, want not.

A week later, Dennis had doubled in size. He was now as big as a Shetland pony and as green as the Incredible Hulk. He had eaten five ficus trees which were Betty Smith's pride and joy, and Tad had been forced to relocate Dennis to a chained post behind the woodshed. He mowed the lawn twice that weekend and fed Dennis the clippings. The demon grew and grew.

The following week a series of thunderstorms rolled through town and Tad learned something else about his Cordovian Tattletail. One of those things they neglected to mention in the text books.

He had gone out to the woodshed around eight that morning, as had been his routine since becoming a pet-owner. He had put on his slicker and galoshes and went out to the chopping block where Dennis liked to sleep. Usually the demon was awake and waiting for him, red eyes gleaming, mouth open and salivating. But not today. Tad found Dennis lying on his side with his back to him. He didn't appear to be breathing.

Tad ran over and crouched down next to Dennis. He felt for a pulse and located it—both of them, in fact—but it was low, very low. And his breathing was very shallow. Tad timed it on his Casio as only two or three breaths a minute.

"Dennis! Dennis, wake up!"

He grabbed the demon's long, scrawny arm and shook it. Two red pinpricks of light appeared in the deep hollows of his eyes. Tad untied him and carried him back to the house. Tad's dad remarked that Dennis smelled worse wet than he did dry and disappeared back behind his paper. Tad's mother told him to take Dennis out to the greenhouse.

Tad did as he was told, carrying the demon out to the greenhouse and placing him on the workbench. He turned on the heat lamp his mother used for the few tropical plants she grew and trained the light onto Dennis. He wasn't thinking about the talent contest. He just wanted Dennis to be okay. He never had a pet before and hadn't expected to feel so attached to it. It wasn't a bad feeling.

"Photosynthesis," Tad said for the third time. He spoke in the tone of someone discussing festering wounds and putrescent corpses. "Photo-stinkin-synthesis."

It was Monday. The thunderstorms had packed their bags and moved on. Dennis was on the mend, but Tad's prospects of winning the Blackloch talent show were not good.

It turned out the Cordovian Tattletail took on more characteristics of his diet than just its colour. One could go so far as to say that feeding on plants had turned Dennis into a vegetable. Literally. As such, Dennis was subject to certain biological requirements. Like sunlight. Without it, Dennis became slow and sluggish. The previous week's thunderstorms hadn't been enough to kill him, but they had sent Dennis into a coma-like state. He was also growing what appeared to be a set of branches out of his back.

Life was funny sometimes. Tad had a demon that need sunlight to live, while his sister Lizzie, who had been turned into a vampire the past summer, would be reduced to dust if she so much as stepped outside to fetch the mail. Oh yes, life was just a laugh-and-a-half.

Dennis looked like a skinless pony—a *green*, skinless pony—and compared to some of the demons the other kids would be bringing, that was about as scary as a game of patty-cake. If Tad was going to make Dennis scarier, he would have to feed him something a bit more exotic than ferns and ficus.

Tad checked the chains for the seventh time, confirmed that they were fastened tightly, and returned to the chopping block where a pair of boxes were stacked one on top of the other. Dennis blinked questionably at his master with his large, expressive eyes.

"Don't look at me like that," Tad said. He felt bad about chaining Dennis up, but it was in lieu of adult supervision.

He opened the first box, which was full of frozen porterhouse steaks Tad's parents had bought at the Price Club. He took one out and tapped it against the cordless phone sticking out of the waistband of his pants. The steaks were for Dennis: he needed a new diet if he was going to make an impression at the talent contest. The phone was for Tad, in case the New and Improved Dennis decided he wanted something more to eat than frozen steaks. Like Tad, for instance.

"Okay, buddy. It's magic time." He raised the steak high over his head, which Dennis had quickly learned was the signal for dinnertime. "Open wide!"

Tad tossed the steak and Dennis made it disappear. They repeated the process until the box was empty. As Dennis was downing the last steak, the transformation began. *It's happening faster now*, Tad thought, fascinated and a little frightened, as the demon's long limbs grew even longer. His teeth were growing, too. It looked as if knitting needles had inexplicably grown out of his gums.

Tad touched the phone with a reassuring hand, ready to punch in 911 if Dennis showed any sign of biting the hand that had fed him. But Dennis wasn't making any such motions. In fact, he wasn't moving at all.

"Dennis? *Dennis?*"

He reached out and gave him a slight shake. The demon's skin (it had changed colour from fern-green to the pinkish-red of raw hamburger) was cool to the touch. Cold.

Frozen.

Tad bit his lip.

"Oh damn."

On the day of the talent show, Tad and his father secured Dennis to the roof of the family station wagon with bungee cords and drove over to Blackloch. The demon was still a gruesome thing, John Smith opined, and he still smelled like dead fish set on fire, but he commended Tad on a fine job of raising Dennis and keeping him docile. Tad almost told him that if anything should be thanked it was the frozen porterhouses, but then figured his mother and father could find out about that in their own time (and if he won the talent contest and was able to replace the steaks with the prize money, they needn't know at all).

After they had unloaded Dennis at the rear of the school gymnasium, where the contest was being held, Tad walked his dad back to the station wagon.

"Make sure you get him inside before he thaws."

"I will, Dad. And thanks for driving us."

"You're sure you don't want me to stick around?"

"No parents allowed. You remember what happened at last year's Science Fiction Fair?"

John smiled reflectively. "Oh yes. I forgot about the no-parental-influence rule. It's probably for the best."

"I'll call you after it's over."

"Good luck, son. And good luck to Dennis." He stuck out his hand.

Tad shook it. "Thanks, Dad."

The judge was Mr. Farley, one of Blackloch's art teachers. His area of expertise was still-lifes, but he wasn't impressed with Tad's frozen Cordovian Tattletail.

"Master Smith," he said in the lofty cadences that only art teachers can reach, "you should know better than to try and pass off this . . . this *model* as the real thing."

A few of the other student-contestants snickered. One of them was holding a scraggly, red feline—a were-cat, as it were—with the unfortunate name of Hexxy. Its owner had trained it to fetch sticks.

"It's not a model," Tad protested. "Dennis is a real Tattletail. But he's also—"

"Dennis?" Farley said. "What kind of name is that for a demon?"

It beats Hexxy, Tad almost said.

"I'm afraid the only tattletale here is you, Master Smith. But if you'd like to submit *Dennis* as your art final, I'm sure something could be arranged."

This time the students laughed openly. Hexxy the were-cat hissed and took a swipe at one of the other contest entries, a Bolo Jumping Spider; it leaped up onto one of the basketball nets and glared down balefully.

"I assure you Dennis is very much alive. But he's so ferocious I have to keep him in this frozen state or else he might . . . well, he might run amok."

"Run amok, huh?" Farley said, grinning wryly. "So why don't we take him outside into the sun and see what happens?"

Tad said, "I wouldn't recommend that."

"Come, come," Farley said, clapping his hands for emphasis. "We can bind him to the megaliths on the grounds. Just so he doesn't 'run amok.'"

The students laughed again. Tad seemed to have no choice. He manoeuvred the push-cart on which Dennis stood outside, into the sun. Mr. Farley and Tad tied Dennis's arms to a pair of the runic pillars that were scattered across the grounds of Blackloch like strange stunted tree trunks. He seemed to take great pleasure in hamming it up for the students—tiptoeing around the inert demon, binding its arms in a mincing burlesque of fright. The students snickered and laughed, but it was clear to Tad that most of them thought Farley was pouring it on a little thick. On the other hand, if this is what it took to prove that Dennis was truly a flesh and blood Tattletail, then so be it.

"So here we are," Farley said in his rich and mellifluous voice. "Just you, me, your classmates, and your demon. Are you ready to confess, or shall we waste more of everyone's time?"

Tad was feeling the pressure of being the subject of attention. Dennis seemed to be feeling it, too, because he appeared to be sweating buckets.

The Bolo Jumping Spider had come out with the students and hopped onto one of the pillars to which Dennis had been tied. Now it leaped onto the wide, football-shaped head of the demon and made as if to scamper down its quickly thawing body. It was skittering across Dennis's chest when the demon regained its *savoir faire* and plucked the spider up in one enormous hand and deposited it in his mouth.

"Gross *out!*" cried a red-haired girl named Tart Williams. In her hands was something that looked like an octopus spliced with a Brillo pad.

Dennis let out a thunderous growl that heralded the fleshy explosion of another four limbs that erupted out of his sides. His voice degenerated into a loud insectile buzzing that sounded to Tad like the hum of high-tension wires cranked up to a deafening volume.

Despite Mr. Farley's shortcomings in the personality department, he was no coward. He leapt between Dennis and the students, picking up one of the ropes that had bound the demon's hands, and pulled it so hard the cords in his neck stood out.

"Down! Down! Hie!"

He jerked the rope, but he might as well have been trying to bring an ocean liner to heel. Dennis gave a jerk of his own and Mr. Farley was suddenly airborne.

Tad watched as the art teacher landed in a crumpled heap, and thought: *If I don't get expelled for this it'll be a miracle.*

Joey Lawson, the kid who had trained his were-cat to fetch sticks, was standing a few feet away from Dennis, staring at the demon with an expression that could have been total amazement or paralyzing terror. Hexxy hissed at the demon, leaped out of Joey's arms, and bolted into the Avebury Woods.

"*Joey!*" Tad called. "*Get out of there!*"

Joey turned to Tad, dropped the sticks in his hand, and ran screaming after Hexxy. Into the woods.

The woods.

The wood.

Tad ran over and picked up one of Joey's sticks. Dennis had managed to free his other arm, and was now looking at the kids running helter-skelter across the school grounds. *Fast food*, Tad thought crazily. He had to hurry before this really did turn into a bloodbath.

He gripped the stick tightly and raised it high over his head. "*Dennis! Over here, boy!*"

Whatever metamorphosis the demon had undergone, it still recognized the voice of its master. Its eyes (there were eight of them now) regarded Tad with alacrity.

"*Open wide!*"

Dennis opened his mouth. Tad threw the stick. It tumbled through the air, end over end, and even before it had left his hand, Tad knew he had thrown too high. It went over Dennis's still-changing head, missing his mouth completely . . . *and landed in one of the demon's extra hands.*

He stuffed it into his mouth and swallowed it without fanfare.

Tad tossed the rest of the sticks and Dennis ate them as well. By the time Mr. Farley had regained consciousness, Dennis had devoured three of the trees on the edge of the woods and was halfway through his fourth.

Farley thanked Tad for saving his life and the life of Tad's classmates. Then he disqualified Dennis for eating one of the other contestants. First prize went to Tart Williams and her oven-cleaning octopod. Tad didn't mind much. Mr. Farley had helped him to see the positive side of not being expelled from Blackloch for bringing a dangerous demon onto its grounds. Tad saw it very well.

His parents let him keep the Tattletail. Tad didn't tell them about the incident at the talent show, only that he had lost; he suspected it was their feeling sorry for him that prompted them to let him keep the demon.

Tad kept Dennis on a wood diet—*All that you can chop*, his father told him brightly—and he soon developed a smooth oaken coat. Once a week Tad polished him with Pledge.

His dad no longer complained about the smell.

CHARLOTTE'S FREQUENCY

Morris Hardy was standing in his front yard watching the delivery truck with SHARF ELECTRONICS on the side back into his driveway when Eddie Giles came over.

"Hey, neighbour. How's it hangin'?"

Eddie was wearing a plaid bathrobe and moose-slipper ensemble that might have been stolen off a homeless person. He was holding a coffee cup with TEACHERS DO IT EIGHT MONTHS OF THE YEAR printed on the side. Eddie taught history at the community college—a fact that confirmed to Morris that education in this country was going right down the toilet.

He and Eddie had been living next to each other on Alder Lane for two years—two years that, to Morris, felt more like ten—and at some point during that time Eddie had come to the debatable conclusion that he and Morris were best friends.

"Hi, Eddie," Morris said. "I thought you were headed up to Groverton this morning."

"We're leaving this aft." Eddie scratched himself with his free hand and yawned. "Kim's got morning classes. You can't believe how much I miss that kid."

Morris nodded even though he was pretty sure Eddie's daughter didn't reciprocate the feeling. Kim had escaped to university the previous fall, and, after landing a waitressing job at a seafood restaurant, had stayed on through the summer. She had been home to visit only twice. Watching her father openly scratching his balls through his bathrobe, Morris understood completely.

"Tell Kim that Jude and I say hello," he said.

"Will do," Eddie said distractedly. He was staring at the truck.

That, Morris realized, was what had lured Eddie from his fortress of suburban solitude. Here in the 'burbs, the arrival of a delivery truck was to adults what the arrival of the ice-cream truck was to kids. As if to further prove this truth, Morris spied a curtain open at the house across the street, and a face peek out.

The truck stopped and two men in brown coveralls climbed out. One of them had a clipboard with a piece of yellow flimsy attached to it.

"Mr. Hardy?"

Eddie slapped Morris on the back. "He's your man."

The deliveryman gave Eddie a passing look and handed the clipboard to Morris. As he signed, the other deliveryman pulled up the rear door of the truck and started shimmying out a large cardboard box—the widescreen television Morris had wanted for years but had only recently been able to afford. Jude had tried to kick up a fuss, but she couldn't come up with any specific reasons against the purchase. Morris knew she was sore because he hadn't consulted her before placing the order. But the way he saw it, if they had to move out of the city—against his own wishes—then he should be allowed to take the necessary measures to make himself comfortable.

Morris returned the clipboard and the deliveryman tore off his copy.

"I knew you were getting a new toy," Eddie said slyly.

"How'd you guess?" Morris said, going along.

"The dish," Eddie said, and jerked a thumb over his shoulder at Morris's roof. The new satellite dish gleamed in the early-morning light. "That's a hell of an antenna, too. You get Skinemax on that?"

Morris nodded even though he wasn't really listening. He was watching the deliverymen. They were speaking in low, furtive voices. A moment later one of them came over and said, "Uh, Mr. Hardy, I'm afraid we have a bit of a problem."

"What's wrong?"

"Well." The man took off his hat and raked his fingers through his greasy hair. "It appears we left the cart back at the store. And we need it to—"

"Couldn't we just carry it in?" Eddie piped.

The deliveryman looked at Eddie, then turned to Morris with a questioning look. "Well . . . we *could* carry it. It's not so much heavy as it is awkward. But . . ."

Morris understood what the other man was trying to say: *Yes, it* could *be done. But do you really want to put your new toy in this guy's hands?*

He looked at Eddie, trying to see past the patchy robe and grungy moose slippers. He didn't hate Eddie, but he felt something, and irritation seemed too small a word to describe his feelings for a man who punctuated his every accident with the word "oopsie." As in, *The other day I was in the front yard taking a few test swings with my new five iron and—oopsie!—now I need to replace the windshield on the Subaru.*

There had been an oopsie just a month ago, in fact, on a Sunday afternoon when the couples had gotten together for a barbecue. Eddie had manoeuvred Morris's new hibachi next to the hedge wall that separated their backyards—*to give it some shade*, was Eddie's oblique explanation—and a large section of it had caught fire. Morris would never forget the expression on Eddie's face that day, a look of complete and total perplexity that seemed to say, *Damn, were those things flammable?*

If Eddie helped carry the television, the odds were there would be an accident (an oopsie, if you like). But with the deliverymen helping . . . and it only had to go into the house . . .

"Okay," Morris said finally. "Let's do it."

The deliverymen used the hydraulic lifter to lower the box to the driveway, and when everyone was ready, each man took a corner and lifted with an enthusiastic grunt. To his surprise, Morris found himself to be the weakest link. While Eddie and the two deliverymen hoisted their quarter of the box effortlessly, Morris struggled to keep his off the ground. His arms began to tremble, and he finally had to set his corner back down. It wasn't heavy, as the deliveryman had said, but he felt inexplicably drained.

"Jude keep you up last night?" Eddie chortled.

Morris couldn't see Eddie's face over the top of the box, but he could picture his sly grin quite easily. He took a deep, cleansing breath, shook his arms to loosen his muscles, and said, "Okay, let's try it again."

The box wouldn't fit through the front door, so they brought it around to the back of the house. Walking up the short set of steps to the deck, Eddie stepped on one of Jude's potted azaleas, pulverizing it. As he watched Eddie shake the dirt off his tacky slipper, Morris had a sudden, brief image of Godzilla wearing a plaid bathrobe and laying waste to Tokyo, punctuating each cataclysmic footfall with—

"Oopsie," Eddie said, smiling sheepishly.

Morris closed his eyes and took another deep, steadying breath.

They carried the box through the sliding glass door and into the dining room. Eddie tracked dirt on the carpet. They passed through the kitchen, guiding the box around the refrigerator and the dishwasher, and came to a stop at the top of the stairs leading down to the basement.

Morris leaned against the doorway, breathing heavily. He looked at Eddie and thought, *If you have an oopsie going down these stairs, you'll be wearing this thing like a hat.* But it was Morris who was huffing and puffing and hunched over with his hands on his knees. If anyone was going to have any oopsie, it was probably going to be him.

But there was no oopsie. It was slow moving the box down the tight confines of the stairway, but they made it without incident, setting the box on the clean patch of carpet where Morris's old television had recently held court.

Everyone stood around catching their breath. Morris needed more time than anyone else. He leaned against the doorway that communicated between the den and the laundry room, his face as red as a cooked lobster, sweat rolling down his cheeks like tears. One of the deliverymen offered to get him a canister of oxygen from the truck, and everyone had a chuckle over that.

When the deliverymen had gone and Eddie had wandered back to his own house, Morris returned to the den and began the business of setting up his new television.

He loved the den. It was his place. He had installed shelves on one entire wall to accommodate his extensive DVD library. Framed movie posters—as beautiful as any work of art, in his opinion—

graced every wall. Tall Bose speakers stood like sentinels in each of room's four corners. A glass-fronted cabinet held his DVD player and stereo system. The only furniture was a leather couch and a recliner, both of which had been strategically positioned to take full advantage of the surround-sound system, thereby ensuring a true theatre-going experience. Jude referred to the den as his shrine to the great god Hollywood.

As he was admiring the setup of television, sound system, and furniture, like megaliths in some postmodern Stonehenge, he noticed something out of the corner of his eye, near one of the speakers.

It was a spider, a little grey one, constructing a web in the corner near the ceiling.

Morris picked up a copy of *Entertainment Weekly*, rolled it into a tube, and made to brush away the web.

Then he remembered the crickets.

They had moved in sometime around the start of the summer. He didn't remember exactly when because they didn't bother him, but Jude started to complain about their incessant chirping. She claimed to hear them all through the house, though Morris was fairly certain they were located somewhere in the laundry room. That Morris couldn't hear them in any place except the den didn't matter. According to Jude, he usually had the volume turned up so loud he wouldn't have heard World War III even if the first nukes landed on Alder Lane.

He figured the crickets were holed up behind the water heater, or maybe under the wash tub. Jude only went downstairs to put on laundry, but lately she was making him do it. The chirping, she said, was becoming too much to bear. She told Morris to hire an exterminator, but he had refused. Surely he was capable of taking care of a few crickets.

Except now he wouldn't have to. The spider could do it for him. He had seen a program on the Discovery Channel that said spiders were the sheriffs of the insect kingdom. They were tough little rascals. The program had also said that spiders couldn't die of natural causes, and if kept safe, a spider can continue to live and grow for a theoretically unlimited amount of time. Apparently there was a collection of "holy" spiders in China that had been hatched some 2,800 years ago. One of the geeks on the show said that a spider's carapace, if sufficiently scaled, could adequately shield a nuclear blast.

It might take a few weeks for this particular spider to catch the crickets, but in the long run it would be worth the money he'd end up saving on an exterminator. And so what if Jude had to suffer a bit longer. She didn't seem to care about his own suffering at having to leave Portland.

Okay, he thought, putting down the magazine, *you've just been pardoned, my eight-legged friend.* But he wouldn't tell Jude. No way. She'd think the solution was worse than the problem.

Morris spent the rest of the day setting up his new television, adjusting the settings on his new television, and then playing with his new television. By nine o'clock he was beat and dragged himself to bed, answering Jude's few, polite inquiries about the television, and then falling quickly into sleep.

He dreamed of Eddie.

His first thought when he saw him, coming down the stairs into Morris's den, was: *Don't I see you enough when I'm awake? Now you've got to barge into my dreams?*

He watched as Eddie, dressed in his plaid bathrobe and moose slippers, came over to the new television. Eddie smiled as he took a metal canister out of one frayed pocket. He held it up with both hands, displaying it like a prize on a television game show, and Morris saw it was a canister of starter fluid.

What are you doing here, Ed?

Eddie continued to smile as he upended the canister and poured starter fluid all over the television. It splashed across the black plastic housing and ran down the polished screen. Eddie produced a wooden kitchen match and scratched it across his thumbnail. Still smiling, he dropped it onto the console. A wave of flame leapt up with a *whomff!* sound. Morris stepped back, shielding his face from the bright flames.

Damn! Eddie bellowed. *Was that thing flammable?*

Unable to move, Morris watched as the fire ran down the screen in burning rivulets. There was loud pop and a fan of sparks exploded off the back of the console. The television screen blackened, cracked, and coughed glass onto the carpet. Acrid smoke billowed out of the hole.

Eddie danced puckishly before the quickly spreading fire. *Oopsie!* he said with a shrug, and ran up the stairs. Morris followed. He moved quickly, but when he reached the living room, Eddie was nowhere to be found. He looked out the big picture window and there was Eddie, outside on the lawn. He wasn't alone. It looked like the entire neighbourhood had come out to watch his house burn. Eddie smiled and waved.

House is on fire! he shouted. *It's the antenna! It's throwing off sparks like a sonuvabitch!*

At first Morris thought he misheard him—then a shower of sparks came down from somewhere on the roof. But there was no antenna up there. The only thing he thought it could be was a downed power transformer. But there weren't any that crossed over the house.

Morris heard a crash behind him, followed by a tinkling sound like the ringing of tiny bells.

As he was turning around, he woke up. For a second or two he thought he could still hear the tinkling, as if the sound had followed him into the waking world. But the house was dark and silent.

He picked up the glass of water on the nightstand and drained it in a single gulp. He looked over at Jude's side of the bed, but it was empty. The door to the connecting bathroom was closed and he could hear muffled retching sounds from within. He wanted to get up and make sure she was okay, but he was so exhausted he could hardly move. All was quiet on the digestive front, but he felt weak and oddly used up. His body was slick with sweat. He pulled his nightshirt up over his head and tossed it on the floor. His skin was ghostly pale and there was a purple bruise the size of his fist under his left armpit. He didn't recall hurting himself there. Maybe when he was moving the television? But that didn't explain why he felt so drained.

Probably picked up a bug, he thought. In the bathroom, Jude made another heaving sound. *Both of us.*

A damn flu bug. And on a Friday, no less! He had the whole

weekend planned out. He was going to clean the gutters, mow the lawn for what he hoped was the last time this season, and go to the hardware store to pick up a new set of hedge-clippers. His old set had vanished last year into the Bermuda Triangle that was Eddie Giles's tool shed.

He heard the toilet flushed, and Jude came shuffling out of the bathroom, wiping her mouth. "I barfed," she said unceremoniously. "Must've been those fish sticks."

Morris gawped at her. She was pale as a ghost. "Maybe," he said.

Morris didn't bother showering the following morning. Instead, he went down to the den and put on a movie. Fifteen minutes into it, he started to feel drowsy. He found his attention drifting over to the spider, still building its web in the corner.

As he watched, the spider crawled up to the ceiling and skittered across to a spot directly above the television. Morris felt something move along his arm and brushed at it instinctively. But when he looked there was nothing there. The feeling remained for a moment—like a slight breeze blowing through the hair on his arm—then it was gone. He looked back at the ceiling and saw the spider floating down on a thin, almost invisible strand of web. The moment it landed on top of the television, the picture on the screen went out. There was no flash, no pop, no spark. It just went out.

Morris went into the laundry room and checked the fuse box. He replaced the blown fuse (a thin curl of smoke rose off the cooked end) and returned to the den.

The television was back on. He dropped back onto the couch and looked into the corner. The spider was back in its web, racing busily back and forth.

Morris droned. *Coffee break's over, fella. Get back to work.*

He slept.

The day drifted and so did Morris. Time dissolved into a grey mist that, in his mind, looked like a spider web in which his thoughts were caught like flies. He did none of the things he had planned for the day; he never even left the den. He slept, he woke, he shifted around on the couch, he slept some more. At one point he woke up and saw the spider on the armrest beside his head.

Howdy, sheriff? Catch any varmints today?

The spider remained still, legs curled up to its sides, which wasn't grey after all but a deep, almost reflective, silver. Morris was struck by the crazy idea—it had to be crazy, didn't it?—that the spider was watching the television.

"Too much of this stuff will rot your brain."

He picked up the remote and put it on the Discovery Channel.

"You might as well learn something." He looked down at the spider. It still hadn't moved. "You're a smart little fella, aren't you?"

Morris shook his head and slunk down lower on the couch.

Then he drifted off again.

The next time he woke up the spider was gone and there was a test pattern on the television screen. He turned it off and went upstairs. He was so tired when he reached the top of the stairs that he made a proclamation to join a gym next week. This was starting to get embarrassing. He went to bed and slept through most of Sunday with Jude curled up beside him.

He dimly recalled going into the bathroom at some point, but the memory was distant and intangible. It might even have been a dream. A part of him hoped it was because he recalled looking into the mirror and seeing a face that was not his own. It was the gaunt face of a concentration camp refugee. His eyes looked like ice chips staring out of sockets that seemed much too deep; his cheeks were sunken and carved with dark lines of shadow; and his lips were bright red, as if he had been eating cherries. He didn't look sick—he looked diseased.

The following morning—was it Monday already?—Morris tried to take out the garbage. He made it halfway to the curb before a wave of nausea came over him. It felt like someone was jabbing him in the stomach with a stick. He stumbled back up the driveway and and along the flagstone path to the front porch. For a brief moment he glanced up at the roof. He saw the new satellite dish and, next to it, a silver antenna.

Had the satellite people installed that?

For some reason he associated the antenna with fire, but he didn't know why. It was just a silver rod, about eighteen inches long, with a ball-bearing on the tip. And yet something in his mind was convinced that wasn't all it was.

He went back inside and picked up the phone in the kitchen. He had to call work and tell them he wouldn't be in today, maybe not for a few days. As he put the receiver to his ear, a horrible screeching sound came out of the earpiece. He drop the phone and it smacked loudly on the linoleum floor. He picked it up, replaced the receiver, and went back upstairs to check on Jude.

She was curled up on her side of the bed. He crouched next to her and gave her arm a reassuring squeeze. When he let go, his fingers left dark impressions on her skin. Bruises. Morris shook her—gently at first, then progressively harder—but she wouldn't wake up.

"Jude," he said with a slight tremor in his voice. "Jude, wake up."

She muttered something unintelligible and fell silent.

Morris raced back downstairs and grabbed the car keys off the cork board. He went outside and the nausea fell on him again. It felt as if his head was wrapped in a hot, wet towel. He stumbled down the porch steps and zigzagged across the flagstone path to his car. The early morning sun felt hot enough to burn holes through his skin.

He fumbled the door open and collapsed into the driver's seat. He closed the door and stabbed the key at the ignition slot. It took him three tries to find it. He just couldn't seem to *focus*. The nausea continued to close around his head like a bad weather system. His stomach clenched, suddenly and violently, and before he realized it, he had vomited all over the steering wheel. The smell was so awful he vomited again. Then he passed out.

When he awoke the smell inside the car was so bad it was almost miasmic. He opened the door and hauled himself out, breathing in great snatches of fresh air. He looked at his watch to see how long he had spent in that putrid sauna, but it had stopped. He shambled back to the house, his head throbbing with every step.

He saw the antenna on the roof.

It looked taller.

❖

He couldn't make it back upstairs to Jude. It seemed to require too much effort to go anywhere. He managed to slink down the stairs to the den. It was cooler down there. He flopped down on the couch and stared at the web in the corner of the room.

It was the spider, he thought deliriously. It was feeding on them somehow, draining them. A couple of days ago he would have laughed at such an idea. It was a regular Eddie Giles special. A spider that fed on life force instead of bodily fluids. But it didn't seem so crazy now. When one's mind was hanging by a thread (*a spider-thread!* he thought crazily), it was easy to accept all kinds of things that might ordinarily seem unbelievable.

It's been working overtime, but the real web is this house.

Which made him and Jude flies.

Houseflies.

In the horror movies he sometimes watched, the killer insects were always huge, radioactive abominations. But this spider had not gotten big; it had gotten smart. Like the one in that children's book, the spider that wrote messages in its web. *Charlotte's Web.* Charlotte.

Is that who you are? Charlotte? A spider for the new millennium?

He wondered how long he had before he became as comatose as Jude. A week? A day? Maybe only a few hours? He knew he should have felt concern for his wife, but it just seemed like too much work. It was horrible to feel that way, but it wasn't personal. He didn't care about anything. He had never felt so apathetic in his entire life.

He thought back to *Charlotte's Web*, specifically the ending, when Charlotte's children emerged from the egg sac and flew away like dandelion seeds on the wind. He didn't think this particular spider had flown in on a thread, but he had an idea . . . something about fire . . . and sparks.

He managed to muster his strength and go upstairs. He went out onto the porch and craned his head around so he could see the roof. Yes, the antenna had indeed gotten taller. He thought about getting the ladder and taking a closer look, but he'd probably fall off and fracture his skull. Besides, he didn't really need to go up there. He knew in some unexplainable way that the spider and the antenna were somehow connected. He had to figure out what to do about it. While he was still able to do anything.

He went back into the house, found a flashlight, and went downstairs. The web in the corner of the ceiling was finished, but the spider, Charlotte, was nowhere to be found. He looked behind the television and saw something among the rat's-nest of patch-cords and coaxial cables.

The spider had spun a number of threads from the wall to the back of the television and the other pieces of electronics equipment. They looked like very thin silver wires.

Morris reached out and touched one and his finger immediately went numb. He tried to bend it, but it wouldn't move. He bent the rest of his fingers, and they worked fine. He put the paralyzed finger between his teeth and bit down on it gently. He didn't feel a thing. He bit down harder and still felt nothing.

He picked up a magazine, rolled it into a tube, and brushed it through the strands of webbing. They were strong and tensile, almost like chicken wire, but they broke.

The lights went out.

Morris picked up the flashlight and made his way to the fuse box. Another fuse had blown. He replaced it—this one wasn't just smoking; it had melted into the socket—and was closing the panel door when he noticed something.

In addition to the black insulated cables and other assorted wires, Morris counted six silver threads running into the fuse box. After the experience behind the television, he wasn't as quick to touch them.

He tapped one with the end of the flashlight, and the bulb went out with a small pop. Morris shook it and heard the tinkle of broken glass. He dropped the flashlight on the floor and looked back into the fuse box.

The spider threads gave off a faint silver glow that pulsed slowly like respiration.

Morris went back upstairs to the kitchen, and then out to the main foyer and up the stairs to the second floor. By the time he reached the landing he was huffing and puffing like a man of seventy. He leaned against the railing for support and saw a row of bruises along his arm. His body was starting to look like an apple that had fallen off the tallest branch. He stumbled down the hall to the master bedroom and stood wheezing in the doorway, staring at Jude lying on the bed.

She was dead, of that he was sure. Her body was wrapped not in blankets but in a thin, translucent sheet of spider-web. It covered her from head to toe like a death shroud. He could almost make out her face, ghostly and insubstantial through the gauzy material.

Tears seeped out Morris's eyes. It hurt to cry—in his heart and in his head. He felt a sudden, powerful resolve burning through the grey haze that had been fogging his mind. He was angry, and a part of him was glad to be able to feel something so strong and distinct again. And he knew exactly where to direct it.

He went back downstairs and went into the garage through the connecting door in the kitchen. The sledgehammer was leaning against the wall in the corner. He picked it up with an effort and carried it into the living room.

The wall opposite the wide picture window was as good a place to start as any. He took down the wall's only decoration, a Rembrandt print Jude had bought at a garage sale, and leaned it against the couch. He had to work quickly. He could feel his strength ebbing away like the tide.

Spreading his legs, he lifted the hammer over his shoulder and swung it in a wide arc. It sank into the wall with a dull *thunk*. Drywall crumbled in a puff of plaster dust. Morris pulled it out and swung again and again, until the floor was littered with chunks of drywall and a thick cloud of dust hung in the air.

He rested the sledge on his shoulder as a coughing fit came over him. He covered his mouth and when he brought his hand away it was sprinkled with blood. He was running out of time.

He had made an enormous hole in the wall, revealing pipes, wires . . . and half a dozen silver threads.

I don't know whether to call an exterminator or an electrician. He started to laugh, but it quickly dissolved into another fit of coughing. The sledgehammer slipped out of his hands and landed on the floor, narrowly missing one of his feet. The coughing stopped and he was laughing again. A stomach cramp doubled him over. He dropped to his knees thinking, *It's over, that's it, it's too late.* He squeezed his eyes shut, and when he opened them again, he saw her.

Charlotte.

She came out of the hole in the wall and went scrambling up toward the ceiling. Morris managed to get his legs under him once more.

One more swing, that's all I ask, just one more swing.

He picked up the sledgehammer, drew it back, and swung. He felt something pop in his chest, and a burning sensation raced up his left arm.

The sledge struck the wall and went through it. Morris let go of the handle and fell to the floor. The sledge hung there, embedded in the wall, like a piece of modern art.

Did I miss? he wondered. He didn't know. He had closed his eyes at the last second.

Then the sledge fell to the ground, and Morris saw the small stain on the head.

He did it. He killed her. Charlotte was dead.

The heat in his arm had moved into his chest. It felt like his heart was being clenched by a hand made of fire. He crawled over to the picture window that looked out on Alder Lane. He was wondering what the neighbours would think of all this when he heard a sound behind him. The tinkling of tiny bells. He turned back to the wall.

Spiders—thousands of spiders—were coming out of the hole. Silver spiders. Charlotte's children. They looked like a river of ball-bearings pouring out of the wall, some of them crawling up to the ceiling, the rest moving across the floor. The ringing sound of their tiny, marching legs filled the dusty air.

Morris thought they would come for him, swarm him, devour him. But they didn't even go near him. They moved across the floor to the stairs, then went up the steps. A glimmering silver waterfall flowing up instead of down.

He knew where they were going. And why. They were Charlotte's children, after all, and they had to fly. Places to go, people to see. Morris turned back to the window.

They were going up to the roof, to the antenna, where they would take flight—not on kites of thread but on a radio wave, or a satellite signal.

Spiders for the new millennium, transmitted through the air on their own special frequency.

Morris stared out the window and waited for the sparks to fly.

Eddie knocked on the door again. He stood on his tiptoes, trying to peer in through the fanlight, and dropped the stack of plastic-wrapped newspapers cradled in his arm.

"Oopsie," he muttered to the empty yard, and crouched down to pick them up.

He gave the front door a final concerned look and started back to his own yard. On the way he stumbled over the trashcan Morris had left in the driveway and dropped the newspapers again.

Across the street a kid on rollerblades yelled, "Hey, stupid! First day walking?"

Eddie shot the kid a dirty look and continued on his way. He wasn't stupid. A lot of people thought he was, but he wasn't. He was a little slow sometimes, sure, but that didn't make him stupid. Sometimes he just didn't notice things. Like that time with Morris's barbecue and the hedges. Or just now with the trash can.

Or the silver antenna on the roof of his house.

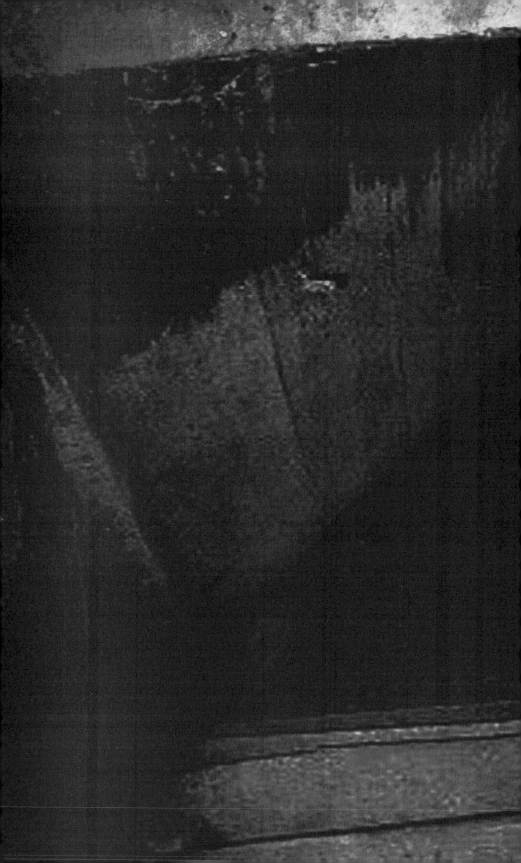

THE CELLAR

Relaxed Best

Ryerson pulled over to the curb and watched as Jonathan Marchand stepped out of the taxi in front of an establishment he assumed was a bar of some kind. It was hard to tell for certain. The windowless façade was dark, crumbling brick, and the only adornment was a plank-board hanging on a pair of hooks above the oaken door. The two words burned into the grain seemed to glare out of the dark like mad eyes. Al Azif.

Ryerson checked his watch. It was a quarter of one in the morning. He jotted the time on his notepad and tossed it on the passenger seat. He had been following the Blue Fairy's husband for over fifteen hours.

The day started at nine o'clock when Jonathan left the Park Avenue brownstone he shared with his wife and went for breakfast at Sorrento's. Afterwards, he went for a manicure and massage, strolled through Central Park, and met a female acquaintance for lunch at the Crystal Cave Restaurant. Ryerson doubted if this was the fabled mistress, seeing as how their only physical contact over the course of the meal was a kiss-kiss on the cheek before they sat down to eat. After lunch, Jonathan went suit shopping at Landry's on 42nd Street. Then he played racquetball for two hours at the New York Fitness Club, took in a three-hour dinner at The Hartencourt Bistro, and met a pair of suited gentlemen who looked like members of the Hair Club for Men for drinks at the Biltmore. Jonathan stumbled out at 11:40 PM, hailed a taxi, and came here, to Al Azif.

Strange name for a bar, Ryerson thought. *Is it a Muslim place?* But then he wasn't getting paid for his opinion; he was paid to follow, and follow he had, like a puppy dog. A very well-paid puppy dog, he reminded himself.

They called her the Blue Fairy because it was said that if you worked yourself into her favour, she would make all of your dreams come true.

Ryerson hadn't come for wish-fulfillment. In fact, you could say the shoe was on the other foot. The Blue Fairy, Veronica Marchand, had summoned him.

She lived in one of the Park Avenue brownstones that Ryerson had only ever seen from the outside. The room where he waited was not very large, but living space in New York wasn't measured in square-footage, it was measured in dollars. A lot of money had been spent in this room, from the gilt-framed oil paintings on the walls, to the pieces of statuary sprouting from every tabletop, to the Turkish rug under his feet.

The Blue Fairy, Ryerson had learned from his hurried research, had made her fortune on the stock market. She had done unusually well in blue-chip stocks—which were about as easy to predict as next week's weather—and had acquired a reputation as someone who put her eggs in all the right baskets.

"Good morning."

Ryerson almost jumped at the sound of her voice. The Blue Fairy was an ordinary-looking woman in her sixties. Medium height, slim, and possessed of a cherubic youthfulness that hadn't come from a surgeon's scalpel. She was dressed casually in a white blouse, untucked, and a pair of faded jeans. She padded across the room in bare feet and extended a long, well-manicured hand.

Ryerson crossed to meet her. "It's very nice to meet you, Ms. Marchand."

"It's *Missus*, actually."

"My apologies."

She made a dismissive gesture. "It's no matter. I've only been married a year, and quite frankly I'd be surprised if it lasts another. That's why I asked you to come. I'm told you're efficient and discreet."

"You heard right," Ryerson replied.

"I suppose you've heard what they call me."

Ryerson smiled.

He drummed his fingers on the steering wheel and listened to the rain tip-tap on the roof. The minutes dragged by slowly. Like Tom Petty said, waiting was the hardest part. Ryerson's intuitions told him this was Jonathan's final stop of the evening. He could probably call it a night, but the kind of cash the Blue Fairy was paying granted her some overtime. And he still had yet to see the mistress—assuming there was one.

A thought struck him then: *What if she's already inside? What if Al Azif is their rendezvous spot?*

That decided it. He got out of the car, debated taking the gun (he called it Patricia for reasons he no longer remembered), and decided it would probably be a bad idea. Al Azif didn't look like much, but in the city even the shittiest watering holes that couldn't afford a metal detector had a couple of goons to pat down everyone who came through the door. He wasn't about to hand Patricia over to some goon who'd probably "lose" her later on. It wasn't like checking your coat.

It had started raining earlier that evening, and now it was really starting to come down. Ryerson turned up his collar and sprinted across the street. It was so dark he tripped on the curb and almost went sprawling on the sidewalk. Stepping up to the door, he wondered vaguely why the streetlights hadn't come on.

He put his hand on the door's metal pull-handle, and froze. Thinking about the streetlights led to another question. Why couldn't he hear any street noise? He cocked his head to the side, but couldn't hear anything except the rain. He should have been able to hear the traffic a street or two over. New York was famous for its street noise, but this particular avenue seemed to be the exception. Maybe it was some trick of acoustics, a fluke arrangement of buildings that blocked out the din.

A homeowner's dream, Ryerson thought, and pushed the door open.

❖

"The Blue Fairy," she said wistfully. "Isn't it funny how we feel the need to label those things we don't understand? I've been investigated, you know." She managed to sound both amused and annoyed. "Mostly by people who didn't know how to label *me*. The government gets very suspicious, as I'm sure you already know. We as a society don't trust those who achieve great wealth and success. The ironic part is that my secret"—a playful smile touched her lips—"my secret is there is no secret. Two things helped me to become the person I am today, Mr. Ryerson. Contacts and contracts. Finding those who could help me and binding them to my service. Marriage isn't all that different, if you really think about it. Promises are made, contracts are signed. Does that sound cold to you, Mr. Ryerson?"

"I have no opinion," the detective said truthfully.

She seemed intrigued. "Really?"

"A private eye with too many opinions doesn't find very much work."

"Proverbs?"

"Dashiell Hammett," Ryerson said with a small grin. "Or maybe it was Ross Macdonald."

"Regardless, I treat my marriage as seriously as I do my business. My husband made certain promises, and I expect them to be carried out."

"You think he's running around?"

Veronica Marchand crossed her arms. "I don't know," she said. "But with Jonathan I've found it's prudent to expect the worst."

Ryerson stepped into an anteroom that smelled of ancient leather. It was darker inside Al Azif than it was on the street. He craned his head around and felt water rush down the back of his neck, chilling his spine. He waited for his eyes to adjust to the darkness. After a moment, he could make out a pair of unlit candles set in wine bottles on a ledge, and another door. He opened it and passed through.

He was in a larger room now. The muffled sounds of jazz music came from beyond a heavy red curtain. To his left was the dim outline of a vacant coat-check booth. He brushed water off his jacket, smoothed down his shirt, and stepped through the curtain.

The sudden bombardment of sound and light almost caused Ryerson to cry out. He stumbled backward, gripping the curtain for support.

The room was packed full of people. Men in expensive suits sat at a long mahogany bar or at small, round tables. Some of them had a woman on their arm, some had two. The women were unbelievably beautiful. To Ryerson they looked like Greek goddesses in designer dresses and evening gowns. A room full of Persephones and Junos and Athenas. Each one wearing an outfit that seemed to defy gravity in some strange yet alluring way.

The air of the club was hot and thick with smells: the harsh fug of cigarette smoke, the sharp scent of men's aftershave, and the floral bouquets of a dozen or more perfumes. It was a heady mix that only added to Ryerson's disorientation. A heavy bank of smoke hung in the air like a blue fog, making the place seem ethereal, dreamlike. People moved about like ghosts. A silver-haired man in a burgundy smoking jacket was moving from table to table, shaking hands and making chitchat.

On the left side of the club, past the bar, a set of stairs curved up to a section cordoned off with a velvet rope. A sign on the newel post said VIPERS.

Ryerson blinked his eyes against the smoke and squinted at the sign.

No. It said VIP.

"Welcome, sir!" a voice boomed.

Ryerson turned and saw a black man leaning against the bar and snapping his fingers. He smiled and disclosed teeth so white it almost hurt Ryerson's eyes to look at them.

"Good evening," he replied.

"Yes, sir!" the man agreed exuberantly, as if Ryerson had made a statement.

Ryerson moved to the far end of the bar and sat on a stool that gave a view of the rest of the club.

It looks like a Philip Marlowe novel exploded in here, he thought.

He turned to the bartender, a young black man who didn't look old enough to be in a bar much less tending one. "What can I get you?" he asked.

"Rye and ginger."

"Straight up."

"This is some club," Ryerson remarked. "I've never seen one quite like it."

The bartender set the drink on a paper napkin, dropped in a plastic stir-stick, and slid it across the counter. "It has atmosphere," he agreed. "But the real draw is the music."

On that note, the music abruptly stopped and the audience erupted into applause. Ryerson picked up his drink and swivelled around. Next to the stairs leading up to the VIP section, there was another, wider set of steps leading down to a sitting and dancing area in front of a stage. There was no one up there at the moment, just a cloud of yellow smoke dissipating in the air. When it was gone, a spotlight snapped on, throwing a jaundiced glow on the floor. An ancient black man with hair like steel wool came shuffling out. He raised a gnarled, claw-like hand and tapped the microphone, sending off thumps of amplified thunder.

"Tonight," he said in a grating voice, "is a special night, here, at *Al Azif!*" Feedback shrieked off the mike and the audience applauded again. A few people whistled loudly.

"As you know, we like to present our performers at their relaxed bests." A few people nodded their heads knowingly. "And so, without further ado, I present the trombone of Danny 'L'il Joe' Johnson."

The crowd whooped and hollered as the old man shuffled off stage. A short black man in a suit the colour of dried limes came out. He was holding a trombone that was almost taller than he was. He put the mouthpiece to his lips, and the spotlight changed colour, from jaundice-yellow to pumpkin-orange.

L'il Joe started to play a slow, mournful song, all warbling notes and quavering drawls, pulling the sounds from the instrument in a way that seemed painful to him. His eyes squinched shut and his cheeks puffed out to a cartoonish size. The crowd stared in mingled awe and anticipation.

Ryerson tried to find Jonathan in the crowd, but the smoke was too thick to see much of anything. The whole place seemed faded, washed out of all its life and colour. The only thing that stood out with any real clarity was the neon FIRE sign above the emergency exit to the right of the stage. Jonathan was probably up in the VIP lounge—the only place in the club Ryerson couldn't see from where he was sitting.

He paid for his drink and made his way across the room, skirting the stairs that led down to the sitting and dancing area, and took a seat at a table with a slightly better angle.

He loosened his tie as he sipped his drink and glanced around the club. He looked toward the emergency exit again, and noticed something different about the neon sign above it. It said EXIT, even though he was sure when he looked at it a moment ago it had said FIRE. He stared at it for a long time, thinking about how the other sign had seemed to change as well. The red neon still said EXIT. And of course that was what it was supposed to say, right? He couldn't recall ever seeing an emergency exit sign that said FIRE.

He looked up at the VIP lounge. From his vantage point, he could see three tables lined up against the railing. A single person was sitting at each one, but none of them was Jonathan Marchand. One of them, an older woman in a black dress with a mink stole over her shoulders, was tapping her foot along with L'il Joe's trombone. She seemed to feel Ryerson's look, and turned and smiled at him.

Ryerson stared back, unable to tear his eyes away. He found himself transfixed by the rhythmic rise and fall of her foot. Maybe it was the smoke in the air, but the rhythm of her tapping seemed relaxing, almost soothing. It seemed to grow louder as he stared. At the same time, the sound of the trombone began to decrease in volume. The smoke was very thick, an opalescent tide that ebbed and flowed, obscuring his view by turns. It cleared for a moment, and Ryerson was startled to see the woman's foot was no longer a foot. It had become an animal's cloven hoof. He squinted his eyes and saw that the leg attached to the foot was now covered in tufts of thick, white fur.

His gaze drifted upward, as if by some inexorable force, to discover the long, gruff face of a goat. Its eyes were a burning red split by sharp, triangular pupils. A pair of curving horns sprouted above its downturned ears. It was still wearing the woman's dress.

"I feel he's up to something," Veronica Marchand said. "I suspect he's trying to locate someone to nullify our contract."

"Excuse me," Ryerson said, "but if you believe your husband's been unfaithful, why not cut to the chase and ask him? It would save you a lot of time and money."

"I don't want him exposed," she said firmly. "I just want to know where he's going. What I do after that . . . well, that's my business." She took out a pack of Kools and lit one with a gold-plated lighter. "I don't believe in divorce, Mr. Ryerson. In my twenty-eight years of trading I've never gone back on my word. I expect the same respect from my husband."

Ryerson nodded. The business analogy was getting a little tired, but he understood the message perfectly. He had already decided to take the job. Shadowing a cheating spouse was as routine to a private investigator as filling a cavity was to a dentist, but there was nothing routine about the money. That aside, Ryerson found he liked Mrs. Marchand and genuinely wanted to help her. There was something about her gutsy, no-apologies approach to life and business that he respected. It wasn't his way, but he didn't meet a lot of people with convictions, much less the fortitude to stand by them.

Ryerson finally managed to tear his gaze away from the goat woman. He closed his eyes and counted to ten. When he opened them, Jonathan Marchand was sitting across the table from him. He looked like his picture: a dark-haired, dark-eyed man in his early thirties with a scar on his chin and a smarmy smile that looked just as permanent. He looked like the kind of guy who was used to getting his way, and with minimal effort. A man who looked at the world with lazy confidence, with emphasis on the lazy. He was wearing a suit and tie under his overcoat. He was also wearing leather gloves, which Ryerson thought strange considering the cloying heat of the club.

"You've been following me," Jonathan said, grinning. "I don't know you. Do I?"

"Where did you come from?" Ryerson felt ill and off-balance, like a man suffering seasickness.

"Philadelphia," Jonathan replied, and tittered. "But I don't think that's what you really want to know. You're a detective, aren't you? Hired by my wife? The Witch of Wall Street." He scoffed. "I'm surprised she sent you in *here*. That was very irresponsible of her."

"She didn't send me," Ryerson said. "I followed you here."

"How resourceful of you. But this isn't a very safe place to be, detective. Although," he add thoughtfully, "it's the only place to go if you want to get out of an uncomfortable predicament."

"If you want out, then hire a lawyer."

Jonathan smiled contritely. "A lawyer is of no use to me. My marriage is no ordinary union, just as Al Azif is no ordinary club. As you may or may not be coming to realize."

Ryerson thought of the goat woman, and had to force himself from looking back at her table. Jonathan turned to face the stage.

"The performers here are presented at their relaxed best."

"So they say."

"Yes, but do you know *why* they're presented? Do you know what happens to those who are put on stage?"

L'il Joe had finished playing. He stood motionless, trombone held close to his chest, almost protectively, and tilted his head up to the sickly glow of the spotlight. He looked like he was waiting for something. The silence spun out. His mouth suddenly fell open in a silent scream. Yellow smoke began to rise up from the stage. It quickly enveloped L'il Joe. He didn't run, he just stood there while the smoke closed around him. When it dissipated a few seconds later, he was gone.

"Tricks," Ryerson said, but his voice wavered slightly.

"There are no tricks here," Jonathan declared. He took off his gloves and held up his left hand. There was an angry red scar across the palm, as though it had been slashed open with a razor, and not too long ago. "It's all business, detective. Transactions. I made a mistake when I signed on with that witch—I concede that—but I'll be damned if I'll let her take me without a fight. This," he raised both hands to indicate the club, "is a pocket. A kind of purgatory. Time doesn't pass in this place. I like to come here and think, have a martini or two, enjoy some live music. Al Azif has played host to many performers. Sometimes you'll meet people you haven't seen for years. Sometimes you can even find those who have died." He tittered again and put his gloves back on. "Rarer still, you can find people who are just passing through. Special people. Like someone who can break the bond between a witch and her familiar." He shrugged. "Expensive, but doable."

Ryerson found himself repeating something the Blue Fairy had told him: "Promises were made, contracts were signed."

"Yes." Jonathan sounded disgusted as well as annoyed. "But how could I have known? How could I have *known*?"

❖

"So you want me to follow him?"

"Yes. He's a regular man-about-town. He'll keep you on your toes."

"Do you have a picture of him?"

Mrs. Marchand raised the hand that had been holding the lighter. It was gone, and there was a photograph in its place, held between her thumb and index finger.

Neat trick, Ryerson thought, and reached out to take it.

She pulled back at the last second. "Don't let him see you."

"I'll be just another one of the shadows."

❖

"I'm leaving," Ryerson said. "Your wife can find someone else to play these games."

Jonathan threw his head back and laughed long and hard. "You think this is a game?"

Ryerson stood up, knocking his chair over, and made his way across the room, past the bar, and through the curtain. He glanced over at the coat-check booth as he went by, then came to an abrupt halt.

The door leading into the anteroom was gone. In its place stood a wall with an advertisement for something called Fireball Whiskey. It showed two women bent suggestively over a flaming bottle. The slogan proclaimed IT BURNS! Neither woman was entirely human. One of them had the head of a hawk, while the other's face was an explosion of squirming tentacles.

Ryerson went back through the curtain. The black man with the blinding grin was still leaning against the counter, snapping his fingers. "Evening, *suh!*" he rasped.

Ryerson ignored him and went past the bar. He came to the foot of the stairs leading up to the VIP lounge. The sign on the newel post said VIPERS. He heard a sizzling sound like water striking a hotplate. He looked up the stairs and saw the velvet rope had become a length of barbed wire. Beyond it he saw a couple sitting at a table. They both had the heads of snakes. The woman was wearing a strapless green dress with a sapphire broach around her scaly throat. The man raised a fluted glass to his lipless mouth and drank the amber liquid with quick darts of his forked tongue.

Ryerson tried to scream, but it got stuck in his throat. He uttered a weak choking sound and stumbled down a short corridor. He pushed through the door of the men's room and stood for a moment bent over at the waist, hands propped on his thighs, catching his breath. The cloying smell of pine filled his nostrils. He straightened up, went over to one of the sinks, and splashed water on his face. He took a deep breath, held it, and released it in a pathetic whimper. There had to be an explanation for what was happening here. He just had to calm down and figure it out.

Jonathan must have found out he was being followed. He had set a trap, maybe put something in his drink, a hallucinogen of some kind, and now he was playing with him.

The first thing he had to do was find a way out of here.

He went past the row of stalls to the window. It wasn't barred, and Ryerson silently thanked God for small favours. The lock was a simple thumb latch, but it had been painted over and wouldn't budge, no matter how much pressure he put on it.

Desperation started to set it. In a panic, Ryerson drove his elbow through the glass. A jagged piece slashed his arm, but he was so keyed up he didn't feel it. His attention was focused on the view outside the window. He was staring at a night sky scattered with thousands of coldly twinkling stars. He should've been looking at the wall of the adjacent building. He took an unconscious step closer. He stuck his head out the window and looked down. He couldn't see the ground, or anything else for that matter, just blackness. He looked back at the stars. They began to twinkle faster and brighter.

Ryerson watched them, utterly transfixed, until he realized they weren't twinkling.

They were blinking.

"God . . ." he muttered.

Eyes. He was looking at eyes. Thousands of them.

And they were looking back at him.

Ryerson screamed and threw himself away from the window. He bounced off the side of a stall and collapsed on the floor, sobbing. He was vaguely aware of a buzzing sound coming from the window. It was growing steadily louder.

He wiped his eyes and saw blood on his hands. He went over to one of the mirrors and squinted at his reflection. Tiny rivulets of blood were trickling from the corners of his eyes.

He turned on the hot and cold faucets full blast and flushed his eyes. Bloody water splashed the sink, the mirror. He looked at his eyes again. The bleeding had stopped, but it looked like he had gone a week without sleep.

The buzzing was very loud now. It sounded like a hive of extremely large and extremely pissed off bees. The cut on his arm bled freely, but he didn't have time to take care of it now. He'd patch himself up after he got out of this fucked up jazz club. *If* he got out. He still had to find an exit.

Exit.

The emergency exit.

He burst out of the men's room and ran briskly across the room. He didn't look up at the VIP lounge, skirting the stairs and the table where he had sat with Jonathan Marchand. Jonathan was gone, but that didn't matter anymore. He had done his job like the well-paid puppy dog he was. Getting out of this place was all that mattered now. Being able to look in the mirror and not see blood pouring out of his eyes was high on his list, too.

He weaved through the crowd to the emergency exit. The sign over the door had changed again. Now it said BURN. It could have said DISCO INFERNO for all Ryerson cared. He was getting out. He put his hands on the push-bar, relishing its cool, firm reality. Then he slammed the door open and stepped out into a wall of mist. It was like the atmosphere in Al Azif, only much denser. And yellow. Ryerson could barely see his hands in front of his face.

The door snapped shut behind him, and he jumped. He took a breath, then let it out. His hands cut smoothly through the mist, up and down, side to side. There was nothing within his reach. He took a few tentative steps forward, arms outstretched.

He turned right and tried moving in that direction. A minute passed. Then five. It was hard to tell how far he had come. He had lost all sense of distance and direction. He considered backtracking to the fire-door, but wasn't sure he could find it again. He thought he heard something up ahead. Something that might have been a voice.

He allowed himself to walk a little faster. He looked down to see how his feet were doing, but couldn't see anything past his belt buckle. The sound of his shoes slapping the ground was distant, almost dreamlike.

Gradually, the mist began to clear. He stopped moving when he saw it was actually flowing past him, as if propelled by a strong breeze. Ryerson didn't feel anything, but the voice was getting louder and clearer.

He started moving forward again, expecting to see the mouth of the alleyway opening onto some side-street. Instead he saw faces. Lots of faces. They seemed to be staring up at him, as though the ground up ahead slanted downward at an abrupt angle.

His shoes made an abrupt clomping sound on ground that was unmistakably wooden. The mist was gone, and Ryerson realized he was back in Al Azif. On stage. Under the spotlight.

He looked out at the crowd. Jonathan Marchand was in the VIP lounge, sitting next to the goat-woman. She held a cigarette in an ebony holder and was staring at Ryerson through the rising smoke.

The crowd waited. Ryerson thought of the eyes outside the men's room window, the one that looked out on some unimaginable border. Someone started tapping their foot, which was joined by the snapping of the black man's fingers. The crowd broke into applause that became a loud buzzing. Ryerson looked up into the spotlight, feeling its putrid glow on his face, and waited for the show to begin.

Hunger

It begins with fire and it ends with fire.

I step out of the smoke. A man rushes toward me. He takes my hand and leads me away from a burning building. He is the first.

He passes me off to another man who helps me into an ambulance. He is the second.

A woman in the back of the ambulance puts a plastic mask over my face. She is the third.

I am taken to a hospital.

After that I lose count.

I spend the night in the hospital. I visit a lot of rooms.

In the morning the doctor comes to see me. She asks if I remember anything yet. I shake my head. She says it will all come back to me in time. I smile.

A nurse comes in with breakfast. He says he hopes I like scrambled eggs. I smile. The doctor is writing on my chart. Then she stops and looks at the nurse. She drops the chart and leaps onto his back, sinking her teeth into his neck.

I smile.

I leave the hospital shortly thereafter. No one notices I am gone. They have bigger problems to deal with.

I wander around the city. I have never been in one before. I meet a man in ragged clothes. He lives in a cardboard box. He says the city has done this to him. He holds out his hand and asks me for help.

I help him.

❖

I go back to the building. All that remains is a crown of smoke-stained bricks. I go inside and find the charred remains of a table. Before it was a table it was a piece of wood. Before that a log. Before that a tree in a deep northern forest.

My home.

❖

The next day I find a man on the steps of my building. He is eating a human arm.

He says he can't help himself. He is hungry. So very hungry.

I wonder how he found me. Then I recognize him.

He is the first.

❖

I meet a lot of people over the next few weeks. Some of them come to me. They see me in dreams.

Some people don't like me. They say they know me. They say they know what I really am. They try to stay away from me, but the city is being closed off.

One man tries to kill me. He sneaks into my building one night and puts his hands around my throat. I do the same to him.

He goes away hungry.

❖

The people outside the city call me different things.

They call me a virus. They call me a myth. They call me a terrorist. They call me mass hysteria.

They tell the people still in the city to stay indoors. They tell them not to leave.

People attempting to leave the city are being shot.

I spend my days walking around the city. The streets are filled with bones. I touch many people. They collect the bones and use them to rebuild my home.

I smile.

My people eat each other. My building grows.

It's almost time to move on.

❖

The people outside the city have set fires.

They say the spirit of the city is dead.

They say I killed it.

I will show them.

The spirit of the city is alive.

Alive and well.

Alive and well fed.

INHERITOR

Daniel Ramis thought the only thing he inherited from his father was insomnia, but as it turned out, he got a house, too.

He received this news at three o'clock in the morning, about a week after his father collapsed in his London flat of an apparent heart attack. He had grabbed onto a china hutch for support and ended up taking it down with him; the sound of it crashing on the floor was what prompted the neighbours to call the police. Daniel was notified the following day, but had made no arrangements to attend the funeral. To say that Daniel and his father weren't close would be like saying the Chernobyl nuclear power plant suffered only a minor mechanical problem.

It should have ended there, but it seemed his father had come back to deliver one final lick—this one via a probate lawyer, a Brit named Kingsley who seemed oblivious of the time difference between London and Seattle.

"Strange as it may seem," Kingsley said, "your father actually left instructions for you to be contacted at this exact time." He chuckled good-naturedly. "It seems that he wanted to wake you up."

Daniel had not been awakened by the call. He had been sitting in his favourite chair and watching a thunderstorm perform its final act over the bay. Having lived with insomnia for almost twenty years, he knew that a window helped pass the time much better than a television.

"What can I do for you, Mr. Kingsley?"

"First of all, let me tell you how very sorry I am for your loss."

"Thank you."

"I had the opportunity to meet your father, and he was an exceptional man."

Daniel thanked him again; he hoped the man would get to the

point before the sun came up.

"I had planned to speak with you after the funeral, but I understand you were unable to attend."

Daniel said nothing.

Kingsley went on as if he had spoken. "That's most unfortunate. I had hoped to discuss your father's will. He's left you considerable assets, as well as instructions that he wished you to carry out after his passing."

"What instructions?"

"It's more of a request, actually." Kingsley cleared his throat. "Your father would like you to return to Sycamore, which I understand is the name of a town."

"Yes," Daniel said evenly.

"According to his records, you have a house there."

"*Had* a house," he corrected. "My father sold it years ago. Before he ran away to London, as a matter of fact." He closed his mouth before anything else came out.

Papers rustled on the other end of the line. "Actually, Mr. Ramis, according to the last codicil, which was drawn up in March of this year, the deed to the Sycamore property is still in your father's possession. I verified ownership myself. Perhaps he merely closed it down for—"

"He told me he sold it," Daniel said brusquely.

"Be that as it may, he has requested that you return there."

"Why?"

"I'm sure I don't know. I can send you the documents on the transfer of the deed, as well as the keys and—"

"Save yourself the trouble, Mr. Kingsley. I have no intention of going back to that house."

Kingsley was silent for a moment. Thousands of miles of air hissed between them. "It was your father's wish," he said finally.

"Yeah, well he can keep on wishing."

He hung up.

Well done! a voice cheered in his head. It sounded like Beth. *You sure put him in his place. Teach him to do his job.*

"Shut up," Daniel said to the empty living room.

You hung up on him, she said. *You like hanging up on people, don't you?*

"I didn't hang up on you. I just . . . I just didn't want to talk about it."

He stood up and went over to the calendar on the wall. The November sheet showed Rainier Avenue at night in the rain—in fact, every month showed some prominent Seattle landmark in the rain. Beth had given it to him as a gag after she moved to Reno, where the annual rainfall was measured in single digits, when there was anything to measure at all. They had been married for three years before deciding they couldn't live in the same house together anymore. A year after that, Beth decided the city was too small for them, too. They still exchanged birthday cards, the occasional phone call, and Daniel thought that was better than some couples who had gone through the train wreck that is divorce.

You asked a lot of questions about my dad, he thought, turning back to the window. *Too many.* He ran an unsteady hand over his stubbly cheek and decided to call it a night—or a morning, if you wanted to be technical about it.

He dragged himself up the stairs to bed. The storm was breaking up, anyway. The good parts were over.

The following morning the sky was clear and the sun etched the tops of the mountains with red filigree. He glanced over at his alarm clock and saw he had gotten an hour of sleep. He grinned wearily.

It was a good night.

Kingsley's package arrived a week later. Postmarked London and stamped half a dozen times by the customs people, it contained a number of curious items: documents pertaining to his father's will (written in a British legalese Daniel couldn't make heads or tails of), a folded map with a note paperclipped to it, three keys attached to a cracked-leather fob, and a thick stack of Polaroid pictures.

Daniel picked up the map and shook his head. *I can't believe he sent directions. Does he really think I don't remember?*

It was true, Daniel had been trying to forget the house in Sycamore (and everything that had happened there), but the basic truth about memories still held: the things you wanted to forget were often the same ones you remembered most clearly.

He tossed the map on his cluttered desk and picked up the Polaroids. He flipped through them, not really looking at them, and put them down as well. He started to crumple the big padded envelope everything had come in, and realized there was something else inside. He turned it over and shook out a small key. He looked at it closely and wondered why it wasn't on the key ring with the others.

The number 089 was engraved on the tiny keyface.

He picked up the map again and read the note attached to it.

Dear Mr. Ramis,

First of all, I would like to apologize if I upset you in any way during my telephone call last week. The loss of a loved one, especially one's own father, is a terrible experience, and I apologize if I conducted myself poorly.

I have forwarded you the documents pertaining to the house at Sycamore, along with the deed and keys to the property. I have also included a number of photographs your father took of the house. He wished for you to have them. Likewise, I have included a key to a safe-deposit box located at the post office in Sycamore. I have attached a map with directions, supplied by your father, to help you find it. I don't know what is waiting for you there, only that, like the house, your father wanted you to have it.

Respectfully yours,

Philip P. Kingsley

Daniel put down Kingsley's letter, feeling abashed. He wasn't exactly choked up with guilt, but he thought he probably owed Kingsley a letter of apology.

On the other hand, he still felt he owed his father nothing. And even though he spent the next hour gathering items for the trip to Sycamore, he told himself the only reason he was going was to find out what was waiting for him in safe-deposit box 089. If he decided to continue onward to the house (which was actually located on the outskirts of town), he probably wouldn't even get out of the car. He'd just cruise up the driveway, take a quick swing around the dooryard, and leave.

Daniel put an overnight bag in the trunk of his car, next to his toolbox. He didn't intend to spend the night in house, nor did he plan to complete any repairs, but he thought it was best to be prepared for anything. He had no intention of making a return trip.

With his gear stowed, he slipped behind the wheel, catching his reflection in the rearview mirror.

Drive up and drive down and that's all, he told himself.

But his eyes seemed to say something else.

Daniel left Claremont Bay and travelled east on the I-90. He left the turnpike at Ellensberg and headed north on US 97. After an hour of trees, fields, and lakes, he started passing rows of tract houses set tastefully back from the road. Each one seemed to have a picket fence or a board fence or a natural border of trees or hedges. The houses were alike in another way, too. Each one had a garden gnome or pink flamingo or some other piece of cheap statuary standing on the front lawn.

He passed a trailer park where rows of double-wides gleamed in the late-morning sun like miniature Quonset huts.

Finally, he passed a green reflectorized sign the that SYCAMORE POP. 2400. The post office was in town, but Daniel knew he wouldn't be stopping. The urge to see the house was too strong.

Main Street was in rough shape. Peeling facades, crumbling brick, and shifting foundations had turned the buildings into enormous tombstones canted on ominous, horror-movie angles. He passed the post office, one of the few buildings that looked as if it had been built sometime after the Depression, and the sign in the window said it was open until nine. Daniel continued on.

On the other side of town, Main Street turned back into US 97 as it climbed a steep hill. *Hunter's Hill*, Daniel thought, grinning in spite of himself. *I don't remember if that was its real name, but that's what Sissy and I called it.*

At the top of the hill, the road zigzagged around thick copses of trees before disappearing into the mountains. The feeder road which branched off to the house was still there, but the mailbox—and the post it sat on—was gone. In its place stood a pair of metal posts with a length of rusty chain hanging between them.

This is new, he thought, and pulled off to the side of the road.

He sat in the idling car, fighting a powerful urge to drop his foot on the gas and simply plow right through. It wasn't about the time it would take to remove the chain; what bothered him was that his father had put it on in the first place. The chain was proof that he had been back to the house. The house they had vowed never to return to again. The house where Sissy had died.

There it was. The part of his past that had pushed Beth away. The part that almost certainly was the cause of his sleepless nights. Death was supposed to be the end, but it hadn't been in Sissy's case. She was still with him, riding his shoulders like a bad habit he couldn't kick.

Eighteen years ago Sissy had gotten sick and died. Daniel didn't know the exact nature of her disease, except that it kept her indoors. He had asked his father about it on only one occasion, not long before they went their separate ways, and he had replied vaguely: "Cancer."

Daniel remembered how it had been at first. Sissy had been allowed to roam the house, and she had prowled around ceaselessly. Then she had been restricted to her bedroom, and Daniel didn't see her very much. He tried to, but his father said Sissy was much too sick to see anyone. Finally, she moved down to the cellar, where she eventually succumbed to whatever ailment had plagued her for all those years.

Daniel and his father had left the house soon after her death. Later, Daniel's father told him the house had been sold. He said it was important to put these bad times behind them and move on. If you didn't, they would come back to haunt you.

But his father hadn't sold the house. No more than Daniel had put the bad times behind him.

I guess that makes us both liars, he thought.

He turned off the engine and got out of the car. He went over to the padlock that secured the chain to the post. He fished out the key ring Kingsley had sent, found the key that fit the padlock, and turned it. It wouldn't budge. It wanted to, he could tell, but the tumblers wouldn't perform. The lock was very old and rusty.

He went back to the car, opened the trunk, and took a ball peen hammer out of his toolbox. He hit the padlock until it snapped open. He dropped it on the leaf-covered verge and the chain slunk to the ground. He put the hammer back in the toolbox, closed the trunk, and slipped back behind the wheel.

He stared through the windshield at the tree-lined corridor before him. Branches stretched across the gap on both sides to form a vaulted roof.

I'm going home, he thought, and started down the road.

He was standing right here, he thought, *or somewhere close to here.*

Daniel stared at the old house where he had spent a large portion of his childhood. It was here he had received his first lesson in death. He was holding the stack of Polaroids, shuffling them like a deck of cards. He took the top one and held it up and away from him, like a movie director trying to figure out the best angle for his next shot. He took a step backward, his arm still outstretched, then took three steps to his left.

The house had been boarded up and left for dead. Creepers had taken over one entire side of the structure; the chimney was gripped in a stranglehold of vines. The paint had turned the lifeless grey that seemed to be the colour of all old houses. Some of the board panelling had come loose and there was some roof damage, but not nearly as much as Daniel had expected. The place still pulsed with a low, tenebrous life. Like a cancer patient holding on even though the chemo has stopped working.

Did Sissy have chemo? Beth asked in his head. *She didn't, did she? She didn't fade away. She just . . . died.*

A strong gust of wind swept through the yard, kicking up leaves and throwing them together with papery explosions. Daniel was reminded of last night's storm and felt a pang of loneliness for his house on Claremont Bay.

He stuck the pictures back in his coat pocket. His Maglite was in there, but he wasn't ready to use it yet.

He walked around the yard, instead, staring at his boots as they swished through the drifts of leaves that covered the yard. He was building up the nerve to walk up the porch steps and enter the house. It made him feel young and stupid. Like a kid trying to gear himself up and go inside the local haunted house.

But you don't believe in haunted houses, Daniel.

No, he didn't.

Just haunted people.

He looked at the woods that surrounded the house. Nature had been at work here, too. *Give her an inch and she takes a mile*, he thought.

The trees had encroached like rubberneckers at a car accident. No one had been around to perform the maintenance necessary to keep the yard from turning into a jungle. And yet something strange was happening here. He couldn't tell exactly what it was. Something in the way the branches bent and curved away from the house . . . almost as if they were recoiling from it. Instead of following their natural growth paths, they had been forced into strange, sinuous shapes that suggested some kind of intervention.

Daniel took out the Polaroids and looked at them more closely.

There were twenty-five of them, but only a few showed the house clearly. Most of them were off-centre, showing only a portion of the front deck or a piece of eave. At first he had thought his father was just a lousy photographer, but now, walking around the yard, Daniel understood. His father hadn't been taking pictures of the house; he had been taking pictures of the yard.

The trees in the pictures were not much different from the ones he was looking at today. But he could see the bigger picture they formed: a perimeter of trees whose branches would not enter the space of the yard, as if was protected by an invisible barrier.

There was a single tree in the yard itself, but it was dead. Daniel's father had set up a tire swing when he was a kid. The tire was gone, but a piece of the rope remained, swaying in the breeze like a lyncher's forgotten lariat.

Daniel wandered back to the porch steps. He gripped the wood railing and a piece broke off in his hand. A long, moaning creak emanated from the house. He patted the Maglite in his pocket as if it was a talisman.

He climbed the steps.

A single wooden plank had been nailed across the front door. Someone had written on it in what looked like grease pencil, but Daniel couldn't make out the words. Without knowing what he was doing or why, he ran his palm across the plank and smudged it out. Then he gripped the board with both hands and pulled. It came free with a rusty squeal, and he tossed it dismissively over his shoulder.

He took a deep breath, turned the doorknob, and pushed. The hinges screamed, and plaster dust came raining down from somewhere above. He couldn't see anything, only blackness. The smell of mildew and long years wafted over him.

He turned on his Maglite and a beam of light leapt down the front hallway to the kitchen.

The floorboards creaked as he stepped inside. Everything was faded and yellow, like he had stepped into an old daguerreotype. Every surface was covered in a thin patina of dust. He put his hand on the banister and felt a low thrumming sensation race up his arm. He took his hand away and realized it was he who was trembling.

You're not really going up there, are you? Beth asked in his head.

"No," Daniel said. "Not yet."

He turned away from the stairs and stepped into the room to his left—what had been the parlour. It was empty except for a single straight-backed chair standing in the corner. The windows had been boarded up. Boarded up from the inside. Nothing was written on any of them, though.

He turned right, passed through another empty room, and into the kitchen.

The stove and the refrigerator were gone, but he could see the outlines of where they had once stood. The cabinets were open and empty, and again the only piece of furniture was a solitary chair.

Daniel crossed the hilly linoleum to the back door. A plank had been nailed across it. He turned to his right and looked over at the cellar door. There was another plank, but this one had writing on it, three rows of gibberish that weren't any kind of letters Daniel had ever seen. It hurt his head to look at it. He didn't recognize the words—if that's what they were—but he recognized his father's spiky backhand script.

Again, Daniel felt an urge to reach out and wipe the writing away. But this time he stayed the impulse and continued his trip through the main floor of the house.

When he was finished, he found himself back in front of the stairs. He put his foot on the first riser and his hand on the banister. He was no longer shaking. He took a deep breath and climbed up to the second riser. He moved closer to the railing, away from the wallpaper which hung in long, thick tongues, and sidled up the rest of the stairs, feeling both juvenile and justified.

Standing at the head of the second-floor hallway, he knew his time here would be short. The house—or rather, the memories of the house—was pressing in on him like the contracting walls of a torturer's press. Whatever it was he had to do up here, he had to do it fast.

He went straight for Sissy's bedroom.

Like the other rooms in the house, it was mostly, but not entirely, empty. The bed was gone, but the frame had been left behind—a corral for the dust kitties that covered the floor.

Sissy's dollhouse sat in one corner, looking eerily like a miniature version of the house in which he was currently standing. Except instead of vines and creepers, it had been taken over by cobwebs.

He caught movement over his head, and turned the beam of his flashlight on a spider the size of his fist. He let out a strangled cry as its long legs fluttered in the air, reaching for him.

He stumbled backwards and tripped over his feet. He pointed his flashlight back at the ceiling, but the spider continued to hang there.

Not a spider, he realized, only the sun—or rather a paper cutout of the sun his father had glued to the ceiling about a thousand years ago. Back when Sissy was bound to her room.

Daniel remembered that day. Sissy was standing in the corner while their father read aloud from a book. He said it was an instruction manual. Something to help make Sissy's room more comfortable for her. After he read from the book, he and Daniel had glued the sun and the moon and a whole bunch of cotton-ball clouds to the ceiling. Sissy stood in the corner the entire time, watching them. Not sad, not angry. She was just . . . Sissy.

Most of the clouds were still up there, Daniel noticed, panning his Maglite across the ceiling. They were thick with dust and looked absurdly like thunderheads now. What he had thought were the legs of an oversized spider were actually the light-rays of the sun.

He lowered the Maglite and noticed a large wooden chest under the room's single, curtainless window. A smiling clown was still discernible on the lid, though time had transformed its happy, cheerful face into one bordering on the insane. Daniel wasn't interested in looking inside. He had never liked that clown.

He walked slowly, reflectively, to the window and looked down at his car parked in the yard. He tried to imagine his sister standing in this very spot, staring out at a world she was permitted to see but not to touch. He tried to imagine himself through her eyes: a towheaded boy playing in the yard, waving up at her with awkward feelings of happiness and guilt. He supposed some things never changed. He didn't know how to feel about her then, and he didn't know how to feel about her now.

For a moment it seemed as if she was there in the room with him. He could almost feel her eyes burning a hole in his back. He turned around, but of course no one was there.

Of course.

He went back downstairs, slipping quickly past the wallpaper again, and into the kitchen. He stood before the cellar door, and when the urge returned to wipe out the writing on the plank, he didn't fight it. He dragged his fingertips across those strange curves and dips and curlicues, and felt something loosen in his chest. He gripped the plank and pulled it off with a loud screech.

At the same moment he heard a strange sound from outside. A great torrent of wind rushing through the yard.

He went out on the porch. Something had changed, but at first he couldn't tell what it was. Then, once he saw it, he couldn't take his eyes off it.

The trees.

They had unfolded their branches into the yard.

Panic gripped him like the vines gripping the house. He looked at the greasy pencilmarks on his fingertips and heard Beth's voice again: *Are you going to hang up again, Danny?*

No. He wasn't going to hang up. Not yet.

There was something he had to do first.

❖

The girl behind the counter at the post office was deeply engrossed in an issue of *Entertainment Weekly*. She didn't look up when Daniel came in. Nor did she look up when he asked her a question.

"To your left," she said, and pointed to a recessed wall with rows of safe-deposit boxes.

Daniel found box 089, unlocked it, and removed a mahogany case. He thought about opening it there, then tucked it under his arm, and left the post office.

❖

Daniel thought the only thing he inherited from his father was insomnia and a house, but as it turned out, he got a gun, too.

There was also a note. He read it once, but couldn't bring himself to look at it again. It was easier to look at the gun, sitting in its bed of red velvet. There was a compartment that contained six bullets.

He drove back to the house. The trees were still as he left them, branches stretching out into the yard. He barely noticed them.

He walked up the porch, opened the door, and went directly to the kitchen. He sat down in the chair with the case on his lap like an old woman with her knitting. He stared at the cellar door. He didn't have to wait very long before he heard the slow, steady creak of someone climbing the stairs.

He had never handled a gun before, and it took him a moment to get the cylinder open. He loaded the bullets with fingers that threatened to drop them, then snapped the chamber shut. He took a deep, steadying breath and let the gun hang limply between his thighs.

His grip tightened as the cellar door swung slowly open. He stared into the blackness beyond, and two thoughts chimed loudly in his head, like a clock announcing the second hour.

The first was that he had known deep down that his father hadn't sold the house. It was the thing that had been keeping him up nights, the thing that filled him with an inexplicable underknowledge that his life here had never truly ended.

This realization should have terrified him, but it didn't.

The second thought did.

Sissy. . . .

At first he saw nothing in the black maw of the cellar door. Then a grey shape began to materialize, developing slowly like the image on a Polaroid picture.

He saw something tall and gaunt with arms and legs as thin as rails.

Eighteen years had passed, but Daniel still recognized his sister. She was a sickly, sallow thing with long, greasy hair. Her bony shoulders supported the frayed straps of a garment that might have been a nightgown once upon a time. Her eyes, once a deep glacial shade of blue, had turned completely white: no irises, no corneas.

She stepped out of the doorway. Her feet looked normal enough until he saw her toenails: thick, black talons that clicked on the linoleum.

Daniel felt adrenalin flood his veins, and although he was overcome with fear and guilt, thoughts of running away never entered his mind. He had been seized by another, stronger emotion: responsibility.

Sissy opened her mouth. Her voice drifted out like smoke.

"Danny . . ."

The mahogany case slipped off his lap. The note fluttered onto the floor, face up. Daniel glanced down and saw his father's final message, the deposition of a coward:

I'm sorry. I couldn't do it.

Sissy came forward, arms outstretched. Daniel stood up and raised his own.

Don't worry, Sis. I'll take care of you.

TWILLINGATE

It was a few minutes before dusk and we were out walking along the shore below the cliffs. The sun was beating a fast retreat, bleeding the colour out of the day and making everything look grey and lifeless. The waves lapped the beach with a marked lack of enthusiasm. The receding water sluiced through layers of sandy grit and water-polished pebbles, making a sound like crackling fire.

I sat on the wooden stairs that ran up the side of the cliff, breathing in the sharp tang of saltwater and decomposing seaweed. I wondered if my memory of that smell would be enough to adequately recreate it once our vacation was over. I doubted it.

I looked over at Toby. He was walking with his head down, looking for flat rocks. He spied one, picked it up, and weighed it on his palm. After a moment he dropped it and went back to conning the beach, his eyes narrowed to slits as he struggled to see in the diminishing light.

Jill and Eva had wandered off down the shore, their arms linked companionably, huddled inside their fall jackets.

"Hey, where you going?" I called out to them.

"We want to see the lighthouse!" Jill called over her shoulder.

"The lighthouse?" Toby said. "It's way the hell out on the end of the Point."

"We just want to see it!"

Eva suddenly bolted away from Jill and ran along the beach. After a moment, Jill followed, kicking up sprays of wet sand in her wake.

They came to the point where the sand ended and the big rocks began. Giant boulders and long, flat slabs of rock that bore the constant brunt of the waves. Eva and Jill started to climb.

Toby and I exchanged a look: that was all it had ever taken with us.

We ran.

The girls had a good lead by the time we reached the rocks. They were moving quickly and carefully, making sure they had secure footholds and handholds as they went. Overhead a pair of seagulls watched their progress, unusually silent in the violet sky.

Toby and I climbed over the rocks like a pair of crabs. The girls were far ahead, but we had longer arms and legs, and we managed to catch up to them as they reached the edge that marked the end of Twillingate Harbour. At that point they changed direction and started moving up the cliffside.

I looked back over my shoulder. Toby was making steady progress, his face contracted in an expression of intense concentration. It was the same look he wore when we played chess. Further back, the whitewashed houses along the rim of the harbour gleamed like lanterns. From this distance you couldn't see the peeling paint or the weather-beaten boards; they looked brand new. Past them, up on the hill, the dark brooding hulk of the hospital stood over everything like an enormous totem.

As Toby passed me, I saw that he had put on his toque—the one we thought made him look like a fisherman. He had it cocked on a jaunty angle that caused me to chuckle.

"Don't be makin fun of m'hat, b'y," he growled in a faux accent that sounded more Nova Scotian than Newfoundlander. "A curse on anyone who laughs. A curse!" His voice echoed in the dark cavities between the cliffs.

The girls, already a fair pace up the cliff, looked down and showered us with their loud, raucous laughter. Toby started climbing after them.

I looked back once more, out into the harbour this time. The tide was still slinking away like a bully who had received some of his own medicine. A single buoy bobbed in the water. It was shaped like a wine bottle and the shadow it threw on the water was perfectly formed, no ripples.

A light breeze washed over me and made hooting sounds in the cliff pockets.

I started after Toby. The cliff wasn't very steep, but it was high and wet. I moved slowly, aware of how easily my rubber-soled sneakers could slip on the rocks.

The girls were moving slower. I could hear them puffing exhaustedly. Toby and I closed the gap.

"We'll make sure you don't fall," Toby said. He had swapped the bad East Coast accent for a lecherous tone. "I'll keep my eye on you every step of the way."

"Keep an eye on this, Toby m'boy." Eva turned around and flipped him the bird.

Toby clapped one hand over his heart. "That hurts, babe. I was just watching out for ya."

Eva pulled herself up to a slender ledge of stone. "I'm sure," she said, out of breath. "But who's going to watch out for you?"

Toby snapped his head back in my direction. "Joey's got my back. And my backside, too! Don't you, Joey? Can't take your eyes off it!" He gave his rear end a little wiggle and slid down the cliffside a bit.

"Maybe in one of your better dreams," I replied.

Jill grabbed two thick handfuls of the tough grass that grew along the top of the cliff and pulled herself up. She let out a long theatrical sigh and called down: "Let him fall, Joe. Then we won't have to watch any more reruns of *Danger Bay*."

Jill crouched down and stuck out her hand. Eva took it and pulled herself up. Then they looked down at us together, grinning.

"Keep stepping on those wet rocks, Tobe. You'll slide all the way down and *that* will hurt."

"*All* the rocks are wet," he grumbled. "We're on the g.d. ocean."

"You're going to *faa-aaall*," Eva said in a malicious singsong.

"Nope . . ." Toby grunted. ". . . Joey'd . . . break my . . . fall . . ."

As he reached the top, Jill raised one sneaker-clad foot over Toby's questing hands. She turned her head to Eva and said, "Don't suppose you've got a life insurance policy out on him?"

"Alas," Eva lamented.

"You'd go to hell," Toby huffed. "Where all the rocks are sharp and wet, and the air smells of dead fish, and the only thing on TV is *Danger Bay*."

Eva glared at him. "My hell sounds like your heaven."

Toby dragged himself up over the edge. "That's how you know we're in love, Eva m'dear."

I found a good handhold and looked up in time to see Eva administer a light kick to Toby's ribs. He made like she'd caved in his chest, rolling back and forth and groaning loudly. "It's true," he bugled. "Love hurts!"

The gulls continued to circle in the sky above us. They still hadn't made a sound, and there was something ominous in their silence.

I made a final mad scramble to the top of the cliff. Jill offered me her hand, but I reached over and latched onto one of Toby's big shore boots instead. He looked at me, and I made a deep, slobbering growl in the back of my throat. He slapped his hands to his cheeks and pulled them down in mock horror. "*No, NO!*"

I sank my teeth into the tough material that covered his ankle, tasting a mixture of old leather and seasalt.

Jill pointed an accusing finger at me and squealed. "Zombie!" Her voice leaped across the harbour and came back again. "Zom-*BEEEEE!*"

"Gross-*out!*" Eva said, laughing. "But I guess it's cleaner than biting Toby's foot."

Toby snapped his head around and glared at Eva. His mouth gaped open and now he was growling.

"*No!*" Jill cried, but she was laughing, too. "Our men! Our men are zombies!"

The girls took off across the grassy slope. Toby and I clambered to our feet and went after them. We could see the sun now, or what was left of it—a bright pastel smear bleeding between the gaps in a line of spruce trees. Ahead of us, on the far end of the Point, stood the lighthouse.

The wind chilled the sweat on my face. I felt like I was freezing and on fire at the same time. Toby took off his toque and waved it over his head like a flag. His hair flew around his head in a blond corona that made me think of how halos looked in old religious paintings.

We ran and ran, out toward the end of the Point, where the cliffs dropped to the sea and the lighthouse kept its constant vigil.

The girls suddenly stopped running. We were about fifty yards from the lighthouse, and the pine forest was behind us. The sun was dipping below the horizon now, laying a burning track across the water. Below us, the long rock breakwater looked like a bony finger pointing at that part of the Atlantic known as Iceberg Alley.

In the sun's dying glare, the foam kicking up along its craggy length looked like blood.

Jill was looking at the lighthouse. She collected them the way other people collected coins or butterflies, except she didn't have an album or a killing jar. All she had was the camera of her eyes and the album of her memory. That was all she needed. She told me that if all she wanted were pictures, she'd stay at home and order postcards off the Internet.

We stood there on the Point, catching our breath as the sun sank below the horizon and the wind buffeted our bodies. The light drained away as if it were controlled by a dimmer switch, leaving us in a sterile purple twilight. It felt like we had slipped seamlessly into another world.

And we were no longer alone on the Point.

The cliffs and bluffs and the breakwater below us were crowded with wispy, insubstantial figures that glowed with a deep pearlescent light. *Ghosts*, I thought immediately. But that wasn't exactly right. They had vaguely human shapes, but their arms were too long, and their legs were jointed in too many places. They wavered from side to side, as if drawn by the currents of the air or the water, ebbing and flowing, ebbing and flowing.

Jill was still looking at the lighthouse. She threw her arms in the air and yelled, "Number seventeen!"

Toby and Eva held hands and watched those white wisps that were not ghosts. I don't think they saw us, or took much notice of us if they did. I don't think we were of their world. For a brief moment we existed in a special place, on the terminator between day and night. Then the stars started coming out, dotting the darkening sky with their chilly, indifferent light.

I stared at them for a moment, and when I turned back, the white wisps were gone. It was like they were never there. Jill looked at us and we looked back. She had seen her lighthouse, and we had caught a glimpse of something else. Just a glimpse.

We started back across the Point, but I didn't recognize anything we passed.

THE CANDLE

"Did you blow out the candle?"

Tom lowered his book and turned toward Peggy.

Peggy lowered her own book and bit her lower lip. Why was it that she could remember what she had for breakfast every day this week, could even remember what she was wearing on most of those days, but couldn't remember if she had blown out the candle in the living room? *Is this what middle age is*? she wondered. *The loss of short-term memory*? She hoped not. She was forgetful enough as it was; she didn't need to help it along.

"Yes," she said finally. Then: "No. I don't know."

Peggy watched as Tom laid his hand on top of his book. She noticed the wrinkles on his fingers, the white hairs on his knuckles, and thought, *We've gotten old, how did this happen*?

He looked at her fully now. "Well," he said, "which is it?"

"Huh?" She looked at him quizzically; her own book had slumped forward and was now lying open on her chest. "I'm sorry, Tom. I must be sleepier than I thought. What did you say?"

"I asked if you remembered to blow out the candle." He was getting impatient. "In the living room?"

She bit her lip again, and Tom had to repress an urge, one that had been growing stronger over the twenty-six years of their marriage, to reach out and pull her lip from under her perfectly capped teeth. It drove him crazy. Biting her lip while she was trying to remember something was one of her half dozen or so little gestures. It was enough to drive a man nuts.

"I really can't recall," Peggy said at last. "I remember lighting it, of course, because the window was open and the smell of oats was really strong tonight. And I remember turning off the lamp after the movie was over. You put the DVD back on the shelf and I picked up the glasses on the coffee table. . . ." She trailed off, lost in thought. "But I don't remember if I blew out that darn candle."

"Well, can you go check?"

"Why can't you go?" she asked, a little testily.

"Because you lit the damn thing," Tom replied, a little testily himself.

"Because I lit it?" Peggy repeated. "What are you, six years old?"

"Are you?" he shot back. "What is it, are you afraid to go into the living room in the dark?"

"Are you?"

"I'm already comfortable." Then, as if to accentuate this fact, Tom nestled a bit further down under the covers and picked up his book again.

"I'm comfortable, too," Peggy replied, a bit indignantly. She opened her own book as if she was deeply engrossed in it, a tight little frown squiggled on her face.

Tom heaved a big sigh. "Listen, Peg, I've gotten up twice already. Once to make sure the side door was closed and locked—because you couldn't remember if you did *that*—and again to feed the stupid cat."

Peggy looked at him and decided it was probably easier to submit now than to continue arguing about it. On the day she had married Tom, her mother had given Peggy two pieces of advice: *Don't sign anything until your lawyer's looked at it first* and *Never go to bed angry*.

"Okay," she said, closing her book and putting it on the nightstand. "But this means you're making breakfast in the morning. Blueberry pancakes," she added.

From behind his book, Tom snorted good-naturedly to show that he was a good sport, that bygones were bygones.

Peggy flipped back the coverlet and slid her long legs out of bed. She was quite tall—taller even than Tom's considerable five feet ten inches—and while she had always taken pride in her long legs, she didn't much like looking at them anymore. Like Tom's hands, they were starting to show their years. Not that it mattered. Her legs had the years *and* the mileage. When the floor creaked under her feet, she thought that part of the sound—surely not the greater part, but some part at least—was the joints in her knees letting her know that her days of junior varsity soccer and ringette were over—long over.

She pulled up the baggy cotton boxer shorts she was wearing, the ones with the Peterborough Petes' logo on them, and reflected that her days of sexy lace underwear from I See France, the lingerie store downtown, were over, too.

This is where I ended up, she thought as she ambled out into the dark hallway. *This is where life has taken me.*

It wasn't as bad as she made it out. She had a satisfying marriage to a man she was still in love with, they had no major financial concerns, and they were both healthy. There were no kids because they had planned to wait until Tom's first novel put them on easy street, and when it didn't, they decided that the window had passed and, really, would it be such a tragedy if they didn't have kids? They had a house that was paid for, a car that was only three years old, and a large nest egg for their steadily approaching retirement. *All of these things have brought me here*, she thought, walking down a dark hallway to the living room where they watched a lot of movies but not much living really took place.

Tom tried to get back into his book, but he couldn't concentrate. He was distracted by vague feelings of guilt. He felt a bit like a guy who had taken a girl out on a date, then told her, no, he wouldn't walk her home, even though it was dark out. Like a bit of a louse, if he was perfectly honest.

But it was just their living room, he reasoned. Nothing scary about that. He listened for Peggy's footsteps, which should have been audible on the old hardwood floors, but he didn't hear anything.

All of this over a stupid candle.

"Peggy?"

The house was an old Colonial, and even the cat, who weighed a whopping seven pounds, made the boards creak and pop as he padded around. It was not a house where you could sneak up on someone undetected; they could hear you coming a mile away. It had even gotten so he could tell, just by the different groans and creaks, exactly where someone was headed, from the living room to the kitchen, from the bedroom to the bathroom. The sounds had become as much a part of the house as the smell of oats from the Quaker factory across the river that wafted in through the open windows when the wind was blowing right.

From where he was lying in bed, he could see only a small sliver of hallway through the open doorway. The bedroom was located at the very back of the house; the living room was at the front.

He looked over at the clock on the nightstand and tried to figure out how long she'd been gone. Two minutes? Three? Surely not as long as five minutes. Long enough, he figured, to walk into the living room, check to see if the candle was still burning, and if it was, blow it out.

"Peg?"

No reply.

She's screwing with me, he thought. *She's not answering because she's pissed off.* Soon he'd hear the creaking floorboards and she'd stroll into the room and slip back under the covers as if nothing was wrong.

Fine, let her be that way. Two can play that game.

He picked up his book again. He tried to read.

Thirty seconds passed. It felt like thirty minutes. Tom closed his book with a clapping sound that seemed extraordinarily loud in the silent room. *Silent house*, he corrected. *Why is it so quiet*? He was so distracted that he had forgotten to put in his bookmark. He swore under his breath and jerked back the covers. He was sliding out of bed when he heard the sharp, unmistakable sound of a woman screaming.

His first panicked thought was that it was Peggy. That's why she hadn't answered him. Something was wrong. Had someone broken in? His guilt was no longer vague; it was as solid as the obstruction that had formed in his own throat and kept him from calling out.

But the scream hadn't come from the house. No, he was sure of that. Tom's gaze flicked toward the bedroom window. It had come from outside.

It wasn't Peggy, he told himself, *assured* himself. It was someone in the house next door, or maybe even from one of the houses further down the street—it had certainly been loud enough. But it was muffled, too.

That's because it came from inside one of the houses. Not from someone on the street.

He didn't know how he knew that, but he did.

He climbed out of bed and walked over to the doorway.

"Peg? Where are you?"

Nothing.

He stepped into the hallway and out of the glow thrown by the bedside lamps. He was alone in the darkness. The smell of roasting oats was very strong. It was not an unpleasant smell, but it was one that had gotten old very quickly. His stomach made a protesting, groaning sound.

He walked into the darkened living room, the hardwood floor popping and creaking under his bare feet. He moved past the dining room table, the futon they had bought for guests to sleep on because they didn't have another bedroom. The shapes of the couch and the loveseat were limned against the orange glow of the streetlights. He saw the candle, a smaller silhouette on one of the end tables. It was out. There was no sign of Peggy.

He started to turn around, to search the rest of the house, when he suddenly realized the room wasn't empty.

Someone was sitting in the old wicker rocking chair, which was no longer in the corner of the room but in front of the wide bay window that looked out on McDonnel Street.

He was straining his eyes to see who it was when the candle on the end table suddenly flickered into low-burning life. Tom's eyes were drawn to it instinctively. His mouth fell open. In the dim light he saw it was Peggy sitting in the chair.

It rocked forward and Tom jerked backward. He didn't scream. *Not like the woman next door,* he thought randomly. *What had that woman seen? Her husband, maybe, sprawled out in his favourite recliner? What had he gotten up to do? Check to make sure the front door was locked? Bring in the dog?*

A cold sheen of sweat formed on his back. His pyjama top clung to him like a greasy second skin.

Peggy began to speak, but not in any tone Tom had ever heard in all the years he had known her.

"No questions, my sweet," Peggy said in a sharp, clear voice. "No questions tonight. Just the answer. Your answer."

What in the hell is going on? he thought frantically.

The candle flickered, and Tom glanced at it again. A smell wafted over to him. It was a sweet smell, a ripe smell that he couldn't identify. It didn't make any sense. The candle was vanilla-scented. It was a smell he and Peggy both enjoyed, along with Autumn Spice, Apple Pie, and Desert Rose, a smell that had filled the room earlier that evening.

Something was wrong. Peggy was staring at the candle, too. He had seen her profile a thousand times over the years—a hundred thousand times—and he knew it as well as his own reflection. But there was something different about it now. Different in the same subtle way that the smell of the candle was different. It was clearly Peggy sitting in the rocker . . . and yet it wasn't. Something was missing, or something had been added—something that changed her entirely and made her a stranger.

Tom jumped as another scream split the night. Was it someone else making a similar discovery? Was it someone he and Peggy knew, someone in their circle of friends, someone, maybe, who had spent the night on their futon?

He had sent his wife out here to do something. Now he bent over to do it himself. He felt Peggy's eyes watching him. He could feel them crawling on his skin like beetles. His eyes looked up at the window, and from this angle he could see the moon. It was different, too. The shape was right, but the colour was all wrong. Tom took two deep breaths, one to steady himself and one to do what needed to be done.

Just pretend it's your birthday, he told himself.

Peggy whispered, "Make a wish."

He blew out the candle.

ACKNOWLEDGEMENTS

The stories in this book represent my first six years in the publishing industry, from my very first sale, "The Tattletail," to my most recent, "Aces." As a collection, I like to think this book shows my evolution as a writer over that period of time. But the one thing you might not get from these stories is the number of people who have helped me out along the way.

So I'd like to take this opportunity to thank them.

First of all, I'd like to thank Brett Savory and Sandra Kasturi for publishing this book and making one of my dreams come true. And to my editor, Helen Marshall, for her tireless work, her quick response to e-mails, and for coming down to the bar (along with Michael Rowe) to find me so I wouldn't miss the announcement that ChiZine had accepted my book for publication.

Thanks to Paul Tremblay for the extremely kind introduction. Paul, the cheque is in the mail.

Thanks to Erik Mohr for the incredible cover art, and to Samantha Beiko for the stunning design work. This book is like a haunted house itself, and you were both the architects. I'd also like to thank Laura Marshall for coming up with some great ideas for marketing and promoting this book.

Some other people I'd like to thank for their friendship, their advice, and their support of my work over the years: Laird Barron, Craig Davidson, Peter Darbyshire, Kurt Dinan, Gemma Files, Richard Gavin, Orrin Grey, Nicholas Kaufmann, Michael Kelly, John Langan, Nick Mamatas, John Mantooth, Gary McMahon, Andrew Pyper, Michael Rowe, Robert Shearman, Simon Strantzas, Joel Sutherland, Jeffrey Thomas, Shayne Winters, and Rio Youers.

I'd also like to thank the editors who originally published some of the stories in this collection.

Last but not least, I'd like to thank my friends and family for their love and support. Most of all to my wife Kathryn who's been with me since the beginning and that very first short story sale. It takes a lot of heart and a lot of patience to be married to a writer, and Kathryn has both in abundance. I love you, Peach.

About the Author

Ian Rogers is a writer, artist, and photographer. His short fiction has appeared in several publications, including *Cemetery Dance*, *Supernatural Tales*, and *Shadows & Tall Trees*. He is the author of *SuperNOIRtural Tales* (Burning Effigy Press), a series of stories featuring supernatural detective Felix Renn. Ian lives with his wife in Peterborough, Ontario. For more information, visit ianrogers.ca.

Publication History

"Autumnology" (as "Autumn Burns") first appeared in *Writers Post Journal* (September 2007).

"Cabin D" first appeared in *Supernatural Tales #17* (April 2010).

"Winter Hammock" first appeared in *Revelation 4:1* (August 2007).

"The Nanny" first appeared in *Nossa Morte #3* (May 2008).

"The Dark and the Young" first appeared in *Bound for Evil* (2008, Dead Letter Press).

"The Currents" (as "The Man from the Currents") first appeared in *Touched by Wonder* (2007, Meadowhawk Press).

"Leaves Brown" first appeared in *Shades of Darkness* (2008, Ash-Tree Press).

"Wood" first appeared in *Black Ink Horror #2* (September 2007).

"Vogo" first appeared in *Northern Haunts* (2009, Shroud Publishing).

"The Tattletail" first appeared in *Dark Wisdom #9* (May 2006).

"Charlotte's Frequency" first appeared in *Horror Library, Volume 2* (2007, Cutting Block Press).

"Relaxed Best" first appeared in *Not One of Us #38* (October 2007).

"The Candle" first appeared in *Shadows & Tall Trees #2* (August 2011).

"Inheritor" first appeared in *Cemetery Dance #58* (February 2008).

"Twillingate" first appeared in *Salt* (2007, Naked Snake Press).

EMB
RACE
THE
ODD

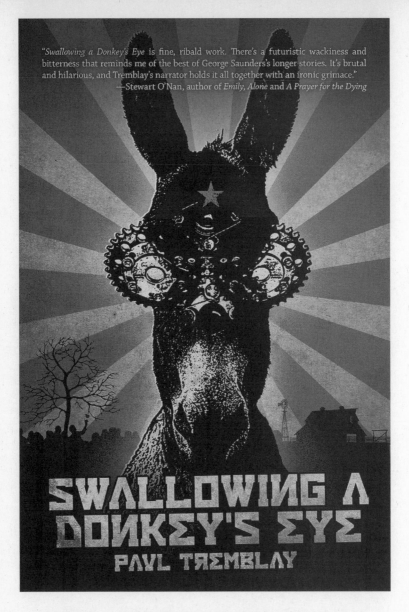

"*Swallowing a Donkey's Eye* is fine, ribald work. There's a futuristic wackiness and bitterness that reminds me of the best of George Saunders's longer stories. It's brutal and hilarious, and Tremblay's narrator holds it all together with an ironic grimace."
—Stewart O'Nan, author of *Emily, Alone* and *A Prayer for the Dying*

SWALLOWING A DONKEY'S EYE

PAUL TREMBLAY

AVAILABLE AUGUST 2012
FROM CHIZINE PUBLICATIONS

978-1-926851-69-3

BULLETTIME

NICK MAMATAS

AVAILABLE AUGUST 2012
FROM CHIZINE PUBLICATIONS

978-1-926851-71-6

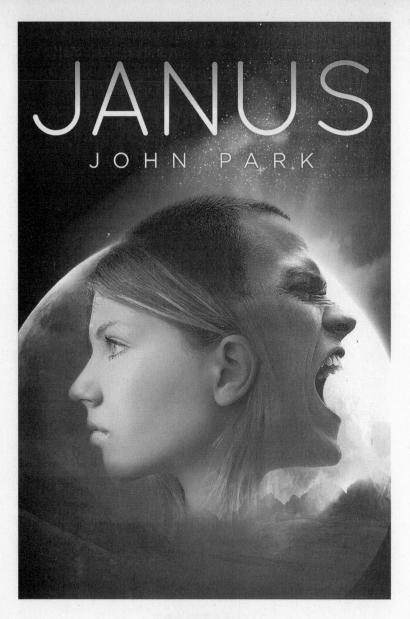

JANUS

JOHN PARK

AVAILABLE SEPTEMBER 2012
FROM CHIZINE PUBLICATIONS

978-1-927469-10-1

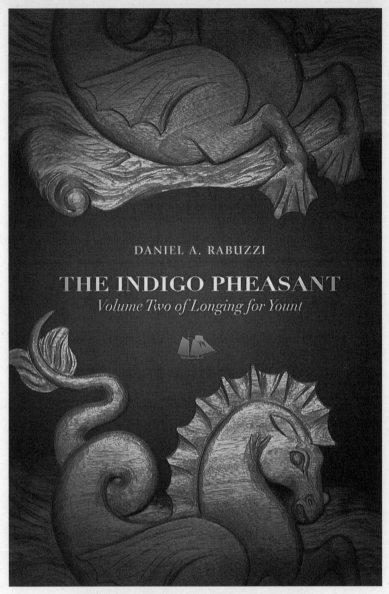

THE INDIGO PHEASANT

VOLUME TWO OF LONGING FOR YOUNT

DANIEL A. RABUZZI

AVAILABLE SEPTEMBER 2012
FROM CHIZINE PUBLICATIONS

978-1-927469-09-5

WORLD FANTASY AWARD-WINNING AUTHOR

THE BEST DARK FICTION OF **ROBERT SHEARMAN**

REMEMBER WHY YOU FEAR ME

INTRODUCTION BY STEPHEN JONES

REMEMBER WHY YOU FEAR ME
THE BEST DARK FICTION OF ROBERT SHEARMAN

AVAILABLE OCTOBER 2012
FROM CHIZINE PUBLICATIONS

978-0-927469-21-7

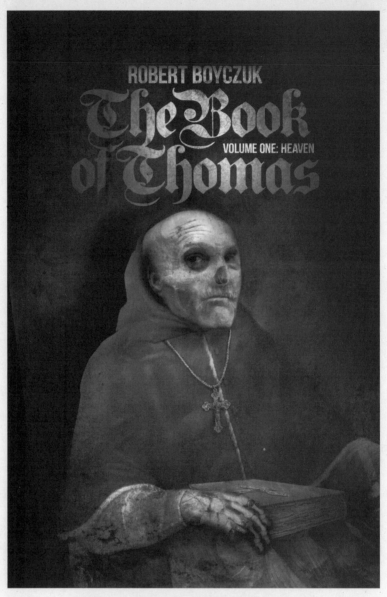

THE BOOK OF THOMAS

ROBERT BOYCZUK

AVAILABLE NOVEMBER 2012
FROM CHIZINE PUBLICATIONS

978-0-927469-27-9

BEARDED WOMEN
TERESA MILBRODT
978-1-926851-46-4

A BOOK OF TONGUES
VOLUME I OF THE HEXSLINGER SERIES
GEMMA FILES
978-0-9812978-6-6

BRIARPATCH
TIM PRATT
978-1-926851-44-0

CHASING THE DRAGON
NICHOLAS KAUFMANN
978-0-9812978-4-2

CHIMERASCOPE
DOUGLAS SMITH
978-0-9812978-5-9

THE CHOIR BOATS
VOLUME ONE OF LONGING FOR YOUNT
DANIEL A. RABUZZI
978-1-926851-06-8

CITIES OF NIGHT
PHILIP NUTMAN
978-0-9812978-8-0

THE DOOR TO LOST PAGES
CLAUDE LALUMIÉRE
978-1-926851-13-6

ENTER, NIGHT
MICHAEL ROWE
978-1-926851-02-0

EUTOPIA
DAVID NICKLE
978-1-926851-11-2

EVERY SHALLOW CUT
TOM PICCIRILLI
978-1-926851-10-5

THE FECUND'S MELANCHOLY DAUGHTER
BRETN HAYWARD
978-1-926851-13-6

FILARIA
BRENT HAYWARD
978-0-9809410-1-2

THE HAIR WREATH AND OTHER STORIES
HALLI VILLEGAS
978-1-926851-02-0

HORROR STORY AND OTHER HORROR STORIES
ROBERT BOYCZUK
978-0-9809410-3-6

IN THE MEAN TIME
PAUL TREMBLAY
978-1-926851-06-8

ISLES OF THE FORSAKEN
CAROLYN IVES GILMAN
978-1-926851-43-3

ISON OF THE ISLES
CAROLYN IVES GILMAN
978-1-926851-56-3

KATJA FROM THE PUNK BAND
SIMON LOGAN
978-0-9812978-7-3